Julian Rathbone is the author of man  *Fisher Lives*, both of which were shor in Dorset.

'Lyrical, amusing . . . entertaining'
TLS

'With remarkable imagination, cutting between the Norman side and the English, Rathbone plunges us into the gore of battle, the heartache of hopes lost for ever, in a fiction that sings with conviction. The result is a superb story that breathes on its own, larger than text-book history, but with the savage bite that only a backbone of truth can give'
Scotland on Sunday

Also by Julian Rathbone

King Fisher Lives
Joseph
A Last Resort
Nasty Very
A Spy of the Old School
Lying in State
Intimacy
Blame Hitler

THE
LAST
ENGLISH
KING

JULIAN
RATHBONE

An *Abacus* Book

First published in Great Britain by
Little, Brown and Company 1997
First published by Abacus in 1998
Reprinted 1998 (nine times), 1999

A CIP catalogue record for this book
is available from the British Library.

ISBN 0 349 10943 5

Typeset in Bembo by M Rules
Printed and bound in Great Britain by
Clays Ltd, St Ives plc

Abacus
A Division of
Little, Brown and Company (UK)
Brettenham House
Lancaster Place
London WC2E 7EN

On the field of battle it is a disgrace to the chief to be surpassed in valour by his companions, a disgrace to the companions not to come up to the valour of their chief. As for leaving a battle alive after your chief has fallen, that means lifelong infamy and shame. To defend and protect him, to put down one's acts of heroism to his credit – that is really what they mean by allegiance. The chiefs fight for victory, the companions for their chief.

Tacitus, *Germania*

AUTHOR'S NOTE

Anachronisms and Historical Accuracy

The reader will find three sorts of anachronism in this book. The first group are those that are unintentional and of which, at the time of going to press, I was not aware. They are fair game for swots, letter-writers, anoraks and so on. I don't think there are any serious enough nor are they frequent enough to spoil the ordinary reader's enjoyment.

The other two types are intentional. *The Last English King* is written, dialogue as well as narrative, in modern prose. It may be thought I have gone too far in this direction, allowing dialogue especially to be unreconstructedly modern. Thus, for example, royalty are allowed to use bad language much as they do today. But why not? Assuming, and I am sure it was the case, that Anglo-Saxon lords were as quick with the odd expletive as their modern counterparts, and bearing in mind that, apart from Edward the Confessor, most of them were pretty rough types, why not make their expletives as modern as the rest of their speech? The fact that most of the vocabulary of profanity and obscenity is what is jokingly, though often accurately, called Anglo-Saxon, makes it doubly absurd to deny them the odd 'fuck' and 'shit'.

For similar reasons I have used modern versions of proper names wherever they exist. Why bother the reader with Cnut instead of Canute, Wintanceaster for Winchester?

The third type of anachronism may be a touch more problematic.

Occasionally characters, and even the narrator, let slip quotations or near quotations of later writers or make oblique references to later times. Better writers than I have followed the same pattern: Heller, for example, in *God Knows*. Some will find this irritating. For reasons I find difficult to explain, it amuses me, and may amuse others. But it also serves a more serious purpose – to place the few years spanned by the book in a continuum which leads forward as well as back, to remind readers, especially English readers, that it was out of all this that we came.

I have tried to be accurate with historical personages, events and dates in so far as these are known through the few and often contradictory sources available, though, of course, I have put my own interpretation on them in a way that is disallowed to historians. This is, after all, a novel. Thus an important part covers the relations between Edward the Confessor and the Godwinson family. It seems clear to me what they were – and it is my privilege as a novelist to say so. A historian must be more circumspect. And another factor which should be kept in mind is that William, like most successful bastards with guilty consciences, saw to it that history was written the way he wanted it to be written.

I have made only one conscious alteration to actual events for artistic reasons – historians 'surmise' (their word) that Harold was in Normandy in 1064. I've moved the trip to 1065. And, of course, I've left things out where they got in the way of my main story-line, and, where no source I could find covered a particular theme or span of time, I have felt free to invent.

PROLOGUE

PROLOGUE

1070

The Wanderer stepped over the side into shallow clear sunlit water. His feet stirred fine glittering sand into brief swirling clouds above a shingle of small smoothed fragmented seashell and flint. He gave the small black coracle a push and waved a farewell at the oarsman who had ferried him from the tubby cargo boat that lay anchored a hundred paces out in the horseshoe bay. With his face set to the land, he climbed to the top of the shingle bank and walked along it to a point where a steep chalk track climbed to a saddle of grass between the white headland and the country inland. Salmon-coloured valerian still bloomed in spikes above its waxy leaves, choughs wheeled against the cliff faces.

In his left hand he grasped a staff of hazel he had cut more than two thousand miles and a year away on the southern slopes of Asia Minor's Taurus Mountains. From a strap over his right shoulder hung a small bag or large wallet in which there was some bread and cheese, both now stale. He kept the strap in place with the smooth, rounded stump which was all that was left of his right hand and wrist. He was wearing a natural-colour woollen jerkin held in by a belt which supported a smaller wallet holding three gold coins and a handful of bronze above woollen leggings with leather-thong cross-gartering. His old shoes were made from cow-hide but sound, though the stitching had begun to unravel.

He was of middling height, deeply suntanned beneath fairish hair, fit, but looked a lot older than his twenty-six years – his more or less hand-some face was marked with lines of pain and grief.

The sun went in. He glanced up at the dark clouds that were gather-ing in the west and north, then, as he reached the saddle between the two headlands, he looked back over the sea. The sun still shone on the boat that had brought him; its sail was now up again, the coracle safely lifted and stowed in board. The sea gleamed silver to the high horizon beyond but, even as he watched, the white cliffs turned grey and purple cloud shadow slid across the waters in pursuit of the ship. The Wanderer turned his face inland again, and followed the track down into the woodland and scrub on the northern side. A host of starlings whirled like dust motes over the valley ahead, gathering for an autumn moot. Summer was fading.

As he walked on, following the track round the shoulders of the downs, through coombes and valleys nothing of what he saw looked right. Fences made from hurdles had been put up where none had been before, closing off what he knew had once been common land or deer-forest open to all; in other places fences had gone, so sheep and cattle grazed and browsed across vegetable lots and through deserted, unkempt orchards.

Worst of all, the stench and the howling buzz of a thousand flies led him to the bodies of a man, a youth, a woman and a baby, lying in a ditch with the man and the youth on their backs, the spear thrusts and sword slashes that had killed them in their chests, throats and stomachs. They had been dead, what, a couple of days? Carrion birds had gouged their bodies for the softer, richer parts, the livers, hearts, eyes, but not the men's testicles, which remained where their killers had left them – in their mouths.

The woman's clothes had been pulled round her head leaving her naked and exposed first to the men who had killed her then to beaks and claws. What shocked was not the wrecked and raped cadavers – the Wanderer had seen many such before – but the fact that here, in Wessex, no one had seen fit to give them a decent burial.

He pressed on and a flurry of cold rain swept down the hillside and briefly soaked him. He made no attempt to find shelter.

A distant clatter of clip-clopping hooves came up the hill behind him. Mindful of the bodies he'd seen, he bundled himself over a low stone wall and into a thicket of bramble. Swearing because the suddenness of the movement and the awkwardness of managing it with only one hand had caused him to twist his ankle, he crouched down and waited.

There were ten of them. All wore uniform plate-mail hauberks beneath high cylindrical helmets with cone-shaped tops. Their nose-pieces almost obscured their faces. The mail came most of the way down their thighs leaving polished leather boots with pointed toes and wicked sharp spurs. Big shields shaped like pointed leaves swung aslant from their backs, long scabbarded swords slapped their thighs, their lances were eight feet long. Small scarlet swallow-tailed pennons fluttered below the polished steel of flanged spear-heads.

Their horses were big, bay or black, glossy, well-fed. They were well-shod and sparks flew as they clattered over the flints in the metalled track which climbed to a ridge a hundred yards above the briars. There was a solid coalescence about them all, the men welded to the horses to make fighting machines, the machines joined to each other by discipline and the invisible threads of a common cause.

They paused at the top, and for a moment milled about, horses snorting, stamping, steam rising from the rain that ran down their flanks. The Wanderer could hear the jangle of their accoutrements, marked the way cold dark eyes scanned the countryside around – not warily but with arrogance. Then one of them barked an order, raised a mailed fist and in a flurry of hooves they turned away. Stones and chalky mud flew up behind them, and, tails lashing, lances and pennons swinging across the iron sky and the rain, they were gone.

For a full five minutes the Wanderer shook as if with fever, gasping, retching from an empty stomach so his rib-cage felt it would burst. He was filled with anger, hate, fear and, worst of all, despair. At last he clambered back over the wall and scouted up to the ridge, careful not to raise his head above the skyline. From the top he looked down into what had once been a pleasantly bosky vale with fields and orchards in the clearings and a slight eminence between higher hills at the far end. A small village had nestled round a mead-hall and a daub and wattle chapel with a rush roof. Corfe, the gate to the Isle of Purbeck. On the top of the hill there had been an earthwork with a small stone keep not more than twenty feet high – enough to protect the villagers if pirates or Danes came harrying inland from the coves and bays on the coast or across the marshes of Poole harbour.

All gone now. The woods had been cleared, fences broken down, the small individual lots of land split into unfenced narrow strips, the orchards clear-felled, the common pasture ploughed, too, but in one wide expanse. Charred stakes and burnt ground were all that was left of the village and manor though a handful of twenty round hovels huddled together in a hollow below. Not all was destruction, however – there had been building too.

The stone bailey that had taken the place of the earthwork was three times the size in circumference and was as high as the old keep. There was a deep dry moat all round it. A huge stone structure had been begun on the highest point of the hill where it perched above a small natural cliff. Already the highest point was sixty feet above the raised ground below and looked, because of its unevenly unfinished state, like a huge broken tooth. The soldiers who had passed him were just crossing the bridge over the moat and more patrolled the crest of the baillie. Men and women laboured all round, carrying stones in huge sacks, mixing mortar, climbing ladders with filled hods, hoisting larger, shaped rocks on rickety derricks perched on a wooden frame of scaffolding.

There was a gallows at the gate. Eight bodies slowly turned in the rain or swung more sharply as a carrion crow or raven flapped on to a shoulder or perched on a head, so its heavy wedge of a grey beak could tear at a mouth or a neck.

The Wanderer took a wide circle round the settlement and headed inland, crossing rivers not by bridges but by fords where he remembered they existed or wading through up to his chest or neck. He guessed the bridges would be guarded by the fighting machines. After the rivers there were more downs to be climbed and deep valleys to be followed, most of which were still forested as they always had been, the birch just turning to bright yellow, the oak and beech still heavy with the tired green of mid autumn. He avoided all dwellings and villages. Once his bread and cheese had gone he fed off hazelnuts, blackberries already over-ripe and fly-blown, acorns and beech kernels carefully separated from the mast. These gave him painful stomach cramps as well as some nourishment.

Late on the second day he came to a wider, deeper river that threaded for a time a narrow valley whose wooded sides were almost steep enough to form a gorge. Running roughly north to south it took a wide ninety-degree bend round two hills that stood out on account of their isolation from the rest. One was low and almost square, Hod Hill, the site, it was said, of a Roman camp. The other was much higher, longer and crowned with turfed ramparts that snaked a long ellipse enclosing the whale-back top. Hambledon. He climbed the southern side through hawthorn whose red berries looked like drops of newly shed blood, came over the switchback of the ramparts, crossed the crown and at last looked down into the Vale of the White Hart.

Rain swept across the fields and coppices, and beyond them the charred timbers, where the roof-tree of the mead-hall had fallen, his mead-hall, and the bowers of the women were roofless shells. Flattened by the rain a few wisps of smoke rose above the hovels and cottages that were all that remained of the village that had stood a hundred yards or so outside the broken fences of the manor. His gaze moved to the right, to the foot of the hill, to another, nearer settlement. The story here was the same except that a large barn made from mortared flint had been raised beneath a shingled roof and the tiny church where he had been married had been pulled down to make way for it. He had seen such fortified barns in Normandy and knew what they meant: riches and over-abundance for the lord, short commons for the men and women who worked the land – mules and horses were treated better.

A small flint core landed in the turf by his feet and skittered on down across the sheep-grazed grass. Heart pounding, staff raised to defend himself, he turned. On the rise above him, silhouetted against the grey sky, there stood a youth, a grown boy about thirteen years old. His dark brown hair was unkempt and long, he was dressed in animal skins above his thighs but wore patched woollen leggings below. He was barefoot and held a short spear. A small bow and a quiver were slung across his back.

'Walt,' he said.

'Fred.'

The boy tried to kneel, to grasp his thighs, but Walt lifted him up, embraced him, slapped the boy's shoulders with his stump on one side, his left hand on the other.

'Fred,' he repeated. 'It's good to see you.'

'We heard they never found your body. You should have come back sooner. We needed you.'

Rage, sorrow and despair flooded through Walt's brain and chest.

'How could I come back? I should have died there.'

'You should have been killed. If no one bothered to kill you then that's not your fault. Did you lose your hand there?' Fred nodded down to the stump.

'Yes.'

'That was enough. You should have come back.'

Walt longed to explain – his right hand had not been enough. If he had put his whole body in the way of the blow and died as a result, then that would have been enough.

'It's been bad?'

'You cannot believe how bad.' The boy laughed, high, hysterical, then stuffed his fist in his mouth. 'I'll show you.'

He pushed on beyond Walt, down the switchback of the iron age ramparts, threading through hawthorn, briar and mountain ash, all splashed with bloody droplets of fruits that clung to black twigs. At the bottom there was a clump of elder, leaves and berries now gone, just the twisted thickly textured boughs against the agate clouds.

For two miles or so they pushed their way across a mixed landscape of copses, small fields, hedges and low wilderness where, especially close to small brooks that fed the bigger river to the west, nature in the shape of dogwood thickets and alder and willow left unpollarded for three or four seasons was slipping back over land that had been farmed for five hundred years. They passed the skeleton of a cow.

A gentle slope, an overgrown track led them towards a second ridge of downs, riven with wooded coombes. Presently they passed the ruined huts and cottages and came to the broken fence of what had been a farmstead, a small manor. The buildings here had been more substantial – a mead-hall for feasts and folk-moots, five bowers, three with two rooms or more and a second floor, a well into which the rotting cadaver of a pig had been thrust so what was left of its trotters and tail still stuck above the low stone drum, barns, and an oast-house for malting barley.

All had been fired but much of the centuries-old seasoned oak framework, deeply charred though it was, had survived.

In the largest bower, nearest the mead-hall, sitting right in the centre, on an ancient blackened chair, two figures sat, a woman and a child, burnt down to an armature of blistered, black clinker. Hair and clothes had gone, though traces of swaddling bands could be seen round the baby's torso.

On the woman's head someone, Fred himself perhaps, had placed a small chaplet of spring flowers, hellebore, Christmas Rose. They were withered now, but kept their shape and something of their greenish-white hue. Erica – the Wanderer's wife, and the child conceived before the battle.

Walt was home again, at last. He stooped, picked up an oak-twig. The three or four leaves were brown and crumbly. There were three acorn-cases on it, but the acorns had dropped.

PART I

THE WANDERER

CHAPTER
ONE

He had travelled for three years, or was it four? At first he had not known where he went and did not care. First, after crossing the water (ill, probably dying, friends had paid a boatman for his passage across the Channel), he went into barren, frozen fens where people lived in stilted houses above the rushes, and beneath them too, for their homes were roofed with them. They fished through holes in the ice, snared the wintering wild-fowl, skated with marvellous agility and speed on skates carved from the shoulder-blades of cattle. Their Germanic language shared with his English enough basic vocabulary for him to get by.

Among these people there was a healer. Three months had passed since the battle and still the stump at his wrist suppurated, smelled foul, extruded occasional shards of shattered bone. The healer, an old man, bathed it in hot suffusions of herbs and bound it with cobwebs torn from the gaps between the ridge-pole of his house and the timber that supported it. Then he bound it with clean rags. A fortnight later he unwrapped the rags. Most of the inflammation and the smell had gone. The healer repeated the process and in another fortnight the stump was healed. It was ugly though, swelling into a knobbly cap like some mushrooms or even the warted glands of a giant penis, the pizzle of a donkey. For a time it itched dreadfully, but within a few weeks all feeling went and the obscene end of it became numb.

Fever and nightmare receded but a greater clarity brought no joy – in the stark, cold light of these foreign fens Walt now knew for sure just how deep his treachery had gone. It was simple enough. When the sword fell, he had tried to parry it with his own sword, his own arm. Had he taken the blow upon his body, as a king's companion should, then the king and lord he was meant to protect might have lived.

Through January and February he worked like a serf for the healer and learnt to cope with only one hand. He emptied slops, prepared vegetables for the pot, went about the settlement with a sledge and dragged the sick and dying to the healer's house. When the ice cracked and the water flowed, and the geese and duck who had strutted in their thousands on the ice flew north leaving the muddy mussel and oyster beds where the water was salt and did not freeze, the healer said he could go. Walt set his face to the rising sun, or the sun at midday, eager only to get as far as he could from the place of his spiritual annihilation.

He discarded the leather jerkin, padded to support chain-mail, the heavy woollen hose cross-gartered with leather thongs. The healer gave him a cloak from a patient he had failed to cure; he worked a week for an old widow who gave him stout boots with leather uppers and soles made of two thicknesses of hide – deadman's shoes.

Through the spring he followed the course, but against the stream, of a great river that meandered out of the south through farmed and forested plains, pushed on through gorges or hills so steep you could not believe they supported vines, now bursting into bright green leaf. He heard horns and woodland birds and maidens singing of stolen gold. The river became a lake and on the day of St John the Baptist, midsummer's day, when men leap through the flames of bonfires, and the hills and valleys are filled with wild roses and lilies, and the women dance with garlands made from both, the Wanderer saw huge black mountains soar above the southern shore, sheeted across their peaks with glancing snow. Rivers of ice tracked down from them into the valleys below.

He was a tall, gaunt figure from whom the women and children in fields and villages would cringe or even run with fright – until they saw his stump. Then some would mock and throw stones but others would express in tongues he could not understand curiosity and even pity. He drank from springs, he begged bread, and as the season turned he gorged on nuts and grapes. Heading east he found another river, wider, slower, more sluggish than the first but all along its banks were hamlets and villages and sometimes cities almost as big as the biggest city in the country he had left.

The further he went the more troubled were the lands he walked through. For every village with fields ripening with corn, and wine, milk, and indeed honey, with fat cattle and glossy horses, there were five that were burnt. The naked bodies of raped women festered in doorways, babies were impaled on seven-foot lances, dogs fed on the bones of their masters. He had seen such things in the past, in his own country even, but never as bad as this. Men with swaggering moustaches and fur caps, curved swords, galloped by in squadrons and fought each other beneath parched skies of azure blue. Yet Walt passed harmless and unharmed through it all, a grey wraith lost in the mirages of the plains, spared as soon as his stump was seen.

It was good land, he could see that, better than any he had seen since he left his own country, and he knew too well how good land attracts marauders the way a plum tree in September attracts swarms of wasps. And now he felt a stirring of nostalgia for what he had left behind – a land where there was abundance but order too, where all were fed, and most content.

The cold he had expected as the year turned never came, though to the north of the river more snow-capped mountains lay along the northern horizon. Then the whole landscape changed once more. The great river split and split again. Keeping to the south of it, he nevertheless found himself in a wilderness of huge rushes. Insects abounded, and carapaced amphibians, huge birds who strutted on stilt-like legs, whose sinuous necks raised their pink and black heads with axe-like beaks above his. The people were wild and savage, melting into the forest of reeds and rushes as he approached them, some mother-naked, and none to beg food from. For the first time he began not just to feel hunger but to fear it.

He headed south again and reached fertile and well-ordered plains where the churches were domed and the lords with their soldiers wore helmets inlaid with bright gold but the people laboured like slaves on huge estates or huddled in villages made from sun-baked mud. Bulgars, the lords were. Walt knew the word as a term of abuse for these people were believed to practise contraception through sodomy and so Bulgar or bugger were the words he used for a sodomite. But at that time he had had no idea that these handsome people who had clearly subdued the native population of peasants were Bulgars. It had been the same in the kingdom of Hungary. He had not known that the marauding, fur-clad horsemen with their curved swords were Magyars.

Then there was a huge forest of oak, but not even in spring – for spring it was again – the bright, brilliant green of the oak forests of home, but a dull, dark, oily green. Still, it fed him. He knew how to follow the dancing bees to their nests and steal their honey without being stung, he discovered hidden groves of wild cherry, he rooted like a pig for onions, garlic and truffles, he raided nests for eggs and tickled trout from streams.

Often he glimpsed parties of brightly dressed Bulgarian noblemen and ladies, gaudy with bright silks and gleaming armour, flying falcons or hunting boar to the blast of horns, the hullooing of their servants, and the musical confusion of their Thessalian hounds. On one occasion a mastiff treed him in a giant oak. He swung into its branches and climbed like a monkey, one-handed though he was, before its baying brought huntsmen and their beaters round its massive trunk. They peered up through the dense foliage and even loosed off a couple of arrows and a cross-bow bolt but they could not see him. Then, in the very crown of the tree, he suddenly heard a sound that for a moment scared him more: the hiss and spit of a giant cat.

Not five paces from him, and on a massive lateral bough, she faced him, back arched, brindled fur spiked, yellow eyes staring, tail as straight as a broom-handle, lips hauled back to expose white fangs and a scarlet throat. And even though she was not far short of him in length, and in weight too perhaps, he had to laugh, she so much put him in mind of the cats in the farmstead where he had been a boy. Especially he remembered a kitten called Wyn.

Steadying himself with the stump of his right arm, he plucked a bough heavy with acorns and thrust it in her face. She managed a turn, scampered down the bough and made the leap into the next tree. The men below saw her, and set to to hunt her with much laughter and hallooing on of dogs, but she was soon clear away through the forest's canopy.

Walt stayed where he was and faced a fact that filled him with remorse. For a moment, more than a moment, he had been happy, ecstatically happy, the way a man can be in the midst of battle or in the arms of his wife. And then he realised that for all the weeks he had spent in the forest he had been happy, more quietly happy, soaking in contentment with the dappled sunshine. And happiness, he knew, was not his lot. For him it was a sin. He stayed in the forest another month or so and brooded on this, mortifying himself the way he knew monks did through Lent – whipping himself with birch twigs, not eating until he fainted with hunger, exposing himself in the very tops of the trees to the summer thunderstorms that raged, hurling bolts that came close, very close, but never struck him.

The days became shorter, the nights shed dew, the restlessness returned and he knew again he had a destination, a place to go to. He could not visualise it but it was there. He walked again, south and east again, mostly east, and after two days came to an escarpment which made a natural belvedere from which he could look down out of the forest and on to a new world – new, that was, to him.

Across the roofs of marble palaces he saw a sheet, a sleeve of deepest indigo streaked with white wavelets, where gilded ships with sails and oars ploughed the water between two continents and dolphins twice the size of the porpoises he had seen in the river estuaries of his homeland tore the surface of the strait. And presently, following the forested ridge, he looked down across a narrow estuary to high walls, sturdy turrets and towers that cradled the huge domes of buildings bigger than any he had seen in his travels, and palaces more magnificent. The roofs of many flashed with beaten gold. He felt a surge of hope that this was the goal he had been heading for, but first he had to cross that river mouth and a smaller city that lay on the nearer bank. He threaded his way down through shanty towns and then the alleys and markets of the north side, but always he tried to keep in view the eminences that soared beyond the river.

He was now remarkable only because of his height, for there were many beggars more deformed than he – lepers with their faces eaten away, men whose legs had been severed at the hip, either in war or as punishment, men blinded by an executioner's brands. He passed through ghettos where, caged behind screens of iron fantastically wrought, Jews traded gold and gems weighed to the last scruple in brass balances. He picked fresh dates and crusts of bread from the gutters and drank from marble fountains set by philanthropists in the outer walls of their great houses. In a small square he saw how the poor had gathered, women with babes in arms for the most part, and how a huge cart filled with the severed heads of goats, their glazed brown eyes with horizontal pupils dilated in death, was tipped amongst them and how the women scrambled and even fought for them.

The stench and the noise were intolerable and he hurried on until at last he came to the water-side, a crowded quay which faced the walls and ramparts almost half a mile away on the further shore. On both sides scores of ships were moored. Hundreds of stevedores, mostly only in trousers or baggy loin-cloths, ran up and down steep narrow gangplanks, carrying huge baskets on their backs attached by leather thongs round their foreheads. Amongst familiar things like hazelnuts and cobs, sweet chestnuts, grapes, apples, pears, medlars, quince, green vegetables and salads there were strange orange and yellow fruits with dimpled skins. And then there were three boats filled to the gunwales with loose charcoal, another with bales of silk, five loaded with marble chips. Bemused by the variety and the sheer size of the amounts involved Walt moved through the bustle and the noise, tripping on cobbles and hawsers, peering past the sails and through the cat's cradles of rigging, but always aware of a presence on the far side that seemed to be calling him.

On the highest acropolis and dwarfing all the huge buildings and columns around it, a confederation, a congruence of small domes and half-domes nestled around a larger one that seemed to brood above them. On each a gold cross blazed in the sun. But how to get to them? There were no bridges, none in sight at any rate, and he was loth to move west and north up river, away from those domes, in the hopes of finding a crossing. But, of course, it was not a problem. A swarm of smaller craft, some with triangular sails, most rowed from the stern by oarsmen using huge black sweeps mounted on twisted posts that looked like blackened and etiolated limbs sculpted by the wind, scurried back and forth across the brown and scummy water.

Walt joined a group, a meandering line of people above a flight of steps set into the quay, some twenty or so in all. Among them were three men he took to be some sort of priest since they were robed in black, had black beards and wore high round hats, and women in mud-coloured skirts and shawls, holding baskets filled with fruit.

All of these and indeed most of the ordinary populace of this city, or pair of cities, had pasty dun-coloured skin and very black glossy hair, and eyes so deep a brown they were almost black. A tall man with a wispy beard and blue eyes stood out from the rest. He wore a leather hat with a wide brim, a leather jerkin studded with shiny rivets which came to his knees and shoes that were little more than soles held on to his ankles by leather thongs. He had a large purse on one side of his belt and carried a big sack hung from straps on his back. There was a cockle-shell on the front of the crown of his hat, and he carried a staff from which hung a gourd.

A skiff took off the first eight in the line, and a little later one of the long, thin rowed boats nudged in against the quay. The nine of them who were left descended the steps, the bottom three of which were slimy with bright green weed and studded with limpets. As he stood behind the man with the pack on his back Walt suddenly caught the smell of estuaries and the sea, the sweet rottenness of decayed fish and birds, the raunchy odours of shellfish, the salty promise of clear water beyond. A small boy tugged at his sleeve, then stood back with a curse on his lips at the sight of his stump. The tall man with the misty blue eyes looked up at him from under the brim of his leather hat. He was already standing in the boat.

He spoke. He spoke in Walt's language, but in a dialect he had not heard before, nevertheless it was the first time in nearly two years (or maybe three?) he had heard his own tongue, and it drew tears to his eyes.

'He wants,' said the man with the pack on his back, 'the fare. The fare for the ferry.'

'I have no money.'

'I'll pay.'

And he drew a second brown bronze coin from his purse.

A narrow bench rimmed the gunwale of the boat and they sat next to each other. The small boy gave the side of the quay a push with a boat-hook, the oarsman dipped his oar and with a twisting motion pushed it through the glaucous water. The Wanderer and his new friend were facing east, out across the mouth of the estuary to the swirling deep blue-black of the water beyond and the woods and villas a league away. A breeze whipped snowy crests from its surface, and the bigger ships, galleys with high prows and banks of oars, slipped effortlessly between. A flock of shearwaters skimmed the wavelets, almost touching the scything dolphins, and the Wanderer, momentarily forgetting the domes he was heading for, recognised the souls of sinners seeking repose. If he were dead he would be one of them. But his companion, the traveller, had his mind on other things: his eyes were fixed on the quays they were approaching and the great gate set in the towering ramparts above their landing place.

'I have sailed the seas,' he said. 'And here I am.'

CHAPTER
TWO

They passed between the huge towers of the gate and, leaving an inside line of smaller, older crumbling walls on their right, now converted into caves and hovels, began a steep zig-zagging climb up cobbled, narrow streets between buildings taller than any dwelling places Walt had ever seen before. Most were faced with grey plaster, sometimes moulded or carved into fantastic patterns. In places this stucco had fallen away, exposing walls of narrow bricks.

The streets here were less busy than on the other side of the horn-shaped estuary but not much; there were many priests and monks, but in robes and cloaks quite different from those worn by the clerisy of his own country. There were soldiers too who guarded the greater doorways of the bigger buildings, or strolled with a martial gait beneath plumed and gilded helmets. There were many pedlars like the women who had crossed in the boat with them, who shouted their wares to the blank windows or set up stalls on the street corners. As well as fruit, there were men who sold fish from the crowded sea. Mackerel, sardines, grey and red mullet, anchovies, octopus and squid filled shallow baskets scattered with salt. Others carried huge trays on their heads filled with crisp loaves covered with seeds, tiny and black or white like fresh-water pearls. A large cart passed, pulled by a glossy mule and filled with amphorae containing oil or wine. The seller exchanged full amphorae for empty ones with money added for the contents. The people who bought from this perambulatory market were, from the clothes they wore, servants at best but more probably slaves. Some were black, some had high cheek-bones and ochre complexions.

About half-way up the zig-zagging stopped and a street on their left ran straight to the crest. Here on this corner the traveller paused, slipped his gourd from his staff and offered it to Walt, first removing the bung.

'You look thirsty, tired, too. Drink – it's water, spring water.'

Indeed Walt, perhaps because he was, he thought, coming to the end of his quest, was now shaking as if with a fever; and sweat, more than the hot sun might have caused, streamed down his cheeks and neck.

They toiled on up the slope until it opened out into a wide, uneven space, flagged with striated marble, white, cream, rose-pink and black, flat and smooth enough to dance on. In the middle was a lofty column supporting a huge equestrian statue of a bearded emperor or warrior, bronze but gilded. Behind it there stood a big building with a portico of six noble columns with acanthus fronds decorating their capitals, and to the right a great gateway sumptuously carved with emperors in their niches, their armour not the chain- or ring-mail of the times but clad in the shaped breast-plates and crested helmets of another age. The gates themselves were bronze, also moulded in relief with the stories of ancient wars. They were guarded by tall soldiers, many fair-skinned and blonde, whose freshly cleaned and polished mail glittered in the noonday sun.

Walt rode waves of dizziness, vertigo. He was bewildered, confused.

'What is it all for?'

His new friend shrugged.

'Monuments of their own magnificence?' he suggested, with dismissive wryness.

But most magnificent of all, to their left as they entered the square, were the domes and half-domes climbing like foothills to the huge domed drum in the middle. Walt seized the traveller's thin, freckled bare arm.

'What is that?' His voice was now a hoarse whisper.

'The Church of Holy Wisdom.'

'Then that is where I shall find what I seek.'

Walt turned and headed across the marble towards the big, black, round arched door, open like a whale's mouth. As he approached the steady beat of a repeated note sung in a deep bass voice came to his ears, and the tinkling of bells.

Once inside he knew he was in heaven. The huge interior was far brighter than it had seemed from across the sunlit square. The base of the central dome was ringed with forty arched windows, and beneath it four more arches, the east and west ones themselves half-domes, also pierced with lights. Below these, four galleries, each with fifteen columns, were supported by forty taller and larger columns rising from the floor. No two capitals were the same but all intricately and fantastically carved.

Everywhere there was light and colour. The dome and semi-domes seemed to float on light or on the smoke from countless thuribles and candles. Every wall was revetted with marbles of various hues and patterns, often cut in veneers that echoed each other in mirror fashion. The columns were all of marble, save for the largest eight on which all else rested. These were a deep-striated, glimmering red – porphyry, from the Temple of the Sun in Baalbek.

Weaving between them or grouped around altars a hundred priests and acolytes, all in vestments and copes studded with jewels, embroidered with gold, some wearing high hats that swelled at the crown beneath jewelled crosses, sang masses in a language Walt did not recognise, swinging gold and silver thuribles and chanting in the long, deep repeated way he'd heard from outside – a quite different chant from the undulations of the one used by the monks at home.

More wonderful still were the mosaics which filled every space available, but especially the curved three-sided spaces where three circles or semi-circles touched. In most the background tesserae were gold. In the four spaces below the dome there were colossal cherubim; round all the walls angels, prophets, saints and doctors of the church. On the circle of the apse the Virgin sat enthroned, flanked by archangels with banners inscribed in an alphabet Walt could not read.

But the greatest of all, filling the inside of the great concave semi-globe of the central dome, was the Pantocrator Himself – the creator of all things, He who made Heaven and Earth and all that therein is, the Creator-Redeemer, throned against a lapis lazuli heaven studded with gold stars, the Judge inflexible yet compassionate, his complexion the colour of wheat, hair and eyes brown, grand eyebrows, and beautiful eyes, no beard or moustache, clad in gorgeous clothing, humble, serene and faultless.

Walt, drowning in incense, his mind bereft of rational thought by the chanting and the chiming bells, span on his heels and fell backwards, stunning himself on the marble floor. His eyes met those of his Creator, precisely one hundred and seventy-nine feet above him, before he sank away. Out of the darkness that closed around him, a cowled but female figure, huge but not threatening, Mnemosyne, memory, the Titan mother of the Muses, led him down dark labyrinths which finally opened out, as if he were emerging from a cave in a hillside on to just that, a hillside steep and stepped . . .

Whirling axes caught fading sunlight, arrows like hail sliced down the airways, swords crashed and cracked on helmets and shields. Horses neighed and screamed, blood spattered and ran in rivulets, mingling with that of their riders. The chorus of warriors eager for battle had faded and gone, only the cawing of carrion birds hung high in the air. Hewing and slashing, their arms weighted with woe, the housecarls laboured, silent in pain, too weary to lift their lime-wood shields. Crushed by despair the fight had gone from them, knowing no miracle now would amend it. Empty of hope, they welcomed the death stroke and those who were lucky fell to its falling. Yet one duty remained, blazoned with splendour, the calling and doom of all who stood near him, to die by his side or fall by the fallen . . .

'Are you all right?'

His head was cradled on the traveller's thighs. The traveller let water drip from his gourd on to a rag and gently soothed Walt's brow. A priest and an acolyte or two looked over his shoulder. Concern and scorn chased each other across their faces.

'If you are well enough to walk, we should go, you know? There are rules, regulations, about how one should behave . . .'

The traveller's hand shifted to the back of his neck, applied an upwards pressure.

Walt resisted it. He focused his gaze and met the eye of the Pantocrator above him, Jesus in judgement.

'I thought, when I came in here, I was in Paradise. I was wrong. Paradise is where I came from and now I am in hell.'

Slowly, but with more ease than he had expected, he pushed his feet beneath him and momentarily placing his stump on the traveller's arm for support, he hauled himself to his feet.

'Now, I want to go back.'

And he headed towards the semi-circle of sunlight, brighter even than all the brightness around him.

But when he was out, and the heat hit him like a wall, he sank to his knees again at the foot of the column that bore the Emperor Justinian, lifted his stump into the air and bellowed.

'But I can't. I can't, can I? Not after what I have done.'

'They do say,' the traveller said, correctly interpreting the broad gist of this remark, 'that a pilgrimage to the place of Our Lord's Crucifixion, and the Church of the Holy Sepulchre, undertaken in a spirit of contrition, wipes out all but the most mortal of sins.'

With his hand under Walt's elbow he lifted him up again.

'I'm going that way myself, though not, I have to say, out of any desire to wipe out sin.' He continued: 'Perhaps we could travel together. After I've seen what this place has to offer. I go by the name of Quint. No more and no less.'

Walt put his left hand on Quint's right shoulder, and wiped a tear on the sleeve that flopped over his stump.

'I am Walt, Walt Edwinson. How far is it to the Holy Land?'

'I reckon we're about half-way there. Perhaps a bit more.'

In fact, he never made it to Jerusalem for at that moment, in the Constantinian Forum of Byzantium, Walt's redemption had begun.

CHAPTER
THREE

Quint was in no hurry to leave Constantinople. It was, he said, the greatest city in Christendom, perhaps even in the world, though other travellers he had met talked of an even greater city in far-off Cathay.

'Perhaps I will go there,' he said, 'when I have seen you safe to Jerusalem.'

He had some money hidden, apart from the coppers he kept in his purse, in seams and odd crannies of his clothing. He was always able to find a gold coin to buy them out of trouble, the change from which refilled his purse with bronze and silver. He considered himself a pilgrim and self-consciously kept the traditional gear of the pilgrims who go down the Milky Way in north Spain to the Field of Stars in Santiago. That, he said, had been his first pilgrimage and he kept the staff, the gourd, the cockle-shell and sandal shoes of those who make that trip.

From Santiago he had taken a tin-trading boat to Porlock, the nearest port to Glastonbury, where the merchant Joseph of Arimathea, uncle of Jesus, had taken the infant Christ on a trading trip ('Nice country,' said Quint, 'pleasant pastures, clouded hills, that sort of thing.' 'I know,' Walt replied), then Rome and the shrine of St Peter and the Colosseum where so many Christians had died in the jaws of lions or at the hands of gladiators, and to less important places whose names he had forgotten.

There was no piety in any of this, or none that Walt could see. Quint had one purpose in life – to move, relentlessly on and on, punctuating his journey with the greatest marvels he had heard tell of. When he reached them he stopped – for a few days, a week at most, and gawked at the sights with some understanding but little awe until they bored him, then he shouldered his back-pack again and was off.

On this occasion, perceiving that his new companion was weak and needed rest, he took him back down the hill to the remains of the old Constantinian fortifications they had passed just after disembarking from the ferry, and found an empty cave or burrow which was enough to keep him out of the sun during the day and protected from the dew at night. He unslung his pack and from it pulled a sack made of quilted stuff and spread it for Walt to lie on, found a fountain and refilled his gourd which he left by Walt's side. Then he touched the brim of his leather hat and was off.

He returned at dusk with a small loaf of sesame-seeded bread, a handful of the golden downy plums which he said were called apricocks, and a pair of coddled duck eggs. Side by side they sat on the quilted sack and slowly ate what really was, when Walt thought about it, a very adequate feast. They were quite high up and could see over the wall and a strip of the now black Bosphorus to the woods of Asia beyond. A crescent moon, thin as a fingernail, hung above the continent. Round them, in caves hollowed from the bricks and stones of the old walls, a small tribe of Athinganos, Egyptians some called them, played their pipes and strummed their primitive guitars to the muted wailing of their songs.

Quint was excited by the crescent moon.

'What,' he said, 'the people of this doomed city do not know, what they have not been told, is that even now a nation of the most warlike people on Earth are sweeping out of Syria. They have captured fortresses by the score, routed armies by the dozen and by now are probably entering the ancient city of Iconium.'

'Where is Syria?' Walt asked.

'Oh, down there,' Quint waved his hand in roughly the right direction, south-east, 'and you see their emblem, the standard they fight under, is the crescent moon. Already Asia is theirs.'

'Who are these people?'

'Turks. Seljuk Turks. And their leader is called Alp Arslan, which in their language means lion, and he is the greatest warrior since Alexander.'

Walt thought he remembered the name, Alexander, that is, but wasn't sure.

Quint was quiet for a time, finishing his supper. The warmth of the city flowed over them, the smells of woodsmoke and charcoal, the lights in the streets and houses, the stars and the moon, the Romanies' soft laments.

'You know,' he said at last, 'you spoke of a paradise lost, better than heaven.' He stroked the air in front of him. 'Better even than all this?'

'Yes.'

'Tell me.'

'I can't.'

'Try.'

'All right.' He spread his knees, let his hands loll between them, his chin rested on his collar-bone and he closed his eyes. 'Picture this,' he said.

I am on a long high hill whose lower slopes are covered with hawthorn in blossom, blackthorn now finished, the sloes like tiny green tear-drops just forming. The upper slopes and crest have few shrubs for here the chalk beneath is only a few inches below the turf and the thin top soil supports grass only but in high summer a garden of flowers as well. It is an ancient place, for the old people dug out two ditches one above the other, throwing up high ramparts of earth and chalk now grassed over. And on the top within the ramparts and along the whale-backed ridge they had a town, or so the slaves we have, descendants of the old people, still say. And still they climb the hill on certain days in the year and perform ceremonies . . . but this is not to the point.

From this hill I look down upon a plain called the Vale of the White Hart. It is part lush pasture watered by the brooks that run from springs in the chalk hills to the River Stour, it is part fields of waving corn, green now as I look at it, blue green, just on the cusp of turning – bearded barley, nodding oats, tall rye, and wheat for the white bread the thegns, earls and royal house demand. And much of it is woodland oak, beech, sweet chestnut and holly where deer roam, foxes, but not wolves any more, though the oldest of us can remember wolves. Nobody claims ever to have seen a white hart.

'Hang on a moment. How old are you in this dream of paradise?'

'Sixteen. I think. I have just returned from my first campaign, the first time I served my lord in the field.'

'Your lord?'

'Harold Godwinson.'

Quint drew in breath, glanced at the stump where Walt's arm ended, and let out a slow whistle.

'Go on,' he murmured.

Two farmsteads or manors. The nearest, half a mile away, lying to my right and right under the steepest slope of the hill, is called Shroton. The further, nearly three miles off and nestling beneath another line of hills that run roughly north to south, is called Iwerne.

'That has a Jutish, Ytene ring to it.'

This time it was Walt who looked across with wary surprise.

'Perhaps,' he said. A monk from Shaftesbury Abbey had said much the same to him.

They have many similarities, these farmsteads. The dominant building in each is a hall, timber-framed, with a second floor at the inner end beneath a roof of shingles. Around it cluster bowers for the children and women, outhouses, barns, stables and the hovels where the poorest live.

'Slaves?'

'Slaves, but—'

'But you treat them well, like family, really.'

Walt sensed irony, felt a tremor of anger.

'Very well.'

He could have gone on to say how most were eventually freed one way or another and took their place in this well-ordered society as free gebors, moving out to the village beyond, gaining some land they could call their own, but he was aware that in many ways the status of a freed-man, forced to give endless labour in return for the right to work a few acres of land he could just about call his own, was not, if at all, preferable to that of a straight slave.

All this fenced, and outside maybe ten or fifteen cottages, each housing a family of churls or freemen, and then, in the case of Shroton, Iwerne did not have one, the church. This was no more than a shed really, timber-framed, the walls of daub and wattle like the cottages, but painted with scenes of Our Lord's life, done by an artist from Winchester, His nativity, changing water to wine, the Resurrection. No resident priest, but a pastor comes from Shaftesbury Abbey every Sunday and Holy day to say Mass and, when sent for, to celebrate weddings, christenings and funerals. Round this the fields, those in the lord's demesne, those held by lease or freehold by the cottagers, those held in common, are worked by all and, at the time Walt is remembering, it works well, it all works, better than ever it has before. That's what the old people say, and they bless King Edward who is surely a saint and keeps all things just and smooth and kind and well. And, Walt adds, his servant Earl Harold Godwinson and his sibling earls who keep the coasts and borders so well that harrying and ravaging from intruders are things of the past, almost forgotten.

Lord? We are not lords, neither my father at Iwerne nor Erica's at Shroton. We have our place in the order of things. Every man should have a lord. So my father is the manor lord of these people, but above him is his lord, the Earl of Wessex, Harold Godwinson, and above Harold, saintly King Edward, and above Edward – God.

'The Pope?'
'Fuck the Pope.'

And because there is order, an order we all accept . . . listen, we did, I'll tell you how. The serfs and the gebors meet together and if they have an improvement in our lives to suggest or a complaint to make, they pass it on. The freemen all sit in the village or hall moot once a month. Under the shire's sheriff representatives of every moot meet twice or four times a year in the hundreds moot, that is representing the people of all degrees who live in a neighbourhood originally sustaining a hundred families, though latterly the number has risen. And the Witan of the land, the earls, bishops and abbots, the greater thegns and ealdormen meet with the King twice yearly. It works. It is a system where every voice in the land is heard from the base of the pyramid to the top.

'The Greeks have a word for it.'
'They do?'
'Democracy.'

Anyway, that is paradise, that is how things should be. Even when the great storm came the year before I was born, and the earthquake when I was eight, and the murrain that killed the cattle, things were put right, made the best of and soon the swallows return, the grapes ripen on the southern slopes, the honey flows like honey and is made into mead and the girls dance, how they dance, and the cattle give creamy milk and the pigs die in November for the Christmas feasts, and though there is hard work, hard work for everybody, nobody suffers needlessly and even the cottars and gebors and slaves know that their lord and his lord will protect them and feed them when times are bad, and that is better than grubbing a meagre living from your own few acres . . . It is better than anything I've seen in all my travels . . .

But Quint was asleep and snoring.

Four days later he came back in a vile temper.

'This place,' he said, 'is shit. We're off.'

'Why?'

'They have here in the treasury of the Church of Holy Wisdom a reliquary, one of many hundreds. This, gold and crystal, jewelled with pearls, amethysts and garnets, houses a withered head. And whose do you think they say it is?'

'How should I know?'

'They say it is that of St James, the cousin of Jesus.'

'So?'

'The head and body of St James are buried in the Field of Stars at Santiago in Iberian Galicia. These Greek people are liars and cheats.'

Even as Walt stood, Quint rolled up the quilted sack and stuffed it in his back-pack.

'Jerusalem! Yes?'

CHAPTER
FOUR

Four bronze coins got them across the Bosphorus. They disembarked at Chrysopolis, a bustling town with a frontier air to it not unconnected with the fact that behind it lay the great hinterland of Asia Minor, its forests, mountains, plains and deserts sparsely populated, except on the coasts, by ancient tribes who acknowledged the Eastern Emperor as their lord, paying him tribute, but no loyalty. Indeed, already many had sided with Alp Arslan and his Seljuk horde. Walt and Quint followed the quay until it ended in a gate and then set off along what was little more than a sandy path, but a delightful one nevertheless since it skirted the north bank of the Propontine Sea, the almost land-locked water that is the gateway to the Pontus, the Black Sea, which gives it its name.

The shore was sandy, a fine white sand, scalloped into small bays, the water shallow and calm so they could paddle along in it and keep their feet cool. Behind it lay aromatic woods of pines whose canopies were shaped like the ceremonial umbrellas carried by Nubian slaves above the heads of viziers, ambassadors, counsellors and the like. A breeze nicked snowy scars from the blue-black wavelets and fleets of fishing boats dragged their nets through the teeming sea.

'Quint,' Walt said, after walking an hour in near silence, during which they had remarked only on the beauties about them, 'I cannot continue to use and abuse your generosity. I have no money. I have no prospect of gaining any unless I take to brigandage. And a pretty poor brigand I'd be with only this,' he raised his knobbly red stump, 'and no other weapon.'

Quint smiled at him, his lips lengthening beneath the sandy, thin, unkempt moustache. But he said nothing. They splashed on for five minutes and Walt felt his heart grow heavy and tears of frustration began to prick his eyes.

'I am, when all is said and done, a useless thing, a tattered cloak upon a stick and good for nothing.' His voice was bitter now, bitter and angry.

'You're company. Travel with no company is bread without salt. I like the way you talk. To hear a man talk of what he has done, where he has been, who he has known, who he has loved and who hated, of the passions that have possessed him, is worth a few coppers.'

Quint's head was up now, the strong almost beaky nose questing from under the brim of his hat, his eyes on faraway places.

'You see,' he went on, 'I have actually done nothing. Oh, I travel. I look at things. I learn languages – very easily – and I listen and sometimes I talk. But I do . . . nothing. I have no wife, no children. No occupation. I do not labour, I do not fight, I do not hate, I do not love. I have neither killed a man nor fucked a woman. I like to hear the tales of those who have.'

Presently, shortly after noon, with the sun now hotter than was comfortable, they came upon a wider bay than the rest with a promontory of rocks and a ruined hermitage. As they walked the wet sand towards it both men noticed how small dark holes appeared every now and then in the surface, emitted a small bubble, and then closed again.

'Clams,' said Walt.

'Yes.'

Quint unslung his pack, delved in it and pulled up first a long wooden spoon, then a wooden bowl. Stooping he scooped in the sand with the spoon and presently came up with a handsome bi-valve, a good four inches across and coloured bright chestnut with mother-of-pearl at the join of the shells. The long pseudo-leg of the creature slipped inside and the shells clicked shut. He stooped again.

'But how will we purge them?' Walt asked. He knew about clams, had first dug for them in the sands of Wexford Bay some seventeen years before. He had learnt then that if they are not placed several times in fresh water, which the clam is forced to take in and spew out, the meat will be filled with unpalatable grit.

Quint gestured towards the hermitage. 'Anchorites are, if you ask me, the silliest of men, but even they do not set themselves up in sanctity without a reasonable supply of fresh water close at hand.'

He continued to spoon away at the sand and, when they had four each, declared more would be greedy. A short causeway followed by a brief climb over rocks brought them to the tiny chapel and the even smaller cell abutting it. This had a shelf five feet long, two from the ground and a scant foot wide.

'His Holiness's bed,' Quint remarked.

'But where's his water?'

They scouted about but there was no sign of spring or well.

'Perhaps he went up into the woods?'

'No. Lazy bastards, hermits. That's the point of being a hermit.'

They went back into the chapel. It was now bereft of any moveable ornament, though the plastered walls were painted with remarkable representations of the Temptations of St Antony – the devils disguised as naked courtesans were especially lifelike and painted with a natural vigour more in keeping with Roman than Byzantine art. Or so said Quint. Meanwhile Walt noticed how a flagstone near the door rocked beneath his foot. Stooping he got his one set of finger ends in the crack and heaved. When Quint saw what he was doing he came to help him and together they lifted the stone. There was a ring on the underside and a rope attached to it, and sure enough a staved bucket at the other end. The water was sweet and cold.

'You see,' cried Quint, 'already you have earned the coppers I paid for your ferry fare.'

To anyone in a hurry the next hour or so would have been tedious. Seven times they changed the water in the bucket before they were satisfied that the clams had ceased to exude sand and grit, and then they had to collect stones to make a fireplace, enough wood to boil a pot of water, and enough tinder to light the wood. Quint's capacious pack, of course, held flint, an iron lode to strike it on, and a pot – the latter being tinned copper and just big enough to hold the bi-valves.

'So,' said Quint, at the outset of all this, 'how was it you learnt the purging of clams?'

A summer's day, but unlike any he remembered from previous summers spent on or beneath Hambledon Hill. For a start he has never seen so much sky, not even from Hambledon's highest rampart. Then there is the sea. A very different thing from the monstrous deep he crossed three days earlier from Porlock to Wexford. In the open boat he was terrified, drenched, and of course seasick. Now it is a matter of white breakers storming out of water grey-green where the sun shines, bruise-purple beneath the rolling clouds. They rush their swirls of foam up the sands, a great swath of sand stretching as far as the eye can see, with a grassy dune behind it. Only to the south and behind him is there a break in it, the turreted mole of Wexford harbour hiding the small town, castle and port.

There are four of them, all boys between the ages of eight and twelve, Walt being the second oldest at eleven. Dragged from their pallets in the stables before daybreak, they have spent most of the morning in various forms of pre-martial exercise directed by an ancient Sergeant-at-Arms who bellows at them most horribly. He makes them fight each other with a variety of toy weapons which yet can leave a cut or nasty bruise, and he slashes the bare backs of their legs with a cane if their exchange of blows lacks conviction.

At nine in the morning they are given a breakfast of rye bread soaked in milk still warm from the udder and told to wait in a corner of the castle yard until a Father Patrick comes to teach them their catechism. But that particular morning the reverend never came. They grew bored. They especially resented the way they were ignored. There was much bustle and toing and froing. Harold and his younger brother Leofwine came out of the great hall and mounted their horses . . .

'Harold? Harold Godwinson?'
  'Yes.'
  'Already you were part of his household? So young?'
  'I was to be a housecarl . . .'
  'Explain.'
  'One of a chosen group of warriors, closest to their lord, sworn to fight for him and defend him. Such men must be brave, loyal, well-skilled in all the arts of war, and, of course, fit for their duties in body and mind.'
  'So the training starts early?'
  'Yes.'
  'How were you chosen?'
  'I'm not sure. I remember a retinue of people came through. We had

a kitten. Called Wyn. Frightened by the horses she ran up an apple tree and would not come down. I went up after her and she jumped like a squirrel into the next tree and I followed her, caught her – a brindled little thing she was, all tiny claws and teeth and spitting – but I caught her and brought her down. The earl's men praised my agility and courage and took me away with them.'

Presently, the oldest of us, Wulfric, who knows about the sea since he was a Dane from Sandwich in the Earldom of Kent, says, 'Bugger this, let's go down the beach.' And that's where we are now and he is teaching us to dig for clams. We have perhaps a score or more, smaller than these, bluish in colour, and he has just finished explaining how they should be purged in fresh water before they are put in the pot when we hear the racing thudding of hooves through sand and water and looking back towards Wexford see nine or ten riders on horses thundering towards us, the sun behind them so they stand out black against the sea and sky, with the standards and pennants streaming above them, and these men, in cloaks and chain-mail, helmeted too as if for battle, wheel round and about us, herding us together, smacking at us with the flats of their swords, bumping us with the shoulders and rumps of their horses, and throwing back their heads in mocking laughter.

But two stay apart from the rest and watch. One was Harold Godwinson . . .

'What was he like? In appearance, I mean.'

'Then? Then he was what? Thirty years old or thereabouts. He was . . . magnificent. He had long brown hair that shone with fire when the light caught it, moustache and beard which also he wore long but kept well trimmed and curled. The English fashion for shaving beards came a few years later. His eyes, grey or blue according to the light, were kind when nothing angered him, but flashed bolts if something did. But mostly kind and laughing. Three things made him laugh. In battle he laughed like a trumpet, in wine he laughed like a river, and in bed, with a woman, or even if he saw a woman passing by in all her beauty, in a dance, or bearing a cup, or with a baby at her breast he laughed . . . like a god.'

With him now he has a lady. She is young, perhaps no more than sixteen, mounted on a palfrey filly that is restless but she has a switch of willow which the filly is learning to respect though she continues to circle and kick the sand. The lady has long dark hair braided beneath a snood held in place with a gold circlet. Her cloak is purple but the robe beneath is white. She rides with both knees on one side, with a special saddle. Her hands are long and white, but strong on the reins. Her eyes smile and laugh like Harold's, save when she shows temper at her mount, and her mouth, unpainted though it is, is full and red. But her most striking beauty is her neck which gives the name she is known by . . .

'Edith Swan-Neck.'

'Exactly so. The only woman he loved. She bore him a child seven months after he left Wexford.'

'What happened then? These other men, who were teasing, goading, bullying you? Who were they?'

'Housecarls. Harold never went anywhere without some in attendance – as bodyguards, messengers if need be, whatever . . .'

The taunting and railing, the blows and shoves and pushes, are now frightening, have become more than a game. One housecarl especially, a red-headed brute, seems determined to drive us into deeper water, drown us perhaps. He has us herded almost up to our waists to just the point where the waves break and he shouts with laughter at us or abuses us in foul language as he heads each off in turn who makes a break for the shore again. I can feel shingle beneath my feet, and the slimy embrace of great belts of seaweed and I am almost ready to panic when one of my companions does just that.

He is the youngest of us and has been snivelling and weeping ever since his stepfather handed him over in a lordly hall in a place called Cheddar, one of the biggest and richest halls I have been in, where the King himself sometimes stays a week or even a month. Poor soul, he weeps for his mother openly, and since we all weep for our mothers, but secretly, we mock him for it. We call him Timor, though his name is Aethelstan, for every night before he sleeps he mumbles again and again in Latin 'the Fear of Death distresses me' – *Timor mortis conturbat me.*

This poor lad, just eight years old, thin and shivering, with the waves breaking into his face, now lets go a long, long scream. Resolutely he turns his head to the east, to Cheddar perhaps, but more immediately the ocean, and pushes his way further in.

I know he cannot swim. I can, albeit I learnt in the mill-ponds on the Stour on the further side of Hambledon and the only sea swimming I have done has been in the sheltered harbour of Wexford in the last week or so. Nevertheless I launch myself after him, but as I reach him he turns on me and seizes my throat, just as the undertow of the ebb scythes my feet under me, and down we go together, the salt tide flooding our lungs, the roaring in our heads, the certain knowledge of imminent death. *Timor mortis* indeed.

But through the swirling foaming murk I mark just as the darkness of death begins to fill my head the massive breast of the great black gelding the son of Godwin rides and indeed his strong thighs and stirruped boots. To cut a long tale short my lord it is who rescues me, hauling me across the withers and banging my back to expel a bucketful of water from my lungs.

This is wonderful in itself, but yet more wonderful is it that Timor's saviour is the Lady Edith, although the red-headed housecarl who was the cause of all this has now seen the error of his ways and comes to help her.

Soon we are all safe on the sands again and all crowd around us while the Lady Edith rubs our heads with borrowed cloaks and then wraps them round us, although her own dress and cloak are black with water to her waist. Then Harold pinches my cheek between his finger and thumb and pulls me round to face the rest.

'Walt Edwinson,' he says, 'you owe me a life, I think. When will you repay me?'

'As soon as the shrouded ones decree.'

He frowns, perhaps at my allusion to the Fates of the old religion, then turns to Timor.

'And you Aethelstan owe Walt a life.'

The boy blubbers and nods.

At that up speaks Wulfric who has been set to one side through all this, and that's not a place Wulfric likes to be.

'I think not,' he calls. 'I think Walt Edwinson was simply following Timor, was as frightened as he and wanted to get away.'

A silence falls now broken only by the sighing of the wind which has freshened and blows stinging grains of sand against our legs.

There's nothing for it. I don't wait. Hesitate or doubt and you're done for, we've already been taught that lesson. I go straight for him and catching his jerkin in both hands head-butt his chest, just beneath the breast-bone. He's well winded and for maybe half a minute I have the advantage and I pummel away at him at his chest and arms and face, but then he recovers and smacks me to the sand, and turns my face in it, then wrenches me round and begins to beat my eyes and nose and mouth with his fists. At last he reaches out and finds a hefty pebble, a smoothed flint core, just uncovered by the receding sea. He raises it above his shoulder, and . . . my lord is there again to catch his wrist.

Again he sets me on my feet.

'Two lives now Walt Edwinson, and that's enough for one day,' and he laughs – like a trumpet.

By now they had finished the clams. Quint had two small loaves in his pack which served well to mop the broth. He hauled up one more bucketful of water, rinsed the bowl, the wooden spoon and the small copper cooking-pot, before packing them away again.

'You tell a good story,' he said as he did all this. 'Three lives saved but not paid for. I sense a sequel. An ongoing narration. At all events, I am more obliged to you than you to me for the meal we shared.'

Soon they were striding along the strand again, savouring the odours of the pines and the sea.

'Surely very different,' Quint remarked, 'to the wide and stormy vast-ness of the Irish ocean. But tell me,' and he paused in mid-stride, 'just why were you there in Wexford, in Ireland?'

CHAPTER
FIVE

A t the time Walt had had very little idea indeed of the answer to
this question. All he knew was that he had been plucked out of
the bowers, the warm and barmy nests of mother, sisters, aunts;
out of a farmyard where calves butted their mothers for milk, where the
pain of seeing the slaughter of an eighteen-month-old hog, who had
become a bit of a friend, was outweighed by the succulent meat and
crisp crackling that came after, together with smoked hams and smoked
sausages through to Lent; away from his gang of boys, the sons of
freemen, whose leader he naturally was since his ageing dad was the
thegn, a gang which marauded about the orchards, the forest's edge,
swam in the mill-pools and fought the gang from Shroton, slinging and
throwing flint cores up and down the ramparts of Hambledon.

All this gone in a day! And simply because he had shown some agility
and courage in rescuing a kitten called Wyn. The first pain was quickly
swamped by the wonder of it all: five hundred mounted housecarls, and
a couple of hundred from the fyrd – the levy of freemen a lord can take
for a limited time – armourers too, sutlers, cooks, smiths and a wagon
filled it was said with coin so each could be paid his daily hire, administered by a tonsured cleric who carried, just, a huge bound and clasped
book of vellum under his arm wherever he went and noted every item
of expenditure in it. And in the midst, but always near the front, not
Harold, but his father, Godwin himself, Earl of Wessex, mounted on a
big bay gelding with tufts of fur about its fetlocks and a nose longer and

broader than most horses have, a real brute of a beast, with his standard-bearer beside him, the standard a gold dragon on a red background, the gold real gold, and closest to him the most trusted of his housecarls.

There were Roman roads for much of the way, and older tracks where these did not lead where they wanted to go. They passed through village after village, past farmstead after farmstead, and the people turned out as Godwin and two of his younger sons went past. They cheered, danced and even knelt by the roadside, offering piglets, fruit, garlands of flowers. In one place the Earl would stop and praise a thegn for the good upkeep of a bridge (for that was a condition of his book-right, the written char-ter which confirmed on him the rights of the land he held and of his heirs); or, in another, fined the local lordling for letting a fort lapse into disrepair.

The sixth night they stopped at Cheddar where there was a great feast of cheese and cider and some talk of subterranean chambers infested with witches a mile up the gorge but none knew the truth of it. There poor Aethelstan, Timor, had been forced to join the cadets, dragged scream-ing from his mother's bosom, his stepfather happy to see him go. The next day they climbed through the winding gorge up into the Mendips from which they could see the hill at Glastonbury where the infant Jesus walked with his merchant uncle, and where Arthur and Guinevere were buried. Also up there in the Mendips there were the hollow mounds where lead-bearing ore was dragged from the ground and smelted by a clan of idiots, diseased, deformed and mad and treated by their masters worse than brutes simply so the great new churches, abbeys and palaces just then beginning to be built could be roofed in material more weather-proof and permanent than thatch or wooden shingles.

On the afternoon of the ninth day, they came to Gloucester, a burgh snug within its Roman walls, huddled about its church and abbey, and there, not in the town but in the meadows on the eastern bank of its river, the River Severn, three miles away, they met up with Harold, Earl then of Kent, and all his troops and three others of his brothers with theirs. The whole company numbered some two thousand trained housecarls with perhaps another five thousand levied from the local peasantry, the fyrd. Most were camped in small huts made from hazel branches bent into hoops and covered with skins or spare cloaks, blan-kets, and so on, but the Earls themselves and their closest bodyguards were in big tents, almost as big as the halls they had left. In the very largest of these, hurriedly erected after their arrival, was that of Earl Godwin himself. And in it they feasted as though it was all a high holiday and not a serious matter of state likely to end in the greatest evil that can befall a commonwealth, a civil war.

For on the other side of the river a host as large was gathered around the standard and tent of the King himself with all the housecarls of the Earls of Mercia, York and Northumbria and with the King's fyrd too.

'Of course,' said Walt, as Quint spread his quilted sack in front of a fire of pine cones and on a bed of pine needles and sand warm from the day's sun, with the water of the Propontine Sea lapping twenty yards away with streaks of ghostly green phosphorus rippling along the crest of every wavelet, and the moon now half-full casting rippling wires of gold across the blackness and a nightingale pouring forth its liquid song from the thickets inland, 'of course no one thought to tell us what it was all about. What I most remember is being called into the big tent to serve at the long table, carrying mead, wine and ale in big jugs, of being threatened with a beating if any great man's cup or drinking horn remained empty for longer than the time it takes to count to ten. There were oxen roasted whole and sheep too and basketfuls of bread and fruit and the rich orange-coloured Gloucester cheeses of the neighbourhood and Godwin and the Godwinsons, all together in the one place.'

'That must have been a sight. Few crimes known to man did not sit upon their shoulders. What did they look like? First, Godwin himself.'

Walt was confused. These men had not then been nor were they now criminals for him, but heroes, but he did his best, though a memory seventeen, eighteen years old was not easy to conjure.

'Godwin himself was, I believe, about fifty years old, big, tall and broad, thickening at the waist with arms like a smith's and thighs like a wild bull's. His hair was dark but grizzled and his beard long and broad. He preferred a mutton's leg to other meats though at that feast he ate two partridges and three quail as well. I personally filled his cup, a giant affair holding a quart, three times with mead. And then, as the feasting got less, the poets and harpers came on and sang and improvised grand epic lays in praise of the Godwins, and presently Harold himself took a harp and sang the Battle of Maldon, which all knew and joined in . . . and they were all in such finery, such finery as I had never seen. Their cloaks were scarlet, deep blue or saffron; all wore gold armlets and bracelets and circles in their hair and rings on their fingers, the men as

much as the women, who were for the most part war-wives or mis-
tresses – the real wives remaining at home to mind the children and their
hearths—'

'The Godwinsons?' Quint reminded him.

'Yes. Sorry.' Walt went on, 'There was Sweyn. He was the tallest and
the darkest, and, despite the pock-marks on his face, perhaps the most
handsome. Then Harold. After Harold, Tostig. He was the fairest in
colouring of them all, and then just twenty-six but with a bloom of last-
ing youth on him. He wore his hair long and fastened with a gold toggle
so it fell down his back in ringlets below the toggle, and some of his
brothers mocked him for his maidenly looks, indeed the second to
youngest, Gyrth, had a blackened eye for saying so.'

'So,' said Quint, 'we're in Gloucester but not yet across the water in
Wexford. And the year is still 1051?'

'That's right.'

'Explain.'

Clearly Quint already knew in broad outline the answers to the questions he posed. But curiosity was his passion; history, the past, and the
future, too, were his obsessions. He knew many languages, and was lettered and well-read in several of them, but he preferred what he called
the 'horse's mouth'. Wherever he went he questioned and listened, and
it was now a fascination for him to speak with a man who had actually
witnessed so much he had already heard of.

'I'm not sure I can.' Walt yawned. Always a doer, and by no means
reflective, he could no longer recall the ins and outs of it all. 'There was
a big dispute between the Godwins and the King, and the lords from the
north took the King's side. The upshot was we went first to London to
settle it and then the Godwins were sent into exile. Godwin himself
went across the Channel to Bruges but Harold to Wexford, and I was by
then attached to Harold.'

'And there you dug for clams and Harold saved your life. Twice.'

But Walt was already asleep.

CHAPTER
SIX

At the end of their second day they came to the end of the Propontine Sea or rather to that point where the coast turns right round the compass and slices back to the west and south, and there, in the late afternoon, just as it was reawakening from the somnolence of the hottest part of the day, they entered the city of Nicomedia, a pleasant town set on a narrow isthmus between the sea and a fresh-water lake. Here Walt discovered one of the ways in which Quint supplemented or replaced his hidden store of gold. Entering the market place or forum they saw how three Frankish merchants moved about asking questions which few could understand while those that did replied in tongues the Franks were ignorant of.

Quint asked them, in an approximation of the Frankish language they could grasp, if he could be of assistance. Their leader, a rough-looking man with an eye short of full eyesight and missing several teeth, explained to him how they had been commissioned by an abbey close to Frankfurt itself to come to Constantinople to buy lapis lazuli. The retailers there had none of the stuff, or what they had was not good quality since all had been bought by icon painters attached to a monastery within the city walls. However, these advised the Franks that the principal wholesale dealer resided in Nicomedia. But they could not find him and did not have enough demotic Greek to seek out his address.

Quint offered them his services. Walt noticed that his communication was more by free use of gesture, a winning smile, an easy manner and the

same few words repeated often, slowly and loudly than by any facility
with either language. Nevertheless he got through and soon a small flock
of urchins led them out of the markets and into the alleys of the com-
mercial quarter. On the way Quint explained that, while he was at home
with the language of the Ancient Greeks, and with the baser variety used
in the Gospels, the dialects spoken in Bithynia were not easy to follow.

The traders in all manner of rare and valuable commodities turned
out, as had been the case on the north side of the Golden Horn, to be
Jews. The mystic signs of their persuasion were carved or painted on
their walls next to their barred gates – the seven-fold candlestick, the
interlaced triangles that make up the Star of David and others more
arcane. In most cases a small delightful courtyard filled with flowers lay
behind a heavy gate, wrought iron or cast bronze, and that of Shimon
ben-David, dealer in lapis lazuli and other rare stones, was no exception.

An urchin had run on ahead, a circumstance which later seemed significant, and they were waited for. A slave, not a Jew, opened the
creaking gate, took them down a short flagged path beside a small
alabaster fountain and so to a door of silvered cedar-wood where a lady
was waiting for them. About thirty, she was still strikingly beautiful with
long black hair, piled on her head in coils and curls much like the well-
born ladies of Constantinople. She wore a thin but pleated cotton muslin
robe which, although it reached her sandalled feet, revealed more than it
concealed. Her eyes were almond-shaped beneath a high forehead and
above prominent cheek-bones, her complexion and skin were the pale
ochre of dried olive leaves, embellished with occasional moles. Her
breasts were full, her waist clamoured for an arm to be set around it, her
thighs pillars of perfection.

Smiling modestly she turned and led them down a short passage on
whose walls oil-lamps glowed brightly enough to show how the muslin
shifted over her callipygian behind. She knocked on another wooden
door and they, that is the three Frankish merchants together with Quint
and Walt, heard a choked reply that presumably was an invitation to
enter. The lady pushed open the door and stood aside to let them in.

'Jessica, you may go now. I shall call you when it is time to let these
gentlemen out.'

That was what Quint later said was said – in demotic Greek.

'And it did not occur to you,' Walt asked, 'to wonder why a Jew
should speak to his Jewish daughter in Greek?'

'She was not his daughter.'

'At the time we both thought so.'

The room was not brightly lit. An old man, with a copious grey beard and long grey hair beneath a skull-cap and the prominent drooping nose of his tribe, sat behind a large table on which most of what light there was fell. It came from a high, grated window, part curtained. He, swathed in a copious gabardine, appeared to be in some distress from an ague or fever. He coughed and snuffled a lot, and for all it was very hot in that room, wore woollen mittens that all but covered his hands. But these were not details his visitors paid much attention to. All eyes were on the table.

The surface was filled with a pile of rubble. But such rubble! Stones as small as hen's eggs, as big as small squashes but not regular in shape save for one, a rhombic dodecahedron, a good eighteen inches on its longest side. They were all blue, but blues shading from that of a clear sky, just as the afternoon turns to evening, to the deepest ultramarine, the deepest blue beyond sea blue. Some had a purplish tinge. The surfaces of many were dusted with tiny dots which lent them the appearance of miniature heavens at night – the night-sky inlaid with flecks of bright gold.

'Mother of God,' Quint muttered. He turned to the Franks. 'These are worth . . . thousands. Their weight in bullion and more.'

Walt was impatient.

'How do you know that? What is this stuff anyway?'

Quint took him to the back of the room, near the door, grasped his jerkin up near his throat.

'This,' he whispered hoarsely, 'is lapis lazuli. Azul stone, blue stone. But the best I have ever seen. No one knows for certain where it comes from. Some say Tartary, though it has been found in Persia. But the best, and this is the best, is said to come from Badakshan, in the valley of the River Kokcha which runs north into the Oxus. Many thousands of miles to the east, north of the Roof of the World. But the exact spot remains a secret.'

'But what's it for?'

'What is it for? It is for itself. It is. It exists. But if ever you have seen a true deep blue in the margins of a text or admired the sky in a painting in a book of hours then a thimbleful of its dust has been ground down and mixed with Arabian gum. And now Arab pharmacists have introduced it into molten glass so they can make the lights in the domes of mosques look like heavenly light-shows to gull the credulous into believing paradise exists. Christians of both east and west are working towards similar ends to colour the windows of these new churches they are building. And of course princes and their consorts are not averse to mounting especially fine specimens in gold. It has also been used to colour enamels and faïence . . .'

But one of the Franks had plucked his sleeve and asked a question.

'How much?' Quint hollered. 'How *much*? Dolt! Every last scruple of gold you have save what you need to get back to Frankfurt. Though if you go short you'll surely be able to pay your way in lazuli. But, before you buy, you pay me my interpreter's fee.'

The Franks spilled gold coins from bags and pockets and hidden places, thrusting one of them towards Quint. He asked for a second and got it. The bearded man with mittens scooped it all into a capacious leather bag. The Franks now filled their bags with the blue stones. All were panting somewhat with the effort and stress but at last straightened above the now bare table with the shamed conspiratorial half-smiles of those who believe they have won out handsomely on a crooked transaction, when plop, a large drop of thickening blood splashed in the middle of the spaces from which the azul stone and the gold had gone. All eyes to the ceiling. It was coffered and also made of cedar wood. A patch of red grew to a heaviness in a crack between two timbers and another plop dropped.

The man behind the table took off his beard, hair, skull-cap and nose, they were all in one piece, a toy with which Jewish children like to frighten each other in sport or maybe it had been fashioned in mockery by anti-semitic gentiles, revealing himself to be a tall blond man no more than twenty years old, perhaps less. His right hand dipped below the table and came up holding a long broad-sword. His left hand did likewise and produced an axe, not a big one, the sort an Englishman or a Dane might throw. It was bloodstained.

Walt, using his stump and his good left hand, tipped the heavy table and pinned the blond man against the wall behind him.

'Fuck you, Oswald,' he said, but one of the Franks had a better idea. Drawing a sharp knife from somewhere in his sleeve he reached across the top edge of the table and slit the blond man's throat just below his ear, severing the jugular. Walt and the other Franks held the table in place. They watched till the pulse behind the blood-flow faded and stopped and his eyes grew dark with death. Then they righted the table and let him slither to the floor.

'Who was this Oswald, then?' Quint asked.

'A Northumbrian. One of Morcar's housecarls. I knew him by sight.'

What to do now? The Franks, especially the one-eyed one, were all for getting off as quickly as possible with both gold and lazuli, but Quint said no. That would throw suspicion on them all. Presumably there was a dead man upstairs, certainly there was a dead man downstairs, the gold and stones gone, they would clearly be suspected and, since they had no horses and no doubt the constables of the town did, they would soon be caught. Much more sensible to go straight to the magistracy and tell the truth. They took the gold and stones with them.

In all this they quite forgot Jessica's dark beauty, until, that is, they returned with two magistrates and a guard of five foot-soldiers. And by then she had gone. There was no sign of her at all, nor indeed of her clothes or jewellery. Her husband, a man much younger than the dealer aped by Oswald, not in fact much above forty-five, lay on the floor of his bed-chamber dead from a single axe-blow delivered to the crook of his neck. It had smashed through collar-bones, scapula and ribs and deep into his chest, a terrible blow and one which the Danes of Northumbria were noted for.

The slave who had first answered the gate for them was encouraged by the sight of the magistrates' fasces, which could be used to give him a beating, to fill in the background. A year previously thieves had broken into Shimon's residence and made off with much of his stock and some gold. At about this time Oswald appeared in the market-place declaring he was willing to hire himself out as bodyguard, guard, whatever. He had his full kit of helmet, chain-mail, sword and axe, but no shield. No one knew what his story was or how or why he had come to Nicomedia, though it was rumoured he had applied to join the Emperor's guard in Constantinople, but English already there had told of his reputation for cowardice and deceit. At all events, Shimon employed him, and such was his stature and the way he exercised in public with his weapons, he had nothing to do – no thief went near the place again.

The Devil and idle hands. It was not long before Oswald had his on his master's wife's breasts and then elsewhere. And she found things of his, much younger and more virile than her husband's, to toy with.

Shimon had caught them at it that very afternoon, during the hot part of the day. He turned Oswald out and vowed to put Jessica away – already he was more than friendly with a rich widow much his own age.

Oswald had hung about the market-place – there was nowhere else to go – where he heard how the Franks were seeking his ex-master. He hurried back, slew Shimon and he and Jessica set up the deception whereby they hoped to sell Shimon's entire stock and make off with the proceeds and any other valuables they could carry.

And that really was it, though Quint and Walt lost two days while all was wrapped up, statements made on oath and so on, before they could continue on their way, this time south and into the mountains, hoping to reach Nicæa in two days' time. But first they spent some of one piece of the Frankish gold on salted meat, bread, grapes, peaches, and a leather bottle of wine, as much as they could reasonably carry without it all being more of a burden than it was worth, for, said Quint, we'll go to Nicæa by the country route through mountain passes, thus avoiding the constant flow of traffic on the main road: there will be brooks and springs for water, but no crops to scrump.

CHAPTER
SEVEN

'So,' said Quint, as the track began to climb away from the olive groves and into a sparse forest of cork oak and ilex, with aromatic shrubs and coarse grass beneath, 'at eleven years old you began the training that makes a housecarl. That must have been hard.'

'It was at first, but we soon adapted, and once we grew to be comfortable with it, it was a good life.'

'Tell me how it was.'

Walt thought for a bit.

'First you must understand all was unsettled and on the move for the next two years. We were only a few months in Ireland before news came that Godwin, heartened by reports from Wessex that the thegns preferred him as a lord to some jumped-up Norman, was coming out of Bruges. In fact it was more serious than that. The Bastard William himself had visited London in the Godwins' absence and many thought Edward had promised him the succession. So. We took ship again, a terrifying business—'

'What were these ships like?'

'As long as from here to that grey-lichened boulder—'

'Twenty, twenty-five paces.'

'No more than three paces across at the middle and less than a pace at the ends. And when they were beached no taller than a tall man in the middle, though they swept to high and pointed ends at prow and stem.

But in the water, laden, you could, in the middle of the boat, reach down and scoop the water with your hand—'

'How built?'

'Clinker-built of oak, each plank nailed with iron nails to the one below, the gaps closed with hards—'

'Hards?'

'The coarser fibres from flax. They have to be picked out of the softer fibres from which linen is made.'

'Ah, oakum. Which was then covered with pitch made from pine trees?'

'That's right. Though shipwrights also obtained a similar substance from the outcrops of coal-rock that occur in Kent. Then there was a deck set above the hold where cargo or ballast was stored – in our case, arms for the most part such as we did not actually carry and wear above the deck and some provisions in case an adverse wind got up; transverse benches for the oarsmen, twelve or so to each side, a mast and a big red sail often emblazoned with a lord's device or something threatening like Raven the Land-Waster. As well as the oarsmen, who were of course housecarls themselves, there could be up to another thirty or so men on board, or horses to provide mounts for some of the oarsmen. In calm water with a gentle breeze blowing the right way it could be very pleasant. Even without a breeze it was fun so long as you were still too young to man an oar, but in a swell even, let alone a storm, they were hell.'

'But a hell seaworthy enough to get you across the Irish sea.'

'Just.'

'But you English, and especially the Danes and Norsemen amongst you, pride yourselves on your seafaring qualities. Could you not have designed and made something a touch larger and more reliable?'

'I suppose so. But what people do not realise is that these ships were expendable, throw-away vessels. Each port has its shipwrights whose normal occupation is to make boats for fishing or trade. Such ships are built to last with copper nails that do not rust, built on a frame of seasoned wood. They are costly to build and costly to keep up unless they are, as it were, earning their livings. So, when a king or an earl needs fighting ships to defend his coasts or harry those of an enemy, he sends out orders that they should be built and the shipwrights put them together very speedily since they have most of the materials to hand and many already shaped. Their purpose served, those that are still sound are often disassembled and the timbers stored, the iron nails already rusting, thrown away . . .'

Quint was one who believed that the proper study of mankind is man. He was not interested in the mysteries of the shipwrights' craft.

'All right, but take me back to the high seas between Wexford and . . .?'

'And Porlock. In Somerset. There was a battle there with the King's men, thirty thegns were killed, but our ship was somewhat off course, caught by the tide behind the others and we missed it. There were also messengers from Godwin waiting for us—'

'One thing puzzles me,' Quint interrupted. 'Why were you with Harold, whose Earldom was that of Kent, rather than with Godwin Earl of Wessex, who had recruited you in the first place?'

'I'm not sure. But I believe it was because, when we left, Godwin felt his days were numbered – he wanted Harold to succeed him in Wessex and so surrounded him with Wessex thegns and housecarls. Or maybe our departure was over-hasty and things got muddled. Anyway, these messengers—'

'I'm sorry. Please go on.'

'These messengers were from Godwin and told how he, Sweyn and Tostig were about to sail along the south coast from east to west, harrying as he went, and ordering Harold to do likewise first to the west along the north Devon and Cornwall coasts, round Land's End, and then to the east to meet Godwin in Portland harbour . . .'

He paused for a moment, and drew breath. The last fifty paces or so had been steeper than the rest and the sun was now hot in their faces.

'Let's stop awhile,' Quint suggested. 'My legs, which are older than yours, are aching. I could, as they say, crush a grape,' and he pulled a bunch from the bag of woven straw the greengrocer had sold him for a penny.

They sat on two smooth boulders, looking down over the hills and forest they had walked through, ate grapes, and Quint spat out the pips. 'They stick between my teeth,' he said.

And then:

'This harrying business. It does not seem, if I understand the word correctly, to be the best way of winning friends and influencing them to do your bidding. And presumably what Godwin and the Godwinsons were attempting was to win support in their argument with the King and his Norman entourage.'

Walt laughed.

'There is, you see,' he said, 'harrying and harrying.'

'There is?'

'Nearly always, nowadays at any rate, it is a way of sending a message, especially when carried on by ships along a coast. In the first place every village with a harbour, every river with an estuary, for that is one thing about these war-boats, with their shallow draught they can often go many miles inland, as many as twenty or thirty in the case of the great rivers of our land, anyway, every port and estuary mouth has coast guards who watch out for raiding parties. Thus warned, the towns around put themselves into a state of defence: the nearer villagers flock within the walls of the burghs good King Alfred caused to be built, taking their herds and valuables with them, while the more distant ones hide in the hills or forests. The worst the raiders can now do is burn a few crops and farmsteads, unless they have sufficient numbers to organise a siege. And sieges take time, time enough for the king or the earl to raise an army and come to the rescue.'

'So what was the point of Godwin's and the Godwinsons' harrying in the summer of ten fifty-two ?'

'To see how things stood between them and their erstwhile vassals. They had been stripped of all their titles and no one in England, or any-where else for that matter, owed them a thing. Indeed, to offer them aid or comfort could be taken as an act of treason. But that did not mean that, when threatened with harrying, and perhaps after seeing a few barns burnt down or whatever, the local thegns could not meet together and offer to buy Godwin off. Thus he collected the funds that were, by almost everyone's consent, his due anyway. So much was true of Godwin's company. For us, those of us with Harold, it was a different story.'

'How so?"

'The Cornish are Celts, speak their own language, still practise their old religion openly, and acknowledge the suzerainty of the English crown but grudgingly . . .' Walt's eyes grew unfocused again, and presently he stood, and walked about a bit, arriving at a platform of rock above Quint's head. He stayed there before returning with a shake of his shoulders which displaced the memory of a twelve-year-old's first expe-rience of the savagery of war.

The fifteen ships turn Godrevy Island and race each other towards the sands just east and north of the estuary, leaving to the west the headland with its hermitage dedicated to the Persian bishop St Ive. Instead they aim for the large and prosperous village of Hale. The swell mounts higher as they close upon the shore, with the brightness of the clear sky above them and the deep blue of the sea beneath. And now the waves surge and roar like wild sea-horses determined to unseat their riders. The sails rattle down, the men ship their oars, only the helmsmen work their great sweeps to hold a true course for if their ship goes at all across the surf then surely it will go over. The surf thunders in my ears, we are speeding now faster than a horse at full gallop, the wave breaks around us in a great crashing wall of foam and suddenly we bump and skid and grind up the soft white sand as yet another breaker smashes over the stem and rushes through us like a wind.

The men are shouting, roaring and laughing with the joy of this, tossing the salt water out of their hair, jumping over so they can help the last push of the waves to get the ship a few yards further up the strand. Timor takes a tumble, bangs his face on an oar handle and is bleeding from his nose, howling, and refusing to get out of the boat until Eric, our Sergeant-at-Arms, throws him out into the wet soft sand. Down the line one ship has overturned and snapped its mast. Harold Godwinson is raging at the helmsman and telling him he'll have to bear the cost of a new one. Fortunately none drowned for if they had the helmsman would then have had to pay the drowned man's wergild.

Some of the men are now shrugging themselves into mail corselets, but most don't bother – shields, swords and axes are enough and all are eager now to climb the dune in front of us and walk along the crest the half-mile which will bring us to Hale. The men, three hundred or so, scramble up the loose sand, slithering and laughing at the slipperiness of it and, with Harold and his Raven standard in their midst, are soon moving at a slow run along the skyline. We boys follow with Wulfric in front, I'm on his heels, doing our best to catch up, but, encumbered with clubs and round shields as we are and with our clothes sodden, we trip and tumble more often than we should.

Soon the dune becomes a dyke keeping the sea from fields and marsh land on the other side and we see a small settlement below us, a hall thatched with reeds from the marsh, some stunted apple trees, two substantial bowers, some hovels or barns and a wattle fence around the whole. Eight or so of the men break away from the main body, down the side of the dyke, smash their way through the fence, set hens scurrying in every direction and a dog to bark at the end of his tether. They break into the hall and, just as we boys come level with it, two come out with firebrands which they hurl into the thatch. Red flames blossom along the roof tree.

'Come on,' cries Wulfric, and he charges in bounding leaps down the turved slope. I hesitate, but follow, and three or four other lads do too.

Inside the hall which is dark and filled with smoke, one Cornishman, small, dark and with the big black beard all Cornishmen wear, is not quite dead though his head is half off – I can see the white rings of his windpipe and the snapped tendons of his neck. Another is trying to put his guts back where they belong through the hole left by a slashing sword blow. At the far end of the hall an old man with a white beard and wearing a long jerkin stands in front of an old woman, a younger one and two girls about my age. He has a big two-handed sword and, filled with the war madness, is howling with rage.

The eight men facing him watch him for a moment with narrowed eyes, then one then others hurl their axes before rushing in with flailing swords. Within a moment the old man is chopped, literally, to pieces. Then they seize the women and drag them kicking, screaming, biting, tearing with their nails down the hall to the doorway just as the flaming roof timbers and sheaves of blazing rushes drop about their heads.

Out in the yard the men rip the women's clothes from their backs right down to sheer nakedness and then tumble them about in the earth and chicken shit and falling ashes, taking them any which way they can but mostly from behind as if they were bitches. But one of the girls breaks free. She has black hair and elfin features and she sprints for the fence like a whippet. Wulfric, throwing aside his shield, is after her, catches her leg as she rolls over the fence and tumbles after her. I hear her screams and dash round by the hole the men made in the fence to see how he tries to straddle her but on his own he cannot master her. She has his hair in one hand, is scratching his face with the other and her knee is in his groin. But he still has his club, a heavy baton of seasoned and polished ash in his right hand and somehow he manages to jab the end fiercely in her face. Her grip slackens and he pulls free enough to hit the side of her head, then filled with war-rage and war-lust he kneels and stoops above her and batters her head and shoulders with the club until she screams and moves no more. She is dead and I watched her die. And I watch how Wulfric raises his head and crows like a rooster and I think to myself probably he is relieved to have killed her since he is too young to do what the men are doing to the other women and he would have made a fool of himself had he tried.

Walt shaded his eyes and peered down the road they had climbed. A mile or so back he could for a moment, before the twisting of the road took it out of view beneath the trees, discern a figure cloaked and cowled in some dark stuff. He felt, though could not specifically remember, an instance when it had happened, that this figure was always there, had always been there behind him since that day when he was twelve and had allowed a girl his own age to be battered to death before his eyes.

Behind him Quint coughed.

'There is, or so I was told in Nicomedia, a spring just below the watershed on the further side where the water is renowned for its purity and sweetness. I think we should try to reach it by nightfall.'

Walt pulled himself together.

'Of course,' he muttered.

'We've wandered well away from where our conversation started this morning,' Quint went on, shouldering his pack as he did so, pulling the brim of his leather hat over his eyes, and picking up his staff with gourd attached. 'You were, you know, about to tell me how you were trained to be a warrior and a housecarl.'

'Yes. And you are right to make the distinction. The warrior side of it was straightforward enough.' Walt fell into step beside his companion and continued. 'First we had to be fit. We were taken to a place called Tidworth Camp, north of Sarum, where Eric, our Sergeant-at-Arms, saw to that and much else too.

'This was all done in some secrecy, for after the King reconciled with the Godwins, a condition was they should relinquish their private armies, that there should be no armies but the King's or those commanded in the name of the King. That all should be the King's men. So it was in this remote fold of the Wiltshire Downs that our initial training took place.

'On the one side Eric built up sheer strength – he made us walk and run and walk and run for miles and miles across or rather up and down the bare Wiltshire Downs carrying loads carefully chosen always to be a pound or so more than we could manage with any degree of comfort. And on these marches he made us sing or chant: silly ditties like "We hate the Norsemen and they hate us, we all think they're full of pus," or

"The Scots and Picts are a load of shits, and we're going to chop them into bits."

'But as well as building up sheer strength he saw to it as well that we were fast and agile. One trick was to take us to a forested valley and there, giving us a short start, set Irish wolf-hounds on us. If we were quick enough we'd get to the other side and he'd call them off. If we were not quick enough then we could let ourselves be treed, but that could only be justified if we could show a claw mark in our backs or a bite in the buttocks. He had many other exercises of that sort.

'And then there was weapon training. Basically the proper handling of a shield, how to make an overlapping wall of shields. The skills that make an axe a deadly weapon whether thrown or used to hack and maim. And finally the use of the sword, both to slash and stab. And also, of course, the proper repair and maintenance of these weapons—'

'No spear or javelin, then.'

Walt's eyes narrowed.

'Certainly not,' he replied. 'The spear was the arm, as too was the round shield, as opposed to the leaf-shaped shield, of the fyrd, the churls and sokemen.'

'And horsemanship?'

'We had horse-races, we hunted from our horses and went hawking from them, for most lords love both sports, but that has little to do with the warrior side of being a housecarl.'

'Did you not ride horses into battle?'

'No. Of course we rode from one battle to the next but we did not take them into battle.'

'Why not?'

'A fighting man should stand on his own two feet and exchange blows with his adversary until one or other drops. Besides, good horses are valuable, and can get killed in battle. I saw three die between William the Bastard's thighs on Senlac Hill. I could scarce afford one horse, let alone three.'

'But . . .'

'If you are going to say they won because they fought from horses, forget it.'

His face was suddenly suffused with angry blood again and Quint wisely chose not to pursue the subject.

CHAPTER
EIGHT

'You spoke of the difference between a warrior and a housecarl.'

'A warrior without a soul is a mere weapon. The most handsome sword – with a gold pommel set with garnets, with filigree gold on the hilt, a scabbard of gold and garnet bosses, with a well-tempered blade kept bright and sharp and inlaid with the lightning flashes of old Thor – is but a commodity, an article of exchange which can be passed from hand to hand and used for ill as well as good. Such are the warriors who go into the market-place and fight for one lord one day and for his enemy the next . . .'

'Perhaps. But soldiers are always required at every hiring to swear an oath of loyalty to each new lord in turn.'

'Even an oath can be bought and sold, especially when men grow evil and forget the ways of their fathers.'

Quint pondered this for some fifty strides or so. Then:

'We have already seen in the ranks of the Emperor of the East house-carls who fought by Harold's side. Perhaps, had you the use of your sword hand, you might be one of them.'

'Be careful, Dutchman, or whatever it is you are. I can give a good account of myself with what I still have.'

Bless us, but he's in a touchy mood today, thought Quint.

'Frisian actually. Like you we are Saxon stock. But there is something about oath-taking I do not fully understand,' he said, adopting a conciliatory tone.

'Yes.'

'Well, then. Put me right where I am wrong. Your pupil awaits the attentions of his teacher.'

Suspecting sarcasm, Walt threw him a quick look but found only bland interest on his companion's face.

'The oath of the housecarl comes from a heart that has been schooled from birth by example, by story-telling and nights spent in the Hall listening to the exploits of his forebears when as a boy he served as cup-bearer and later joined in the mead-drinking and the harp-playing himself. These are the nights when men make promises and boast of what they will do, boasts which are not bravado but solemn declarations of the lengths to which they will go in service of their lords. Above all they will promise again and again to serve their lord expecting no reward save the honour of serving him. And one other loyalty he swears – to his fellow housecarls he will always be true and faithful too, when standing shoulder to shoulder in the shield-wall, yes, especially then. When a man has lived thus for twenty years you may trust his oath. Yes, indeed, you may trust him.'

And he strode on, swinging his stump, holding his head in the air as if indeed on a march, a march into battle at his lord's bidding. Dear me, thought Quint again, not just touchy, but a touch humourless too, taking himself very seriously today. But worse was to come. Walt began to sing. Quite well, in the middle register a man might sing in, not too low nor high.

> Think of all the times we boasted
> At the mead-bench, heroes in the hall
> Predicting our own bravery in battle.
> Now we shall see who meant what he said.
> I will make known my ancestry to one and all:
> I come from a mighty family.
> My grandfather was a mighty ealdorman.
> No thegn shall ever reproach me,
> Now that my Prince has been hewn down in battle.
> This is the most bitter sorrow of all:
> He was my kinsman and my Lord . . .

And suddenly Walt threw himself at the foot of an ilex and clung to it with his left arm while he chewed on the stump, chewed the way a cat can chew your fist, and if you tease it, draw blood. Quint ran to him, pulled his good arm free and cradled him in his arms for a time, sitting beside him and rocking him like a child – he sang too, but in a very different way, a song his mother had sung when he had the toothache, about a fox going out one cold and frosty night, to get a goose . . . And as he sang, he thought – this is not tetchiness or bravado, this is madness. Walt has a devil in him, not an actual devil, not possessed so it's a matter for exorcism, but a deep devil, a deep distress, yes, perhaps exorcism is the right word, but not the silliness of bell, book and candle, but a deeper probing, a slow drawing forth of ancient poisons.

The immediate crisis passed soon enough, a spasm racked Walt's body, his face relaxed, the stump dropped from his mouth, and his face changed to that of a sleeping child as if a cloud had passed from it and the sun shone through again. He lay like that for almost an hour, then woke slowly and naturally.

'Are you all right?'

'Fine. Never felt better.'

Walt stood, shook his head, fist and stump to his ears, elbows out like wings, and yawned.

'Well then,' he said, 'we'd better get on.'

And the strange thing was, it seemed he had no recollection at all of the fit he had fallen into.

They set their faces to the slope again but now the hour was advanced to a time when the sun, though still with a long way to go before it set, had dipped beneath the escarpments above. The warmth of the day still lingered about them, and presently the oak gave way to aromatic mountain fir and pine. With the sun gone birds began to flit about again and above their heads a speckled warbler with red breast and a long tail poured forth a stream of song from a pine bough.

Quint, curious as ever, wanted to know whether or not or to what extent his friend had suffered an amnesia of the events preceding his fit.

'You have told me,' he said, 'of the hardships and companionship that go with learning to be a warrior, and of the teaching, the deep teaching . . .' For a moment Quint's mind played with words, as it often did, in several languages. To teach was in Latin *docere* and so it was that teachers were called doctors. There was teaching and teaching. By rote for practical purposes, such as a craft, a language, to read or write. But a deeper, more inner sort of teaching, doctoring, made a man and woman what they were, how they acted, tutored their souls. 'Indoctrination?' Perhaps; '. . . the deep teaching that turns a warrior into a housecarl.'

'I did?'

'You did. But surely there is more to it than that. The lord has responsibilities towards his housecarls.'

'Of course he does. Of course. No man would give his all without expecting some return. And, indeed, for what we did, substantial return.?'

'The lord is the ring-giver. Gold, of course. He stands up for you in the courts or in disputes, defends your kin. And when your fighting days are done he gives you land. There remain obligations. You can become one of his stewards, ambassadors even, or from your new estate supply more thegns, more warriors to become housecarls. And there are taxes and dues to pay as well. But at the end of the day you have land. Not just the five hides of a thegn but, according to the services you have rendered, maybe hundreds of hides. And these are like a little kingdom of your own to administer, according to the laws of course, but your own. To be passed on to your heirs.'

This, thought Quint, is very far from the indoctrination inherent in poems like the Battle of Maldon. So different, to believe both at once must be like a soul facing two ways, torn in contradictory directions. A mind split. That could almost be a disease. Again, his own multifarious mind searched for a word and stumbled into Greek. *Schizo-phrenia*?

He put it to Walt, bluntly.

'How can you reconcile these things?' he asked. 'You serve your lord completely, you are his man, out of the oaths you have sworn, because it is a noble thing to do. Yet really you take lands and rings of gold from him, and that's really why you do it.'

Walt looked at him as if he were an idiot.

'How would people know,' he said, 'that I had served my lord with total loyalty if I did not have his rings and land to prove it?'

'So the reputation these things bring is more important than their actual worth?'

This time there was no mistaking the sarcastic incredulity in his tone and Walt, turning away, decided to rise above it. There are some things common folk just do not understand.

Meanwhile Quint, whose search for understanding was as much the very core of his being as seeking after self-worthiness was Walt's, turned it all over again and again in his mind. On the one hand, he surmised, this Walt is riven with guilt because he survived the battle in which his lord died, and that crumbles his soul within him. But on the other he dreams of the lands he should have had, his own hall, his thegns and churls and freemen and slaves, and above all a wife and children, heirs of his own – things good in themselves and to be lusted after, but also proofs of his stature as a man amongst men; all, when you think about it, very Anglo-Saxon, and of all this he is deprived and that makes him bitter, but it is a bitterness riven with guilt, guilt even that he should feel bitter against his dead lord.

Welladay, he thought, I must do what I can for him.

CHAPTER
NINE

They passed the tree line into a rolling climbing country of coarse pasture, low hemispherical shrubs of thyme and lavender, where long whale-backed boulders pushed their lichened humps through seas of grass. In places there were banks of spiky asphodel, white and black, such as grace the Elysian Fields. They reached the watershed as evening fell. On the other side they found the spring. The water was indeed very pure and icy cold, but bubbled slightly with tiny luminescent bubbles; it had an almost indiscernible blue depth to it when one peered into the cup.

They made up a fire, boiled up the salted meat with some wild garlic Walt found, finished their bread and drank much of the wine. By then darkness had almost fallen and again they spread the quilt but because the air was chill Quint showed how they could get into it — there was room for both.

Quint was soon snoring, but Walt lay awake and his mind dwelt on some at least of the things he had been thinking about during the day and describing to Quint. Shortly, through Quint's snoring, he thought he could hear a distant sort of wailing or singing, or something between the two, perhaps an owl of a breed peculiar to these mountains, he thought, but it went on, and eventually he nudged Quint's shoulder, until the traveller turned off his back and stopped snoring.

Now Walt could hear it clearly, a lilting rise and fall, but sad, keening and some way off and below them on the north-facing mountainside up which they had come. For a time he was frightened, thinking of sprites or succubi, demons who take on female forms to seduce men in their sleep. He even thought of the Cornish girl, heathen as she was and probably not baptised, a troubled spirit come to haunt him for not saving her from Wulfric. But the singing came no nearer and finally sank away in a dying fall and Walt slept. Before dawn he woke again, was perhaps awakened, and in the very earliest greyest light, with a mountain mist thick and pearly around them, saw again the cowled and robed figure he had seen before, but now very close indeed and kneeling over Quint's pack. His drawn-in breath startled it and it was gone, flitting away into the mist which wrapped it out of sight in seconds. Walt's heart pounded as he tried to make up his mind whether to follow or not, but he could see no point: it could lure him to a precipice, or, if it was corporeal, have the advantage to take him from behind, so he decided to stay where he was, but determined to remain awake.

However, the dawn was a long way off, he was still heavy from the wine, the climbing walk, and perhaps too from the effects of the fit he had had, and he soon slept again. And now, the way it often is in the latter part of the night, when dawn is near, it was a heavy deep sleep and when he awoke he was ready to dismiss it all, the keening and the figure, as the figments of a dream. He said nothing of it as they breakfasted off grapes and bread, and drank from the spring.

The mist had gone with the first shafts of sunlight though it lingered in the river valleys far below. The view in front of them was now even more magnificent than that to the north, for the southern slopes were more broken and rolled on further without much descent but disappearing into the mauve distances of further mountain ranges. Above them larks sang and around them brown mountain swifts skimmed faster than the eye could hold them, plucking insects out of the air only inches above the thyme and grass and rocks.

'Come now,' cried Quint, 'a sparse six leagues or so and all downhill will bring us to Nicæa well before nightfall, and as we go you can tell me what happened at Portland and after – what, some sixteen years ago?'

'This was before we went to Tidworth Camp.'

'I understand.'

It's quite a sight: a hundred ships or more anchored in the lee of the castle Alfred had built and Canute had enlarged, or pulled up on the eastern landward side of Chesil beach; the tents of a host some two thousand strong and most of them housecarls or men-at-arms, thegns committed to providing their lord with one man-at-arms (usually the thegn himself or one of his sons), helmet, shield, corselet of mail, two saddle horses and two pack animals — all these had come in from Devon, Dorset, Hampshire, risking the King's displeasure. But all were happy to reassert their loyalty to Godwin and the Godwinsons. And no doubt across the bay where the gulls swoop over the refuse of the camp and the terns plummet for sprats in the breakers some nine miles distant along the white cliffs of Osmington and Durdle Dor, the King's men and perhaps those of Robert of Canterbury and Siward of Northumbria watch and mark the extent of Godwin's support.

'We all met up there and feasted in the great hall outside the castle for three days, a time not just for revelry but for reaffirming at the mead benches old loyalties and oaths. Then the combined hosts re-embarked and sailed back east again through the Solent, sailing into the estuaries to make landfalls at Portchester, Bosham, Shoreham, New Haven and so forth right along to Pevensey and now there was no pretence at all of harrying. Some say Folkestone but it was Pevensey. I was there. It was a triumph, a progress, that brought burghers and thegns alike out on to their walls or into their harbours, all promising support should the King not reinstate Godwin and his sons, for all feared the country would be sold to the Bastard and the Normans if the Godwinsons remained ousted.

'Our march from Pevensey took us by Ton Bridge Wells, where there are springs much like the one where we have just passed the night, then Ton Bridge itself, where a small burgh straddles the upper Medway. We were on one of the three tracks, and there are only three, that cross the mighty forest of the Andredesweald, more than a hundred miles from east to west and often as much as forty from north to south. From Ton Bridge we climbed the North Downs into a place of pastureland crowned with a circle of Seven Oaks. Here the Celts amongst us, and there were a few, not just as slaves but some come as mercenaries from Ireland, some from Wales, grew restive and sad and talked amongst themselves of their Old Religion. It was said among them that many still lived like wild animals, elves or goblins in the green wood we had passed through, and that they came out at certain seasons, like St John the Baptist's Day, to celebrate their awful ceremonies and sacrifices within the circle of these oaks.

'The churchmen, the Norman churchmen that is, want to hew these ancient oaks down but the local thegns say no – the peasantry about the place believe to do so will bring plague, pestilence and murrain on the cattle and they will likely fight the churchmen's foresters to save them—'

'You say the Norman churchmen? Were they so very different from the English?'

'Yes indeed, especially the monks and those who served in the bigger churches like Canterbury, London and Winchester. They were very strict in many ways – about collecting tithes and other taxes granted them by the King, but also about church discipline and doctrine – and the one thing they could not stand was any truck with or respect for the old religions and the customs that go with them, whether those the English brought with them or those the Celts observed. And, of course, they will not marry. They demand celibacy from the entire clerisy – though nothing in scripture adjures it, as I understand. In short, they are a joyless bunch, interfering and bossy, do everything by rote. Even alms-giving and support for the sick and needy comes not from the heart but from the rule-book.'

At all this Quint nodded his head in fervent agreement and his nose, which was often pink, became redder, but he did not then enlarge upon the subject beyond muttering: 'Cluniacs, damned Cluniacs.'

'Anyway,' Walt resumed, 'we came thus by the shortest route from Pevensey again to Southwark, on the south bank of the Thames opposite London, just nine or ten months after our ignominious departure. The people of London, whether out of love for Godwin, or fearing a sacking, support us. At a great meeting of the Witan in the new Great Hall at Westminster, the biggest in the land, Godwin and the Godwinsons make a huge ceremony of oath-swearing – of their loyalty to the King, of their innocence of all the crimes they stand accused of, and perforce the King must accept them!'

'Because the host they have gathered is bigger than the one the King can bring against them.'

'Well, partly.' Walt frowned, sounded a touch puzzled at Quint's igno-rance. 'But mainly because when such great men swear oaths together then, perforce, they must be believed – unless an equal or greater number of great men can be found to swear them false.'

'And the facts of the case,' Quint sounded quite scandalised by what Walt was suggesting, 'that Godwin some sixteen years earlier blinded the

King's elder brother and brought about his death, that Sweyn kidnapped and ravished an abbess and murdered his cousin Beorn, and all the rest, all these count for nothing?'

'Well, something, yes. I suppose. But only if the oath-swearing leads on to consideration of them. That is, if sufficient men can be gathered together to swear oaths in contradiction.'

'So this oath-swearing is no more than a sign signifying the physical power the defendant, or plaintiff, can bring to bear upon the case?'

'I am no lawyer,' Walt was clearly irritated at his companion's apparent attack on ancient custom; English custom anyway, 'and all I can say is that oath-swearing is the basis of justice, and the greater the man the more powerful his oath. For instance, if a lord of several manors swears one thing, then some twenty lesser thegns must be found to swear him wrong. This is justice. It upholds the framework we live by. If we took each man's word as equal in weight then there would be no rule of law at all.'

'So. All your oath-swearing law does is shore up, or rather express, the power of those who are already mighty.'

'Exactly so. Is that not the meaning of all law? To uphold the status of the mighty but without resort to war, tumult, death and destruction?'

Quint stopped in his tracks and caught Walt's sleeve. His eyes gleamed with intellectual excitement.

'In one phrase,' he cried, 'one sentence, you have slashed through whole libraries of disputation as to the nature of law and justice.'

'Not I,' replied Walt robustly. 'The English.'

A pragmatic nation, Quint thought to himself, but capable of self-deception to an extraordinary degree. Perhaps that is the true definition of pragmatism – an ability to deceive oneself and so turn one's back on principle, law or custom if they stand in the way of what one wants. Meanwhile, Walt went on.

'At all events no one challenged their oath-swearing on that occasion and Godwin and the Godwinsons got all their titles back and all their lands. The Norman Robert, Archbishop of Canterbury was sent packing and many other Normans with him. The Englishman Stigand, a married man and already Bishop of Winchester, took his place. The only concession the Godwins made was to agree Sweyn should make a penitential pilgrimage to the Holy Land. He set off but died on the way.'

Quint continued to shake his head and mutter.

'What a nation, what a nation of hypocrisy! A lord's men are bound by oaths they are taught from the womb not to break yet in reality they hope for lands for their service. They go through complicated rituals in the name of justice and law but in reality what counts is the number of helmets a lord has behind him.'

Fortunately 'hypocrisy' was a word Walt had not come across.

By now they were perambulating the grassy bank of a pleasant stream which quite suddenly cut its way into a narrow rocky gorge where it tumbled in waterfalls from pool to pool.

Quint unshouldered his pack, delved in it and pulled out a shapeless lump of lardy soap made from goat's tallow and beech ash.

'You shared my bag last night,' he said, 'and I could not help wondering, now that we are away from the noisome smells of towns and cities, when you last washed your clothes. Or indeed yourself.'

'I really c-c-can't remember.'

The stutter signified very well that he could. It was not far off a full two (or three?) years – in Waltham Abbey on the way from Stamford Bridge to Senlac Hill. No. That was wrong. He no longer had the leather jerkin he wore then – he remembered as if it were a dream the widow he had worked for in the fens of the Nether Lands, who had given him the cloak and the deadman's shoes he still wore. They had held up well.

'A long time, at all events. Now what I propose is that as soon as we find a pool big enough to bathe in, we will first wash our clothes, and then, while they dry, wash ourselves.'

Walt blenched at the thought. Too much washing smacked of femininity. After all, women have to wash at least once a month, they would be impure if they did not. But men need not wash much and only for important occasions. And how could their clothes be washed with no women there to do it?

They continued downwards and, as Quint predicted, the pools became bigger, but surrounded too by thickets of crimson-stemmed dogwood beneath willows, alders and poplars through which soft breezes whispered, setting the sibilous leaves to chatter. As they clambered down a rockfall to such a pool they heard a sudden heavy splash, which Walt thought might be an otter, but almost instantly, through a gap in the branches below, they saw the naked form of a woman haul herself on to a smooth boulder, then with a flash of creamy thigh and buttock she was gone into the thickets on the further side.

'Good Lord,' Quint exclaimed, 'what the devil was that?'

'The devil, perhaps,' Walt cried, rigid now like a statue. 'He can assume many seductive shapes to tempt us to evil.'

'Rubbish!' Quint replied, with some force. 'Either it was a shepherdess—'

'I see no sheep.'

'Or perhaps an antique survival of the distant past.'

'What do you mean?'

'A pagan naiad, the spirit or fairy of this stream.'

'All that vanished on the day of Christ's Nativity.'

'I doubt it. No Christian came here for two or three hundred years after Our Lord's Birth. Perhaps we are the first ever to pause beside this pool. Anyway, there was a lot to be said for a tradition that invented nymphs of the wood and stream to gladden our hearts with their beauty and their dancing. Often in such places as this I feel their presence.'

He fell silent and became very still, his eyes misted. When he spoke again it was in the solemn privileged voice poets use when they wish you to be moved by what they have to say.

'"The sighing nymphs depart from their haunts by spring and pool, edged with pale poplar. With flower-woven tresses spoiled, and unreconciled in the twilight shade of tangled thickets, they mourn."'

'You might have rhymed.'

'I might. Come on, let's go down there.'

'Are you sure?'

'Of course I'm sure. Whatever we saw, it was nothing that could harm us.'

They pushed through the dogwood and came to the mossy boulders at the water's edge. There Quint stripped off his garments without shame or embarrassment, though kept his hat on, and plunged them one by one into the swirling water, hauled them out, scrubbed them with his soap and then rubbed and rolled and beat them on the rock on which he squatted much in the way Walt remembered women did in the villages back home where there was a stream or walled-in fountain.

Quint's body was very thin and scrawny but muscled too. A rubiginous rash spread across his shoulders and below it his back was scarred with white lines and knobbles which here and there still wept a colourless ichor. At the sight of this and of his meagre but slightly floppy buttocks, legs thinly covered in a light red hair, and white misshapen feet,

Walt was suddenly overcome by an entirely unexpected and to him inexplicable wave of tenderness. Quint looked up at him, over his shoulder.

'Come on. You must do the same.'

'Must I?'

'If you wish to remain in my company, yes.'

'Very well. But I have pins and fastenings below I cannot manage one-handed. And I doubt I'll make as much of a job as you do of washing them.'

'I'll help.'

When both had spread their now clean clothes across some low bushes of bog-myrtle, the leaves of which Walt recalled are called 'gale' in Wessex and are used to add a piquant flavour to ale, they climbed down into the pool, and soaped themselves but not each other, even though Walt let the soap slip several times and Quint had to retrieve it for him. Walt's body was quite heavily tattooed – a barbaric habit learnt from their Germanic forebears which the English, the men anyway, have not forgotten.

Then Quint removed his hat and they swam and splashed and generally carried on like little boys playing in the stream. But it was cold, and Walt was first out, but again, one-handed as he was, he slipped on the mossy rock and could not get a purchase with his knee until Quint got a hand under his buttock and bunked him up.

Perhaps feeling awkward at this mild intimacy Quint, still up to his waist in water, turned away, leaving Walt looking down on the top of his head. The water had pulled his sparse but long hair down evenly all round exposing what Walt had never noticed before (for Quint kept his hat on almost all the time) a large round, unnaturally round, patch of much shorter hair no longer than the hair on a donkey's pelt. Since he was feeling piqued and a touch humiliated at having been made to wash, and embarrassed too by the way he had rather liked the feel of Quint's hand on his bottom, he took the opportunity to get his own back.

'Quint, you rogue,' he shouted, 'you're a priest, a vicar or a fucking monk. A By-Our-Lady renegade!'

'I was,' said Quint, turning and looking up at him through eyes squinted against the sun behind, 'indeed a monk. But as I told you before, never *a fucking* monk.'

Walt was abashed.

'Oh, it's just a word. English housecarls use it all the time.'

Quint continued his counterattack, trying to deflect Walt from pursuing the subject of holy orders.

'And your tattoos. All over your arms and legs and on your chest. That's hardly a civilised habit, you know?'

He hauled himself out of the water and his finger flashed over Walt's body but without touching it.

'A dragon here, an eagle there, "Harold Rules, All Right?" inscribed within a scroll, and here's another dagger, with wings this time, and a legend beneath I cannot quite read, it's in Danish runes, is it not? What does it say?'

'"Winners dare". I had it done in Hereford.'

'And this. "Walt 4 Erica." What does that mean?'

'Walt for Erica.'

'Oh, very droll. And who is Erica?'

'None of your business. Quint, why are you a fucking monk? A monk on the run?'

This was a question Quint was still not disposed to answer. He turned their clothes over.

'They're not as dry as I should like,' he said. 'Let's eat now and press on when they are.'

He turned to his bag, pulled out some oddments, rummaged, and then began to swear, but in Greek and Latin for the most part and other languages, too. What it came down to was that all their remaining food had gone and possibly a gold piece or two, though he did not keep count as carefully as he should and he wasn't sure how many.

CHAPTER
TEN

'A fox,' suggested Walt as they set off again, but hungry and, on Quint's part, ill-tempered, 'or a beaver? I've known very cheeky beavers on the River Stour near Iwerne, where I was born.'

'No. It was that . . . er, bothersome woman.'

'Not a nymph, then, sighing in the thickets.'

Quint stopped, made Walt stop too, faced him and swung a finger in his face.

'Walt,' he said, and his blue eyes narrowed and a frown line creased the space between his brows, 'I like you. But you can go off people, you know?'

Walt shrugged; they walked on, side by side for a league or so, saying nothing. The track undulated, passed through woods and then signs of cultivation. Sheep and goats nibbled short, dry grass or reached to browse the lower branches. They were guarded by small boys who hallooed and threw stones to head them off if they strayed towards a crop. Presently they came to a low escarpment with a gentle slope beneath it and there, two leagues or so beyond them, was a shanty town, then battlemented walls of brick and within, just discernible above the walls, the roofs and domes of a considerable city.

'Nicæa,' Quint proclaimed. 'The birth-place of modern Christianity, albeit it took place seven hundred years ago.'

'The birth-place of Our Lord and therefore of our faith was

Bethlehem,' Walt said, but timidly, not wishing to raise Quint's anger again.

'Tell me,' said Quint in a voice already loaded with concealed sarcasm, 'the circumstances that surround the conception and birth of Our Lord, in so far as you understand them.'

'There's no difficulty about them that I can see,' Walt maintained staunchly. 'I was taught all that first by my mother who was a good lady, wise and virtuous, then by the priest who came specially from Shaftesbury to teach the young of our manor and prepare us for Mass.'

'Go on then.'

'The Holy Spirit came to the Blessed Virgin Mary in the likeness of a dove, and she conceived, and bore a son, who was Jesus, Our Lord and Saviour. Is this not right?'

'And who sent the dove? From whom did the dove . . . proceed?'

'From God the Father.'

'And what is He like?'

'I've seen Him pictured often enough. He sits on a throne in heaven and he has a white beard.' He remembered something. 'But in the Church of Holy Wisdom he did not have a beard.'

By now their track had made a junction with the main road from Nicomedia and Constantinople and they joined a stream of traffic, of convoys of camels, of herds of sheep brought into town for the next day's market, carts filled with vegetables and fruit, and a squadron of cavalry, the men not in full armour but with mules in the rear carrying it for them. Quint paid no attention to all this but, eyes almost closed, began to chant, somewhat in the style of a monk, but derisively:

We worship one God in Trinity, and Trinity in Unity
Neither confounding the persons nor dividing the substance
For there is one person of the Father, another of the Son, and another of the
  Holy Ghost
The Father uncreate, the Son uncreate and the Holy Ghost uncreate
The Father incomprehensible, the Son incomprehensible, and the Holy Ghost
  incomprehensible
The Father eternal, the Son eternal, and the Holy Ghost eternal
And yet they are not three eternals but one eternal
And also there are not three incomprehensibles, nor three uncreated but one
  uncreated and one incomprehensible . . .

Walt broke in – he had had enough.

'What is all this stuff?' he cried.

'You might well ask. Not a lot to do with a Father God in the Sky, the likeness of a dove, and a baby in a manger, than which I find it difficult to imagine three more different, un-unified entities.'

'So where did all this come from?'

Quint waved a flowing arm to the battlements now a scant mile off.

'Here,' he proclaimed, 'the year of Our Lord three hundred and twenty-five the newly converted Christian Emperor, Constantine, called a council of all the bishops, doctors and teachers of the church to meet in Nicæa.'

'Why?'

'First you must understand that Constantine's conversion was a political act. More than half the Empire was by then Christian and mostly drawn from the better sort of people, hard-working, law-abiding and so on, including a very large part of his army. But there was a problem. Although most people were united in the faith the church itself was split. And what Constantine wanted was peace, and tranquillity, and, above all, agreement about the exact nature of the religion he had embraced. So he called this council and told them to sit down and get on with it and not give up until they were agreed. I'm hungry and thirsty.'

They were approaching the northern gate, threading their way through a ribbon of small inns and eating-places where men hawked meat ground, grilled and set in small loaves of bread smothered with anchovy sauce, or triangles of flat round loaves baked in ovens with a topping of anchovy sauce, onion, garlic and chopped olives. Quint bought two of each and had his leather wine bottle refilled with red wine. The purse he kept on his belt did not yield quite enough in coppers and he had to delve in his pack before he could pay.

'Bitch!' he mumbled. 'I'm sure she took at least two pieces of gold as well as our lunch.' But he found one at last and took a couple of handfuls of bronze from the vendor in change as well as two meat-filled buns.

There was a small crowd near the gate happy to be entertained by a couple of mountebanks, one who ate flames and spewed them back again, another who twanged away at a tuneless lute and wailed nasally above the noise he extracted from it. A sad ditty about how the answer to everything was blowing in the breeze. None of this was to Quint's liking. Away from the road and in shadow cast by the walls they found a small gymnasium, open air, where young men wrestled, practised sword drill with wooden swords, threw javelins, lifted weights and so on. There was a low, grassy bank from which they could watch the youths at their exercise.

Through mouthfuls of bread and meat, with the brown salty spiced sauce dripping occasionally down his wrist, Quint continued his dissertation on the Council of Nicæa.

"The main split was between the Arians, led by Arius, and Athanasius, a clever young man, who wrote the words I sang to you and which started us off. And what they argued most about was the status of the Son of God. Pass the wine.'

Skilfully he raised the leather bottle above his face and by squeezing directed into his mouth a stream of it which he lapped down, much in the way a dog copes with a jet of milk or water.

'That's better. Arius argued that the Son of God was necessarily, if he was to be called a Son, created by God the Father. That is, there was a time when God the Father was and God the Son wasn't. Athanasius said they were both equally God and uncreated. Constantine, being tidy-minded, slightly favoured Arius, but accepted the Council's decision to back Athanasius—'

'But what has all this got to do with the things that matter?'

'Which are?'

'The Nativity, the Crucifixion, the Resurrection, and the Redemption of us all?'

'Nothing, nothing at all. But it had a lot to do with allying a unified church with a unified state, giving the all-powerful state the legitimacy to interfere with our lives at any point and whenever it chooses. Come on. Let's find ourselves an inn.'

'Can we afford one?'

Quint stopped in his tracks.

'Probably not,' he said. 'We must shift about a bit, then. A night in the open is one thing, a night on the streets is quite another. In the open we were robbed. In the streets our throats might be slit.' He wiped his hands on the broad chestnut leaf his meal had been served in, crumpled it and threw it. 'More wine, please. I need to lose a few inhibitions.'

'What?'

'Loosen up my soul. So I can make a fool of myself.'

They walked back to the great northern gate and edged through the crowd. There was only one busker there now, a tall but compact man with very dark balding hair and a neat beard which did not conceal the deep creases that ran from cheek-bones to the corners of his mouth, and lent his face a look of unconsolable melancholy. His eyes too were tired and pained. Walt felt sure he had seen him before, but could not remember where – perhaps he had come across him in those months or years during which he had traversed Europe, the memories of which were confused and dream-like.

He was a magician. An old woman in the forefront of the crowd had a basket of fruit with three eggs on top. He took one egg, opened the empty hand that had taken it, plucked it from the air with his other hand, let it drop and break at the old woman's feet. She screamed with rage until he pointed to her basket. Not three eggs there now, but four.

Meanwhile, ten paces away, Quint passed Walt his pack, his purse and his hat, did a handstand and walked on his hands.

The magician riposted by cutting a cord in two places with a pair of shears. He pushed the three pieces into his mouth and pulled them out restored to one cord. Walt was put in mind of the Trinity in Unity, the Unity in Trinity. If a mountebank at a city gate could perform such a trick then probably God could too.

The odd thing was someone else in the crowd took the same meaning, and hollered blasphemy. Well, perhaps not so odd. For seven hundred years the town had had a reputation for being pernickety about theological niceties. This was a thin, nasty-looking man with eyes that looked two ways and was obviously known to the crowd because they jeered at him, calling him by name. He cursed them and ran off through the gate.

Quint did a back flip, then a rolling series of hand-stands like a catherine wheel, ending in two aerial somersaults, landing with a thump in an attempt to do the splits. He was obviously jarred by the fall, even hurt. No one but Walt paid any attention, except a new arrival, a woman. Walt, running to his companion's side to help him up, remarked her too. She was above-average height, had red hair, hennaed perhaps, piled high and held in place with a gold band and covered with an emerald-green silk scarf. Her neck was also circled with gold. She wore a peacock-blue cloak over a white shift, silky and pleated, and had gold slippers. For all her magnificence she was unattended, and Walt felt, as he dusted Quint down and enquired how he was, that her attention was covertly fixed on them both. He shuddered, but did not know why.

Meanwhile the melancholy magician had performed three more illusions and was about to perform, he announced, his concluding trick after which he would walk amongst them with a bag into which, if they had enjoyed the show, and he very much hoped they had, he felt sure they would place a small token of their appreciation thus enabling him to eat that night and perhaps sleep safely too. Threatened thus the crowd, as crowds will, began to disperse. He ran amongst them, caught an old man by the sleeve, called out loudly so all turned after all to watch, plunged his hand down the old man's back, his smock was quite loose at the neck, and pulled out . . . a white dove, a beautiful white dove, which he threw in the air.

'See,' called the mountebank, 'how this dove proceeds from the father. You are, are you not, a father?'

'Grandfather, too,' the old man replied proudly.

Meanwhile the dove climbed into the sky in a graceful, spiralling flight, above the battlemented walls, so all who looked up (and some thereby had their purses filched or slit by a young boy who slipped through the crowd) expected it to pass from view.

But suddenly it was coming down again, in a strange tumbling flight, dropping a foot or two at a time so it seemed it had been shot with an arrow then recovering, and then twisting and turning again, until it at last alighted . . .

Beneath a slender palm, on a low bank or mound, a young girl sat, dark of hair but beautiful, hooded modestly and dressed in blue, and the dove alighted first at her feet, and then fluttered up into her lap where it cooed, cr-croo, cr-croo, and she fondled it and stroked its head. She seemed almost to push it into the pit of her stomach.

Some cheered and clapped, and did indeed put money in the magician's bag, but others sensed there was more here than met the eye and began quickly to move off in a variety of directions, though the grand lady, the one with red hair and a peacock-blue cloak was almost the last. And they were right to do so.

Hooves thundered, dust swirled, four armed and armoured horsemen burst through the scattering throng. Two dismounted, pushed the reins of their mounts into their companions' hands and seized the magician. Quint, with a great cry of anger, hurled himself on the back of one, fastened arms round his neck and tried to drag him down. One of the mounted men swung his horse round and drew his sword above Quint's head. Walt leapt between them and took the blow, fortunately from the flat of the blade, right across his ear and cheek. Pain and a noise worse than thunder, bright lights, brighter than the sun, flashed in his head, then darkness came down like a soothing blanket.

He came to, with the coolness of water from Quint's gourd splashing about his face, but it was not Quint who held it. His eyes focused on black eyebrows which met above the nose of the pert face, now smiling but anxiously, of the girl in blue. His head was in the lap of the boy who had slit or picked the purses of the less wary in the crowd.

'What happened?' Walt asked, naturally enough. His head sang, the inside of his mouth raged, his cheek and ear smarted dreadfully, but he had suffered worse in the past, much worse.

'Our Father,' which art in heaven, Walt's errant mind supplied, 'is in the town jail. Your friend is with him.'

It was the boy who spoke.

'I followed them there,' he went on. 'It's not far, just the other side of the gate.'

'What will happen?'

'They'll be tried in the morning. Hopefully for disturbing the peace, assault on a constable, that sort of thing. But I'm afraid there's talk of blasphemy.'

'Daddy's so *silly*,' his sister interjected, and there were tears in her voice. 'He thinks it's so *clever* what he does, and it always gets us into trouble.'

With his arm round the boy's shoulders and holding the girl's hand, Walt and the two children walked away from the gate and back up the thoroughfare that led to it, past the vendors of quickly prepared food and stalls selling bread and fruit. Dusk was lengthening the shadows now and some of the stalls were lit with flaring torches or oil-lamps. They seemed as busy as ever, with clouds of aromatic smoke swirling round those where food was cooked.

'Where are we going?' Walt asked, in English but spoken slowly.

'To the inn where we have been staying. It's quite comfortable. You can borrow Daddy's bed for the night.'

The children spoke in a mixture of English and Norman French, occasionally throwing in demotic Latin or Greek when they were at a loss for a word. In spite of the singing in his now swollen ear and the general noise and bustle of the street Walt found he could follow most of what they said. The girl's name was Adeliza, the boy's Alain; she was, Walt guessed, fourteen, he twelve

They came to the inn. It was a two-storey building built of brick, plastered and painted white, with a gateway high enough to take a mounted man. Beyond lay a large courtyard, fifty paces by fifty paces with a well in the middle. Most of the ground floor was taken up with stabling, though half of one side was given over to a tavern with tables and benches where men, and a few women, prostitutes or dancing girls, were already drinking, singing, and shouting raucously.

Alain checked their horse and mule were still safely stabled, watered and fed, while Adeliza led Walt up one of the staircases, along a short wooden verandah or balcony roofed with red tiles and through a narrow door into the room they were sharing with their father.

It was small, with one raised bed of wooden planks, a straw-filled palliasse and a threadbare blanket. There were two more palliasses on the floor. All this was lit from a tiny window, which had been left shuttered against the heat, but Adeliza pushed back the shutters as soon as they entered.

Along one wall five large, strapped saddle-bags made of leather had been stacked and there was a small assortment of cast-off clothes and shoes scattered about the floor. Adeliza made Walt lie on the bed.

'I'll soon be back,' she said, and smoothed his brow with a cool white hand.

'Where are you going?'

'To get water, and dressing for your wound.'

'It's not a wound. Just a graze.'

'You can't see it. It's a wound, silly, believe me,' and she squeezed his shoulder.

When she was gone he ran his hand up his cheek and winced with pain when he came to his ear. The whole area was crusted with dry and drying blood. And, he now realised, at least four of his back teeth on that side were shattered. He swung his legs off the bed, thinking to find a mirror or a polished surface that would serve for one. He felt a wave of dizziness and had to put his hand on the rough-cast wall to steady himself and lean forward so his head was level with his chest. And then he saw it – the gleam of mother-of-pearl, polished sandal-wood, inlaid gold and the light running up and down the twelve or so cat-gut strings. It had been part-hidden by one of the saddle-bags against the wall, clearly visible from where he was now. He shifted the saddle-bag and looked at it.

It was a harp. One of the largest he had ever seen, and instantly he knew he had seen it before, and knew, too, who its owner was. The body, forming the sound-box, was at least two feet long and swelled at the base to nine inches across. Its belly was a further nine inches deep. It was built like a ship of slats of seasoned hardwood, fastened to a hidden frame by copper or brass pins, the body or hull of it inlaid with mother-of-pearl and gold filigree. The beam, projecting almost two feet from the top, curved like a wave, was of some dark wood, highly polished and seemingly so hard that inlay was not possible, though of course it had been bored to take the pegs that tightened and tuned the strings.

And now too he knew who the magician was whose blasphemous illusions had led to the arrest of Quint, and for him to a blow that might, had its perpetrator had a mind to it, have taken his head off. Three, four years since the first time he saw him? In the great hall at Rouen? No, Bayeux. Singing and playing at the end of a great feast in front of William Duke of Normandy and Harold Earl of Wessex. And what had he sung? Why, nothing less than the *Chanson de Roland*.

But how could this be? On that later day, Saturday the fourteenth of October 1066, the man he was thinking of had been the first to fall, felled by the axes thrown from the shield-wall – Walt himself had seen him fall. Walt himself had thrown an axe. How could Taillefer, Sharp-iron, the minstrel, magician, jester and jongleur kept by Duke William and known throughout the West as the greatest entertainer of his time, be alive and busking for a living outside the wall of a city in Asia Minor nearly two years later?

Walt's head swam, he got back on the bed, rubbed his eyes and tried to remember not the singing warrior on Senlac Hill whose face was masked with blood but the man who had sung and played this harp in the great hall a year before the battle. He had been dark and thickset, certainly, but surely of more noble bearing? The face certainly less melancholic, those lines less deeply etched. He shook his head a little, not much, it hurt to do so. Certainly the harp had been the same. There could not in Christendom be two harps like that.

And why had they been in Bayeux at all, Harold and his eight best housecarls, the inner guard, their prince's last defence? Again Walt shook his head. There had been a reason, a good reason, the King's command, or Harold's business. But for the life of him he could not remember how it went.

He slept, was briefly roused when Adeliza and Alain returned. Alain held his head while she sponged his face with oil and honey and then water, and gave him watered wine to drink. The King's command? What King? Why Edward the Confessor, of course. It was because of him they'd gone to Normandy, he was almost sure. He slept again.

PART II

THE CONFESSOR

CHAPTER
ELEVEN

Early in 1065 Edward the Confessor was forced to recognise that the disease he had suffered from for a year or so was soon to prove fatal. He tired easily, was forced to piss frequently and found that if he held on he would wet himself. His piss smelled of honey. His vision became blurred, his feet numb. Constantly he wanted to scratch himself. He suffered from terrible and unpredictable thirst. If he drank mead or ate honey all these symptoms worsened immediately; roots were as bad as fruit – parsnip, to which he was partial, and even cabbage stalks. He consulted his doctors. They knew of the condition, called it by the Greek words for honeyed urine, told him to eschew all sweet things, and, since the illness was now well-advanced, gave him six months to live.

He was at Westminster when he heard the news, in the Great Hall he had caused to be erected between the river and the new abbey church he had ordered some fourteen years before. He went there whenever he could to supervise, or at any rate interfere with the erection of an abbey church he hoped would rival those being built in Normandy and Lorraine. It was to be a monument in stone to God, to the reformed Christian ideal as propounded by the monks of Cluny, and to his own holiness.

A tall lean man, but at sixty stooped and grey, he left the upper chamber of the hall where the doctors had examined him, allowed a page to help him down the steps to the floor below, called a couple of young housecarls and a clerk to follow him, walked the length of the hall, acknowledging the obeisances of clerks, scribes, monks, sutlers and cooks, to the big door at the far end, and so out into the open air of a mellow March, filled, where they had not been trampled by the toings and froings of his court, with daffodils.

He hardly needed the cloak he had thrown round his shoulders, for one of the blessings of his reign, or at least the last twelve years or so of it, had been a gentle warming of the climate, a succession of warm but damp winters and sunny but not over-heated summers. Many of the simpler folk believed this was due to his saintliness, and he did nothing to disabuse them. After all, in less miraculous respects he had served them well.

He had settled disputes between the earls – untutored war-lords, really – and between them and himself, appearing to give way rather than plunge the country into civil war. In his entire reign there had only been one Viking raid and his ships had seen them off before they could do much damage. He had employed Harold Godwinson, Earl of Wessex, whom he at first despised as an illiterate ruffian but whom he later learnt to respect, to subdue the Welsh, and he had kept the Scots from trespassing south of the Great Wall.

But more than that he had encouraged agricultural improvements to feed a rising population; he appointed good justices and promulgated good laws, most of which left intact the ancient barbaric but homely customs of councils, moots and Witans. He realised that these, tedious though they were, gave to a feuding, clannish people, proud of their right to shape their own lives and take responsibility for their own actions and those of their closest kin and dependants, the illusion that, in most respects, they were free. As if anyone were ever free.

All this he ruminated on with some satisfaction, plunged as he was into that mood of nostalgia and sadness which all of us must feel when told our time on earth is, if not over, then definitely rounded with a date. Of course one knows one will die – but to be told when, while it does not, if it be not now, necessarily concentrate the mind, at least provokes the sort of mood he was now in. Thus abstracted he passed the stabling, the long huts where his personal bodyguard lived, the bowers of the womenfolk in the largest of which his childless wife, Edith, was no doubt now spinning or copulating with her latest boy-toy.

Unbidden the great gate opened: as they do – for kings.

Edward stood for a moment on the threshold beneath the big beam above and looked out. To his left, a hundred yards or so away, the rounded east end of his abbey church rose above an improvised town of huts where the labourers lived, and more pleasant houses occupied by draughtsmen, stone-masons and overseers. The building itself was shrouded in a net of wooden scaffolding and platforms up and down which men scurried like ants searching out aphids on a rose bush while others used hoists to raise ready-shaped blocks of stone to a height of seventy feet or more. For many years he had watched its growth with excited pleasure. Now it was with dread: for behind that eastern wall, and he now knew more or less when, he would be buried.

Hopefully in years to come it would be known as the Chapel of St Edward the Confessor – but that seemed less of a consolation than perhaps it should have done. It dawned on him he would not be there to see it. Stumbling occasionally on the uneven ground but waving away the assistance of the men who followed him he turned instead to the river and walked to its bank.

It was edged, save for where there were landing stages for ferrymen or muddy churned-up places where cattle came down to drink, with willow and alder – already hung with catkins shedding yellow pollen in the breeze and furry pussy-willow buds which, where they caught the sun, glowed like pearls.

The brown tide was in a racing ebb going with the current and knowing it would soon reveal brown mud-flats, oyster-catchers, dunlin and curlews whirled and mewed, waiting for the clams and worms that lay beneath. It had its inevitable effect and he had to hoist his tunic, lower the front of his leggings and piss into the stream.

For the twenty-three years of his reign the turning seasons had brought in, more or less at their expected times, the blessed progression of green corn, hawthorn and the lark, swallows, hay and harvest of grain, bright autumn and the huntsmen's horns. How he had loved to hunt through forests teeming with red and roe deer, beneath the bright red-gold of beeches and that more sombre gold of the oaks! And so to Christmas . . . suddenly he shuddered with presentiment. The seasons turned and on their back the Reaper rode.

This would not do. The news, both good (an untroubled passage to paradise if he was the saint some said he was), and bad (considering certain proclivities he had thrown off long ago, and, with some embarrassment, confessed to and been absolved of), carried with it duties. He glanced across the swirling brown stream towards Lambeth. Smoke above Archbishop Stigand's hall. Archbishop? Pluralist since he refused to relinquish Winchester, uncanonically married, refused the pallium by the Pope and excommunicated. Above all, English crony of English Godwinsons. No. Keep the news from him for as long as he could.

He turned north. Partially hidden by the bend in the river he could still see at the end of the road they called Strand, just beyond the place where it crossed the River Fleet, a corner of the Roman walls of London, and above the tongue of land which came between, where the smaller town of Southwark lay, the smoky haze that always, whatever the weather, hung above it.

He called the clerk who had remained with the housecarls a spare twenty paces behind him.

'Write me a note,' he said, 'bidding my lord bishop of London to come to me as soon as he can. I want him to say vespers with me and then consult privately on a matter of some importance.'

He walked slowly back to his hall, stumbling more often now as the too familiar weariness descended upon him, head bent and fingering beads at each one of which it was said he murmured the Paternoster and a new prayer to the Blessed Virgin, beginning Ave Maria – Hail Mary. The fact was though that he just fiddled with them when he was tired, irritated or anxious.

He climbed the stairs again, pulled back the curtain, a fine tapestry depicting the laying of the footings for his abbey under his direction, with angels swooping above, and stretched himself out on his bed. Yes, he was weary in the afternoon, long before a man in good health should be, and his mouth had dried up with that damned thirst. There was a pitcher of water by the bed and a leather cup. He hoisted himself up again and drained it three times, although the water was brackish and carried the slightly musty taste it had picked up from standing too long in unglazed clay, but he felt better.

In none of this did any of his servants attempt to interfere. Two decades ago their predecessors had learnt to come only when called for and had felt the force of his temper if they tried to pre-empt his wishes. The lesson had been passed on, though the King's temper had become less wilful and fierce with age.

Again he lay on the bed, and this time pulled a coverlet up to his chin, and, still meditating on the doctors' diagnosis, thought back over the years, and as the visions and memories came he tossed and turned, and occasionally sucked his thumb, sometimes chewed on his knuckles to choke back a cry. Bitterness and anger were at the root, bitterness and anger against Godwin and the Godwinsons. Not to mention Edith, the old monster's daughter.

Chapter
Twelve

1042. Harthacanute, son of Canute, was a drunk, and died of a stroke while drinking. He left several possible successors to the throne. One, his half-brother, was Edward, later the Confessor. The other was also Edward, Edward the Atheling or Prince, the son of Edmund Ironside and grandson of Ethelred the Unready or Redeless – he who would not take advice. Edward, later the Confessor, was actually Ethelred's son – but by his second wife, Emma of Normandy. He, however, was there, in England, when Harthacanute died, and he was nearly forty years old; whereas the Atheling was in exile in Hungary, and still a stripling.

Under English law the Witan, the supreme council of the land, was the final arbiter, and by custom chose not necessarily the most direct in line, but the candidate most suitable for the job. The succession remained unsettled through the winter of 1042–43. The Witan was dominated by two factions – Godwin and his sons in the south and Siward and Leofric, Earls of Northumberland and Mercia, in the north. By getting their own personal choice on to the throne, each faction hoped to be rewarded with the lands and earldoms of the other.

Godwin backed Edward, later the Confessor, but there was a snag. Eight years earlier, when Canute died, Godwin, who had ruled England in Canute's name during Canute's campaigns in Scandinavia, won the favour of Harold Harefoot, who was Canute's eldest son and first heir, by blinding and causing the murder of Edward's elder brother Alfred, thus clearing the way for Harefoot's succession and brief reign. The murder of his elder brother was the first reason why Edward's relations with the Godwins remained ambiguous at best.

Since there was no king, and Winchester was the old capital of Wessex, and Godwin was Earl of Wessex, the mead-hall at Winchester was, in effect, Godwin's hall. Edward, unattended, was kept waiting at the great door. It was cold, the ground like iron, horse-shit like brown stones, the frozen puddles sprinkled with fine snow. Above the palisade he could see the squat grey stone of the old minster. God, he thought, deserved something better and, when he was King, God would get something better. Either here or in London. He had, however, already learnt to admire and indeed be moved by the Winchester school of painting and illumination. It flowed, was real, had feeling. He'd commission something from them when it was in his power to do so, a full bible, something like that. Then, just as the cold was getting to him, the door behind opened.

'Earl Godwin asks you to come in.'

A lackey? A servant? Or a thegn? It was hard to tell with these English. In armour, yes, or garbed for a feast or a festival, the rich and powerful stood out all right – but day-to-day they slouched around in the same drab clothes, often grubby, that their servants wore.

He followed the man up the central nave of the hall between the squared pillars of oak which supported the high roof. Much of the considerable space was dark, but warm. Small charcoal braziers were set at intervals all the way and right in the centre there was a much larger one – so hot that the iron basket glowed and Edward and his guide had to skirt it by several feet. Not only did the charcoal burn hot, it gave off no smoke. Charcoal, though principally used for metal smelting, was a luxury most could afford in England with its still abundant oak and alder forests. In Normandy, where metal smelting, particularly for the making of armour and the forging of weapons, was a far more important industry, Normans burnt wood, breathed smoke and stank of it. Edward had spent most of his life in Normandy, the guest of the Dukes, his mother's nephews and cousins. In England, as Ethelred's son, he was always a threat to Canute and his Danish dynasty. Consequently, by upbringing and inclination, Edward was more Norman than Saxon – and remained so until the day he died.

Thirty or so housecarls, most of them young, played dice, chequers,

drank ale, and occasionally squabbled. Large dogs shifted about and
scratched themselves. The air was heavy, foetid with heat, damp, and the
smells of beer and mutton fat. Somewhere, someone strummed a harp,
accompanying a melancholic though melodic lament played on a block-
flute. Edward, out of habit, passed a cursory glance over the more
youthful faces he could see, or lissom figures, but none caught his attention enough to make him want to pause. They all looked so grubby.

At the far end of the hall ladder-like steps climbed to an upper chamber. The servant, whatever, motioned to them.

Edward climbed the steps and pushed the tapestry aside. Tall and thin
as he was he had to stoop to get beneath the lintel. The room he was
now in was better lit than the hall below. The plastered walls were
washed with plain white; there was also a small glazed window set
beneath the gable. There was a lowish table in the middle on which
stood simple clay jugs filled with mead and wine, a lot of broken bread,
a couple of half-finished chicken carcases and a large cheese. There were
bone-handled knives too, the single-edged seaxes the English favoured
for pub-brawls or indeed anything less serious than a battle. The floor-
boards were covered with straw.

Above the table and more or less in the middle Godwin slouched
across an arm-chair, elbow on one arm, hand with forefinger against his
chin, supporting his big head. His left hand fiddled with one of the
knives, used the bone handle to tap quietly to the rhythm of the harp
below. His dark hair was grizzled, his brows met above a nose which
was just beginning to show signs of dissipation, his dark eyes were a
touch bloodshot. But for the rest, at forty-two, his strong, thickset
body and ruddy, scarred hands showed little sign of being beyond their
prime.

'Prince Edward. You know my sons. Sweyn, Harold, Leofwine. Tostig
will be here shortly. Take a seat.'

There was only one available, a four-legged stool, lower than the
chairs. Edward sat on it, careful to show no awareness that he was being
humiliated, intimidated even: after all, this man had murdered his
brother. He looked over the devil's cubs. Although he had been part of
Harthacanute's court for over a year, he had not seen them often, and
conversed with them hardly at all. Tostig and Leofwine he had not
even met. The Earls remained for the most part on their own estates,
coming only to court for meetings of the Witan or to receive special

commissions or demands from the King. And when they had been around it was not, after all, surprising that this lot had kept their distance.

Edward looked at them now. Sweyn, twenty-two, dark like his father, but leaner, taller, handsome apart from a pock-marked face, the result of youthful eczema which even now the youngest, Leofwine, just fifteen years old, was suffering from. But there was a meanness about Sweyn, even a whiff of evil, a hint of hell. Leofwine, however, with his spots, was a youth, no more, not yet fully formed in character or physique and so, to Edward, uninteresting.

That left Harold, just nineteen years old. His hair was clean, well-groomed, dark brown but with red and gold lights in it: perhaps he took after his mother, Gyrtha, who was Danish, related by marriage to Canute. His eyes were greyish blue. From beneath dark brows they focused on Edward with an expression that was both cool yet interested, curious even. Edward judged him to be intelligent rather than merely cunning – and so perhaps the one most to be feared. Since there was not a hint of vulnerability in him, Edward felt not the slightest tremor of desire.

Godwin, his voice deep and a touch rasping, was speaking.

'Let's get to the nub. You want to be king.'

Edward took a breath, forced himself to keep calm, sound in control. He even managed a shrug and a sort of laugh.

'I *have* to be king,' he said. 'If I am not, I shall have to go back into exile. But Normandy is closed to me, at least until William is secure. I could join the Atheling in Hungary, I suppose. Though I doubt we'd get on. But I have come to like this country and would prefer to stay.'

'Could you stay and not be king?'

'I think not.'

'You did with Harthacanute.'

Edward shrugged.

'I was his prisoner,' he said. 'And he would have found a way of . . . dealing with me as soon as he took me for a danger.'

Godwin sighed and shifted in his seat.

'So,' he repeated, 'you would be king.'

He leaned forward, stabbed a piece of cheese with his seax, placed it on a crust of bread, chewed on it, belched, drank from his cup, looked up over it.

'And how are you going to arrange that?' he asked.

Edward felt a small surge of confidence. It dawned on him that these gangsters were the ones who were selling, laying out their stall – no matter how much they tried to make it appear otherwise, that was the case. They needed him at least as much as he needed them. Indeed, if he chose to go into exile they could well be in – and here Edward, English as he was, remembered in his head to use the Anglo-Saxon word – shit.

'God will find a way,' he murmured, with a serenity that was not entirely assumed.

Harold suddenly found reason to glance down at the hands laced in front of him. Godwin and Sweyn looked confused. Godwin placed the pommel of his knife abruptly on the table without letting go of the haft, his eyes rose, focused on something beyond Edward's head, and then went blank.

'God,' he growled, 'has fuck-all to do with it.'

Silence. A dog yapped, kicked perhaps by a bored housecarl, the harp and the flute played on. And then suddenly stopped. Those in the upper room heard a high laugh, feet on the stairs and the curtain was pulled back.

The most beautiful young man Edward had ever seen posed on the threshold and then came in, letting the curtain swing to behind him.

'Sorry I'm late, Dad,' and he slapped Godwin on the shoulder. 'And you must be Prince Edward, or should I say . . . Sire,' and he bowed neatly from his waist.

Tostig was twenty-one years old. He had long hair the colour of ripe wheat tied back with a hinged gold clip or amulet so the body of it fell down his back. Unlike the others he was dressed with some style in a short blue cloak fastened on the right shoulder with an old-fashioned dragon brooch, the dragon contorted into an abstract pattern, gold with garnet inlay. His jerkin was crimson wool, belted with studded leather to show a marked waist. The clasp was as ornate as his brooch. His thighs were strong but rounded, in fine woollen leggings, his hands were strong too but with long, expressive fingers. All in all his body promised the suppleness of a hazel bough. But it was his face . . . the face of a mischievous angel, high-browed, straight-nosed, with angel lips that turned up at the corners promising perpetually an unrealised grin which already lit wide-spaced eyes. These shifted from green to topaz depending on the light. His cheeks were flushed a little with the cold, indeed you could smell its freshness still on him.

'I have a new Barbary colt, a roan, just brought up from South-ampton; God, he's magnificent, I just had to see him. Forgive me . . .' his eyes shone round the room, lit on Edward. 'I know you will.'

The Prince's tongue flickered between his lips and he dropped his head in something more than a nod, less than a bow.

'Well,' Tostig went on, 'you managed without me. All settled?'

'Not exactly,' Godwin snapped.

'Oh come!' He dropped to his haunches by Edward's side, put one hand on the table, the other on Edward's knee. 'King, exile, or die. Yes? Of course you'd rather be king. But until you are king you have no army, no support, no following, no one is bound to you by oaths, you can't stir without support.'

Without rising, his head swung to face his father across the table.

'And you, sir. If you don't get Edward's arse on the throne then old Siward and Leofric,' he glanced back at Edward, put on a northern accent, 'our friends from oop North,' turned back to his father, 'will get in a Dane or a Norseman, someone with old Canute's blood in him, and you know what they'll claim for reward when it's all settled? Do I have to tell you?'

Edward, confused and quite carried away by the young man's energy and lightness could scarcely shake his head, but Godwin knew, though Tostig, crowing like a cock, provided the answer . . .

'Why, their reward will be Wessex . . . East Anglia . . . Kent . . . the Thames-side shires . . . do I have to go on?'

'Can we stop you?' Sweyn at last spoke or rather grunted.

'Oh, let's have it all out in the open. Much better, don't you think . . . Sire?' He flashed a mocking smile up at Edward. His teeth were white and even.

They all looked at each other, lopsided grins appeared on the faces of Godwin and the three Godwinsons, then they shrugged, waited.

'Much better,' Edward said at last, 'much better.'

Godwin again let out a long sigh, this time of relief.

'Leofwine,' he said and waved towards the jugs and cups, 'do the honours.'

They drank but still eyed each other suspiciously over the rims of their cups.

'Oh what a lot of grumpy old men you are,' cried Tostig. 'Look, just get a couple of clerks in, draw up a document of intent and then we can all have a good time. Meanwhile I'm going back to my Barbary roan . . . he's sort of sorrel with very fetching white patches and as skittish as a kitten . . .' He paused on the threshold. 'Edward, I know you're a fine horseman, that you love hunting, wouldn't you like to come and see him?'

Edward stood, Godwin waved a hand of acquiescence. He and his sons waited, heard the clatter of steps on the stairs, and, moments later, the thump of the great door at the far end of the hall. Then:

'I think that went off very well,' murmured Harold, and slowly at first all four began to laugh, building up a huge storm of laughter, knocking jugs and cups about as they clung to each other in paroxysms of laughter.

Through it Godwin managed to splutter: 'Cock-queans, fucking cock-queans! That I should father such a cock-quean!'

CHAPTER
THIRTEEN

When they arrived the colt, a two-year-old, unbroken and skittish, was nuzzling at a bucket of corn held by a groom. As soon as Tostig and Edward leant on the top poles, the colt's head came up, knocking the groom in the stomach and sending him arse over tip, and the bucket spinning over the frozen ground. He then backed off, eyes rolling, showing the whites, bucking and neighing.

'Well, he's a pretty boy, but he's got to learn to behave . . .'

Tostig swung himself over the fence, picked up a long raw-hide whip the groom had taken into the corral with him, and advanced on the colt which backed off again, pawing at the ground, snorting, showing its teeth. Tostig felt a firm hand on his shoulder.

'Let me,' Edward murmured. 'You go and sit on the fence for a moment. Take the whip with you.'

Face flushed and with some impatience, Tostig did as he was told. It had been his intention to impress this mild, middle-aged man for whom he had no real respect at all, with his bravery, firmness and mastery. He had it in mind that Edward's particular taste might be for correction, it was often the way with devout, ascetic people, and that he might be aroused at the sight of Tostig giving his new colt a good hiding. But above all he knew he had to please the future King, and that meant doing as he was told.

Edward began a slow walk round the ring. The colt shied, stood still, shied again, snorted, shook his tail. Already his movements lacked conviction. Edward moved slowly, keeping always level with the colt's shoulder and angling his body slightly away from him. In that position he was a presence in the corner of the colt's left eye and, because of his stance, one that did not threaten.

After three or four turns Edward increased the length of his stride but still kept his body and head angled away from the colt, which now stopped and let him pass. It stood still for a moment, as though weighing up this new situation, but then as Edward straightened his body its own head dropped a little and it began to follow him. Within twenty minutes Edward had his left arm over the colt's neck and was allowing it to nibble a carrot the groom had given him out of his right hand. Then he climbed back over the fence.

'That's enough for today,' he said in a voice that was not harsh but expected to be obeyed. 'Tomorrow we'll get a neck-halter on him and the day after a saddle. You'll be able to ride him within a week.'

Tostig eased himself off the top pole and landed a foot in front of him. He took Edward's face in his hands and kissed him briskly on the lips.

'You were magnificent,' he asserted.

That night he came to the small house Edward had been given within the walls King Alfred had set four-square round Winchester seventy years before. They supped together, drank mead and Tostig played the harp for a while before they took a candle to the upper room. There, behind warm tapestries and lit by a couple of beeswax candles, they became lovers.

Naked, Tostig exceeded Edward's expectations. His white body, though still slight, was well muscled and perfectly proportioned, long in neck, limbs, fingers and feet. Standing behind him the future king put his hands in Tostig's armpits and then ran them down his chest, pausing to knead small erect nipples. Tostig leant into him and put his cheek on Edward's shoulder, exposing his neck, which Edward now nuzzled, gently at first but then nibbling while his hands arrived round Tostig's waist where his middle fingers met in the youth's navel. After stroking and combing a pubic bush redder than his hair, one hand finally cupped Tostig's balls and the other closed round a long but thin penis.

'You have a lovely cock,' he said, 'the loveliest in the world,' and

Tostig felt his master's – thick and strong now at the top of his buttocks, pressing into the small of his back.

His master's? Yes, indeed. That was the way it worked out and in a way Tostig was relieved. He was not, after all, that experienced in this sort of thing and had not relished the idea of putting his cock up another man's bum, which is what his father had told him would be required of him. But after the initial shock and some pain he discovered that such was his partner's experience and skill in these matters the act done the other way round was quite wonderfully pleasant . . .

The first of many sessions of pillow talk followed.

'You wooed me, the way you wooed my pony.'

'What will you call him?'

'Ned?'

'I think not. Sultan, perhaps.'

'Why?'

'Because he was bred in Barbary and that is the name they give their rulers.'

'Sultan then he shall be. If you rule England as well as you rule us, then all will be happy.'

'I have no intention of buggering England. Though I suspect your father may.'

'What you did to me was not buggery. It was a fuck.'

'Tell me about England.'

Though he had lived at court for half a year he had kept in the shadows, neither seeking friends nor drawing attention to himself. Above all he had kept well away from the sources of real power.

'Compared with Normandy it's a mess. At times it feels like an ugly, shapeless, heaving mass of conflicting parts – at least five of them . . .'

At the top of the heap came the King and his household which included the nucleus of an army made up of housecarls, the navy, tax-collectors, King's reeves and what-all. The defence of the realm against both internal and external threat seemed to be his chief duty. Then came the church which itself was divided into competing parties – the minsters, the abbeys and the bishops. Third, the Earls and greater thegns – owners of huge estates, capable of raising private armies; only a step away from the warlords of the previous century, they bound themselves with extravagant oaths to their King and broke them as soon as it was advantageous to do so. The only way of keeping them in order, it seemed, was to hold close members of their families at court as hostages – they seemed marginally less likely to step out of line if it meant close kin would be mutilated and killed.

'In that case you shall be my hostage to ensure your family's good behaviour.'

'Suits me.'

Every man had his death price, *wergild*, what you paid his family if you caused his death. If you committed a lesser crime, like rape or adultery, you paid a fixed proportion of the wergild. Wergild was scaled according to rank, and, of course, to Edward's despair, varied from place to place across his kingdom. Oath-swearing and wergild all more or less meant that a man could do almost what he liked if he had enough money to pay wergild to the people he'd hurt. And if his oath-swearing capability outmatched that of the plaintiffs he might get away with it altogether.

Fourth came the boroughs or burghs, seventy or more of them, which could be as big as London, with ten thousand merchants, artisans, shipwrights, manufacturers and all their hangers-on, to a small town of five hundred centred round, say, a handful of weaving sheds or pottery kilns. In many ways these were the easiest to handle – chartered to do so by Alfred the Great, they made their own by-laws, regulated themselves, and instead of paying taxes in kind set at often absurd amounts of absurd goods, like one porpoise out of every three caught, or two tuns of pure ale, seven oxen, six wethers, and forty cheeses, they paid in cash, licensed as they were to mint the coin of the realm.

Most burghs minted coinage. Every four years or so the King called in the old coinage – gold, silver and bronze. The metal was then melted down, made up to the required amounts, and redistributed to the mints where the coiners stamped it from dies they collected from London. Thus the coinage of the realm was standard throughout and always in good condition. It was the most advanced, effective and stable system of currency control in the world at that time.

Finally, fifth, the so-called freemen of England. It seemed everyone was free unless they were serfs. Many of them had commuted their rights to tiny plots of privately owned land for the protection and security a powerful lord could provide. And they still had to pay almost crippling dues in terms of the proportion of their daily labour that they had to hand over to both their lord and the church. And even those who had a hide or two to their own name still had to work for the lord of the manor for two or more days a week, pay the church in kind or cash, and be on hand to turn out as part of the fyrd, the peasant army the King could raise when he needed one. Yet all of these, by far the largest section of the population, called themselves 'free'.

'Free! What – churls, freemen, sokemen, even villeins . . . free!'

'Yes. They even claim the right to get up from where they are, under one lord of the manor, and move to another if they feel like it.'

Frequently Edward said to himself as this and other nights wore on: they order these matters better in Normandy . . .

CHAPTER
FOURTEEN

Through Tostig Edward learnt a lot, but he learnt, too, from experience. Not all of what he learnt was to his liking. On Candlemas, the second of February, after Mass in the Old Minster, when, according to new custom just introduced from France, the year's candles were blessed as well as the Purification of the Holy Virgin and Christ's Presentation in the Temple celebrated, he, Tostig, his huntsman and four grooms set off for Romsey, arriving in the early afternoon.

The next morning they pushed on into the forest and soon raised a small group of red deer. Spurs, crops and they were away, with their horses' hooves crunching through leaf-mould bound with frost beneath the oaks and the mast beneath the beeches. Rooks rose cackling from the bare canopies above them, holly in the more open spaces flashed along their horses' flanks. The most backward of the deer veered off to the right, and the huntsman winding his horn managed to steer the big dogs on to its track. All now thought they'd have an early kill, but the leading dog suddenly checked, sniffed around the crackling forest floor, and the others too soon came back and joined him. They snuffled, whined, pawed the ground and suddenly were off again, at a right-angle from the trail of the deer.

The huntsman trotted back to Edward and Tostig, touched his whip to his cap.

'They've picked up a fox scent,' he said. 'Shall us follow them or call them in?'

'Oh, follow the bulgars,' Edward cried, rather self-consciously aping their ways of speech. 'At least Reynard will give us a good gallop,' and set spurs to the flanks of the bay gelding he was riding. Tostig followed on Sultan.

But they never caught him and only had a view of him once, and then outside the forest, slipping like a wraith along the rim of an ancient turf rampart, white belly to the ground, brush straight out, silhouetted against the grey sky where tiny snowflakes hovered like gnats. Dusk gathered, night closed slowly in and the snow thickened, dusting frozen plough-land. Then one of the huntsmen's horses stumbled, nearly threw its rider, and was instantly seen to be lame. The huntsman winded his horn again and two of the dogs slunk back – the others were never seen again.

'We'll freeze to death if we don't find shelter,' Edward remarked. He was not expressing fear, just making a statement.

'There's a small village over there, or a large manor farm, whatever.' Tostig pointed down a coombe, terraced for rye, to a settlement about half a mile off, still just visible as the night gathered. They could see red lights as of flaming torches swinging about and then a sudden blooming of flames, yellow and orange. At that distance they were like a rose against the blackness.

'What's going on?' Edward asked.

The chief huntsman answered.

'Candlemas. They take down all the green stuff they decorated the bowers and hall with for Yule-tide and burn it. Get everything swept up clean.'

'Candlemas was yesterday.'

'Shrove Tuesday?'

'Not till the end of the month.'

The huntsman licked his lips, muttered something about ignorant peasants who always got the dates of things wrong.

They hacked down the grassy slope, and then through stunted apple and pear trees, the groom with the lamed horse following on foot. There were low cottages and huts outside the enclosure surrounded by field strips and small vegetable gardens. Beyond the palisade the roofs of the hall and three bowers could be seen and no doubt there were smaller buildings too – huts for servants, barns, stabling.

All was thrown into a flickering backcloth by the bonfire which was sited on the open space in front of the main entrance to the enclosure. Most settlements of this sort in England kept such a field free for recreation, country sports and so on. Men and women were heaving branches of yew and holly on to the fire: they crackled and flared instantly since it was some six weeks since they had been cut green; flaring ashes circled into the still air amongst the snowflakes, setting all in a whirling contradiction of heat and cold, light and darkness. There was music too – a couple of drums beat fast in a rattling rhythm, wailing pipes, and the occasional boom of a horn – and as they got nearer they could see that many of the silhouetted shapes were not merely fuelling the fire, they were dancing wildly around it.

Suddenly a group of figures broke away from the fire carrying brands of flaming straw and ran right into the orchard, banging the torches against the trunks. When the brands burnt low they chucked what was left into the branches. They all seemed to be female, in flowing scraps of loosely tied worsted and, in spite of the cold and the danger of sparks, many barefoot or merely sandalled. They threw a fright into the horses and some of the men too with a constant flow of ululating cries.

The women flew back to the fire. Edward told the men to wait to see if they would return, but when the wild dancing began again he told them to push on, albeit warily, ready for anything. Their presence had been noted and as they approached the enclosure, passing between the low round huts of the poorest retainers, a couple of middle-aged men, dressed soberly and with a look of some sense about them, came out to meet them.

The oldest, who might have been the thegn or lord of the manor from the dignity with which he bore himself, demanded to know who they were and what their business.

'Huntsmen,' Edward replied, leaning forward over his gelding's neck, 'from Godwin's household in Winchester. Our dogs picked up on a fox and led us astray.'

'You're not churchmen then?'

'No. But we need shelter and food. We can pay whatever is fair. My name is Aelfric, and this is Eric, my son,' indicating Tostig, who raised an ironic eyebrow at the news. 'The rest are my servants'

'They have names too,' the thegn, if that was what he was, grumbled. But he did not divulge who *he* was. However, he whistled up a couple of lads who were watching the dancing. 'Here, see their horses safely stabled.'

Edward, Tostig and the rest followed him into the hall. Tostig, looking over his shoulder, saw how the men outside were now leaping through the dying flames of the fire.

The hall was laid out for a feast and lit with flaming brands and candles, too. The tables were already piled with bread and apples, no doubt taken from the straw they had been kept in in the roof of a barn since September. Heavy with the smell of roasting mutton clouds of blue smoke occasionally blew in from some outer room. The thegn found his visitors a corner up under the high table and bade them sit down. It would not be long, he said, before the feasting began.

He was right. With the dying of the fire, the rhythm of the music changed to something less wild and the people of the village trooped in in family groups, passing beneath an arch of hooped quickbeam. Quickly but in due order, knowing their places, they seated themselves about the tables, the thegn too, but on the daïs with his own family ranging from a very old granny to a new-born baby. And all set to as youths and girls went amongst them with great platters of meat and flasks of mead. The visitors were not forgotten and got their share.

As the plates were cleared a youth with long, dark, brown hair, Saxon perhaps, with no Danish in him, came down from the daïs.

'My father has asked me to show you to the bower we keep for guests,' he said. 'A fire has been lit. He wishes you a very good night.'

The timber-framed house he took them to was warm with a fire of seasoned wood glowing in a central fireplace and giving off little smoke and what there was aromatic, pine perhaps. There were two bed-frames covered with yew and then linen sacking and woollen blankets and similar on the floor for the huntsman and his grooms. The youth was polite but firm.

'Do not let any noise we make disturb you,' he said. 'Stay here and sleep well.'

Tostig's face flared but Edward put out a restraining hand.

'They don't know who we are, ' he said. 'If they did they would treat us more graciously.'

'Then let us tell them.'

'No. That would be an abuse of the hospitality they have given us.'

Presently the music started again, at first in slow rhythms but, as the night wore on, faster, louder, more frenzied, accompanied by shouts and even screams, but not those of terror. Edward's curiosity got the better of him. After all, he needed to know as much as he could about these people he was born to rule and he suspected that what was going on was some pagan rite, the Lupercal perhaps, which, when the time was ripe, it would be his duty to stamp out. Checking the others were asleep, he wrapped his cloak about him, slipped through the doorway, crossed the short space back to the hall.

The music, and it was not what he, brought up on the pleasing of a courtly Norman lute, readily thought of as music, was now very loud indeed. Three drums, made of skins stretched over large barrels, were being beaten by a huge man clad in leathers. Others banged pieces of wood together, rattled vessels filled with stones, and one banged an anvil with a hammer. Above this two long pipes wailed, an old Viking horn boomed, and a couple of men twanged away on rebecs.

Many of the lights that had illuminated the hall were now out or guttered smokily; the beams of those that still burned brightly were broken into rhythmic flickers by the dancers who whirled between. Some of these danced on their own, twisting and stamping, arms flailing, fingers clicking; others faced each other and emulated each others' movements; and some clung to each other, in embraces almost openly lewd. And many formed lines in fours or sixes, arms over each others' shoulders, either side by side or in chains and swayed along, throwing legs first one way then the other.

And while they did all this many of them, all together at a given moment, waved their arms in the air and sang in unison, a repeated phrase, a meaningless mantra, something about the moon.

Bewildered and even disgusted, Edward returned unnoticed to his cot. In the morning the thegn was apologetic.

'I hope,' he said, 'we did not keep you awake with our noise and dancing. The winter nights are long and cold. Cheers us up, reminds us of spring, you know?'

Clearly there was still something that lingered about Edward that people recognised as foreign or at any rate not of their parts.

This experience was the first of many which represented aspects of England he would never get used to, that remained alien to the day he died. He never learned to like the Englishmen's capacity, at all levels, for rowdy, rough enjoyment. Moving with his court round the country, he found that everywhere they drank and ate enormously, especially drank.

Partial though Edward was to mead (and he preferred it not fully fermented so there was still much sweetness in it) he could not see the point of drinking until one was first stupid, then dangerous to others and oneself and finally insensible.

They all seized every opportunity, from heavy rain to drought, to down mattock, spade and sickle and leave the fields for a wide variety of sports and pastimes, none of which required cunning or skill, indeed most needed no more than brute strength and foolhardiness. Many were plain stupid – like putting a pole across a river so two men could sit astride and try to knock each other off with gravel-filled sacks. Or seeing who in a village could throw a leather boot the furthest. Or putting a cow in a small enclosure and striking wagers as to where it would shit first. They would fill a bladder with sand and then all the men of one village or farmstead would try to get it to the centre of another, while the men of the other did likewise. All of which was harmless in itself, but what would happen to an economy where all did not work night and day for the common good? A peasant who, when not actually at work, was not either briefly asleep, or eating just enough and no more to enable him to reproduce tomorrow the labour of today, was a bad peasant.

The noblemen hunted with no concern for their own or anyone else's safety, though they were punctilious about paying for any damage they did. They all loved fighting – wrestling, with fists, with staves – but the fyrd was a joke. Get a hundred Englishmen together with an assortment of agricultural tools for weapons, make them march twenty miles, the first to arrive would be an hour or so ahead of the stragglers.

At the big feasts the men and women danced lewdly together with little decorum, and, according to his Norman churchmen, fornication and adultery were rife and largely accepted. Incest was common – not overt, but tolerated.

More difficult yet to understand was the position of women in this society. Yes, as well as doing the lighter work in the fields, Eve span, looked after the children, made sure clothes were tolerably clean, floors swept, meals cooked, and they kept, by and large, away from the more important concerns of men. But with this difference: here in England these tasks were not thought to be menial, suitable only for chattels, property, slaves (for in most of Normandy that was what women were), but were highly respected and honoured for what they did, and woe-betide any man who tried to interfere. In the women's world the woman was Queen.

The hall was the men's domain. There they drank and decided things, once a month or so formally, at village or manorial meetings, but on a daily basis too disputes were settled, jobs handed out by the thegn's steward, and so on. All were allowed their say, and were listened to – for instance if a man felt he had a better idea of how the time he owed his lord could be spent, he'd get his word in, or if he was in difficulties owing to illness, whatever.

In the winter, if the weather was too bad for outdoor pastimes, the hall was also used for bowling large wooden balls at nine club-shaped skittles with sometimes the prize for the winner at the end of the evening as valuable as a live pig. On these and other occasions they would drink ale to excess while the thegn and his sons passed out on mead or wine.

Often a man would stay on in the hall after his companions had returned to their wives' or mothers' bowers because he was in dispute with his wife or mother over some domestic matter and she would not let him return until he had submitted. In Normandy a woman who behaved like that would end up in the stocks.

And kinship! A woman was naturally and properly constrained to marry outside her nearest kin – but heaven help a husband who then mistreated her, or treated the property she had brought with her as his own. Led by her father a posse of brothers, uncles and cousins would soon be around with staves and stones and worse. And, worst of all, women could hold land and manage homesteads, manors or palaces in their own right if things fell out that way, owing to the deaths or wills of their menfolk. In short, these English actually treasured, even wor-shipped, their women – sought their approbation, gave them fine gifts and mourned deeply when a wife, mother or daughter died.

Throughout his reign, in these and many other areas, Edward's Normans, especially the Cluniac-minded priests and monks, used every-thing from Holy Writ to threat of excommunication and hell-fire to persuade him to change things. But he learnt, not all at once, but bit by bit, to ignore them. It works and it's the way they like things, he'd say to himself, and if every now and then they get into scrapes they'd rather it was so than have me interfere. Or: this is the English way of doing things, these people chose me for their king because I am half-English by blood if not by inclination – I should be betraying them if I did not allow them to be English.

And, anyway – and he repeated it more and more to himself as he grew older, and finally, with his illness, almost senile – God would forgive him his laxity, his willingness to let things be for the sake of a quiet life, since Duke William was surely on his way and would put all to rights.

But at other times, when the sun shone and he had grasped and solved some particularly knotty problem, he had a different sense of it all. One day, shortly after his coronation, during a brief spell of fine weather, he and Tostig again rode into the forest, this time with falconers in attendance with hooded merlins and peregrines trailing their jesses on their wrists, tiny silver bells tinkling. It had been a good ride. Through the downs south of Romsey, there had been primroses in abundance beside the track, cowslips on the downs themselves, the corn was just sprouting green in the fields and the first hawthorn buds were casting a haze of green over the deer hedges round the settlements they passed. Up on the downs there were larks spilling song above sheep flocks where already the young lambs played. There was a harmony about it all that was so palpable he felt he could almost hear it.

On the edge of the forest he suddenly reined in and paused. In front of him was one of the largest oaks he had ever seen, a great tree indeed, spreading huge boughs over a circle almost thirty paces across, and as high as all but the highest buildings in the land. There were no leaves as yet but the brilliant green of its blossom was spreading over it and birds were already nesting in the fastnesses of its innermost boles and holes.

England is, or nearly is, or strives to be like that tree, he thought, and not just the tree, but all the countless animals and smaller creatures who live in and off it. The blossom provides nectar for the bees. Acorns follow the blossom and wild pigs as well as squirrels rummage for them when they fall. There were twigs, small branches, great boughs and the massive trunk. And below ground a vast network of roots including the trunk-like tap-root that found water even in the severest drought. He knew this because there were still plenty of uprooted trees around, victims of the Great Gale that had devastated the south three years earlier. He sensed the extreme differences between each part – the fragility of the blossom, the harsh roughness of the bark, the vulnerability of the robins and tits in their nests to the magpies and pine martens that invaded from outside, the flashing bright red of the squirrels and the wings of moths, so cunningly patterned that they were indistinguishable from the

bark, and others that could simulate the leaves. Then there was the tran-
sience of the foliage in contrast to the permanence of the timber. He was
aware too of how these great trees looked after themselves – if a bough
went rotten with fungus or beetles, the tree shed it. An abundance of
oak-apples brought in the birds that would eat the worms that made
them. If it over-produced blossom and acorns in one summer, in the
next there would be almost none while it rebuilt its strength instead.

Was there a sense in which one could say one part was more important than the other? Was the glorious canopy superior to the deepest
roots, the massive endurance of noble boughs greater than the contribution of passing leaves? Of course he did not know just how the leaves
contributed, but he did know that a tree which lost its leaves through
disease or fire died. Could any part survive deprived of all of any other?
Edward thought not, or was beginning to learn this might be the case.

And so it was, he sensed, with England. Every part was dependent on
every other part and he began to realise where his function in all this lay.
Basically, it was a self-regulating system, responding to outside changes
and to changes within itself, but such self-regulation could take time and
leave it exposed to predators from outside: his job was to foresee such
imbalances and, by fine adjustment, correct them, curbing growth here
or stimulating it there, making sure that no one part got so much more
than the others that the others began to weaken. On one side this could
mean restraining the greed of the large land-holders but on the other it
also meant that the people, these free people, especially those who
worked the land, should not get lazy, doing just enough to support their
kin. There had to be surplus too – and not just to ensure there were
reserves in times of famine but also so the artisans, the merchants, the
potters, the builders and all the rest could make their contributions
without having to wonder where the next loaf of bread was coming
from. The merchants too could commodify this surplus into material for
exchange so they could obtain abroad not just the luxuries and gew-gaws
the noble classes so much enjoyed but staples too when famine or short-
age struck.

And the thing that he found most difficult to grasp and even believe
in about all this was that, by and large, these people believed in it all too.

At their best they were bound from lowest to highest by mutual
respect. There was an easiness between a lord and his man that he had
never seen in Normandy. Sure a man might complain at the long hours

he worked for his lord, but he knew his lord would supply him in times of trouble, protect him when invaders came, provide him with a church, and above all leave him with enough control over his own life and his family for him to retain the self-respect every Englishman deemed his birth-right. Of course this meant they spent hours, days even, in their confounded moots and councils debating endless points which he, Edward, given the chance, would have settled in a moment. But this was England – all were entitled to have their say. It also meant, and it irked him till the day he died, that no one, often not even the serfs, ever addressed a superior by his correct title, as master, lord, sire, majesty.

The thing he learnt most to admire, though it was a difficult thing for his Norman upbringing to accept, was that, while the country was, yes, an intricate web of interconnections and interdependencies seen both horizontally from farmstead to manor, from village to burgh, from sheep-farmer to fisherman, from charcoal-burner to iron smelter, or vertically from King to serf, each community accepted responsibility for itself and all its members – the aged, the sick, the women, the children and even the wrongdoers. Step out of line in a way the community felt brought it into disrepute and it could well treat you more harshly than the laws of the land.

There had to be a word to describe this interlocking of self-interest and genuine altruism. The Latin words *mutuus* and *communis* suggested themselves. English society could be said to live and act *per mutua*, mutually: thus *Mutual Help* was the process by which it all worked.

CHAPTER
FIFTEEN

The coronation took place in Winchester on the third of April, Easter Day, 1043 in the presence of the full Witan. Old Siward of Northumbria and Leofric of Mercia were there. With all of Wessex, Sussex, Kent, much of East Anglia and the Thames Valley ranged against them, they did not have much choice.

The nobles and notables of England remained at Winchester for the whole of Easter week. During the daylight hours a government was put together, and since the weather remained cold, even frosty, much of it was done indoors in smoke-filled rooms since the long winter had depleted charcoal stocks. There was much wheeling and dealing, horse-trading too (sometimes literally), favours were called in and promised.

Ageing housecarls were pensioned off with land of their own and their sons recruited to replace them. The tax to pay for them, called heregeld, the successor to Danegeld, raised to pay for the standing army and navy, was fixed and the extremely complicated ways by which it was to be raised renewed. Appointments were made. The lines between the King's jurisdiction and private justice administered by local courts and moots were firmly established or re-established. The duties of King's reeves were carefully separated from those of Earls' sheriffs, so all knew who was responsible for what.

Clerks scurried about writing it all down, getting Edward's signature on document after document, confirming privileges here and dues there. All – earls, thegns, churchmen, clerks – agreed that Edward was confident and competent. They also could not fail to notice that Godwin's third son was always close at his elbow and that occasionally they touched hands or squeezed shoulders. This neither surprised nor distressed them. It did not surprise because they recognised Godwin's cunning in inserting his third son as the King's favourite and it did not distress either. Relationships of this sort were common, especially between unmarried men, and, being English, though they gossiped about it, most agreed that what they got up to in private was their own affair. Perhaps God's too, but certainly no one else's.

Edward found all this very refreshing. In Normandy he had had similar relationships, but, in an atmosphere pervaded by the puritanism of the reforming monks from Cluny, found it bothersome to be constantly reminded that God had special places in Hell set aside for sodomites, and tortures too, generally involving red-hot pokers.

He learnt most when things went wrong, which they did frequently during the first five years of his reign.

A wet, cold summer followed his coronation. Mould grew in the ears of corn before it could be harvested, and by All Saints' Day, when many taxes and dues had to be paid, the price of grain peaked at the highest level ever; murrain carried off most of the cattle in the warm, wet autumn. By Christmas people up and down the country were starving. And that was when he saw how seriously the rich and great, both secular and religious, took their responsibilities. Barns of stored grain were opened, taxes remitted, food bought in from the Continent. Of course the bluff Saxon Bishop of Wells assured Edward with a belly laugh that if they allowed all the poor to die then there'd be no idle rich – but he could see that compassion and duty played a greater part than mere self-interest.

The same lesson was learned with the terrible winter of 1047, when birds froze in the trees and dropped to the ground; wild animals and the wild men of the woods too, the Celtic fringe, came out of the forests and hung around the enclosures for warmth and scraps, and nearly every homestead and village was cut off for weeks by driven snow. Finally, in 1048 there was an earthquake whose epicentre was in Mercia. It destroyed Worcester, Droitwich and Derby and set off huge forest fires.

But from then on, as far as natural phenomena were concerned, things went well. The climate mellowed and vines were planted again as far north as York, the population grew but agricultural methods were improved. The surpluses produced money and, amongst the many projects Edward instigated using this capital, the greatest was the building of Westminster Abbey. By 1065, the opinion amongst the common sort was that Edward was a saint, and as such people do, they were happy to lay their good fortune at his door.

But Edward was no saint. Moreover, he remained a Norman in all but name. Never mind the quality of the art, sculpture and music that surrounded him, he longed for the hierarchical formalities of Norman courts. He became pious and was therefore vulnerable to the Norman priesthood who looked to Rome and the Pope. The English church had little time for piety, nor popery either, for that matter. Duty, yes, saying the offices, looking after the poor, maintaining the fabric of their establishments, above all producing the best, most marvellously illuminated manuscripts and wall paintings anywhere in the world, far far better than the Normans, for instance – but deep devotion, mortification remained alien. They were suspicious of such enthusiasms.

However, the famines, bad winters, earthquakes came later. The first crises were political and deeply personal at the same time. The first preceded his coronation by a few weeks, though it was not finally settled until the following September.

CHAPTER
SIXTEEN

Housed in the best building in Winchester apart from the Minster, and one of the few built of stone, dowager Queen Emma, Edward's mother, kept her own court. She sent for him, late in February, choosing her time well since Godwin and the Godwinsons were either in their own earldoms, or, in Godwin's and Harold's case, in the north country negotiating with Old Siward of Northumbria and Leofric of Mercia the terms under which the northerners might accept Edward as their King.

Emma, daughter of Duke Richard I of Normandy, was the widow of two kings, the mother of one, and shortly would be the mother of a second. Her first husband, Ethelred the Redelees, married her in a fit of desperation in 1002 – no doubt hoping that an alliance with Normandy, cemented by marital ties, would at least stop the Normans from giving the Danes help and support. In fact, the only thing the marriage achieved was the Norman connection which fifty years later became the basis of Bastard William's claim.

Emma, then not yet twenty, was Ethelred's second wife. By his first wife Elfleda, he had had several children, most notably Edmund, known as Ironside. This meant that Emma's children, Alfred and Edward, were figures of little importance, especially when the heroic Ironside undertook a far sturdier defence of the realm than his father had ever managed, even though their chief assailant was now the equally redoubtable and youthful Canute. Ethelred died and, after exceptionally bloody campaigns against Canute which ended with them agreeing to share the kingdom, Ironside followed his father. The Witan now confirmed Canute as King of all England.

No doubt hoping to strengthen the legitimacy of what was in effect a conquest, Canute took the widow's hand in marriage. Possibly she was flattered – even enraptured. The young Danish King was at least seven years younger than she was, huge of limb, of great strength, and a very goodly man to look upon, save for his nose, which was lofty, narrow and hooked; he also had long, fair hair, and eyes brighter than those of any man living.

Unfortunately for Emma he also had an English/Danish wife, Elgiva of Northampton, alive and well and whom he repudiated. Sort of. In fact she remained Queen in the north and east of the country in all but name and actually ruled his Norwegian Empire for a time as regent for their eldest son, Swein. Her second son was Harold Harefoot. Emma's situation was thus not a lot better than it had been when she was the second wife of Ethelred – in fact in some ways worse. At least Ethelred had been a widower.

By 1043 she was extremely wealthy. When she married Canute, Exeter, the major city of the west, was her dowry and the taxes and duties it raised were paid directly to her. She was the widow of two kings, one of whom had ruled an empire that stretched from the land of the Midnight Sun to Land's End and from Land's End to the shores of the Baltic beyond Denmark. She had treasure in gold coin and jewellery worth many many thousands of pounds – and it was all in the cellars of her Winchester house. Deprived of any real power at almost every moment of her life she had hoarded the next best thing – the wherewithal to buy power.

Edward was welcomed by her chaplain and adviser, a monk called Stigand. A strong, burly man in Benedictine black, he had short sandy hair, tonsured, above a square, reddish face, snub nose, mean blue eyes, thickish lips, jowls that shook. He was Edward's age or a little younger. He had been Canute's and Harold Harefoot's chaplain and one of their principal advisers. With some discretion he had withdrawn into the shadows during Harthacanute's brief reign, acting as chief adviser and chaplain to the dowager Queen, a position he still held. He led Edward to Emma's hall, announced him and withdrew. Worldly, ambitious, sensual, he typified for Edward all that was bad about the English church.

Emma's stone hall was hung with rich tapestries but otherwise barely furnished and heated only by one small brazier. She had no intention of wasting the savings of a lifetime on fuel bills. However, she was not averse to having rich and beautiful things about her – hence the tapestries, the gold drinking vessels, the furs wrapped round her thin but by no means frail body, the jewels and gold she wore, including a circlet with enough ornamentation to be called a crown. All these were saleable commodities. Charcoal ash and chicken bones were not. She did not rise from her throne-like seat when Edward approached but let him kiss a cheek lined like a walnut but fragrant with Indian sandalwood.

'You're not king yet,' she said, explaining why she had stayed in her seat.

'But you are for ever a queen,' he replied and took the armless chair that had been set for him beside hers.

Her red-dyed hair was pulled back beneath her crown-like coronet. Her eyes were bright and sharp, the black pupils bird-like in their darting awareness. She was never quite still – her nails, long, brown, ridged and hooked, tick-tocked on the arms of her chair, which were carved at the ends like lion heads; her feet tapped to some inner rhythm only she could hear. She brushed aside his enquiries about her health.

'So,' she began, 'you would be king.'

'I will be king.'

'Not while those bully boys rule you.'

He shrugged, ignored a spike of irritation.

'I need them now. I shall not need them for ever.'

'So. When you no longer need them you'll say, Dear Godwin, dear Sweyn, dear Harold and so on, thank you very much for everything you have done for me, now kindly relinquish your earldoms and all your power and go and live in . . . Cathay, beyond high Karakoum and the Roof of the World . . .' she cackled, snapped her fingers, 'and just like that they'll pack their bags and go.'

Foolishly (but who can avoid mentioning, as if casually, the name of a secret lover?), he replied: 'You left out Tostig.'

'Oh, keep your bummer boy. He's of no account.'

Irritation shifted to an anger he bottled up.

'Mother, come to the point. Why have you sent for me?'

She leant towards him, fixed his eyes with hers, sank her voice to a whisper.

'Tell Siward and Leofric that if they need money to raise a power strong enough to defeat the Godwins you have it.'

He was so taken aback at this that he had to stand, walk behind his chair, then turn away, strut half the length of the hall before returning.

'If anyone can hear us,' he was thinking of Stigand, 'you have already said enough to have us murdered.'

Her claw-hands ceased their tap-tap and gripped the chair arms so her swollen knuckles showed white.

'Jesus, but you are your father's son.' She meant Ethelred, but her mind was fixed on Godwin. Her voice shook with rage and chagrin. 'That man, that evil bull of a man ruled England whenever your stepfather was away. You and Alfred were in Normandy so you did not know, but he treated me like dirt. And he murdered your brother. Your brother! Does not that count, does that not mean something . . .? Come on, you steer, you eunuch, does that not mean something?'

He swung back at her, smashed his fist into his palm.

'Of course it does. But when the time is ripe. When it can be done with no loss to me, to you,' he hissed, close to her ear, afraid to shout, 'then we'll do it. Do you not understand? Wessex, Sussex, Kent, East Anglia, the shires north of the Thames, the ships, the navy, the house-carls – will your treasure run so far as to buy a host big enough?'

'Yes. Even without Siward and Leofric. There are Normans I, we, can buy. Danes, Norsemen. Macbeth too is a mighty warrior and, being a Scot, always ready to accept a handout—'

'And do you think, once this hired host has come and ravaged the country, this part of it anyway, to ruination, and killed all the Godwinsons as well as their father, for if one of the brood remains alive none will be safe, the people of this country will want me as their King—?"

'The people? Pah! Who are the people? The people will do as they are told.' Ever a good Norman was Queen Emma.

'And do you really believe,' still hissing, 'that out of all that hired host, victorious as it will be, they will not find a prince, a duke or a king they would rather serve than me?'

He took deep breaths, calmed himself a little, and returned to his seat beside her.

'Mother,' his voice took on a pleading, reasoning tone, 'you upbraided me with being my father's son. But he was a fool and I am not. He was foolhardy, and I am not. He was a wastrel of his resources and callous with human life—'

'And I am not,' she chanted with him, rocking her head from side to side in mockery.

He struggled to ignore this, but only just.

'Unfortunate though it is, Godwin and the Godwinsons are the only resource I have. What is fortunate is that they need me. That's the way things are. They will not always be so, but now, yes, that is the way things are.'

He stooped to kiss her, but she shrank back as if from something vile. He turned, walked briskly back to the door that faced her. Behind him she stood, hands still on the lion carvings of her chair and screamed: 'You are a cock-quean, a faggot, a coward, a fool. You'll regret this. You'll be sorry for this. And when you are, remember Alfred, my first-born and your brother . . .'

Chaplain Stigand showed him personally to the street door.

That was not the end of the story. In September of the same year Edward, now King, was in Colchester, the guest of Harold Godwinson, then Earl of East Anglia, with whom he already had some rapport. Together they were reviewing the needs of the fleet: rumour had it, backed by reports from spies, that Magnus, King of Norway, son of the sainted Olaf who had supplanted Swein and Canute's first Queen Elgiva, was planning at least a series of raids, and possibly a full-scale invasion.

Edward and Harold were standing on the quay, watching the grey tide flood over the brown flats below the town and up the navigable channel that led back to the Thames estuary. Beside them an attendant scooped oysters from a bucket, opened them skilfully with his seax, salted their phlegmatic flesh, and handed them in turn to each of the two lords. They swallowed them with relish, even though they were the staple of the very poorest in the area, those who cut reeds in the fens to supply thatch. Gulls, black-headed and the larger predatory brownish ones, swooped and cackled tunelessly about the two men, hoping for scraps. Between oysters they discussed where a ship repair yard should be sited and a naval magazine, and the difficulty of procuring adequate timber in a region where the trees were all willow, alder or poplar.

A distant blast on a horn drew their attention to the causeway that carried the London road across the estuary. Four horsemen came towards
them at a slow gallop. The standard amongst them and the way the sun
glinted off helmets and mail suggested they were people of some note. At
a hundred paces Harold recognised Leofwyne, his younger brother.
Breathless, the youth swung his leg over the front pommel of his saddle
and slipped to the ground, feeling as he did for a parchment in the
leather pouch at his belt. Though he made a brief obeisance to Edward,
it was to Harold that he gave the letter. The seal had already been
broken. Harold took his time, for he was not that well lettered, handed
it to Edward.

'Here, you had better read this.'

Edward glanced first at the addressee and then at the signature and
style given at the bottom. The first was Magnus, King of Norway; the
second Emma, Queen of England. Then he read the matter between,
which was in a clerkly hand, not hers. The gist was plain. Whereas the
Kingdom of England had been given over to her son Edward who was
a cowardly sodomist who allowed himself to be governed by a gang of
murderous rogues, she, mindful of Magnus's sainted father and his
unblemished record as a Christian Prince both just and wise, invited him
to come to England to clean out the midden it had become. To this end
she was ready to put at his disposal gold coin and jewels, worth some
thirty thousand pounds.

'Is it your mother's hand?'

'The signing is.'

Edward, pale, hands shaking, turned the parchment over, fitted the
cracked wax together.

'The seal, too.'

Harold sent an oyster shell, which skipped five times, skimming across
the tide race, which was now almost level with the quay, wiped his
mouth on his sleeve, turned to his brother.

'Has our dad seen this?'

'Yes. He sent me, he said we were to—'

'How did it come into his hands?'

'Stigand got hold of it. In fact she asked him to find messengers who
would carry it for her.'

'All right. Now tell us what Dad says.'

'He says to meet him at the bridge at Putney and to ride as fast as we

can to Winchester. We must get there before she has news that we are on
our way.'

'To what end?'

Leofwine, whose eczema had receded, glanced at Edward. Harold
reassured him.

'This is the King's business, not ours. Speak openly.'

'To take her treasure off her before she can plan any more mischief
with it, and put her in a house of seclusion.' He turned to Edward. 'Not
a prison, but under watch by people we can trust.'

'And the treasure?'

A brief pause.

'Why, to be placed in the King's treasury. Of course.'

Harold turned to Edward.

'Would that be your wish too?'

Just once, Edward thought, you might bother with a Sire, or a
Majesty, or even Your Grace.

'All right. But I ride with you.'

Two days later, they burst in on her – Edward at the front, briefly,
Godwin, Sweyn, Tostig, Harold, Leofwine close behind and overtaking
him. Behind them came housecarls equipped with crowbars and outside
in the street a small fleet of covered wagons waited.

There were no formalities, no laboured reading from a warrant or a
judgement. They went straight to it, the way shown by Stigand who
clearly knew where to go, down to the cellars, breaking locks, dragging
out chests which sometimes needed four strong men to lift them. Emma
stormed about screaming abuse directed mostly at Godwin himself
whose eyes she tried to tear out with her long hooked nails. No doubt
she had her first-born in mind. Roughly restrained though she was, she
yet broke free and turned on Edward, making a grab for his balls and
screaming that, unnatural practiser of forbidden vices as he was, she
would be happy to castrate him herself. Harold and Leofwine bundled
her back into her great chair and Harold tore from her cloak the silver
brooch she wore, depicting a hawk grappling with its prey. It had been
a betrothal gift from Canute.

Meanwhile Godwin and Sweyn rampaged around the room, tearing
down the tapestries, and dropping the few but expensive ornaments,
drinking vessels and so on into sacks. Physically restrained, Emma

regained if not composure then at least some self-control, and at this point Stigand came into the room. There was, he began to say, more to be collected from the upper rooms but the doors were good ones and the locks Moorish work and very fine – it would be a shame to break them . . .

'There, there's your man,' she screamed, and managed to get on her feet again. 'He put me up to it, it was his idea, he composed the letter, the fucking bastard even wrote it . . .'

One glance at the cleric confirmed the truth. It was not transparent guilt that seared Edward's heart but the look of complicity the monk exchanged with old Godwin. The fear, hate and scorn Edward felt for Godwin and all their clan, apart from Tostig whom he loved and Harold for whom he was learning an unwilling respect, bit deeper into his soul. And worse was to come.

CHAPTER
SEVENTEEN

One June dawn in the first full year of his reign he woke in the upper room of the great hall of Cheddar to find that Tostig had deserted their bed, was sitting on a small bench beneath the small window. Since it was near the solstice and the sun had just risen above the gorge the youth was bathed in the magical light of full dawn. The horizontal beams made a nimbus of his yellow hair: he looked like a naked angel, Lucifer before The Fall.

Outside the dawn chorus quite overpowered the crowing of numerous roosters in the enclosures below and the village beyond. A stir in air which had responded to the sudden warmth of the sun filled the room with the fragrances of honeysuckle and rambling roses. White-rumped house martins flashed by, feeding their twittering young in their clay-built nests suspended beneath the eaves. The grey shape of a cuckoo flew by above the trees, and the woods resounded with its trisyllabic call. In June I change my tune.

Meanwhile a very small baby bawled its lungs out at some distance – from the lady's bower. Edward guessed the source: the day before he had stood as sponsor, godfather to the tiny infant. What was the baby's name? Athelstan. What will he be when he grows up? The mother had answered – a bishop. The father, stepfather apparently, the father having fallen to his death down the cliffs in the gorge, raiding a peregrine nest for its chicks, replied – housecarl.

Edward eased himself upwards, put his hands behind his head, spread his elbows. For a month he had been housed here in a timber hall with plank walls plastered with rough-cast while he sorted out the government of the south-west corner of his kingdom. Albeit the only latrine was outside and at the other end of the building and the whole place was draughty in comparison with a decent solid-stone Norman keep with proper conveniences, he had to admit to himself England had its points – at any rate during a fine spell in early summer.

He felt drowsy, over-relaxed, ready perhaps to sleep again, though the noises from below and the smells too of fresh baked bread overriding or mingling with the fragrance of the blossom told him that soon the young thegn who served as steward of the bed-chamber would be knocking discreetly at the door. And the reason for this delicious lassitude was the passion, excessive even by their standards, which Tostig had brought to their love-making the night before, that and rather more mead than he was accustomed to.

He licked his lower lip and found the tiny swelling where Tostig had bitten it; the skin round his groin still tingled from where the young man's stubble had too roughly pushed and rubbed against it. There were odours on his fingers that he savoured . . .

'Last night,' he began, 'you were—'

He was going to say 'magnificent', but in response to his voice, Tostig turned his head from the sun and Edward could see how tears rolled down his cheeks. He was off the bed immediately, kneeling between his lover's knees, holding his face between both palms.

'Don't cry, please don't cry. You know I can put it right, whatever it is . . .'

And he stood and cradled Tostig's cheek against his stomach, smoothed his long hair, continued to murmur love and assurance.

Tostig pulled back, looked up at him.

'I'll tell you the matter.' His voice was hoarse, his eyes frantic. 'They want you to marry. I've been meaning to tell you for weeks, but we were so happy I couldn't. They want you to marry Edith, my sister—'

'Who wants this?' This was a shout, although Edward knew the answer. He clenched his fists, banged them on the folded-back shutter so it banged against the wall. A chunk of plaster fell to the floor, revealing the plank behind. "I'll see them in hell first,' and he stamped about the room, throwing their clothes about, came back to the shutter, banged it again so more plaster fell. 'In hell before I marry,' he repeated.

Tostig looked up at him, shook his head wonderingly, but suppressed a hint of a smile from his lips and the laugh that was in his throat.

'No you won't,' he said, and then his lovely face darkened again. 'I tell you, she's a bitch, a bloody, bloody bitch. And she'll have you to sleep with her here in my place.'

'I won't, I won't,' stormed the King. 'I will not allow it.'

'You will. Oh yes you will.'

'Why?'

'England requires you to provide her with a successor.'

'There are many alive, and no doubt others to be born who qualify.'

'Too many. And where there are too many there will be divisions and strife. Civil war.'

It was not Godwin he was faced with, not a Godwinson, but the man who had betrayed his mother, or trapped her into treason – Stigand, now rewarded with the bishopric of Elmham for his pains, a position which was more important than it sounded, for the Bishop of Elmham was in fact the Bishop of East Anglia. It may not have been a coincidence that Harold Godwinson was its earl.

They were in Bath, in the Benedictine Abbot's private rooms which had been made available to them. Since the Benedictines had been there for a hundred years, and were so far untouched by the Cluniac reforms, the interview took place in surroundings that were certainly comfortable and bordered on the luxurious. The large chairs were cushioned and the cushions were embroidered with hunting scenes rather than religious ones; the jug and cups from which Stigand poured mead were silver, and there were silver plates filled with cherries and wild strawberries. Outside in the cloister butterflies flickered above the flowering aromatic herbs the monks used to invigorate their cuisine and bumble-bees cruised through them.

'You speak as if I might die tomorrow.'

'May the King live for ever,' Stigand replied and spat out a cherry stone. 'A gracious prayer, said at every coronation since that of Solomon, but a vain one. You are mortal. However,' he sighed and shifted in his seat, easing beneath him the chasuble which he had not bothered to remove after Mass; Edward sensed a fart but a silent one, '. . . we do hope you will live long enough to see your son and heir reach his majority.'

'We?'

'All England.'

Silence stretched between them. Stigand was too clever a negotiator to be the first to break it. He carefully chose a second cherry and let his gaze wander across the cloister and up to the squat roof of the abbey church. Edward knew he should either dismiss the man, or himself stand and go. But he felt his temper rising again and wanted to have it all out, get to the bottom of it. He leant forward, banged the table, almost shouted.

'It is, is it not, transparent why Edith the daughter of Godwin should be Queen?'

Stigand looked mildly surprised.

'Transparent? I suppose so. What we need is an English succession, and one which will stick and last. With, once again, an English royal house properly established, then all these Scandinavian connections of Canute, God rest his soul, not to mention the Norman bastard who through your mother also has his foot in the door, will simply have to forget any spurious claims they may now think they have. Edith is English . . .'

'Half. Gytha, her mother, is Danish.'

'And so is about a third of the population of your kingdom and they all consider themselves English. They've been here a hundred years. Nevertheless, the fact that she is a connection of Canute's through marriage will please them too. But she's really English, as English as any of us. As English as apple-pie. All through.'

'So is the Atheling.'

'The other Edward?' Again the bishop spat out his cherry stone. It chimed on the rim of the silver platter. 'He's under age and lives in Hungary. Wherever that is.'

Edward at last got up, stormed round the room, came back to the table, lifted his mead-cup and banged it down so some of the amber liquid splashed.

'The Godwins would rule. That is what all this is about. With a prince who is half Godwinson, who is likely, should I sire him, to be still in his minority when I die (I recall you were kind enough to remind me that I am not immortal), he will be ruled, and all England too, by his grandfather, if that old devil survives me, and by his uncles if he does not . . .' One of whom is Tostig, and the thought filled his soul with a void which his anger could scarcely fill.

'I see no reason for this union,' he concluded. 'I see no advantage to me or the English.'

Stigand shifted forward so he could reach the spilled mead. He scooped a drop up with his ringed pinkie, and sucked it.

'There might be advantage to you.'

'How so?'

'The Godwins fear what might happen when you die. And let's not beat about the bush – you could fall from your horse tomorrow or catch an everlasting cold this winter. A murderer cloaked and hidden from our sight, a man perhaps known to us but not his intent, may even now be slipping through your housecarls . . . And, and this is the crux, no matter who succeeds you, be it Norway or Normandy, they will have no use for the Godwins – unless . . .'

Edward listened to nothing but the rush of his own blood, felt little but the prick of cold sweat in his palms. But the message was clear. Perhaps the shade of Alfred his brother whispered it in his ear.

'Unless,' he said at last, 'one or all of the Godwins has assisted my successor to the throne by murdering me.'

'You may think what you like. I could not possibly express an opinion.'

Edward stood, walked to the unglazed window. Beyond the cloister he could now hear the monks chanting the office of Terce. Like Benedictines everywhere their mastery of Gregorian plainsong was of a high order and filled him with nostalgia for the remembered simplicity of the life he had left, of uncomplicated devotions in places like Bayeux or Lisieux, the fragrance of incense, the sad face of God on the Cross and his sorrowing Mother, the sweet, mindless religiosity of adolescence . . . tears pricked his eyes, his heart felt empty. He turned back to the gross, cunning bishop.

'So. Once I have an heir, they can murder me anyway.'

'The Witan will never elect a child. Ill fares the land . . .'

'. . . where a child is king.'

The distant monks fell silent and the persistent buzz of a trapped humble-bee filled their space. Stigand stirred in his seat again and cleared his throat.

'For the time being,' he said, 'a ceremony of betrothal is what they suggest. They propose this should take place at Lammas-tide, at Cerne, in Dorset.'

And so it did. Edward with Harold and the nucleus of what was becoming a royal, that is Edward's own bodyguard of housecarls, rode out of Sherborne through a steady downpour. Edward's hunting dogs, big, long-legged, grey and shaggy, much like wolves apart from their long, broad, very dog-like muzzles, jogged alongside the horses. Occasionally they'd break away, attracted by the smell of a hare or the sight of a pair of partridges in an open field. Their pelts were soon as wet and mired as the horses, and the cloaks of their riders. Thunder rumbled around the beech-clad hills.

Naturally none of them was in a good temper.

'Could we not send someone on ahead and call this all off for a day or two?'

'Not really,' Harold replied.

'Why not?'

'Lammas-tide. Important day.'

'Certainly. Rents fall due. Let me see, what else? With the harvest, home fences are pulled down in certain parts, opening fields for common pasturing for the months before the spring sowing on Lady Day. A sensible system as the cattle feed the land with what they dump. What else? The name means "loaf-day". Barley cakes made from the new-mown grain are offered in churches. But none of it adds up to a particularly good day for a betrothal.'

Harold was impressed. The Norman aristocrat, brought up in cloisters and stone halls, on the Tales of the Virgin and the gestes of Charlemagne's knights, really was taking on the detail of the lives of his new subjects. However . . .

'The sanctity of the day lies deeper than that.'

They rode in silence. The hooves clipped the flints that metalled the road and clopped in chalky puddles. Harnesses jangled. A frown spread across Edward's face.

'Witches meet at Lammas,' he said at last.

Harold said nothing, but his lips hardened into a thinner line.

'I'll not be party to any pagan nonsense,' Edward declared, and reined in, so his horse snuffled and twisted its head to the side, anticipating a turn. The rain came on more heavily, strings of silver about them, grey curtains against the Downs ahead.

'There's no harm in it.'

'It's devil's work and you know it. I'm surprised you have any truck with it at all.'

'Oh, come on. It's just an excuse for a feast, a bit of dancing and jollity.' Harold repeated: 'There's no harm in it.'

'I've never known this country ever lack a reason for a feast – especially if there's plenty to drink on hand. But I'm going back to Sherborne before I get any wetter.'

'Hang on. There is more to it than that.'

Reluctantly Edward pulled his horse's head back to face south. 'Well?'

'Most round here have Celtic blood – they say the Saxons who came here had no women folk of their own and married the women of the peoples they had defeated, while inflicting serfdom on the men who survived. Sure, they are all Christian now and have been for many generations, but the old customs linger on, especially amongst the women. They are just customs. Not religion.'

'So. Of no importance. '

Harold sighed. This was more difficult than he had expected. The damned rain. Because of it the subject had been raised earlier than he had planned.

'They are slow to pay their taxes, they will not let their sons join the housecarls, the fyrd turns out, marches as far as the west bank of the River Stour and then goes home. They say our kings are not their kings, our queens are not their queens. To be sure of them when we need them, we must change that. What will happen today will help. If they accept you and Edith – Edith is important for they set as much store by the Queen as the King – then they will follow you and yours. Moreover, they will protect you if ever you should need it . . .'

'Are you trying to say that by going through with this flummery today I will gain the loyalty of the peoples who live west of the Stour, the Frome and the Parret.'

'Yes. As far as the Cornish border.'

'Very well. I'll go through with it. But I will not participate in anything blasphemous, in Devil worship, or anything of that sort.'

Harold said nothing but kicked his horse into a trot. Edward, housecarls, dogs, splashed on behind him.

The rain eased a little as they approached Cerne and, once they were in sight of the great Down, crowned then with a grove of holly trees, a rainbow glowed briefly above it. They wound down the valley, following a brook towards the small nuns' abbey and found the track lined, but sparsely, with folk from the settlements around. Some wore animal masks, others held hoops bound with the flowers of late summer, or carried sheaves of barley. A fool or two went amongst them, hitting children with a pig's bladder tied to a stick. But there was something lethargic about it all, uncommitted, self-conscious, or so Edward thought.

They turned left away from the brook before they reached the abbey and the small manor farm that lay around it and began to climb the shoulder of the Down. It was at this point that Edward caught sight, askew and from the side, of the giant figure cut into the turf so the white chalk shows through – the Fighting Man of Cerne.

Then, just in the way he still does today, his right hand wielded a club aloft made from holly, the best of all trees, while in his left he held a lion skin. Between his legs his erect phallus reached almost to his navel. He is Hercules, the Holly King who vanquishes the Oak King at midsummer and is worshipped by witches to this very day at Lammas-tide, then the first of August, now the twelfth. Almost as it were in his honour, tiny white or purplish blossoms clustered on the holly bushes that climbed the lower slopes of the hill.

The rest of the Godwins had already come up from near Dorchester, where they had camped on Maiden Castle, the Celtic hill fort which they, and the local people, took to be holy ground. They were waiting now on the edge of the grove above the Fighting Man. Amongst them, veiled from head to foot in green, was a faceless figure of good stature but not tall. In spite of everything, Edward could not suppress a twinge of curiosity. This was the first time he had seen her. But she crossed the sward with some white-gowned women and entered the grove and all he could see of her were her feet, long-boned and white, bound in her sandals' golden thongs.

The first part of the ceremony, which was conducted outside the grove, was long and tedious and had almost no Christian content at all, though an old priest was in attendance who occasionally mumbled fragments of dog-Latin and crossed himself exaggeratedly and often. For the rest, some was in an old language with a few sounds and words recognisable to anyone who could speak English, but most was in the sing-song lilt of mainland Gaelic. Edward was at a loss as to whether what he was witnessing, and indeed was part of, was a Saxon ritual remembered across six centuries from the forests of Thuringia or a yet more ancient Celtic, even Goidelic liturgy. Perhaps it was an eclectic combination of both.

He was asked to sip strange bitter concoctions from flattish clay beakers marked with spiral patterns of dots which had been exhumed from nearby barrows, the burial places of ancient kings. He would have feared poison, had not Harold with some reverence accepted them, too. He submitted to having a mixture of spittle and mud smeared on his eyes, nose and mouth, was symbolically whipped with hazel, and so on. For a time he wondered if this were all not some elaborate joke the Godwins were playing on him, but looking round them he saw nothing but serious, sober faces. Tostig, whom he had not seen since his meeting with Stigand at Bath, was among them. He was red-eyed with weeping and refused to meet Edward's gaze.

At last he was led into the grove itself, with Harold at his side. It seemed his future brother-in-law was playing the part of sponsor. Inside the grove the dark glossy trees were laden with pearl-like blossom and were loud with the bees that fumbled the flowers. It was all very bright and hard-edged, each detail standing out. The many shades of green pulsated against each other, the blossoms throbbed with inner life, a raindrop caught in a transient sunbeam burnt like the sun itself, the odours of a damp wood, steaming slightly, intoxicated a mind already tilted out of kilter. Worst, or best, of all he was conscious of a warm glow spreading up over his stomach and round his buttocks, emanating from his balls and prick, which he realised, with some embarrassment, was more than partially tumescent beneath his kirtle.

In the centre of the grove there was a round space and in the centre of the space a round, flat stone, yellowed with lichen, set in the ground so it made a step about a foot high. It was about six feet across. For a yard or so round it there was a circle of grass, the only grass in the place, since nothing will grow beneath dense holly.

Ranged in front of the stone were the women who had gone before. Edith, still in green, was set apart, framed in an arch of holly boughs, rich with blossom, the leaves glowing dark with their natural oils. All faced the stone, with their backs to Edward and the rest. At a signal, or perhaps just aware of his presence, she turned, and pulled off the green muslin hood. For a moment he could not breathe.

Her hair was a deep red and threaded with pearls. Her skin was whiter than any skin he had ever seen before. Her forehead was high. Her eyes beneath brows shaped and darkened a little were wide-spaced and large, aquamarine in colour. Her features were small, delicate though her mouth

was full-lipped, her nose straight, her chin firm, her neck a column of
ivory. But most of all it was her head of flaming hair that made her almost
supernaturally beautiful. She was not in the least like Tostig, as she had
been in fantasies he now forgot, but, as far as her face was concerned, there
was no reason not to interpret it as the countenance of a peculiarly beautiful and epicene boy on the cusp of puberty. This, not to put too fine a
point on it, was much how he liked them. Certainly his first sexual experience, at the age of fourteen, had been with just such an angelic form.

She stretched towards him a hand, long-boned and white like her feet,
and her mouth spread in a smile that did not reach her eyes. He placed
a gold ring taken from his mother's treasury upon her ring finger, and
submitted while she did the same for him. He could not repress a shudder at the touch of her fingers. She then led him by the hand out from
under the holly arch, to the rim of the stone.

He was now heavily under the influence of the potions he had
imbibed which were possibly aphrodisiac, and certainly, being distilla-
tions of certain mushroom juices, conducive both to dionysiac behaviour
and hallucinations. To all this she now added alcohol. One of her
acolytes handed her a jewelled gold cup. His fevered mind recalled that
he was not that many leagues from Glastonbury and in an area where
visions if not the actual reality of the Holy Grail had been recorded. She
bade, indeed made him, drink it off in one draught. It was in fact nothing more exotic than cider, but cider kept in cool cellars for a year or two
and therefore clear and very strong, and possibly again laced with addi-
tives designed to exaggerate its intoxicating effect. And the fact that it
was cider had its own significance for by it this being of supreme and palpable corporeality and evanescent beauty was identifying herself with the
apple-goddess.

Indeed, a second acolyte now brought to her a bough taken from an
apple tree, laden with apples. She indicated one, it was plucked. A flint
knife was used to cut it, but not in the normal way, from sepal to stem,
but in the way that is often tabooed – across its equator, so that when it
fell in two it presented a cross-section of the five seed-caves in the form
of a star, with each pip cut cross-wise. Tabooed in part because each seed
cave now had an emblematic, schematised likeness to a female vulva. She
gave him one half and ate the other, watching him with serious eyes to
make sure he did likewise. Thus she was Frigg, Holda, Held, Hild, Goda
or Ostara for those who remembered their Saxon, Germanic origins and

Rhiannon, Arianrhod, Cerridwen, Blodeuwedd, Danu or Anna for the Celts. And he? For a moment he was any hero or god mothered by the goddess, seduced by the goddess, sacrificed by the goddess.

The acolytes now closed round them. Unfastening Edith's robe down the front two of them drew it back like a curtain, while others began to undo his clothes. His head swam, his heart pounded. The fact was that he had never before cast his eyes on a female naked form, naked that is apart from her golden sandals. He was torn in two – by disgust and desire – disgust mainly at the sight of her flame-red pubic hair. He had never supposed that women had hair there, too, indeed he took her to be some sort of monster because she had. And now, forming itself out of the mist and holly behind her, a figure slowly materialised and the disgust this time was unmitigated . . . a ram's head, with ram's horns on a man covered in furs, with a rampant phallus reaching up from between his legs, he lorded it over them both, over all.

Illusion or representation? Edward never found out, but if it was the latter then the Godwins had gone too far. He knew, whichever it was, this was the devil and he was about the devil's business. Filled with the rage that comes over men in battle and which he himself had never felt before, clutching what garments they had managed to undo about him, he tore through the circle of women, then the small crowd beyond, and so to where his own men and their horses remained at the bottom of the hill. Lightning flickered, thunder crashed, and the rain swept down again.

Up in the glade the women did up Edith's dress.

'Damn,' she said, with the rain streaming down her face. And then: 'Fuck!'

Later, much later, when Tostig was married and had returned to court to be Edward's chief adviser and only real friend, he told Edward the truth of the whole matter – which Edward had partly guessed.

'They knew you could not lust after women in the normal way of things, but they thought if they fed you love potions, and created a numinous ambience, then you might be aroused at least once for Edith. And once would be enough, especially in front of witnesses.'

'Where did they learn all that mumbo-jumbo? Is the old religion still practised?'

'No, no. Recollections of it remain in trivial customs at feast-times and scarcely understood superstitions at weddings, births, and funerals.'

'So they made it all up for the occasion?'

'More or less. There's an old woman at Cerne Abbas who pretends she remembers it all and preserves it as, she says, part of our English Heritage. No doubt they consulted her.'

Edward, ten years on, pondered this.

'But, supposing I had achieved the copulation they desired, they could not be sure she would thereby be impregnated.'

'Ah. That was why it was a betrothal not a marriage. Not yet part of your household, she was still free to couple with whomever she liked and as often as she liked, at least for a month or so.'

'And if she had produced a child who looked nothing like her or me?'

'Oh, any child she might have produced would certainly have looked like a Godwin for it was only Godwins that she'd have let near her.'

'Her brothers?'

'Who else? Father too, I daresay .'

'You?'

'Ah, no.' Tostig laughed. 'She and I never got it on.'

Edward and Edith were married with little celebration by Stigand in Winchester on the twenty-third of January 1045. Edward never achieved penetration, though came near it during the short spell between the first wedding night and Shrove Tuesday. He was aroused by her feet – long, white, high-arched, unblemished (she was still only sixteen years old), bound in gold thongs or not – but above her knee he flopped. At first she was puzzled and confused – she was, after all, no virgin and thought she knew what she was doing. Confusion gave way to unbridled anger and contempt. Both felt deeply humiliated. He insisted they give up trying for Lent. They gave up trying for ever. Mourning Tostig, Edward embraced total celibacy for the rest of his life. Edith found discreet consolation wherever she could but was careful not to become pregnant: she knew he would disown her and the child if she did.

On one of the last nights they spent together she hurled at him this final threat:

'Do not believe that because you have left me childless you will prevent a Godwinson from ascending your throne: it is the Witan that will decide your successor, and the Witan is Godwin's.'

From that day he worked to prove her wrong.

CHAPTER
EIGHTEEN

Edward was a man riven with contradictions. Clever, even intellectual, he was yet capable of being moved to tears of exaltation by brief moments of aesthetic emotion, especially when these were inspired by religious artefacts, music or architecture. But nowhere were the contradictions of his nature better exemplified than in his dealings with the Godwin family and in the vexed and related problem of who would succeed him.

Godwin himself he hated. For Harold he learnt a grudging respect. Tostig he loved. And Edith he agreed to marry, albeit it was a marriage which, after the first storms, settled on both sides into refined and distant disdain. Hate, respect, love and a bad marriage . . . whatever – he was bound to the clan throughout his reign and for most of it longed to be rid of them but, try as he might, he could not loosen the knots, for the truth was that neither could survive without the other.

Six years went by during which he felt he was managing better and better without them. In 1048 he saw off the Vikings who harried the Isles of Wight and Thanet, commanding his fleet without their help. He built up a civil service dominated by Normans, most of them in minor orders. He arranged a marriage between his older widowed sister, Godgifu, and a member of Duke William's inner circle, Count Eustace of Boulogne, and invited the Count and his sister to visit him. In 1051 he promoted the Norman Robert of Jumièges, Bishop of London, to the see of Canterbury, and brought over another Norman, William, to be Bishop of London.

The influence and power of the Godwin clan was fading. It only needed now for the northern earls, Siward and Leofric, to agree to come to his aid if it came to an armed confrontation. Edward, Robert of Canterbury, William of London and brother-in-law Count Eustace of Boulogne now met secretly in a manor of the King's in the Chilterns and concocted the provocation which would fire Godwin up to an act of disobedience gross enough to be labelled treason. Eustace arranged to leave by Dover and ordered his followers to cause a riot in the streets there. They did so and, unwitting victims of the schemes of greater men, lost their lives when the burghers retaliated. Edward ordered Godwin to harry the town mercilessly as a punishment for abusing so shockingly the customs of hospitality, an offence particularly serious in an important port where it was essential travellers should feel safe.

Godwin, apprised of the circumstances of the riot, refused, and was summoned to Gloucester to answer charges of disobedience. On the way he and his sons raised an army, among whose youngest members were the young Walt Edwinson of Iwerne and Aethelstan of Cheddar, known as Timor. At Gloucester judgement was postponed until September, by when the harvest had depleted Godwin's army, and the whole clan were forced into exile for a year. Even Queen Edith was banned from the court and sent to a nunnery. However, during the year that followed, Edward, no doubt cockahoop at his success, blundered badly.

First, he invited the bastard Duke of Normandy himself on what was to all intents and purposes a state visit.

William was now twenty-three years old and at last firmly in control of his dukedom which had been disputed throughout his minority. He did not stay long – long enough to accept Edward's offer of the succession and the promise that Edward would name the Duke his successor in due course. In return he promised Edward that when the time came he would press his claim to the utmost.

Second, the choice pickings vacated by the Godwins went not to the northern earls but Edward's Norman friends, so when the Godwins returned the northerners were loth to come to Edward's aid again.

Edward's forced capitulation now must have been the bitterest moment in his long struggle. Robert and many other Normans were sent packing; the Witan accepted Godwin's oath-swearing and exonerated him of all his crimes including the murder of Alfred, Edward's elder brother. Queen Emma, in a fit of rage at hearing of the Godwins' return, fell, broke her hip, and died soon after. Queen Edith was readmitted to the Court and insisted on having her bowers at all the important places the court perambulated through enlarged so she could entertain and be entertained by the poets, musicians, dancers and no doubt lovers she collected about her.

Stigand, already elevated to Winchester, had advised and spied for the Godwins all through, and now was rewarded with the see of Canterbury. Only one pope, and then only briefly, confirmed him in the position. That pope's predecessors and successors excommunicated him, but he did not let that bother him. Succeeding Archbishops of York carried out important ceremonies like consecrations on his behalf – he was in any case bored by all that. Stigand was a politician. The see of Canterbury gave him a considerable power base – not founded on the spiritual authority it conferred but on the lands and huge emoluments that went with both his sees. Both? As far as he was concerned taking up Canterbury was no reason for letting go of Winchester although canon law forbad such pluralism.

One consolation followed shortly. Godwin now insisted on remaining in the King's court, no doubt meaning to be earlier advised of any plots against him. Edward tolerated his presence. He placed him at his side at every great feast – generally speaking feasts were the only times Godwin dragged himself out of the bed he now shared with a succession of nubile concubines – and pressed food and drink on him with a generosity that may have been double-edged.

At all events, on Easter Monday, just six months after his return, Godwin started up from the table, one hand clutched his forehead, the other his chest, a great fountain of black blood gushed from his mouth and he crashed into the table sending all flying. He died two days later.

It was said that he had yet again asserted his innocence of Alfred's murder and called upon God to choke him if he was guilty. In fact his swollen liver had caused the veins in his oesophagus to become varicose. They burst and he bled to death.

After that and for the next twelve years things settled into a peaceful reign. Prosperity abounded on all sides, the climate went through a benign spell and Edward, showing ever-increasing understanding of the ways of his countrymen, ruled well, interfering as little as possible, and only when the self-regulating nature of the nation seemed in danger of malfunctioning. In this his chief counsellor was Tostig. During the

Godwins' exile Tostig had married Judith, kin to their host, the Count of Flanders. He was now in his mid-thirties and age, together with the Godwin vices of eating and drinking too much, had coarsened his appearance. Moreover, he no longer took pleasure in being buggered. Edward too had moved beyond a desire for such practices. However, they remained intimate friends and Tostig proved himself a valuable guide through the intricacies and absurdities of English law and customs.

Meanwhile, in 1054, Old Siward of Northumbria, accompanied by his son, joined Malcolm son of Duncan in an attempt to oust Macbeth from the Scottish throne. In the one battle that was fought, young Siward was slain. The next year, 1055, Old Siward himself died, leaving only one child, Waltheof, not yet ten years old. There were many Anglo-Danish connections who could have succeeded him, but Edward, no doubt following his own inclinations as well as recalling past favours, and possibly yielding to the usual pressures the Godwinsons were able to bring to bear, made Tostig Earl of Northumbria.

This left Mercia, held by Aelfgar, Leofric's son, and one of the most troublesome men in the kingdom. Twice already he had revolted against Edward, or at any rate the Godwins, and been banished too. On the first occasion he went to Ireland, raised an army and allied himself with Griffith, who called himself King of Wales, to whom he married his eldest daughter. Together they ravaged the Welsh borders, and plotted with the Norwegians who made landings in the north. Harold broke the Welsh in his first campaign against them, though Griffith survived. Tostig saw off the Norse and thus left Aelfgar exposed and powerless. Because of the loyalty of his housecarls and thegns, who went through the whole oath-swearing charade on his behalf, and because both Edward and Harold wanted peace, he was allowed to survive. He died, presumably of natural causes, in 1062. He was succeeded by his son Edwin, who was only just twenty years old, and not, for the time being, a force to be considered.

In 1057, and on Tostig's advice, Edward invited the Atheling, son of Ironside, to come home from Hungary and bring his infant son with him, offering oaths that their lives would be safe and that they would be paid the respect due to them (save the crown itself) if they came. Such invitations were double-edged. A refusal could be construed as a decla- ration of hostility, even as evidence that he coveted the crown. If that were believed he could, according to the customs of the time, expect assassins to be contracted to kill him. He chose the wiser course and set off for England. Unfortunately, and for once there is no reason to suspect foul play except in so far as it *was* the custom of the time, he died between Dover and London. His four-year-old son, Edgar, now the Atheling, remained at Edward's court and grew up there – a lonely figure, often to be seen sucking his thumb in the darker corners of bowers and halls.

Because of his celibacy and self-restraint (apart from over-indulging in partially fermented mead) Edward gained a reputation for ascetism which was scarcely deserved: the aesthetic rather than spiritual delights of religion were his passion and he approached them with the instincts of a dilettante. He collected and commissioned beautifully illuminated missals, gospels, and even whole bibles, rich with gold leaf and lapis lazuli and filled with painting of the Winchester school. He would travel the length and breadth of his kingdom to hear a choir of monks whose reputation had reached him. He encouraged his bishops and priests to wear more and more sumptuous vestments. With his support and patronage English gold- and silver-smiths achieved a European reputation for their censers, ciboriums, chalices, reliquaries, processional crosses and the rest. And none of this was a charge on the country – it all came from Queen Emma's treasury. The national treasury was full – partly because of increased revenue from the general prosperity, partly because of good management.

The prosperity of all was also increased, as also was Edward's popularity, when he refused to go on collecting heregild, the burdensome tax that paid for the armed forces. The result was that over the decade the number of trained housecarls diminished and the ships of the navy were laid up.

Did more than mere economy lie behind this? Certainly it must be true that if Harold had arrived on Senlac Hill with double the number of housecarls that he actually had, there would have been no Norman Conquest. Enough, however, of both ships and men were available for Harold and Tostig to destroy, in two campaigns, Griffith, the troublesome Welsh Kingling, who persisted in making cross-border raids. Since the alliance between Ironside and Canute, nearly forty years earlier, these were the only campaigns that the English had to fight and most of what fighting there was took place in Wales not England. Thus was maintained a peace whose length was unequalled anywhere in the western world at that time and not often surpassed since.

CHAPTER
NINETEEN

In March 1065 he knew he was dying of Diabetes Mellitus, honeyed urine, and sent for William, Bishop of London, one of the few Normans who remained in place. The Godwinsons tolerated the bishop. London was not important – certainly the largest town in the country, it was still, according to the way they saw things, peripheral – a port on the edge of the country, for the most part occupied by foreigners, and keeping itself very much to itself, with its own laws and customs. Goods came in and goods went out, the merchants paid their dues and taxes, it ran itself.

Bishop William was a tall, lean man, with an ascetic, sculptured face, almost bald apart from a fringe of black hair round his tonsure. He climbed to the upper room, and wrinkling his nose at the sweet but unpleasant smells that met him there, pulled a chair up to the King's bedside. He recited the office of vespers from memory, supplying the responses where the King mumbled or was slow. Then he leant back in his chair and their eyes met – the King's loosely focused, his white hair an aureole above them, his face drawn and pale; the bishop's dark, alert, considering.

'William, I'm dying,' Edward murmured.

'I know,' replied the bishop. 'But you have, I am told, time enough to assure yourself of a welcome from St Peter.'

'Saints, only, go straight through Heaven's portals.'

William fell silent. A silence that could be interpreted to mean that something might be arranged.

Edward added: 'I sinned often and grievously in my youth.'

'If you are referring to buggery, forget it. There are vastly more serious affairs that should be weighing on your conscience. You have done nothing to reform the English church. You have allowed the priests to marry or take concubines, you have turned a blind eye not only to their concupiscence but also their gluttony and drunkenness. Hardly any of them even know there is a pope, let alone what a pope is.' He cleared his throat, pulled his chair in so the legs scraped on the floor, and went on.

'Naturally all this has affected the natural piety of your people. You have done little or nothing to discourage pagan practices. You have allowed them to live in plenty and squander the fruit of their toil in luxury and wantonness, denying the church and therefore God, the full surplus of their labours . . .' he waxed angry, 'it behoves all men to return to their Maker what they do not need beyond the barest necessities to sustain life. The church, and the Lords of the realm, who are the church's protectors and defenders, require from men who work in the fields everything every man can possibly give them. Only thus will their souls, untempted to profligate consumption of the fruits of their own labours, be assured of salvation and redemption at the Last Trump.'

He was stamping round the room now, waving an admonitory finger at the prostrate monarch, and occasionally spitting on plosive syllables.

'There are other things, too—'

'I need to piss.'

'I am referring first to that running sore on the fabric of the state, the godless family—'

'I NEED TO PISS.'

'Oh very well. Shall I call a servant?'

'No. No time. Under the bed. Please.'

Under the bed? Did his monarch expect him to get under the bed? The bishop stooped, lifted the covers which trailed to the floor, stuck his head and shoulders beneath them.

'Ah,' he said, 'the Jerusalem.'

Backing out from under the bed, he came up with a large chamber pot in the form of a coopered bucket with a handle.

'Is this what you want?'

But the King was now lying back with his eyes shut and a hint of a smile on his lips.

'Too late,' he murmured, and gave the lower part of his body a wriggle below the coverlet. 'You were saying . . . something about a running sore?'

The bishop looked at him with unconcealed disdain then shook himself, as if to cast off trivialities.

'A running sore. Yes. The godless Godwinsons. And then there is Stigand. Excommunicated but strutting his . . . his . . . carcase not just in Canterbury and Winchester but up and down the land as if he were a greater prince of the church than His Holiness himself—'

'Remind me. Who is the Pope, just now?' Edward opened one eye then the other. 'They've changed so often this last ten years or so.'

'I forget. It's what he is that matters. Anyway, these are the sins, sins of omission to some extent, which will doom you to centuries in Purgatory, if not worse, if you don't do something about them. You must put your house in order before you go. Let us thank God He has granted you the time you need to do so.'

'Amen to that. But that is why I sent for you. I can clearly see what I must do. I must see to it that Duke William is my successor. Otherwise the Godwinsons will put the Atheling on the throne and rule through him, or even get Harold himself elected.'

'Right. Absolutely right.'

'William will see Stigand off, and his – your – churchmen will reform the church, and he'll crush the Godwinsons . . . But I would not want to see Harold murdered for I have come to see he is a good man and his blood on my hands would be a stain St Peter might choose not to ignore—'

'Pah!'

'Besides, he has so many brothers . . . No. We must think of something more clever than murder.'

Once more the bishop took a turn round the room, this time with head bent and hands behind his back. He too had a string of the new-fangled prayer beads which clicked rapidly through his fingers. Like Edward he found fiddling with them a great aid to cogitation. And, he had to admit, he was impressed with Edward's grasp of the situation. His body might be going, but his mind appeared to remain lucid and even sharp.

'I think I've got it—'

'How about if we—'

They spoke together. The bishop, mindful after all of rank, insisted: 'You first!'

'Somehow,' Edward said, 'we must get Harold to promise to support Duke William's rightful claim. But how?'

'If we could get him to Normandy . . .'

'If we could get him to Normandy . . .'

'I have it.' The King sat up against his pillows and beamed. 'Duke William has in his court two kinsmen of Harold, close kinsmen, held as hostages. One is his nephew Wulfnoth, the other his cousin Hakon. Harold has often asked me if they could not be replaced by some other surety. I'll tell him he can go to Rouen and plead personally with the Duke for their release . . . But how to make him swear allegiance to William once he's there?'

'That will be up to the Duke. The thing might be to put Harold in a situation where he owes a serious debt of honour to the Duke. If the Duke could save his life . . . something of that sort.' The bishop stuffed the beads in behind the heavy belt which held in his cassock and bit his nails instead. Then, presently: 'I have it, I think I have it. I shall have to write some letters . . . to my brother in Christ at Rouen . . .'

'Encrypted,' Edward suggested nervously.

'Of course encrypted,' the bishop was irritated by the needless interruption, 'and he can pass them on to Duke William, yes, yes, it's falling into place. What's the matter?'

Edward had cleared his throat. His head had now drooped a bit, and he looked ill at ease.

'The fact is,' he muttered, 'that I am now feeling, um, feelings of delight and satisfaction at all this – there's a Germanic word for what I – scaden-something . . .'

'Why not? So you should, so you should. This is God's work we are doing . . .'

'But is it not a sin that I should feel so pleased that at last I may deny the Godwins their final ambition?'

'Good Lord, no.'

The bishop looked down at the picture of penitence that was the King. All right, a man nearing death should look to avoid all occasions of sin, but this was taking sanctity a step too far.

'Good Lord, no,' he repeated. 'Get your house in order, that's the thing.'

He gave the King his blessing, offered him his episcopal ring to kiss, and promised to return to say Mass with him in a day or two.

As he got to the bottom of the steps he called over a young boy who was standing around, apparently with time on his hands.

'Your master,' he said, 'needs a wash and a change of bed-linen.'

Edgar Atheling, who had more right to Edward's throne as far as lineage went than either Harold, William, or Edward himself, gave the finger to the bishop's broad, retreating back. Then, he went and found someone more suitably low-born to carry out the bishop's commission.

PART III

THE OATH

CHAPTER
TWENTY

All of which clears the way for an explanation of why Walt, semi-conscious on a bed outside Nicæa, was trying to piece together in his confused mind just how it was he, and Harold's closest companions, had sat listening to Taillefer singing the *Chanson de Roland* in the court of Duke William some years before. There had been a dreadful outcome, for which Taillefer himself had been responsible. Taillefer? A busking magician whose blasphemous tricks had landed him and Quint in jail? Whose children were now looking after him? Walt groaned. He must be mad. But the harp – the harp had been real enough.

His first recollection of the trip to Normandy was of the quayside at Bosham which lies at the head of the various islands and tidal waterways that make up Chichester harbour. It was late summer, with a stiff breeze from the west rolling bundles of white cloud across the sky. A daughter of Canute was buried in the crypt of the church behind him and the sea-wall, strengthened with chair-like buttresses, had given rise to the story that he had sat in a throne and bad the tide come no further. A spring tide followed and washed away the original wall and he had built another a few yards back, thicker and higher.

Walt was troubled, then and now as he remembered it all, by the recollection that what was about to follow was a sea-voyage and he was finding it difficult to conceal his terror. Especially since the wind was strong enough to rock the boughs of the elms which hid the hall and bowers nearby. At least their ship, moored against the quay, with a proper crew of real sailors who were busy checking tackle and caulking seams in the deck with hot coal-tar, was a proper boat, at least ten feet broad in the beam, and forty from prow to stem with a castled fo'c'sle and a high poop.

Around him were his seven closest companions: together they made up the inner core, the *comitati*, of Harold's bodyguard. They hardly ever strayed very far from each other nor any great distance from Harold himself. Lean, tough, tattooed, they now sat or stood around in a small group, each with a couple of large, heavy sacks or bags made out of stout hessian, containing their chain-mail byrnies, helmets, axes and swords. Although all were in their mid-twenties, all but one had been with Walt since late boyhood. Daffydd was the newcomer, a Welsh princeling, nephew of Griffith who had claimed kingship not only over Wales but the fertile marches along the valleys of the Wye, the Lugg and the Dee.

Wulfric, still the largest and meanest of them, though now totally reliable in the shield-wall or covering you as you scouted through a copse on the Welsh border, was their leader; Aethelstan, known as Timor, still the slightest but filled now with the cunning only the persecuted know how to develop, was Walt's closest friend.

They had learnt their trade, not only from Eric, the ancient Sergeant-at-Arms, but on Harold's Welsh campaigns. Harold, Tostig and a small army of which these lads were the core, had trapped Griffith like a nut in a cracker, since Harold came by sea and river, and Tostig across the Brecon Beacons. He'd slipped away but only as far as a stronghold deep in the Cambrian mountains. There, in the Welsh fastnesses, his own brothers, sick of the trouble their older brother constantly brought upon them, cut off his head and sent it to Harold. Harold in turn demanded hostages and Daffydd was one of these.

He was a dark whippet of a youth and tricksy with it. He now sidled up to Walt, holding a shabby leather purse in his hand.

'Walt bach,' he murmured in his lilting voice, 'I have here a most efficacious charm against drowning and I would cheerfully give it to you, but it came from my aunt so I am afraid I cannot.'

'If it's yours you can give it where you like.'

'It's not so simp-le, see. My aunt Blodeuwedd made me give her gold for it, for that is the secret of its mag-ic. It loses all its potency if it changes hands without gold is passed for it. I am sorree for this since I know you fear death by drowning.'

'What is it, then?'

Daffydd drew a brown wrinkled sack from the purse. It was no more than six inches long and three deep and seemed to be made of some dried animal matter.

'It is the maw,' he said, 'by that I mean the stom-ach, of a ravin'd salt-sea shark.'

'How ravin'd. What means ravin'd?'

'Why, by ravin'd you must understand devoured, eat-en.'

'If this shark was eaten, how come the stomach remains?'

'The stomach or maw of your salt-sea shark is renowned, on account of the bile within, as being inedible.'

'It must have been a very small shark.'

'You must understand that this is a very ancient re-lic and is somewhat shrivelled. If you have no gold about you a silver shilling will probably serve. Like gold, it is a noble metal.'

Walt fished out a shilling but, as he put it in the Welsh youth's palm and took the doubtful object he was offered, the rest, led by Wulfric, burst into howls of laughter they could no longer contain.

Walt hurled whatever it was he had bought as far out into the water as he could and a gull swooped on it and carried it off. Instantly he felt a pang of sheer angst – now, for though he knew he had been tricked, he was certain he would drown, certain as could be.

'Where's the boss then?' he turned and asked, masking his discomfiture, and he saw as he turned how the ship's master, a fat man whose linen clothes were greased with dried pig-fat, took a heavy purse from a postulant in minor orders. They were standing on the poop of the ship and all but Walt had their backs to them. Walt thought nothing of it – the ship's master was receiving his due for ferrying them all across the Channel, nothing more. 'We'll miss the tide if he doesn't show up soon.'

'Who knows where he is?' crowed Wulfric. 'But I know where his prick is.'

Long arms, shapely like the boughs of a slender poplar, tightened behind Harold's neck, long thighs spread and rose on either side of his waist while, below shapely knees, calves angled inwards so the soles of long feet met in the cleft between his buttocks. They too tightened, pressed

him into her. She clenched her own buttocks, contrived to contract the
still pulsing muscles deep inside her, did all she could to hold him there
for as long as she could.

'Oh, yes, oh Jesus, oh yes.'

He grinned. He couldn't help it. She frowned, relaxed and his
member slipped out of her. Then, as she straightened her legs along his,
he rolled off her. He turned on his back and slipped an arm beneath her
shoulder, so the side of her head lay below his cheek. Like that they
caressed each other gently and dozed for half an hour or so as the sun's
beams strengthened between the cracks in the shutters and the room was
filled with morning light.

Presently she murmured: 'Don't go. All you need is here, within these
four walls. '

'The King bids me. I am the King's man.'

'The King is your enemy. Only a fool goes where his enemy sends
him.'

His voice lightened.

'It won't take long, a month at most. Wulfnoth and Hakon have been
too long in Normandy. They should come home and learn to be English
again. Else they'll become little Edwards.'

'It doesn't need you to get them. Why you? Why go to your enemy
on the bidding of your enemy?'

'Duke William is no enemy of mine.'

'He wants to be king.'

'So? If that is the will of the Witan when Edward dies, he shall have
my support. If they choose me I shall expect him to support me.'

Edith Swan-Neck sighed. He would not give in, nor change his
mind, nor listen to reason or intuition. He would argue black was white
rather than concede she might be right. All done gently of course, without loss of temper, but firmly.

Presently she sat up and then swung herself round so she could sit
astride his thighs and look down at him. She saw a head of long curling
dark hair with streaks of lighter red, but grizzled at the temples, a glossy
full moustache but strong chin, clean-shaven now, a mouth whose corners
still tilted up a little and which revealed, when opened, two badly chipped
teeth to the left and a scar that ran into the moustache above them. His
chest was broad and deep with a mat of russet hair, his stomach flat and
solid beneath a midriff ridged when he tensed it. Only his eyes had

changed over the years – although they still laughed when she wanted them to, they were often weary in repose with crow's feet spreading from the corners and bruise-like shadows in the skin below his brows.

He saw a woman strong like him and lean. Her skin was no longer the translucent white it had been when she was fifteen but creamy now and with here and there a mole. Beneath it well-toned muscle had replaced the softness of puppy-fat. Her breasts were still full and he delighted in the used look they had, nipples broader and browner than they had been, the skin about them slightly puckered. She had borne him three children and suckled all of them. Her waist was long, her stomach flat and, while she cursed them for what she called their ugliness, he adored the stretch-marks below. But her neck was still the feature that made her the person she was and always would be – Edith Swan-Neck.

A Danish princess, she had been married at fourteen to an Irish thegn, Cuthbert, as part of an attempt to ally a small Danish kingdom, little more than an enclave, with the local Irish chieftains. He had been an old man, and already impotent. When Harold visited in 1047 she had fallen in love with him and quickly bore him two sons. A daughter came later. When Cuthbert died, Harold had wanted to marry her but the rest of the Godwin family had forbidden it: marriage for him should be saved until the time it could be played like a counter to bolster up an alliance, make a friend of an enemy. Nevertheless, he had so far managed to avoid it and lived with Edith whenever he could.

Leaning forward so her breasts swung above him and shadowed her torso her finger began a journey which started in his scalp, moved to the chipped teeth and the scar that ran from his mouth, and so down his right arm to the deepest scar of all, a gash six inches long, roughly sewn and still occasionally enflamed as shards of bone worked their way out. The Welsh axe that had caused it might have done much worse had Walt not been at hand to deflect it.

She lifted it to her lips and let her tongue run along its length then her head dropped to his chest and found the smallest scar of all, just below his rib-cage where a Welsh arrow had pierced his mail, but only just. She kissed that too, then, with her head now almost on a level with his, lifted her face and murmured: 'Come back as you are, please? I want no more of these. I shall stop loving you if there are any more.'

*

Not the laughter of men nor the sweetness of mead
Gladden the seafarer's heart
But call of the curlew, cry of the gannet . . .
Though he be gift-giving and bold, daring in deeds
Graced with a Lord who is gracious
There lives not a man but he fears seafaring.
Yet nor harp-heartening, ring-having, nor rapture with woman
Can smother his lust for wind-spray and wave-slash . . .

As she rounded the mud-flats off West Wittering, where the grey seals basked and the terns arrowed like lightning bolts into the sea, the westerly breeze filled the big sail and sent the boat lolloping on as the rush of waves blue-black beneath their snowy crests chased, caught, overtook her. Down in the waist of the ship Helmric the Golden, the only Norseman in Harold's guard, and the only one with much pretension to musicianship, raised his voice in the nasal long-drawn melodies which seemed, to Harold, to be the same no matter what the song.

Black porpoises raced alongside them, leaping arch-backed clear of the water or flitting like shadows beneath the surface. Wulfric tried to put together a harpoon but his efforts were clumsy and anyway shortly a shoal of mackerel glittered above the wave crests towards the shore and the porpoises were off after them. Gulls cruised on the wind behind them, scarcely moving their wings at all, and suddenly up in the prow a lookout hollered: 'There she blows,' and again and yet again he shouted, as a family of humpbacks, a half-mile away on the starboard prow, spouted in turn, their backs and dorsal flippers black crescents against the luminescent sea. It was all so rich, so teeming, so crowded with life, Harold felt his heart swell in him at the joy, the fecundity of it all.

He marked off his eight men, each in turn: Daffydd and Timor played with dice, pitching wits in some silly game of bluff and chance; two Hampshire brothers, ruddy-faced and dark-haired, whose names were Rip and Shir – their old Germanic blood untouched with Danish red or Viking gold, they came from a Jutish hamlet called Thornig Hill, Thor's Hill; Wulfric – the cruel killer, but that was no bad thing, he'd not hesitate out of squeamishness or mistaken generosity to give the final blow to a wounded man who might yet have the strength left in him for one last thrust; Albert, a Kentishman, small and gnarled before his age but the toughest when the wood-mist froze in your beard and there had been no food for a week, built like an ancient apple tree; and Walt. Poor Walt, right now, since he had heaved and retched his stomach out as soon as they left the estuary – but good Walt, utterly reliable Walt, who back in fifty-six, on the second campaign against Griffith, had paid back the first of the lives he owed, leaving Harold with a scarred forearm instead of a heart or lungs smashed by an axe.

They were good lads, all of them, wild as young cats at play, always ready for japes, crazy acts of daring, stupid wagers, ready to drink each other insensible rather than be the first to give up, whoremongers and wastrels – but once in the shield-wall as solid as rocks, utterly dauntless when faced with an adversary ready to trade blow for blow, until the red blood ran and the shattered bone showed through.

> *Heart bursts from breast-lock – soul skims spume-crest*
> *Mind rides waves in the whales' acre – wanders afar*
> *Earth-stranded unsatisfied, the shrill gull shrieks to me*
> *Singing of sea-space along whales' way . . .*

And Helmric too, the Norseman with a harp.

CHAPTER
TWENTY-ONE

D awn brought a light breeze from the west, the crew bustled, Wulfric dropped a canvas bucket over the side and doused his companions, the sail was unreefed and presently they were off again, but straight into the red eye of the rising sun. Harold climbed down to the main deck and hammered on the master's cabin door. It was barred on the inside. He called for Wulfric and together they broke it down. The tiny cabin was foetid with piss and booze and the master still snored, cradled in a hammock. Wulfric tipped him out on to the floor and they dragged him up steps on to the poop.

'Why,' asked Harold, 'are we going east when we should be going south?'

'The wind is blowing from the west.'

'But not from the south-west. You could trim the sail to bring her head at least a third of a circle towards the south.'

The master, figuratively, changed tack.

'We did well yesterday, I swear it, Lord Harold,' he blustered, 'due south the whole way. We are off the beaches of Normandy, five leagues to the south lies Arromanches and inland Bayeux. If this wind holds we'll raise Le Havre by noon.'

'You're lying. At least in part. Off Selsey we were heading east . . .'

'The wind changed my lord, I swear it, as soon as we lost sight of land.'

'If you fail us, we'll chop you up and throw you overboard. Maybe, even, we won't pay you.'

Walt, towelling the salt water out of his hair stopped, looked up at them from the deck below. His head was knee high to the men above him.

'But he's already been paid.'

Harold looked down at him.

'Not by me.'

'By a clerk. Yesterday. He gave him a bag. There was coin in it.'

'Just when was this?'

'Yesterday. Towards mid-morning. While we were waiting for you.'

Harold turned to the man by his side.

'Take him back to his cabin, Wulfric. Get to the bottom of this.'

Wulfric the Cruel. The ship sailed on. With no expression on his face, the helmsman let the sun climb to his left as he edged the course degree by degree to a more northerly bearing.

Presently a stain grew along the starboard horizon, the gulls came back, a gap in the land-fall indicated a wide estuary and they could see small black dots, fishing boats, not a lot bigger than coracles. The sailors trimmed the sail, the helmsman pulled the prow back a few degrees on to a bearing almost due east and the estuary opened in front of them. There was a small port or fishing village on the north bank and, a little further upstream, a larger town on the other.

Meanwhile grunts, gasps, thuds and occasional short screams came from the master's cabin.

'Le Havre,' Walt suggested.

Timor frowned.

'Too small,' he said. Timor read easily, talked to people and often found out things about where they were going before they got there.

At that moment the master gave a terrible scream which ended on a strangled cry. Wulfric reappeared, ducking below the lintel of the cabin door. In one hand he had a purse which he tossed to Harold.

'Fifteen pieces of gold, ' he said.

In the other hand he had the master's head which he tossed over-board, then he wiped his big hands down his already bloody kirtle.

'That's not the Seine,' he said. 'That's not Le Havre. It's the Somme. He told me that much. And just up stream on the south bank is St Valery which is where his worship was paid to put us down. I need a wash.'

And again he slung the bucket into the water and pulled it in.

Harold, pale with anger, climbed up on to the fo'c'sle. Walt and Daffydd followed him.

'Ponthieu,' he said, 'is not Normandy at all. It is the domaine of Count Guy of Ponthieu. And we are sailing into his territory uninvited, unannounced, and armed.'

'Can't we turn away,' Walt asked, 'sail out again?'

'I think not. The wind is against us, and look . . .'

Behind them, already only half a mile away, two long-ships, fast, sleek and black, oars dipping in unison, were in pursuit – or, like sheepdogs, driving them further in.

'Uninvited, unannounced, but not, look you, unex-pected,' Daffydd remarked.

Some three weeks later Duke William welcomed them in the great hall of his castle at Rouen. He made them walk up the long high hall to the daïs where he sat throned with his council of viscounts and churchmen about him. He was wearing a coronet above hair much shorter than the English fashion, a long ring-mail hauberk covered with a surcoat across which pranced the lion *passant regardant* of Normandy, gauntlets, boots. He had a sword on his belt, the scabbarded point of which rested on the floor at his feet, and on whose pommel his left hand rested. This, Harold recognised, was, unless customs were different in Normandy, an act of discourtesy – one does not welcome a distinguished guest bearing arms.

He was clearly, even sitting down, a tall man, taller than Harold, but thin and not as solidly built. He had a well-trimmed moustache which came to points which looked as if they had been shaped with wax of some sort, and a small triangular beard – both darker than his hair. His general good looks were marred by baggy eyes and a large, high-bridged nose. His complexion was ruddy, outdoor ruddy, not booze ruddy. He was, at thirty-six years old, six years younger than Harold. He came down into the hall with a long, loping stride, taking a slightly curved approach. Walt was put in mind of a wolf he had seen in the Welsh mountains, scouting across snow towards their encampment.

'My dear 'arold, my dear coz,' he cried, attempting English but with a strong Norman accent, 'at last we meet,' and he put his hands on the English earl's shoulders, kissed him on both cheeks, and then stood back to look at him. 'I 'ave 'eard so much about you, and all good. Please to meet my chief ministers. No need for your men to come too . . .'

But they were already crowding round Harold, ready to move up with him, and he had to wave them back.

With one foot on the step William froze, blood rushed to his face.

'Imbeciles,' he shouted, in Norman French. His voice screeched on the last syllable like a chalk on slate. 'Did I not tell you to clear the table?' His hand made a great sweeping gesture which ended behind him, almost catching Harold on the ear so he had to lean back to avoid it. 'All these parchments, ink and slates, all fiddle-faddle, get it out of here, cannot you see we have a guest, perhaps the most impotent, I mean important guest who has ever graced this hall?' And again his voice fluked up almost to a scream on the last word. 'Council is over. I tell you council is over! Wine? Yes, wine, of course. And water. Of course.'

He turned, put a clinking arm round Harold's shoulder and almost pulling him on to the daïs, tried out his English again.

'You see, 'arold, I cannot bear mess and muddle. Everything in its place at the right time. Council we had, council is over. Guest time is here so out with the parchment-work and in with a little light refreshment. Could you kindly tell your men to stop gossiping amongst each other like washerwomen at a village spring? Please?'

He returned to his throne, which was set on a step that raised it a foot above the other chairs, and motioned to Harold to sit opposite him. His English now exhausted, he slipped into Norman French, which Harold understood well enough, but speaking slowly, and too loud, the way people of his sort do when speaking to foreigners.

'How is my royal cousin, Edward? Not well I . . . understand.'

It was almost as if he had used the word 'hope'.

'Not well. But not so ill either. He has given up mead and sweet fruits. He'll live a few years yet. He sends you warm greetings.'

'A few years? With the Mead Illness? A year or so at most. So it is the greatest good fortune we should meet now and have the first of what I am sure will be many most useful little chats. But first my commiserations on your so unfortunate landfall. I hope Guy Ponthieu treated you well?'

Harold shrugged.

'No? Ah, the wine. A little water too? No? I always take a little water with my wine before dusk. A clear head, you know? Where were we? Guy Ponthieu. So lucky for you I had the wherewithal to pay the ransom he demanded. An inordinate amount. Bishop, how much was it?'

The cleric who had remained in his seat next to him cleared his throat.

'A king's ransom, my lord.'

'No, bishop. NOT a king's ransom. But a worthy one all the same. A hundred in gold?'

The bishop inclined his head, but failed to commit himself. William went on:

'I really do believe he would have hanged you if I had not been on hand to pay for your release. Of course, although Ponthieu is not Normandy, he is my vassal. But then again, he was in his rights, quite within his rights . . .'

He pulled off his gauntlets, plucked a knife from amongst a bowl of apples that had arrived with the wine and began to poke his nails.

'In a way,' he said, and suddenly it was almost a growl, 'you could say I bought your life. You owe me, 'arold. What should we say is the measure of your debt?' Yet again the voice grew harsh, fluked up at the end of each phrase. 'Vassalage, shall we say? Shall we say, dear 'arold, dear coz, that from this day you are my vassal, you are . . . my man?'

Silence fell. All the Normans were watching Harold, their gaze steely but expressionless. A shiver ran up his spine. He straightened in his chair and met the Bastard's eye.

'Here in Normandy and wherever you may rule by law and with the people's consent I shall remain for ever your humble but truest vassal.'

And without flinching he stared the Bastard down.

'Very well, very good. Very well said.' The Duke rose. 'Later we'll talk of this. For now my chamberlain will show you to your quarters.'

A fortnight later they were hacking west through the Norman *bocage* from Caen towards Mont St Michel and Dinan. William and Harold rode together, with their standards beside them (Walt bore the gold dragon of Wessex for Harold), though William usually contrived to keep the head of the big black stallion he rode just in front of the gelding he had lent Harold. Behind them, with a great jingling and jangling, came six or seven hundred 'knights', or mounted soldiers well armed, then a column of foot-soldiers, another thousand perhaps, and finally a caravan of mule-drawn wagons. Marching thus they seemed unable to make more than ten or at the most twelve miles a day, stopping often so stragglers could catch up, or while officers consulted each other about the route.

Slow, but, Harold had to admit, very well ordered. Maps had been drawn, instructions given, marshals appointed who, when the way became too narrow to accommodate the whole host, sent elements of it off on loops or parallel paths. A midday stop was always arranged in advance, usually in the shelter of a castle. There were a lot of castles, especially as they approached the Brittany border, where the lord or seneschal would turn out with some pomp and feed the entire army at his own expense. Or rather at the expense of the villeins and serfs who worked his land. And then the same would happen again at nightfall.

The country was much like that of the English south-west, particularly parts of Dorset – apart from the settlements. The main buildings were almost always larger than those in English manors or villages, and many of the barns especially were built not of timber frames with wattle and daub or plank between, but of stone, brick or mortared flint and many were turreted and had arrow slits. Indeed almost anything of value was walled, fenced or fortified and the great halls were not so much halls as keeps or small castles. Even the churches and abbeys, which were truly often magnificent compared with the thatched affairs prevalent in England, looked to keep people out rather than welcome them in.

And the people! They looked thin, bowed and sullen and their huts and cottages were like those of the meanest English serf. None came out to cheer their duke as he rode by – which certainly was not the case in England if an earl was making a progress through his country or the King himself. Worst of all, if there were cattle in the fields or pigs or even sheep, there was also always an armed man in attendance as well as the herdsman.

Every village they went through had a gibbet as well as a cross at its centre, and more often than not a gibbet laden with rotting gibbet fruit.

'Order, you see,' Duke William bellowed above the clatter of hooves when they passed the third or fourth of these and Harold could no longer hide his distaste, 'order and discipline. Everything in its place and a place for everything.'

There were stocks too and even jails. There were almost no jails in England, outside the larger towns. When a village or manor took care of its own wrongdoers, and carefully judged them at a moot where an individual price was set for each offence from murder to petty pilfering, what need was there for jails? If a man could not pay he was made a serf until he or his kinsmen bought his freedom back, not shut away to fester

uselessly in a tiny cell. But here in Normandy there was no point in setting a fine since none but lords had the means to pay – for all that was
surplus to a man's basic requirements belonged already to his lord.

And what was the purpose of this progress, this march through a land
that flowed with milk, honey and misery? Conan, Count of Dinan had
refused to acknowledge William as his overlord, thus obstructing
William's policy of creating buffer zones between Normandy and his
neighbours, especially the King of France and the Duke of Burgundy,
with both of whom he had been fighting for almost two decades. And
wherever he could arrange it the lords of these buffer zones paid tribute
to him rather than to France or Burgundy. Guy of Ponthieu was one
such to the north and east and this Conan of Dinan another, to the south
and west.

Presently the countryside became flatter with outcrops of rock and the
pasture sourer. Crossing a rise, a new landscape spread below them. A
wide, forked estuary with sands and mud-flats glimmered beneath the
westering sun, marking a right-angle in the coastline. To the north the
low cliffs and beaches faded into the mauve distances of the most
southerly part of the Cherbourg peninsula, while straight ahead a much
lower, flat area of salt marshes and reed-beds stretched to the west – a
carpet of browns and greens shot with silver ribbons of water. It was
dominated by St Michael's Mount, perfectly visible even at ten miles,
with its Norman keep ringed with turreted walls above a small settlement of fishermen and sheep-raisers. An especially delectable mutton
was raised, as it still is, on the salt grasses and reeds around it. Being on
the very end of the right bank of the River Couesnon, and reachable
only by a causeway covered at high tide, the castle marked the most westerly extremity of Normandy and protected the Duchy from Breton
incursions along the coastal plain. Or was meant to.

In fact it was in a state of siege since Conan had camped a small army
at the end of the causeway and for some weeks the garrison had had little
to eat but fish.

William reined in, shaded his eyes, chewed his bottom lip for a
moment.

'Good,' he said. 'Very good,' as if everything he could see had been
arranged in advance, according to his instructions and was exactly as he
would want it to be. Then he raised his right arm behind his shoulder
and brought it over and down in a gesture he clearly imagined could be

seen by the whole army winding up the slopes behind him, but in fact was visible only to the fifty or so men nearest to him. He shook his reins, touched spurs to his horse's flanks and began the descent towards a small village which lay beneath a pall of smoke on the more southerly fork of the estuary.

The village, Pontaubault, had been burnt that morning: bodies lay in the lanes – the men with their throats cut, children impaled, women with their genitals ripped open, indicating the final rape had been done with a sword or spear. William was very angry. Not out of horror or pity for his vassals but because his army would now not be fed that night and because this atrocity was a direct insult to his name, his power, his title and his prowess, a point that was made explicit by a message slashed across a plastered wall: '*Bienvenu, Bâtard!*'

CHAPTER
TWENTY-TWO

A sullen grey silent dawn, with a thick chill mist over the marshes. Only a bittern or two boomed in the distance, just as they had all through the night – an eerie, goose-pimpling sound. The men stirred, armour clinked, harness jangled. On William's orders a couple of trumpets were sounded to get the whole army standing to arms. The men grumbled – no supper and now no breakfast.

'Breakfast,' William shouted, from the back of his black charger, making it wheel and waving his sword above his head, 'will be provided by Count Conan. Forward . . . March!'

Even from the backs of their horses they could see very little of what lay in front of them. Apparently, according to a guide, they were moving into a roughly semi-circular plain bisected by the Couesnon with a diameter of ten miles or so. The landward end of the causeway to St Michel was at the centre of its arc. It was flat and filled with reed and bullrush beds as well as pasture of coarse grass. Much of the vegetation was up to five feet high and the whole area was riven with shallow channels and narrow dykes which split off from the main stream and sometimes returned to it. Even without the mist it would not have been easy to guess where and how Conan had deployed his troops.

The first intimation was a shower of arrows from a bed of bullrushes. This did little harm as it was directed at the leading files all of whom were adequately armoured, and in any case the arrows were fired from the small bows the fowlers of the neighbourhood used – accurate but without much weight or penetrating power. However, William's big black stallion took one in its haunch and he was off as if the Duke had given him a smack with his crop, hurtling through swamps, fountaining black mud to head-height and higher, sending birds wheeling into the air, jumping the wider brooks that came his way. In one of the latter they, he and his passenger – one could not fairly say rider at that point – came across a large coracle into which an oldish man was hauling a net alive with eels. The sight brought the horse up dead, snorting and quivering, and William was at last able to gather the reins into his left hand and draw his sword. With one massive stroke he severed the man's head and, as it rolled into the bottom of his tiny boat, pierced it with the point. With it thus impaled he hacked back to his troops.

'Taught the bas . . . the bulgar a lesson,' he said, and let the head slip off and roll under the hooves of Harold's horse.

'How about,' the Englishman began diffidently, 'if we send some scouts on . . .'

'On ahead to see how, haaa–aaah, the land lies?' The Duke was still a touch breathless from his exertions. 'Just what I was about to ask you to do. Why are you getting off your horse?'

'They won't see us if we are on foot.'

'But they'll catch you if they do.'

'A chance we'll take. Rip, Albert, Daffydd and Timor, come with me. The other four cover us.' Back to the Duke. 'Give us an hour.'

Then to William's amazement and indeed that of his Norman entourage, they not only dismounted but divested themselves of helmets, shields and *byrnies*, which was the English word for hauberk, swords and spears as well, and slipped away into the reeds. But first they dipped their hands into the mud and smeared their faces. With their dun-coloured under-garments, they were immediately almost invisible.

The four Harold had named spread out into open order with Harold at the centre, Rip and Albert at each end and Daffydd and Timor coming ten paces or so behind, making the two base points of a 'W'. Twenty paces behind them but with even bigger intervals between them came the other four. They were thus spread over as wide an area as they could be without losing contact with the man who was nearest or being out of earshot of the one who was furthest.

At about half a mile from the river, Rip eyeballed a Breton picket squatting in the reeds about forty paces in front of him with his back to them. It took him a minute to work out what was happening. The man was shitting, but facing his own people, no doubt so he could stand and cover himself, and thus avoid embarrassment, should one of his mates approach. Rip cut the man's throat with a short serrated seax kept hidden beneath his jerkin. The patrol filtered through the gap in the picket line.

They were back in less than an hour but nevertheless heard William in his high loud voice hectoring those about him.

'You see, gentlemen, what sort of person this Harold is. Slips away like a villein or a slave! Is that how a lord, a prince should behave? Mark my words, gentlemen, that's the last we'll see of them. Either they've used this as an excuse to get away, abandoning their arms and armour and heading back now for England, or they've been caught. Conan is no fool, he'll have patrols out who will soon round them up and deal with them . . .'

'If so, God Bless William, King of England,' a viscount named Robert FitzAlan called out, and all those nearest the Duke banged their shields with their maces or mailed gloves and shouted with laughter, then stifled it.

From where none could exactly say, Harold had appeared among them. He took the nearest available spear and quickly made marks across a patch of mud in front of the Duke's horse.

'The shore-line,' he said, speaking briskly. 'The river, the causeway, St Michel. The Bretons are split into two forces, more or less equal in size, each at about six hundred men armed and mounted, with four or five hundred peasants, mostly archers, in support. The first of these is on the eastern bank of the main stream, covering the end of the causeway, that is on this side, while the second is drawn up along the western bank in a north-south line with their left flank on the seashore where the ground is firmer and drops away to sand and shingle. The river in front of them is wide, with sand banks showing, and is, I suppose, fordable at the moment, though it appears the tide is on the turn. I suspect that as the tide begins to cover the causeway, thus preventing a sortie from the garrison, Conan will withdraw the troops covering the causeway back across the river to join the ones already there. He will have to time this move carefully, with the causeway covered but the river still fordable. If you time your attack while he makes this manoeuvre you will catch him at a disadvantage. If you move your army forward a mile or so in battle order, I will go on ahead with a trumpet and signal to you when the best moment for an attack is at hand.'

He pushed his hair off his forehead, looked up at William and shaded his eyes against the sun which was now behind the Bastard's head, and burning off the mist. For a moment the pointed helmet, the nose-piece hiding much of the Duke's face, the chain-mail black against the sky and the large leaf-shaped shield looked alien, menacing. Harold shuddered, but concealed it.

William wrenched his horse's head to the right.

'I know my business best,' he barked. 'We will demonstrate in front of the enemy's left and centre while a third of our force crosses the river above his right flank and turns it. Then the attack will become general.'

And, ignoring Harold, he issued brisk orders to his chief men.

It did not fall out like that. The force attacking upstream with the intention of taking Conan in the flank found their horses floundering up to their knees or higher in a bog Conan knew very well would protect him. The footing lower down was, as Harold had suggested, much firmer and the Duke's men got across, but in doing so exposed their flank to the troops guarding the end of the causeway. William attacked, drew off, attacked again and soon it became apparent that although he was suffering heavy losses he was bit by bit forcing Conan back and driving a wedge between the two sections of the Breton army. Also, by late morning, the Normans who had been caught in the bog had extricated themselves and were able to come to the Duke's aid. Conan now ordered a retreat and brought off his main force with little loss, only losing some of the section on the eastern bank. The Duke's force had been so badly mauled a proper pursuit was out of the question.

Harold and his men watched most of this from a slight rise in front of the river. Whether or not he was surprised by what was going on, Walt and the others could not tell, but they certainly were.

The men-at-arms on both sides remained mounted and fought from horseback, that is the crack troops, not the drafted peasants. The English onlookers had never seen anything like it. As far as they were concerned, you used horses to get from one place to another as quickly as you could so you would be fresh for the fight when you got there. Once there you kitted up, and went to it. If the numbers were equal you charged at each other and traded blows with axes and swords until a numerical advantage had been gained on one side or another. But if, at the start, your enemy had the advantage of numbers then you formed a shield-wall with overlapping shields and faced out their attacks either until you were all dead or the other side gave up. Those were the basics. And if you had a wise commander, who could, like Harold, first make his knowledge of your enemy's strengths and weaknesses and then his reading of the lie of the land work for him, then that made all the difference and you won anyway.

'Don't they ever get off their horses and fight like men?' Walt asked.

Harold shook his head. He was watching intently, chewing his bottom lip. More than anything he was watching the Bastard. William was everywhere. He led charge after charge, had two horses killed beneath him. The second was speared to death by foot-soldiers he had ridden into. Surely now with ten or so around him, armed with bows and arrows as well as spears and axes, he'd be done for. But, for all the weight of his armour, he was on his feet before his horse's legs crumbled beneath him. Warding off thrusts with his shield he waded into them and within seconds had them running from his flailing sword, while a groom came up with a third horse. At another moment a section of his knights broke, turned and fled back towards the river but he galloped out of the fight at full stretch, came round behind them and herded them back into the fray.

At last Harold sighed and turned to Walt.

'You know what it is about him?'

'He has the Devil in him?'

'Perhaps. It has been said. Whatever. But the thing is – he just does not expect to get hurt. He so believes in himself, so believes in his superiority, he simply cannot conceive that there might be someone opposing him mighty enough to do him serious injury. It's a gift. A dangerous gift, but until he is hurt, he can do wonders.'

They watched the final stages. As the battle slowly petered out and Conan's army melted away into the evening mists Wulfric spoke up.

'I tell you one thing though,' he said. 'Our fyrd will never stand being attacked by armoured men on horses.'

'It's of no consequence,' Harold replied.

'No?'

'No. So long as it's stalwart, no horses will ever break a shield-wall.'

★

Conan fought a skilful retreat back to Dinan – indeed his numbers were not all that inferior to William's. There he shut himself up in the forti-fied part of the town. No doubt he expected William to extract from him renewed oaths of vassalage, take some tribute, and go away. But William's ire was up. He sent back to Rouen for reinforcements and invested the fortress while the rest of his army set about comprehensively pillaging the surrounding countryside. Though clearly he and his men enjoyed this a lot there was policy in it too. The Breton lords and people of the region would never again support a count who got on the wrong side of Normandy.

Three weeks passed before the reinforcements arrived during which William and Harold studied the fortifications. Dinan was at the top of the tidal estuary of the River Rance and situated on a bend in the river caused by a rocky prominence. It appeared to be untakeable. However, Harold pointed out that the actual walls above the highest part of the crag, though of a height and even higher than the rest, were actually in themselves only forty feet or so above the rock on which they stood. In short, if a small force could climb the rock, the walls at this point were vulnerable to an escalade.

William fixed him with his cold eyes and stroked his goatee beard.

'Do it then,' he said.

Harold ordered ladders to be made, giving precise specifications so they could be carried or pulled on ropes up the cliff-face in sections and then reassembled. He also ordered lengths of strong but light ship-cordage to be prepared. He and Helmric the harpist, who had exceptionally good sight, watched the battlements evening and dawn from across the river for a week and plotted the movement of the guards above.

Timor was the expert in rock-climbing, having spent his time on leave climbing the cliff-faces in Cheddar gorge, just as his father had done, raiding falcons' nests for chicks to rear for falconry. On a night at the beginning of October, moonless but frosty and filled with starlight, he and Daffydd scaled the cliff, dropped ropes and hauled up the sectioned ladders.

Harold was first over the battlements but what none of them had known was that the landing on the other side was a mere catwalk, unfenced, only a yard wide with a fifty-foot drop to a small courtyard below where washing gleamed whitely from a line. Carried by the

momentum of his leap Harold swayed over the drop and would have
toppled had not Walt, already with one leg over the battlement, not
grabbed the collar of his padded jerkin and held on.

When they got their breath back Harold took his hand.

'Thanks, Walt. I owe you.'

Later, when it was all over and Conan had escaped using the ropes left
by Harold and his men, they walked through the market square of the
town. All around them houses were burning, while the Normans
butchered all but the old men and young boys out of the males, and
raped and slew females of child-bearing age.

Harold's face was white with anger, loathing, and a sort of fear, but he
listened to what Walt had to say.

'Wexford, Ireland. When I was a lad, a boy. You saved me from
drowning, then stopped old Wulfric from bashing my brains out. I still
owe you one.'

'You saved my life in Wales.'

'Just quickness with my shield.'

They walked on down a narrow cobbled street. The central gutter ran
with wine and blood; the stench of burning houses, charred flesh and
faeces. Harold muffled his face with his cloak and stumbled on. Walt, following, recalled how his lord had always stood back, kept aloof, often
with his eight men about him, when the rest of his army went to it, ravaging a border village that had gone over to the Welsh or a Welsh town
that had resisted too long.

Suddenly Harold turned on him.

'Walt,' he cried, 'we must never let these Normans loose in our own
land. We must do all we can to stop them.'

'Of course . . .'

'Swear it.'

Walt swore.

CHAPTER
TWENTY-THREE

Early the next morning William made Harold a knight, requiring again an oath of loyalty. To William's obvious distress, Harold repeated the oath he had given before – to serve William wherever William ruled by right. When that was done the army formed up and moved across the base of the Cherbourg peninsula to Bayeux. As soon as they reached Bayeux, and the march took nearly a week, Harold sought an audience with the Duke.

He was taken to a hall where William was once more back at parchment work, surrounded by clerks. He was apparently checking the autumn returns of taxes paid in cash and kind by the principal barons of west Normandy. It seemed these lords, none of whom had turned up on the brief campaign, though they had sent armed men and money, were the cross, as he put it, William had to bear. Each had at least one large castle near the borders of the Duchy which meant he could connive and plot with the counts on the other side or even the King of France or the Duke of Burgundy. Although they honoured the Duke as their overlord, and accepted that the land they held was his by right, they had absolute control over it through manorial lordlings beneath them, right down to the serfs who tilled the soil.

'One day, dear Harold, I shall be in a position to organise things more sensibly . . . with your help, I hope.'

No question as to which day he was looking at nor where he was thinking of.

'Then I'll get shot of this lot, let one of my sons have it, and do things my way, in a neat orderly fashion, everything in the right place at the right time. What can I do for you?'

'I have been absent from England and from my duties there for six weeks. I should return.'

'Ah. Yes. Oh, by the way, it's only a formality, doesn't mean a thing, but when you've been knighted it's usual to address the man whose knight you are as, um, Your Grace, Sire . . . I mean, of course, sir. Something of that sort. Eh? Think nothing of it.' He repeated: 'Doesn't mean a thing. Just do it. All right? Tell me. Why are you here? What did you come for?'

'As you will remember, Duke William . . .' there, that was as far as he would go, 'I came to take home my young cousin Wulfnoth and nephew Hakon. And so far I haven't even seen them. I don't even know where they are.'

'Oh, Lanfranc will know the answer to that one. Lanfranc knows the answer to most things.' The Duke put his finger to the side of his large nose and dropped his voice. 'Scholarly type, bit of a schoolmaster. Damned good administrator, though. Couldn't do without him.' He raised his voice again. 'Hey, someone get Lanfranc. He's around some-where. Probably in his office.' He turned back to Harold. 'Sit down. Have a drink. Glass of water for my friend Harold!'

When Harold was settled close to him, he put his arm round his shoulder and brought his face close up so Harold could smell the penny-royal on his breath and the bitter hunger behind it.

'I'll be straightforward, if you will. May I call you Harry?'

'If you must.'

'You don't like the idea? Too informal? Keep things on a proper foot-ing?'

'It's not just that. Harry is a familiar form of Henry, not Harold. Henry is a Norman name.'

'And you are not a Norman?'

There was a long silence that seemed to say it all. You are not a Norman. Yet. The voice dropped to a hoarse whisper. 'Harold – under what circumstances would you unequivocally support my claim to Edward's throne?'

'I should support it if the Witan, unforced and speaking for itself, offered you the crown.'

'How many brothers do you have? Four? Five? And all on the Witan? Plus how many other hangers-on? No. Put it like this. Under what circumstances would you support my claim in the Witan?'

'To stop a war, to prevent an invasion, I would accept you as King of England. But only on one condition. You would have to acknowledge me as your deputy and viceroy in England, as the one who ruled on your behalf and in your name. And you would undertake to stay away, apart from ceremonial visits when you would be guarded by my men, not yours. And when you needed arms and men to protect your interests on the mainland I would see that they were provided.'

William chewed his knuckle, shook his head.

'Won't do. Got to get shot of Normandy. Pain in the – neck. Need to start over again, start new. Get it right this time.'

Harold, sweating now, feelings of despair and desperation closing down on him, twisted his face into an ugly grimace. William watched him for a moment with some bewilderment upon his face. Then:

'Ah. Here's Lanfranc. Lombard. From Lombardy. He'll help us out. Dashed clever sort of fellow.'

Lanfranc, about Harold's age, was wearing the Benedictine habit with a solid but plain gold cross and a ring that looked episcopal. He was heavily built, short, jowly, but pasty-faced and had strong, heavy hands. His eyes were sharp, wary, intelligent.

'Lanfranc, tell Harold here where his cousin and nephew are.'

'At Le Bec, my lord. Studying.'

'Lanfranc has an abbey there which he's turned into a school. Mainly for clerks of course, but he has an annexe where sons of noblemen are taught to read, study law, rhetoric and so on. Lanfranc – Harold wants to be off in a day or two. Get the youngsters up here as soon as you can and we'll have a bit of an old feast, whatever, see them off in style. There you are, Harold. That should please you. Now . . .' he pulled a parchment across the table towards him, turned back to the clerk who was still at his elbow, quill and inkpot at the ready, 'that old rogue Montmorency out at Coutances has fallen short again. Take a letter . . . Harold,' he raised his head for a last time to the Englishman, 'if you've got time on your hands why not go over to the women's abbey and ask the Abbess to show you the tapestries her nuns turn out. Well worth a visit.'

Harold realised that his audience was at an end. He rose, managed a slight nod of his head, and walked off down the hall. Once he was out

of hearing, William caught Lanfranc by the sleeve and pulled him down
on to the stool Harold had vacated.

'Bast . . . Bulgar still won't play ball. Tried twice now. Says he's only
my man where I rule by right. And in England that requires the Witan's
say so, and he's got the Witan in his pocket.'

Lanfranc laced his thick fingers.

'There's a higher authority,' he said, 'an authority that overrules a
gaggle of old men in an island on the fringe of civilisation.'

'Rome. The Pope. Right. So how do we get him on board?'

'Send a delegation. I'll lead it, if you like. Get Alexander to bless
your enterprise, give you a token, papal banner, some relics, that sort of
thing . . .'

'He'll want a *quid pro quo*.'

'Of course. But nothing you can't provide with little cost to yourself.
A promise to bring the English church in line, enforce the Cluniac
reforms, bow to Rome in all things ecclesiastical.'

'You mean increase the church's power within the state.'

'But only as a force to uphold the state – a counterbalance to the
barons, which you lack here in Normandy.'

'We'll need a strong man in charge to enforce these reforms.' A sly
look came into William's cold eyes. 'Have you anyone in mind?'

The Lombard blushed a little; he gave a little shrug which in a big
man looked a touch coy. His face, however, remained expressionless.

'Canterbury?' William urged with the slightly spiteful teasing tone that
was the nearest he ever got to camaraderie.

Again the shrug.

'You'll have to shift Stigand first,' the schoolmaster of Le Bec murmured.

'No problem.'

A moment's silence.

'There's still that damned Witan,' William grumbled.

The schoolmaster's voice sank to a whisper, and he looked over his
shoulder to make sure none of the clerks was listening.

'It can be arranged,' he hissed. 'It will be at least a couple of days
before Wulfnoth and Hakon can be brought here from Le Bec, plenty of
time for that rogue Taillefer to set something up.'

CHAPTER
TWENTY-FOUR

arold, with Walt, Helmric, Daffydd and Timor, walked down from the castle to the nuns' abbey. A pair of monks escorted them to a pleasant area of slender pillars and rounded arches leading to a double door with a Judas-window. Already in front of it a long piece of fabric had been laid out, about sixty feet long and twenty inches wide. Apparently it told, in what we now call comic-strip style, the Miracles of the Virgin as experienced by pilgrims on the Milky Way, the pilgrims' road to Santiago de Compostela.

In almost no time the five Englishmen were exclaiming with great hilarity at the comic crudeness of the figures, the lack of characterisation, the primitive embellishments and so on, finally holding on to each other when Daffydd pointed out that the uniform expression on all the faces suggested the strain one sees on a face attempting to relieve constipation of the bowels. Timor drew their attention to the solecisms in the dog Latin that provided the commentary at the top of each episode, while Harold, who had watched Edith Swan-Neck at her needlework through many a long candle-lit evening, pronounced that what they were look-ing at was not tapestry at all, but embroidery, and not very accomplished embroidery at that.

★

> 'Segnurs barons,' dist li empere Carles,
> 'Veez les porz e les destreiz passages:
> Kar me jugez ki ert en la rereguarde . . .'

'He's very good,' muttered Helmric, 'very good.'

'Nice harp too,' remarked Timor.

Down in the hall below them, a central square rostrum was occupied by a dark figure with a high broad forehead, black but balding hair, who crouched over a magnificent instrument, his face twisted in concentration as between each strophe he improvised an intermezzo echoing the sentiments or content of what he had just sung. The harp was built like a ship of slats of seasoned hardwood, fastened to a hidden frame by copper or brass pins, the body or hull of it inlaid with mother-of-pearl and gold filigree. The beam, curved like a wave, projecting almost two feet from the top, was of some dark wood, highly polished and seemingly so hard that inlay was not possible though of course it had been bored to take the pegs that tightened and tuned the strings.

'What's it all about?' whispered Walt. 'Blessed if I can get my head round this jangling Norman.'

'Shush,' said Wulfric.

'Song of Roland,' Helmric whispered, his mouth close now to Walt's ear. 'New version. Tale of treachery. Ganelon puts Charlemagne on the spot – makes him appoint Roland to lead the rearguard as they pull out of Spain. Listen . . .'

> *Quant ot Rollant qu'il ert an la rereguarde*
> *Ireement parlat a sun parastre*
> *'Ahi! Culvert, malvais hom de put aire . . .'*

'What's he on about?' Walt whined in despair.

'Now Roland's abusing his father-in-law, that's Ganelon, for sticking him with command of the rear-guard detail . . .'

At the far end of the hall a long table had been set on the larger daïs, and behind it, in the middle, William and his duchess Matilda were throned. William was six feet tall, and his consort, who moreover had a wizened monkeyish face, worn out no doubt by far too many pregnancies, was a mere four foot.

'If,' Wulfric remarked, 'she sat on his shoulder . . .'

'Then,' Alfred responded, 'he could pass for a Latin pedlar with one of they new-fangled hurdy-gurdies.'

On the other side of Matilda, as guest of honour, Harold. Food was passed around, mostly served in white blancmanges or sauces, and later there were syllabubs and custards sweetened with crystals from the cane the Moors grew on the coast in the sultanate of Malaga. It was all wishy-washy stuff, over-spiced or over-sweet, and, in contrast to the beef or mutton joints that would have graced an English feast, like to give you the squits, said Wulfric.

But Walt noted how, while the Normans at the high table drank little and watered their wine, Harold drank a lot, and the stewards were at pains to keep his goblet charged.

What happened next was surely illusion. Hypnotism may have had something to do with it, even mass-hypnotism. First the minstrel with the harp, Taillefer himself, concluded the first part of the *Chanson* to great, if somewhat relieved applause – the whole thing is very long. His place was taken by two Moorish dancing girls, slaves sent up from Sicily where there was already a strong Norman presence and, for Harold and Walt too at the other end of the hall it was the same, the hall seemed to darken and fill with smoke as if some of the burning brands had been extinguished, though this was not actually the case.

Harold was not much interested in the slave-girls, except in so far as some of their more sinuous movements put him in mind of Edith Swan-Neck and filled him with an empty sense of longing. To counter it he drank deeply again. The wine this time was apparently Rhenish, sweeter, heavier, and certainly stronger than the thin sweet fizzy stuff from Rheims which the Normans usually drank.

'Slips down like a dear woman's milk does it not?' the count on his left remarked and refilled his goblet for him.

Then, as he peered down the hall over the rim of the silver vessel, it began to happen.

For him, possibly for many people there, the dancers turned into the figures of two young men: instinctively he knew they were his cousin Wulfnoth and his nephew Hakon, son of Swein. They were standing on the daïs with heads bowed, hands roped behind their backs, and nooses round their necks. They lifted their heads and looked across the hall at him with unmistakable appeal.

Harold started up, leapt on to the table scattering cups and platters. Shouts and protests but Duke William stood and signalled that all should be silent, not interfere, but wait to see what would happen. Harold shouldered his way through knights, ran along the top of a long table that stretched between him and the central daïs, scattering more food and cutlery, but just as he reached the gap between the table and the daïs the figures disappeared and were replaced by Taillefer, who now stood facing him holding a large white folded linen cloth. He held a finger to his lips. Harold stopped in his tracks and the whole hall fell silent. Then, holding the cloth by two corners, Taillefer flapped it out so momentarily it floated horizontally like a flying carpet between their faces.

Then it sank but only to waist height where it took the form of a table-cloth, neatly spread so the edges and corners hung down, but the main body was smooth and flat, as if it were indeed spread across a table. But no table was there. All in the hall gasped, some crossed themselves and some cheered and clapped.

Taillefer now pointed over his shoulder directing Harold's gaze to the gallery above and behind him. The youths again but this time standing on the balustrade, blindfolded. The nooses were still round their necks but attached to a beam in the roof.

Taillefer grinned, showing white even teeth between his beard and small moustache.

'Swear,' he said. 'Swear, or else. Put your palms on the table and swear.'

Harold did so.

'I am Duke William's man,' he said. 'I swear it.'

'More!'

'I will support his right, with all my might, to be the next King of England.'

The walls of the hall billowed this way and that and he had to steady himself on the cloth which was as solid as a rock.

'Again. Louder. So all can hear.'

'I am the Duke's man and I will support his right, with all my might, to be the next King of England.'

The torches suddenly burned bright again, the figures of the doomed young men faded before his sight, the whole hall, apart from his eight companions, cheered and banged their goblets, platters, whatever on the tables.

Taillefer whipped away the cloth, and there on a table that had not been there before were two jewelled reliquaries. The illusionist lifted one then the other. And from the top table behind him the deep voice of Odo, Bishop of Bayeux, half-brother to William, boomed out.

'The toe,' he cried, 'of St Louis. And the ear of St Denis.' He pursed his lips. 'No need to tell you, Earl Harold, that an oath sworn on such holy objects cannot be forsworn or forgotten.'

And Harold crashed insensible to the floor.

Yes. That's how it had been. Something like that anyway. Walt stirred on his cot, Taillefer's cot, in an inn outside Nicæa. Taillefer. Bastard.

It was dawn and cock-crow. But more close at hand the gentle and mellifluous strumming of that noble harp. He opened his eyes. The girl, Adeliza, was dancing – a slow oriental dance which Alain accompanied.

PART IV

A SHORT RIDE
ACROSS ASIA MINOR

CHAPTER
TWENTY-FIVE

She was so beautiful, so appealing, that for a time he forgot who her father was, what he had done. Her muslin gown, the only thing she wore apart from some pearls in her hair, was diaphanous and though the light was dim he could see the twisting curve of her torso, the shifting tilt of her tiny breasts, the shadowy cleft between her buttocks and the haze of pubic hair, still sparse, as she turned, especially when she moved so she was not between him and the small window but let the light from it play on her. The lilting rise and fall of the harp had a rhythm behind it achieved or marked by the occasional slaps Alain contrived to give the hull of the sound-box, and it echoed and enhanced the self-conscious and simulated eroticism of her dance.

Walt lifted his head and immediately fell back. Pain shrieked down the side of his face and coalesced on a handful of shattered molars. It made him cry out, a gasping, high-pitched moan. The harp broke off and Adeliza hunkered beside him, knees spread. The muslin gown slowly floated down around her. Her head was so close that her long hair hanging forward almost brushed his brow, and he could see her sweet honey-coloured breasts, small and firm but hanging now, showing their weight, below. She had a small mole on her neck.

'Dear person,' she murmured, 'how do you feel? We do so much want you to get better. You and your friend were so brave and kind. Trying to help Daddy.'

I wasn't trying to help your Dad. I was trying to save Quint. He leant over the edge of the bed and spat out a handful of congealing blood, broken teeth, saliva and pus. Her brother plucked the strings again, and she twisted away, stretching her neck, making wanton eyes, walking and mincing on feet that tinkled beneath the gauze of her robe. There were tiny silver bells around her ankles.

Apart from deep dreams which he instantly forgot Walt had not had an erotic impulse, let alone experience, for . . . two years? Anyway, since the summer before the battle.

He stammered through the dried blood and pain.

'Does your father know you dance like that?'

She span away with some petulance.

'Of course he does. He taught me.'

'He taught you?'

'Yes. We are on our way to the Orient. And in the Orient men pay much to see girls doing these sorts of dances. It will be a useful supplement to what my father earns with his illusions.'

He remembered: her dad's fucking illusions.

Alain placed the harp against the wall — it hummed a high note as if upset not to be played any more.

'We should get ready, you know,' he said. 'Dad and your friend will be arraigned in an hour or so.'

He was a slim youth, almost as tall as his sister, but different in appearance and manner — his colouring was fairer and he was altogether quieter, apparently more subdued, less flamboyant. Outside, in a crowd, he attracted no attention at all, especially when Taillefer or Adeliza were performing. But now, younger than her though he was, he took charge.

'We'll leave the animals and the baggage here and walk. See what happens. Walt can keep an eye on things.'

Walt started up, clutched his head, almost sat down again but stayed on his feet.

'No, no,' he cried. 'I must come too. Quint will need me.'

Alain shrugged.

'Very well, we'll just have to lock up as best we can, as we did before. Come on now. We've not much time.'

Adeliza had already lifted the muslin over her head and was washing herself down with water from the ewer she had brought up from the well the night before. She crouched in a shallow round cooking pan, big enough to make a very large paella in, and endeavoured to reach over her shoulder with a golden sponge in her right hand.

Down below the inn-yard filled with the cries of muleteers and grooms, the neighing and ee-aws of the beasts, the clatter of hooves on cobbles as a caravan assembled, prepared to leave the town, but, in spite of such signifiers of impending departure, Walt could not take his eyes off her.

'No need to stare,' she murmured and slipped on a dun and shapeless cotton gown, pushing her hair back inside the hood as she raised it. She brushed her eyebrows in towards the centre to make them appear bushy and unkempt and suddenly she looked as modest as a nun: not a hint of the houri about her now, nor even of the Blessed Virgin she had been the evening before – just a country girl in from the fields, visiting the city's market. Meanwhile Alain had been out and returned with three small loaves straight from the oven and a pitcher of milk on which they quickly breakfasted. Walt could eat no bread until Adeliza showed him how to soften it in the milk.

The law courts dated back to pre-Nicæan Council times, which was to say that the central atrium was open to the sky and surrounded by Corinthian colonnades. Much of the marble had fallen away exposing brick-work; weeds and plants grew in the gutters and from between the roof tiles.

An immense flock of swallows on their way from the steppes beyond the Black Sea had descended into the spaces above, mixing with the vastly increased families of those already in residence. They squealed up a mewling storm so it was not easy to make out what was being said beneath them.

As the three of them joined the crowd of onlookers in the main body of the courtyard, the colonnade at the far end filled with judges and clerks. Some wore ceremonial robes which recalled the togas worn by ancient dignitaries, whose likenesses, carved in bas-relief, many now noseless or missing a hand or foot, graced the tympanum above their heads. The chief justice stood in the middle, was short, fat, balding, and, unlike those figured in stone above him, had a nose like a strawberry and eyes that did not always look in the same direction as each other. He huffed and puffed and was clearly anxious not to be late for some more important appointment – a visit to the baths, perhaps.

A cracked bell was struck and with a clanking and clinking of arms and chains a squad of prison guards led in twenty or so manacled prisoners. A young boy who had stolen a chicken in the market early the previous morning was identified and taken away to be flogged with cane rods. Presently his screams mingled with those of the swallows. A beggar whose apparently legless state was revealed to be a hoax had three fingers chopped off. A fishmonger caught selling stinking fish lost his market licence for six months.

As each case was dealt with witnesses and connections drifted away and by the time Quint and Taillefer were called there were only five or six people, including Walt, Adeliza and Alain, still left. And one of them was the mysterious tall woman with red hair, an emerald-green silk scarf and peacock-blue cloak over a silky and pleated white shift, who had been by when Quint and Taillefer were arrested.

Neither of the accused looked much the worse for wear following their night in prison. Walt looked long and close at Taillefer and decided that, yes, it was he, the same man who had tricked his lord into a forced yet binding oath. His breast filled with rage and a longing for revenge.

Quint was called first. Breach of the peace, assaulting a constable, resisting arrest. Clearing his throat, and placing one foot on the lower step of the three that ran along the base of the colonnade, he doffed his wide-brimmed leather hat, somewhat awkwardly on account of the manacles, and embarked on his defence.

'That I did intervene on behalf of the man who, in the past twelve hours or so, has since become one of my most honoured and revered friends, I do not deny . . .'

Honoured and revered friend! That monstrous charlatan, or, if not a charlatan, then a man who had made his bargain with Beelzebub . . .!

'But since I could see no fault in any of his actions and while I reacted with possibly unconsidered impetuosity I would therefore ask you to examine not the physical manifestation of what my intellect prompted me to but what the Stagirite in his Nicomachian Ethics calls moral intention. For instance in Book Five, chapter . . .'

'Beware, Saxon, lest you fall into the error of Pelagius, the Briton, whose favourite saying was "If I ought, I can", thus denying the necessity of Divine Grace.' This from a judge whose robes and mushroom-shaped headgear suggested the ecclesiastical, and whose lean but rosy visage indicated both constipation and a certain meanness of disposition.

The secular judge whose eyes sifted truth from lies by looking in different directions intervened with prompt acerbity.

'Guilty, *as charged*,' said with heavy emphasis on the last two words. 'Fined twenty pieces of silver and to be beyond the city limits by nightfall. Don't come back. Next please. '

'Your honour, please . . . your honour.'

'Well, what is it? Be brief and utter no more blasphemy. If you know what's good for you.'

'Your honour. I don't have twenty pieces of silver. Just a handful of coppers. You see, on my way here I was robbed—'

'Six weeks in the City jail on bread and water and *then* banished beyond the city limits. Next case—'

'Your honour!' The voice this time was deep, mellifluous and issued from the tall lady with red hair. 'I will pay his fine, and see he is gone by nightfall.' And with all eyes on her she surged up the almost empty courtyard like a queen and was gone.

'NEXT CASE, PLEASE,' bellowed the presiding judge, and Taillefer was pushed forward.

The charge was blasphemy. Five witnesses described his illusions with the three-in-one and one-in-three piece of rope and then how he had caused to be re-enacted the impregnation of the Virgin by a dove in a lewd and suggestive way. The ecclesiastical judge summed up at some length, citing various verses from Divine Writ and chapters from the Holy Fathers all of which added up to, yes, such manifestations as had been described were indeed blasphemous. Taillefer offered no defence other than a wry smile and shrug of his shoulders.

'Guilty as charged.'

The judges now formed a huddle dominated by the ecclesiastic and deliberated the sentence. At this point Walt felt his left hand taken in Adeliza's right. She squeezed, the pressure became greater. He saw how, under her hood, her countenance had gone white, she bit her lower lip and her fingernails dug into his palm.

At last the huddle broke up, re-formed itself into a line. Walt noted the expression of elated triumph on the ecclesiastic's face. The presiding judge came forward.

'Crucify him,' he bellowed. 'An hour before dusk this evening.'

Walt's heart rose in exaltation but to his amazement, as she released his hand and looked up at him, he found Adeliza's face too was wreathed in smiles.

'Oh, I'm so glad,' she cried. 'Daddy's so good at being crucified. I'm always just terrified that one day they'll suggest beheading. Now *that* could be a problem.'

The show was not over yet. As the guards gave a yank on Taillefer's chain he reached up his manacled hands to the nearest soldier's helmet, contrived to lift it and thereby released two white doves who were roosting beneath it. They soared up, just as the one the evening before had, and again, as she turned and made her way out, descended in their tumbling flight on to Adeliza's shoulders.

And on the way, before she reached the portico, four more doves flew down from the architraves and epistyles to join them.

CHAPTER
TWENTY-SIX

Taken with Adeliza as Walt was, and feeling that for all her confidence in her father she and Alain might still be in need of help, he was disappointed to find that Quint and the mysterious lady were anxious to be off. Apart from anything else he had never seen a crucifixion and to witness one carried out on such a deserving case would add to the interest.

However, before going to the clerk of the court and paying the fine that would release him their benefactress had bound both of them to her service. She was on her way, she said, to Sidé, in Pamphylia, on the south coast of Asia Minor, and she would not part with her money until Quint solemnly undertook to accompany her there as protector and companion, for she had no one to travel with. And yes, of course Walt could come too. She would pay whatever expenses they incurred on the way. Later she told them that she was a widow, and was carrying on her dead husband's occupation as a merchant dealing in small but rare gem-stones, intaglios, cameos and the like, which she purchased in Italy and sold in Samarkand where she bought – lapis lazuli. Her most recent paid companion and guard had been killed by a bear.

Hurrying through the streets, the lady told them they could call her Theodora, for indeed, as far as they were concerned, she truly was a gift from God. First they called at a livery stable, where she had a white palfrey already waiting for her and a mule for Quint. After some brisk bargaining with the horse-trader, she bought an ass for Walt.

Walt took Quint to one side.

'I can't ride a donkey,' he muttered.

'Why not?'

'Beneath me.'

'It will be beneath you if you get on it.'

'You know what I mean.'

Quint stood back, pushed up the brim of his hat.

'Ah,' he said, 'coming all over the gent, are we? You should look in a mirror.'

Walt felt the crusted scabs on his face, looked down at the mess his clothes were in, despite the fact they'd washed them only two days before. Since then he'd been rolled in the dust and bled on them too. He rediscovered something long dead or rejected. Shame. He was feeling ashamed.

'Have you ridden a horse since you lost your hand?' Quint asked.

'No. I don't think so.'

'Then start at the bottom and work up.'

Quint turned away and addressed himself to the problem of mounting the mule. He was hardly an adept himself – for while he did not end up facing the wrong way, he very nearly fell off the other side.

Theodora watched all this with a hint of scorn on heavy carmine lips painted in an exaggerated bow. When they were ready she tapped the flank of her pony with a flexible ivory wand and led the way out of the stables and through the city gate. Her newly employed retainers followed her as best they could. The road led into a wide valley with a river which descended from a considerable range of mountains beyond. The valley was filled with evergreen oaks, but widely spaced, as if in park-land.

In the distance, about a league away, they could see a large cloud of dust which marked the progress of the caravan that had finally left the far side of the city an hour or so earlier. Trotting briskly they caught up with it and were then able to proceed at a more leisurely pace, which suited Walt. The jogging had set off the ache in his battered face and sent shards of pain through his broken teeth.

The caravan consisted of a hundred or so men, women, children and babes-in-arms, and some three hundred animals: mostly asses and mules but with four chains of camels, six or seven to a chain. It was led by a donkey, followed by the first of the camels on which was mounted the

Conductor, an old man but thin and upright with a grey beard, swathed in loose cotton garments beneath a vast turban which swayed like the lantern on a ship leading a fleet. His sons collected dues for the protection the caravan afforded.

The oaks were for the most part topped out for charcoal, leaving them stunted and often with only two or at the most three large limbs that turned the trees into oddly cruciform shapes. Walt was put in mind of Taillefer and his fate.

'I envy no man who is to be crucified,' he said to Quint as they followed the tail and rump of Theodora's pony, 'and certainly I feel for the two children who will be thus orphaned. However, I confess I have no love for Taillefer.'

'Because he tricked your Harold into the mumbo-jumbo of swearing fealty to the Bastard on a couple of dog bones?'

'And because he led the Norman army into battle, singing the *Song of Roland*.'

'That was his penance.'

'Penance?'

'For supporting and encouraging what by then he saw was the wrong side. After all, he was killed in the performance.'

'Evidently not. Anyway, how do you know all this?'

'We talked all through the night. He is a very clever man and I would say a good one. I told him of your past, that Harold was your lord and so forth. He expressed a wish that you should know he did not feel the oath sworn had had much effect on the outcome. At all events, he regrets now what he did.'

'He can't get away with that.' There were things here Walt understood very well but could not express. For all it had been obtained by trickery, that oath had hung over the battlefield like the crows and kites, nagging at men's minds, weakening or strengthening their resolve.

Nevertheless Quint seemed to understand a little of what was in Walt's mind.

'It must have weighed on the Bastard's conscience too, you know, that the oath was extracted by trickery.'

'I don't think so. You don't know that man. He revels in getting things by whatever means he can. And if he can congratulate himself on his own cleverness as well, so much the better.'

Quint nodded serious agreement.

'Maybe you're right. But to return to Taillefer. The old Taillefer really was killed on Senlac Hill.'

'How so? What do you mean . . . the *old* Taillefer?'

'Just that. The court minstrel, loaded with money and respected by all as a great artist and performer, truly died. He was reborn as a wandering mountebank – a person and an occupation with far more honesty about them than the posturing pretension of the court sycophant. Reborn, yes, and he has sworn to follow in body and soul the greatest Mountebank of all.'

Walt jogged on, occasionally kicking the sides of his very small moke (his feet brushed the tops of the etiolated grasses that grew by the road-side). Because of his animal's size, he found it a constant challenge to keep up with the others, especially since the movement again exacerbated the various pains in his mouth and face.

'Well, he's done for this time. And you'll forgive me if, in spite of all you've said, I add – good riddance!'

Soon they left the plain and entered a gorge whose beetling cliffs far surpassed those of Cheddar – the only other place like it Walt could clearly call to mind, though his wanderings the year or so before had taken him through several similar places on the Rhine and the Danube. Choughs gave their whistling call against the lower walls, which were hung with emerald ferns and big blue flowers where water coursed down them. Far higher, so as almost to be invisible, eagles and vultures slowly soared and spiralled.

Presently they heard a distant trumpet, and then a rumbling that seemed to bend the air and shake the ground. An earthquake? But no. The Conductor's sons scurried down the column, urging all off the road and against the walls of the gorge on one side or into the river, now little more than a rushing brook, on the other, and just in time, too. A family of Egyptians at the very rear were ploughed into and ridden down, their baggage animals breaking free and careering away below the boughs of the trees as the outriders of a corps of armed horse galloped into them. The main body were heavily armed, the leaders wearing flat-topped cylindrical helmets of a style Walt had not seen before and plumed too, and they went by, as many as five thousand of them, all at a slow gallop, stirring up great clouds of dust through which the sun's beams flashed from polished metal. The sound of their hooves reverberated like thunder between the rocky ramparts. In their midst they carried a huge banner, supported between two poles, emblazoned with the Chi-Rho of Christ.

'Who were they? Who the fuck were they?'

Quint turned to Walt. The Englishman was white and shaking. The sight of armed men on horseback, in numbers, had clearly recalled memories too painful to be easily borne. For a moment the Frisian feared Walt might succumb to a fit similar to the one that had afflicted him early in their acquaintance.

'Not Normans, not Normans I assure you. I should guess they are the Emperor's men on their way to do battle with the invading Seljuk Turks.'

He watched carefully for a moment or two, as Walt struggled with himself, straightened, shook his head, then, without further comment but a definite grimace of disdain, remounted, swinging his long leg over the back of his moke.

He is, thought Quint, getting better. He has regained the childish pride of a petty lordling and so will not ride happily on an ass; he is coping with the problem of Taillefer; he has withstood the memory of squadrons of armoured horsemen. In a small way all this somewhat saddened Quint – while he wished nothing but the best for his friend, he knew he would become less interesting as an object of study and compassion the more whole he became. Quint was an intellectual and as such not likely to find an adequately reconstructed, barely literate soldier and lordling, with all that those stations in life implied, a compellingly interesting companion.

'This Sidé place we're heading for,' Walt now asked. 'What sort of a place is it?'

'I understand from our mistress that it is a port at the top of the Bay of Adalia. She assures me we should be able to take ship for the Holy Land from there. Oh. Oh, dear.'

'What's the matter?'

'Our mistress. She's not here. She must have been separated from us when the Emperor's horsemen went by.'

Presently they found her some fifty paces further up the column in the company of a Jewish merchant and his family. She seemed to be getting on with them very well, almost as if she had met them sometime in the past, certainly as if she shared much in common with them.

She turned on Walt and Quint and sounded off at them roundly for losing her, telling them that if they wished to continue to enjoy her patronage they must remain close at all times.

All this confirmed Walt in certain suspicions he had begun to entertain concerning her: she dealt in lapis lazuli, she had Jewish connections, he felt sure her red hair was a wig.

The trek continued for another two tedious days, following a road which wound tortuously through ravines and gorges, up to watersheds and down the other side. They passed villages where hovels built of undressed stone huddled round small castles or forts. Out of these came armed men, cloaked in furs from the mountain fauna, bearded and moustached like Vikings, save that their hair was black, to demand tribute more often in kind than cash, for in these mountain fastnesses what use was there for coin?

They stopped the nights inside huge cathedral-like caravansarais with stabling instead of side-aisles and rooms for hire where the galleries would have been, and it was in these that on successive nights their lives were strangely threatened.

On the first night Theodora gave Quint the money with which to buy ground-up mutton and three loaves of bread, telling him to borrow a skillet, fry up the cakes of ground meat, and bring one to the room she had hired for herself in the upper gallery. He bought the food from a cripple with one foot missing, the stump being bound in rags, and hands and nails that were filthy. Quint did not want to buy from him, insistent though he was, pushing his way through other less repellent salesmen, but Walt, feeling a kinship for a man thus mutilated, said why not? Clearly he needs the money.

They took it all into their stable and using straw for kindling and three lumps of charcoal soon had a hot fire going beneath the skillet and the rounds of meat sizzling nicely in their own fat. Walt turned away to cut the loaves and suddenly cried out, dropping his knife.

Embedded in the bread, though not presumably baked in, since it was still alive, a large orange centipede, cut in two by the blade, still wriggled convulsively, rearing its cephalic plate, twisting this way and that, searching blindly with a wicked pair of sickle-shaped mandibles on whose tips tiny drops of poison had already formed. Hearing Walt's cry of anger and fear Quint dropped the skillet and dashed the half-loaf from his hand before stamping as brutally as he could on the beast until it was mashed up with the bread in an awful mixture of legs, chitinic casing which crackled beneath his soles, and fluids yellow and brown. The creature, whole, must have been as long as the span of a grown man's hand spread from the tip of the little finger to that of the thumb.

'Had it bitten you,' Quint gasped at last, 'it would have caused severe pain, inflammation and necrosis, leading to gangrene and death.'

'That pedlar tried to kill me,' Walt shouted.

'Or possibly me. He was not to know which of us would cut the bread.'

'What about the rest of the food?'

'Chuck it. Theodora will have to give us more money or do without.'

'But why? Why did this happen? It surely was not an accident.'

'We could find the man and . . . ask him.'

But of course he was gone, not to be found.

On the second morning, in the second caravansarai, Quint, rolling up the quilted bag they still shared at night, found beneath it a large tarantula – striped and hairy. It should have been crushed but they had spread the bag over flagstones where a small stone had been lying loose. Walt had kicked the stone away, leaving a declivity which was now filled by the giant arachnid. Yet there was no hole in the declivity which might have served the monster as a nest and from which it might have emerged during the night. How it got there remained a puzzle.

'This one,' said Quint, punctuating what he said with loud slaps from the sole of his hand-held shoe as he battered the creature to death, 'would have sent you into a dancing fit which would not have ended until you dropped dead from exhaustion.'

'Or you,' suggested Walt.

'Or me.'

Meanwhile the scabs on Walt's cheeks had begun to suppurate and his jaw swelled on that side of his face so he looked like something a child might have scrawled on an inflated pig's bladder, or overfilled wineskin. The pain was bad too, especially when moving or attempting to eat.

CHAPTER
TWENTY-SEVEN

About four hours after noon on the third day they came to Dorylæum which stood at the point where the road bifurcated. One branch headed south and east towards the ancient city of Iconium and thence to the ports on the south coast which connected with Cyprus, Palestine, and the Levant. Important trade route though this was, it was not to be compared with the other, which was no less than the western spur of the Golden Road to Samarkand and, beyond Samarkand, Cathay. Here the caravan split, many of the merchants being on their way to the other side of the world to buy spices and silks with gold, amber, garnets, pearls, and the sort of goods Theodora dealt in. However, on this occasion it was not to Samarkand she was bound but home to Sidé, having already, she said, sold on her lapis lazuli to a wholesale dealer in Nicomedia.

As their caravan approached the town walls, which were substantial and made from dressed stone rather than brick, Walt and Quint espied a small group standing on a grassy knoll beneath an old and substantial ilex. As they grew nearer they paused, rubbed their eyes and, in Walt's case, a cold sweat broke out on his palms and the back of his neck. There was no mistaking what they could see: a pack-horse and a donkey, both well-laden, a small man, dark and melancholic in expression, a beautiful girl-child some fourteen years old and a boy of about twelve.

'Ghosts,' muttered Walt.

'But they have shadows,' Quint replied.

They broke ranks from the caravan and crossed the small space which still separated them. Behind them Theodora's voice was raised in scolding complaint but ignored. They slid to the ground from the backs of their mounts and Quint ran into the arms of Adeliza, Alain and Taillefer in turn. Walt hung back in something of a dither. His feelings of sudden euphoria when he realised who they were had surprised him – he found it required quite an effort to convince himself he was sorry to see Taillefer alive. Once they had pulled back and allowed the possibility of ordinary speech, the magician shrugged, wrinkled his soft and squidgy nose and remarked laconically, 'You see, I too rose on the third day.'

'Liar,' exclaimed Adeliza. 'Daddy cannot resist a fib. He was off the cross by dawn and soon well on the mend.'

Though not yet entirely recovered: his face was even greyer and sadder than before, with new lines etched in his forehead and cheeks; his hands were still bandaged, and when he walked he limped along with an arm on the shoulders of each of his children. That he really had been crucified was not in doubt; as to how he escaped and managed to reach Dorylæum ahead of them remained secrets he would not divulge.

The caravan now split, the smaller section heading south with a new conductor, a rotund swarthy Greek with a big moustache and a stubbled chin. He led them round the city walls to the caravansarai on the south side. Theodora and her new acquaintance took commodious rooms on the first floor, while Quint, Walt and the rest were told to make shift in the courtyard.

'There are good fires there,' she said, 'and the nights are not yet cold.'

Which was not true – the reason for the fires was precisely because, since they were now past the autumn equinox and high up in the mountains, a deep chill settled over everything as soon as the sun set. However, with twenty or so other travellers huddled together around their particular fire, with leather wine bottles freely circulating and a reasonable abundance of wood, mostly aromatic pine, none suffered greatly from the cold. They dined off chicken pieces stuck on sticks or daggers and broiled in the flames and drank deeply from wineskins, Walt more than the others. The wine was drawn by the landlord through spigots from vast upright barrels. Since it was fully a year old it was very strong and very dry to the palate, but rich and dark.

Almost immediately Quint and Taillefer fell into a deep theological discussion, or so it seemed to Walt, who already felt a little put out by the attention the ex-monk was giving the ex-jongleur. They seemed so ready to pick up from where they had left off after spending a night in similar discourse in the Nicæan jail that Walt found it difficult to resist making a wineskin holding two quarts his own personal companion. And anyway he was still not fully reconciled to the mountebank's presence.

'In the three days or so that I have known you,' Quint remarked, wiping the nozzle of another skin on his sleeve and passing it on, 'I have witnessed performances staged by you which appear to throw derision on the teachings of the church, indeed on very basic Christian doctrine. You have mocked the Unity-Trinity, the Annunciation, the passion of Christ and his Resurrection. I have to ask myself . . . why?'

Taillefer, pausing between swallows. fixed him with his dark eyes. They glanced round the side of the almost empty skin which was tilted up next to his cheek, so in the flickering light it looked like a giant growth. There was suspicion there, even now, that Quint might be a spy for the thought-police.

'I am interested, I must add,' Quint continued hastily, 'because I too find my faith stretched to limits by the many absurdities we are asked to give credence to. I have always felt that Tertullian's assertion that he "believed since it was impossible" to be one of the more stupid of the many stupid pronouncements of the Holy Fathers.'

Taillefer resumed swallowing and, when he was sure he had extracted all he could from the sack, lowered it and burped. No, belched. He passed it to his neighbour, a muleteer, short and fat, who reversed it and shook it before breaking into a stream of abuse in the Pamphylian dialect whose meaning was, however, obvious to all who heard him.

Taillefer looked at him with an expression which was more than saintly in its sudden, wide-eyed, pious compassion.

'My man,' he said in tones of unctuous bonhomie, 'go fill it at the well and you will find it has in it all you could reasonably desire.'

After a moment's hesitation the muleteer struggled to his feet and made off. Quint raised his eyebrows quizzically at Taillefer, who in turn pursed his lips and gave a slight shrug.

The magician now wriggled himself closer to Quint (thus making Walt feel even more marginalised) and began to speak quickly, urgently, but very quietly.

'On what,' he asked, 'are the tenets of our religion based? Or, put it another way, for what reasons does it appeal to so many people? One. In return for promises of everlasting life it asks only that you should believe that you yourself are chosen, are one of God's elect. An easy act of faith for anyone with a sense of self-importance. If, however, you lack high self-esteem, it also promises everlasting life to the humble and meek. Or, look at it another way: on the one side it proposes a tolerably sensible and easily acceptable moral code based on the Ten Commandments reinforced by injunctions that we should love God and one another, too. But on the other side it says that no matter how good you are it matters not if you are not chosen . . .'

'This, I must say, has become the sticking point for me,' cried Quint. 'Which is why, even when I was still a monk, I became a follower of Pelagius the Briton, and was indeed expelled from my order for championing his beliefs. Not to put too fine a point on it, was branded a heretic and was about to be handed over to the secular arm of the law when I escaped.'

Side-tracked, Taillefer took him up on this with some enthusiasm.

'A point the surprisingly learned judge picked up on at your trial. How does it go? "If I ought, I can." But Pelagius went further than that. Or rather he accepted the implications inherent in that simple statement, namely that man has a will, a free will to choose between good and evil unassisted by grace—'

'Yes, yes, YES,' Quint rejoined with that special enthusiasm that is typically present when two men ('men'? – the word is used advisedly) with intellectual, or at any rate academic pretensions find themselves in agreement and urge their hobby-horses helter-skelter on towards a destination both can foresee, 'and in this does he not rediscover for mankind the supreme dignity Aristotle the Stagirite proposed when he delineated the intellectual physiognomy of the Great Souled, the magnanimous man . . .'

But at this moment the muleteer returned.

'I did what you bloody said,' he shouted, 'and instead of getting what I wanted all I got was bloody water.'

For a moment it was clear Taillefer might try to persuade the man that water was in fact all a man already drunk could reasonably desire but, receiving a warning look from Quint, instead found a coin or two in his purse.

'I'm sorry,' he said. 'Please replenish your bottle at my expense with whatever you want.'

The muleteer held the coins to the light from the fire and wandered off back to the innkeeper and his hogsheads.

Taillefer shrugged.

'Some you win,' he said, 'some you lose.'

'I'm sorry,' said Quint, reminded of how the conversation had started by Taillefer's failure to convince a muleteer that the water he drew from the well was wine, 'but I should like to return to the starting point of this discussion. Why do you play these mocking tricks that seem to ape the miracles . . .?'

'I was coming to that. The god in Jesus was, for many, manifested in the miracles he performed. What I aim to do is show that these were not beyond the power of any mortal who has trained himself in the right techniques of illusion and persuasion—'

'You aim then to prove Christ a mountebank?'

'Exactly. The Mountebank of mountebanks but . . . a mountebank.'

This was enough for Walt. He was in no way devout, kept his religion well compartmentalised to certain seasons like Christmas and Easter, and a daily moment or two when rising or going to bed. Nevertheless, this was too much, especially when as he rose, muttering something about needing a leak, he heard Quint reciting doggerel verse which Taillefer joined in with . . .

> If you don't think I'm divine
> You'll have to pay when I make wine
> And bear in mind, as I think you ought to,
> It's a whole lot easier turning wine to water.

Taillefer now stood, and wavering about somewhat, with a new wine-skin in his left hand, first held up a still-bandaged palm then began to chant solo in a quiet, happy, foolish voice:

> I've done some harm, I've done some good
> I've done a whole lot better than they thought I would
> To make quite sure you'll believe in me
> I've let them nail me to a tree.

Fortunately, since he continued to use his own mongrel mixture of Norman French and English, none but his immediate companions could understand him. Nevertheless, Walt felt much of his old antagonism to the charlatan returning.

He moved away, staggering a little himself, wondering if there was a proper urinal or did one just turn wine back to water against the nearest wall? He was very drunk. Had, in fact, had a skinful. Apart from anything else, he found that when he was drunk the pain in his mouth receded, became bearable.

He looked up and around him and his blurred vision fell on a casement dimly lit by one candle. Framed within the narrow space a woman in a white-pleated gown took off a full wig of red hair and shook out black locks that had been pinned up beneath it. So what, Walt thought. Women were deceivers ever. Yet, in some corner of his brain he knew he had seen something somewhere that was significant, important, a warning. It carried a name – Jezebel perhaps? But that he knew was not quite right.

He tripped over a somnolent body on the floor and apologised even as he stumbled against a stable door which opened and let him through though he did not actually fall over. A tethered ass shuffled and resumed its crunchy chewing on the grain it had been given, and a drover between it and the wall looked up over his shoulder from the serving girl he was rogering and swore at him. Walt staggered out again, blundered into the next stable where a mule was already pissing, like a horse, so Walt felt there'd be no harm if he did likewise and did so after the usual one-handed awkwardness involved in getting the thing out. The lengthy stream caught a gleam of firelight and, as it faded, Walt for a moment caressed himself between thumb and forefinger, easing the foreskin back and forth. It's been a long time, he thought. And then he remembered Adeliza dancing in her shift.

Outside again and looking upwards the stars wheeled round a still point above his head, and smoke from the dying fire drifted across them, a glaucous yeast upon the rich, plum darkness of the sky, heaven's rooftree hung with purple fruit. Slowly spinning like a wandering planet torn from its sphere, Walt wove his way through bodies that slept like petrified waves or whales upon a heaving ocean and sank at last into a space between Alain and Adeliza.

Taillefer and Quint, improvising alternate lines, sang on using the plainchant for the *Veni Creator* – not an easy fit but somehow they shoehorned it in:

> *Though one in three, I'm not the third,*
> *My mother's a virgin, my daddy's a bird*
> *What's bred in the bone will help me to fly*
> *So I'm off now dear friends to my place in the sky.*

Adeliza reached out her long brown fingers and took Walt's right wrist, and presently began to caress the knobbled stub – which was nice of her. He slept and dreamt, but boozily and still much bothered with the pain in his cheek and shattered teeth.

CHAPTER
TWENTY-EIGHT

Bravely from the bank he dived, the seething waves received him. Dawn to day to night to dawn fled by before his feet touched bottom. For fifty years, depth, length and breadth, the monster-she had held this lake inviolate from human trespass — now fiercely vengeful, ravenous for blood, she smelt the man who dared her lair. Her loathsome nails slashed out but linked rings of mail saved him, nor could her fingers prise open his armour.

Grasping him greedily she swept down through the deeps where the sea creatures struck at him, tusks bored at his corselet, monsters molested him.

Lured by a flame that was lurid she dragged him through waterless vaults to a hall hung with weapons and treasure. The flame flickered brightly revealing her visage, fearsome, infernal, a face straight from hell. No water impeded the blade that he whirled, arm's strength swung the ring-hilted sword so it sang a war song. Yet the edge failed him, sheared though it had through many a helm and split open the mail of many an ill-fated man — her flesh it was turned by, her bone-chamber broke it. In anger he hurled it, its hilt wound with ringed serpents, heeded no more its damascened steel — his own strength he trusted, the might of his hand, risking his life for long-lasting fame. Her shoulders he grappled in mortal embrace nor mourned he their feud as groundwards in fury he flung her. Lithely she twisted and locked him in clinches, tricksily tripped so he stumbled and fell. Knife-naked and gleaming, she threw herself on him, avenging her son, her only offspring. But the ring-mail denied both the thrust and the slash.

Broke free and back on his feet, he spied on the wall a sword wrought by giants, a warrior's joy, massive and matchless, huge as it was, no man but he could handle it hopefully. Savage the blow he swung at her neck-bone, head severed, her body crashed to the ground. Her blood smoked on the blade and melted it utterly, leaving only the gold of its hilt – so hot was the blood, so poisonous the monster who died in the cave. He who had lived through the onslaught of enemies held jewelled hilt and hewn head and swam up through the water. Purged of impurity by the death of the she-beast, the lake stained with battle-blood at last became calm, and under the clouds the anger abated . . .

And Walt, sweating through his dream, ejaculated like a whale, pumping semen over his stomach, till at last the sword of his prick flopped too. The pungent odour swam up through the covers, filled his nostrils and Adeliza's too so she murmured and sighed in her sleep and turned her face into his shoulder. Two years is a long time.

'Your young friend, Walt,' Taillefer was saying. 'I bet he's a good fuck. I shouldn't like him to take advantage of Adeliza beneath that blanket.'

'Not likely. He's a mess. Traumatised—'

'Eh?'

'Word I made up. From the Germanic word for "wound" – applied here to wounds in the mind. Even before the battle where he lost all faith in himself as well as his hand I doubt he was up to much. He fears the female orgasm, the claws that scratch, the teeth that bite. Anglo-Saxon, you see. Attitudes. Attitudes to the female sex. See the conquering hero comes—'

They were both still coherent, speech unslurred, but slow, as if they were speaking and living in a different sphere where time passed more slowly.

'I think I understand,' Taillefer took up the tale. 'Sound the trumpets, beat the drums! The war-parties in their long-boats. No women with them. The curved prows, the dragons' heads, kill the men, and rape the women. Then settle down. But for ever after the women are alien, a separate race—'

'In smoky byres they spin and weave,' Quint chimed in, 'cast spells, make magic, bleed from their cunts, strangle the first-born with the birth cord and for ever plot their dire revenge. Well, it's understandable. Sins of the fathers, unto the third generation—'

'Oh much more than that. Unless the circle's broken—'

'Circle?'

'Manner of speaking. Unless the chain is snapped.'

Quint nodded approval, preferring the revised metaphor. He spun it along.

'It's stuck there for ever. Leads to endless perversion, constant mangling, twisting, contorting of all relationship between the sexes.'

'A sort of race memory?'

'Bollocks, no. Not if you mean it's literally in the blood. After all, the races are almost immediately mixed and both girl-children and boy-children share the same blood. Just a pattern of behaviour handed on from father to son, mother to daughter. But no. That's not quite right.'

'It isn't?'

'Or rather not the whole story.' Warming now to his theme: 'Men learn as much from the lads they grow up with as they do from their fathers. The sub-culture of male adolescence endlessly renews itself wherever lads are lads. And it all goes back to rape and pillage. Women are cunts, slap them down and stick it in. Then comes the guilt. And finally the fear . . .'

'Oh, yes. The fear!' Taillefer exclaimed. 'Fear they'll get their own back. They gang up on us. In their kitchens, in the fields, in the stables as they gossip amongst the cows and sheep whose teats they pull, hiss-hiss, froths the milk in the pail, in the woods where they gather the nightshade, the foxglove, the henbane and death-cap mushrooms, *Amanita phalloides*, they whisper and snigger. But it's not only the Anglo-Saxons, you know? Not just the English who ravish their women and then feel bad about it . . . make monsters and witches out of the fragile flowers they first set on pedestals, dear me, no. Wherever the men have come from another land without their women, and taken those that were there, having first slain their husbands and sons, then this happens.'

'And,' added Quint, 'there are precious few places where this has not been the case. Jews are different, though. When they came down into Cana they had their own women with them. They respect each other. Their men neither idolise or brutalise, the women have nothing to revenge.'

Walt, old memories stirred, drifted back into sleep, and dream –

dreams which confused, melded and separated the Cornish girl beaten to death by Wulfric, then of Erica, his one true love, the daughter of the thegn of Shroton. In spite of Quint's theorising it had been all right with her. All right? Bloody marvellous! He snuggled closer to Adeliza and slept more deeply and peacefully than he had before.

CHAPTER
TWENTY-NINE

His back was cold and he stirred. The cobbles of the inn-yard floor pushed into his side and buttocks. But his stomach was warm and slimily sticky. Struggling up through the fumes of the wine he discovered why. He was curled up and entangled with Adeliza. His left arm was under and round her back and his one good hand held her shoulder. Her small head was on his collar-bone. He could feel her dark hair about his mouth and nose, and her warm breath on his chest. Most of the lower part of her body was spread across his midriff and one knee was bent up higher than the other. With a sudden wave of embarrassment he realised that the stub where his right hand should be was between her legs. And there was a tingling in it, a raw sense of touch he had not felt for nearly two (or three?) years since the pain died and left the cold nothingness he used to try to penetrate by scratching and gnawing at it with nails and teeth.

For a moment, still part drunk as he was, he wondered if it might not grow again, if a small baby's fist might not push through the stump and slowly form a new right hand. He tried to pull it away but her hand closed on what had once been his forearm and insisted he remained where he was. Indeed she moved her inner thighs briefly along it and pressed it closer into her, giving a little sigh as she did so.

With first light and cock-crow, several cocks in fact, someone kicked some life into the embers of the fire, shivered and exclaimed at the thin powder of frost that lay over everything like dust. Others rose, stretched and yawned and went to the stables for a piss; a bucket was dropped into the well. Two girls moved among them, one with a tray of bread hot from the oven, the other with a churn of goat milk warm from the udder. An hour later the animals were led out into the open plain, the plump Greek settled his skull-cap more securely on his head, his camel lurched forward, and all were on the move.

They journeyed for three more days along a road which continued to wind through mountains, but the valleys wider and the heights not so precipitous as before with wide fields of stubble below. The small village huts made now from baked dung clung to the hillsides, built so much on top of each other that the flat roofs looked like irregular steps and indeed the inhabitants hung out their washing and enjoyed the afternoon sun, which was still very hot, above the ceilings of those who lived below. Not much of note happened, the weather remained fine, and, since they proceeded at a leisurely pace without too much jogging, it was only at night that Walter suffered from his teeth.

Their patroness spent more time with them now, had perhaps had differences with her friends. She begged them to keep close, to have what weapons they had always ready for she feared robbers or worse as the country became wilder and the villages less frequent. She also engaged Quint in conversations of a philosophical nature and when they stopped to refresh the animals or for a midday meal she asked Taillefer to perform magical illusions. This he was loth to do but urged his children on to demonstrate their skills. It was, he said, good practice for them.

At nights they slept as they had before, Walt always entangled with Adeliza in an embrace that was never quite innocent but brought neither of them harm. Indeed, a miracle was occurring: each morning the lumps and bumps on his stump seemed less and the skin became more sensitive, responding again with that warm tingling to the caresses she offered him beneath the cloaks and blankets they shared. But his mouth got worse. The outside scabs had cleared up and healed healthily enough but his broken teeth still ached and occasionally flamed into terrible pain.

In the huge fields where wheat had been harvested long lines of orange flame advanced like armies across the plains beneath dense clouds of blueish-white smoke. Field-workers walked like marshals behind with rakes and sheets of stiff leather mounted on sticks which they used to beat out flames that threatened to spread to the orchards and woods. Wheat was not the only crop. Many fields were filled with yellowish stalks that stood about as high as a woman's waist and were crowned with brown, egg-shaped seed cases that rattled in the breeze and occasionally popped, scattering a thin dust of tiny black seeds. The cases were marked with neat, spiral incisions that had been cut into the flesh when it was still succulent and green but not into the chamber that held the seeds. Many of these incisions were still marked with traces of a brownish-black paste where the exuded juices had dried. This tall stubble was also being burnt. The smoke had a sweet, unctuous smell and made many in the caravan feel drowsy, while others began to giggle for no particular reason.

The third day from Dorylæum ended, as always, in a caravansarai, but this time the town outside whose walls it stood was built up the side of an almost precipitous hill which ended in a crag that beetled over the plain that now spread itself to the east, for they had reached the plateau that lies in the centre of the sub-continent. The crag was crowned with a low black fortress which seemed to hug the rocks on which it stood and from which flew huge banners with the Chi-Rho and other emblems of the Christian religion emblazoned on them. At the foot of the hill, some half mile or so from the caravansarai, a huge camp had been pitched and from behind palisades they could hear the trumpet's martial call and the neighing of countless horses.

'The Black Castle of Opium,' Quint added as they passed through the entrance to the caravansarai. 'That's what the locals call this place, though since Emperor Leo the Third defeated the Arabs here some three hundred years past, the Byzantines have called it Nicopolis.'

'How do you know this stuff?' Walt was more than irritable. At the end of a long day his broken teeth felt like pillars of white-hot steel, filling his mouth and brain with pain.

Quint frowned, looked a touch hurt.

'I seek things out,' he said. 'I have a curious mind and at the very least I like to know where I am at any given time. But to the point. Here, if anywhere, we shall find what's needed to alleviate the pain that still afflicts you.'

They ate and drank as usual by a fire of flaming branches and again Theodora slipped in amongst them preferring, it seemed, their company to the solitariness of one of the upstairs rooms. Quint went scouting along the stalls that flanked the stables and soon returned with a small ball

of black gunge wrapped in a brown and friable leaf. Hunkering in front
of Walt he made him scoop a spoonful on to his finger.

'Smear it,' he said, 'along the gums beneath your broken teeth, and
then masticate the rest with your tongue, being sure to work in plenty of
spittle before swallowing.'

'What will it do?'

'It will take away the pain.'

'And give you dreams, such dreams,' Taillefer added.

'But first, as the pain goes but before you sleep, we must find a barber
or, failing that, a smith.'

Walt sat up.

'You're not pulling them. I'll not have them pulled.'

Adeliza knelt behind him, linked her fingers in front of his chest and
put her cheek against his.

'It's the only way. Besides, your breath smells like a corpse left three
days in the sun.'

Alain appeared accompanied now by a huge man with a shaven head.
He carried an assortment of tools in a pouch attached to the front of his
leather apron. Seeming only to want to inspect the cause of Walt's pain,
he stooped over him, delved into his open mouth with a stubby finger –
but he had palmed a pair of wicked forceps and, as Quint, Taillefer and
Alain joined Adeliza and attached themselves to Walt's head, shoulders
and waist, he yanked out the first broken stump from the back of his
mouth.

Five remained, but the next time Walt was ready., He clamped his
mouth shut, twisted and turned until the blood and pus bubbled up
through his nose and he thought he might drown. The leathered giant's
fist was in again like a flash and out came the second. By now there was
a crowd of onlookers, their faces lit grotesquely by the flames, who
cheered and jeered until four more had gone, their shards clattering into
a bowl Theodora held for them.

At last it was done. Quint gave him wine to swill out his mouth, then
water, then more wine, and finally when the bleeding seemed to have
eased a little, another ball of the brown stuff to chew on. Finally he
wrapped him in blankets and left him to sleep, while the rest of the party
gathered round and, over bowls of chicken soup, continued the discus-
sions that had occupied them on the previous evenings.

'Life,' murmured Taillefer, 'is a phantasmagoria of transitory sensation over which our minds hover like the dove that moved upon the face of the waters. We strive to make some sense of it through words. But their meanings shift and they are as stable a foundation on which to build a structure that might explain the universe as the sands against which the Nazarene warned us.'

'Hence,' Quint replied wryly, jokingly, 'his insistence that we should set our trust in the Holy Church and her teaching, built as she is upon a rock.'

'But with what does she teach but words? And what are words? They are not things. They are signs. Merely signs.'

'A rock is a rock is a rock,' said Quint, plucking a large stone from a pile of rubble rejected by the builders, 'and you'll know it's a rock if I hit you with it. But in what lies its rockiness? The word will do for the stone in my hand and for the great lump of stuff on which that black castle stands. I can hit you with one and push you off the other.'

At this point Theodora intervened, her voice low but strong, first adjusting a lock of red hair that threatened to come adrift from the rest.

'Is there not,' she said, 'a quality shared by the rock from which you would have him jump and the rock with which you would hit him? Is there not such a thing as rockiness?

'Did not the great Pantocrator make rock with one hand and sand with the other? On, let me see . . .' she continued, then muttered to herself and counted on her fingers, 'yes. On the third day. But to return to rockiness. Surely there preceded in the Pantocrator's Mind, before he set to work on the third day, an essence which was that rockiness which permeates all rocks and makes them what they are?'

'Some rocks,' Taillefer interjected, taking the nozzle of a wineskin from his lips and wiping it on his sleeve before passing it on, 'are, I believe, impermeable. But that is by the way. I think.'

'We should not,' said Quint, 'presume to look into God the Creator's mind—'

'Box of worms,' Taillefer muttered. 'Sort of rocky horror, really.'

'. . . but, as you say, on the third day came rocks in all their forms, substances, sizes and types out of which man's mind, on the sixth day, abstracted the idea of rockiness – not the other way about.'

'But man, Adam, when he invented the word rock, was responding to an essential idea of rockiness . . .' Theodora was insistent.

'Essences should not be invented except where necessity demands. Or, put it another way: If you can do without them, you don't need them.'

'Sharp,' said Taillefer. 'Oh, very sharp.'

Walt, already asleep moaned a little. Adeliza bent over him and wiped a trickle of blood that leaked from the corner of his mouth with the hem of her cloak, then snuggled down next to him, and, after pulling as many covers as she could find around them both, assumed again the embrace she had held him in every night for nearly a week.

He dreamed, but this time the dream was free of pain, the cradle of Adeliza's arms seemed less equivocal, and wrapped in opiates rather than wine as he was, Mnemosyne joined hands again with Morpheus to lead him back into an enchanted past.

CHAPTER
THIRTY

She ran when she saw him, and he followed her along the side of the small field of barley, a foot or more high and emerald green, scaring a couple of larks from their nest, sending them skimming the green sea, over which blueish cloud-shadows chased each other. In the far corner, just where the great hill began to climb, there was a small, low copse of elder whose blossom was opening into crowded plates of tiny white stars. They filled the warm air with their sweet but sharp scent.

She? She was Erica, daughter of the thegn of Shroton, whose land marched with his father's, with whose brothers and their followers he had fought stone-throwing battles up and down these grassy slopes or swum in the mill-pools of the Stour. She was just a year younger than he and he had watched her grow. The grubby waif in a smock who sucked her thumb had become a lean boyish figure who rallied her brothers with high whooping cries when Walt and the boys from Iwerne drove them along the turfy ramparts above. And then . . . Gloucester, Ireland, Cornwall, London, Tidworth Camp and the Welsh Marches, learning to be a housecarl, a *comitatus*, his lord's companion and final shield in battle, and he'd hardly seen her at all, just glimpses from a distance across fields or apple-picking in a neighbouring orchard when he came home for Christmas or to help with the harvests.

Now he was sixteen, and carrying the first seax slash of a scar on his neck and left shoulder (not deep, it faded to a white line in a year or so). He'd got it, not in battle, but scouting ahead of Harold's main army on the first campaign against Griffith in the Brecon Beacons, fought through a frozen spring. Home now at the end of May he was welcomed as a hero by his family and all the manors around. And two days after his return his father had met her father who still mourned the death of his two sons two years earlier. They had gone mad and finally sunk into a distressed torpor, their brains addled through eating diseased meat during the cattle pestilence of 1054.

Following the meeting between the fathers a brief betrothal ceremony was held in a bower built for the occasion and filled with the flowers of late spring and early summer, set up by the brook which was streaked with crow's foot and fringed with kingcups and which marked a boundary between their lands. Kingfishers, harbingers of summer, flitted above it. It was agreed the actual marriage would have to wait until Walt's service to Harold was complete.

And then, two days later, a small boy from Shroton had slipped into the compound at Iwerne and sought him out in one of the sheds. There, with Bur, a churl skilled in building fences, Walt had been sharpening ash stakes with an axe, one, two, three blows to the base of each stake, leaving the exposed wood white like snow, supports for an extension of the deer fence. A better use for ash poles than the spears Walt was used to fashioning, Bur reckoned. Not if they are used to defend homesteads like this one, Walt had replied.

'Master Walt,' the small boy had piped, catching his sleeve, 'my mistress says you will give me a penny if I give you her message.'

'And who then is your mistress?' Though he knew, his heart raced a little and a strange constriction grasped his throat so for a moment he could hardly breathe. She had kissed him at the betrothal – warmly on the lips, as was their custom. None of this frenchified dab on one cheek and then the other, but the real thing, English style.

'The lady Erica of course. Don't you want to hear what she sent me to say?'

'Of course.'

Silence.

Walt turned to Bur, who was not much older than he but already married with a small baby and another on the way.

'I don't suppose you have a penny ?'

Bur shook his head.

'I'll have to get one then,' and he put aside the axe.

'It's of no account,' said the small boy, 'she's already given me one.' And he held it up proudly for all to see. 'You can give me yours next time I come. My mistress desires to make your better acquaintance and will wait for you in the corner of her father's barley field, beneath the western end of Hambledon. Bring something to eat and drink.'

'When?'

'How should I know? Now? Tomorrow? This evening? I should try now.'

And he scampered away, dodging the more or less playful swipe Walt aimed at him.

Half an hour later Walt pushed through the brittle elder twigs and lower branches, knowing how unlucky it is to snap the wood from which the Cross was made and from which Judas hanged himself, and that slowed him. When he came out the other side she'd gone – but where?

Shading his eyes he scanned the steep slopes above, which climbed all of two hundred feet or more to grassy ramparts. The slopes themselves were too steep to support more than grass and stunted shrubs – blackthorn whose blossom had shrivelled, browned and dropped a fortnight before, and hawthorn already in fresh green leaf and with its tiny clustered globes of white buds just bursting. The grass too was not just grass but filled with the small flowers that grow on chalk. And then he saw her, up on the crest of the first turf rampart, her lithe brown limbs, long straw-coloured hair, a white shift or smock.

He hurled himself at the slope, hands dragging at the thick tussocks of coarse grass, feet scrabbling. Soon, he was panting for breath and cursing the small bag of bread and cheese and the cured sheep's stomach full of cider. They kept swinging off his back and dangling like udders between his legs. And of course as he hauled himself upright on the crest she was again nowhere to be seen. Should he call for her? She had chosen to hide herself – let her call for him.

There was heat in the deep hollow, the turfed fosse the ancients had left between their ramparts, a heavy buzzing of bees, also the tangy smell of fresh sheep-droppings. In front of him the Vale of the White Hart stretched into blue distances. It was approaching the hottest part of the day and nothing seemed to move, although he could hear the bells of her father's cows in the meadows below.

'Erica!'

Her name bubbled out from between his lips after all, though he had not consciously willed it. He was answered by a rippling laugh from much nearer than he had expected. He turned and caught the movement of her shift beyond or in a low clump of hawthorn only ten or so paces from him and just below the ridge. He rounded the clump and found her sitting, knees pulled up, the hem of her shift about her ankles, a grass in her mouth, looking up over her shoulder at him.

'Did you bring us our snap?' she asked and she shook a tress of the long blonde hair off her cheek as she spoke. Her voice was soft and gentle but with laughter in it. She flirted a bit over the cider, pretending to grumble over the lack of cups and claiming the container it came in had imparted a muttony flavour, not the sort of thing you offer a lady. She recognised the blue-veined cheese as a chunk off the one her father had brought to the betrothal and praised it accordingly.

Awkward with each other at first they began by reminiscing about childhood. Do you remember when? What did your mum say when you got home? I wasn't crying because one of your stones hit me but because I'd fallen in some nettles.

I'm sorry about your brothers.

I'm sorry about your mother.

She was old, she'd had a good life, but your brothers . . .

She wept a little and he comforted her, his hands on the warm, milky skin of her shoulder, his face in the fragrance of her hair.

I must go now. Can you come tomorrow? At the same time?

Meet you here.

This time he brought the cider in a pottery jug with two cups and she had barley cakes filled with honey and wrapped in sweet chestnut leaves. It was the devil of a job to get the cider up the hill without spilling it.

How many children shall we have? she asked, wiping honey from the corner of her mouth.

As many as God sends, he answered.

Don't be stupid, I'm not the Virgin Mary, you know.

Filled with a sudden flower-burst of joy he turned her towards him, and licked the dark, brown honey from her chin.

She pushed him away with a giggle but left her hand on his knee.

When you finish your service as a housecarl what will Harold give you?

All the lands between the Stour and the Avon. He meant the Hampshire Avon that rises near Stonehenge.

Silly, that would be enough to make you an earl.

Some of them, anyway. Enough to make a proper lady of you.

Do you mind? I'm a proper lady already, thank you very much.

Of course you are.

She lay back against the grassy slope with her hands joined above her eyes. Her smock was above her knees.

Do you think I'm beautiful?

Like apple-blossom in April, like a cornfield in July, like cream in a dish, like the woods in October when all the leaves are red and gold, like snow in February.

My cousins over in Childe Okeford say I'm ugly, but that's because they thought one of them should be your wife, not me.

'Young love is a powerful thing. I could lock you up, but like a tom-cat when there's a queen in heat within a league, you'd find a way out.'

He and his old father, white hair unkempt since Walt's mother died, sat alone in the mead-hall at the big table, just the one candle, and all the churls and freemen long gone back to their family bowers.

'And anyway it's right you should see her, get to know her. It's a bad thing when strangers marry.'

He drank, wiped his straggly beard, which, Walt noted, was none too clean.

'I wish your mother was alive. She could tell you things.'

'What things?'

'About women, and their ways.'

Walt had a dim understanding of what he meant. The monthlies, he supposed. That sort of thing.

They drank some more.

'You'll be off again soon.'

'St John's Day. At Winchester. I have to be there. I told you.'

'You did. I forgot. Often I forget things.'

Walt covered his father's knobbled knuckles with his own hand and squeezed.

'It doesn't matter.'

'It does. This place needs a proper man in charge.'

'I'll be back.'

'You'd better.'

They drank some more, crumbled some bread, ate it.

'Mind, you're not to leave her with a brat on the way. Not if you can't come back and be a proper father.'

Walt thought about that. Thought about how she'd lain back against the slope and smiled up at him from cornflower eyes. With a sudden, disturbing flash of perception he realised that what his father was telling him might not be too easy to observe. Not if she had as much a mind for it as he did, and he rather thought she had.

It was disconcerting to find that such carnal impulses ran so closely hand-in-hand with the apparently more spiritual longing the thought of her filled him with. But his father had not finished.

'There are ways . . .' his old fingers writhed on the table, his face was suffused, 'you can . . . make . . . oh, damn it, your mother would have been able to tell you so much better . . .' He was confused, did not know how to say the things he wanted to say.

Finally, he looked up at his son.

'Just, do . . . just, oh, make yourself happy and her, but don't land her and us with a bastard. All right?'

The thegn of Iwerne reached forward, clawed Walt's shoulder, drained his cup and stumped off to his lonely bed.

Perhaps Erica had been talking to her mother. Or an aunt. Certainly, along with all the other children of her age, she had watched and laughed raucously at the antics the animals sometimes got up to, how bulls sometimes licked their cows' vulvae, instead of getting on with it properly, that sort of thing. They drank their cider, ate wrinkled apples, the last from the previous autumn kept in the hay lofts above the barns (it was about all they did keep hay for, feeding the best breeding stock on more nutritious fodder through the winter and killing the rest for food when winter came). Then, with no more questioning she pulled him down on top of her and made him kiss her face, her lips, her neck, her shoulders. He lifted her smock over her shoulders and she shook her head and wonderful hair free of it. For a moment he was shattered by the soft, rounded, milky whiteness of her, the globes of her breasts, the nipples like pale raspberries, the rounded tummy and its blue-shadowed navel, the full hips and the fair reddish brush, redder than her hair (foxy lady), between and her long, smooth strong legs. He bent his head, took her nipples between his lips.

After a moment or two of this she sat up to pull at his leggings and jerkin until he was as naked beneath the sun and the larks as she was. She took hold of his throbbing prick with one hand and with the other arm over his lean, muscled shoulders pulled him down but carefully so his member lay between their stomachs. When, driven by impulses stronger than earthquakes and tempests, he tried to wriggle a little lower, find his way in, she seized his buttocks and with nails tearing into them ground her stomach against him until he came before he could get there. Gasping, almost retching with the uncompleted agony of it, he pulled up and back and looked down at her, spread like a universe of potential joy beneath him.

Her hands reached up his arms and on to his shoulders.

'You're not done yet, oh no Walt, you're not done yet,' and shifting a hand to his sweating forehead she pushed him down across her stomach streaked with viscous pearl as it was, right down to where she was moist too and filled with fragrances. She opened her knees and put her legs over his shoulders forcing his mouth into her. His body slipped on the grassy slope beneath them, the wild thyme prickled his stomach and his balls, and he had to scrabble again with his feet to gain a purchase and push himself upwards, and again gather handfuls of grass on either side of her waist.

She pushed with her hands at the back of his head, his neck, twisting them and herself, and once got hold of his hair and yanked his head upwards so his lips and tongue were where she wanted them to be and he felt the small hardness within swell and throb until suddenly she was writhing and moaning as he sucked the rush of wetness into his mouth – sea without the harshness of salt, honey without its cloying sweetness.

And when that was done and the hot flush spread across her breastbone was fading and her head ceased to rock from side to side, when that was over they lay face to face and kissed and gently played with their fingers until it all happened again less urgently but even more sweetly than before. And, of course she found his tattoos. The winged dagger: 'Winners dare'. And 'Walt 4 Erica' inscribed within a heart. That pleased her like anything, because now she knew he had fancied her all along, well before the betrothal.

At last she said: 'Wait here. I don't want to be seen leaving with you.'

And she pulled the smock back on over her head.

He watched her – part walking, sometimes driven by the steepness of the slope to run a little, once slithering and almost slipping on to her backside so she looked back with a grin and a wave. His heart burst with a happiness which enveloped all he could see and smell and touch. The whole landscape from the plants around him, some it must be said a little the worse for being lain on, to the distant hills was hers, was subsumed into her. She was the spirit whose corporeality infused it all.

The grass was a garden, a chalk garden filled with wild flowers, thyme, vetches, clovers, wild flaxes, cranesbills, spurges, borages, mallow, forget-me-nots and harebells. The hawthorn blossom was full and out now and the scent of it, the most sensuous odour that any blossom has and the why of that was something he had discovered first on his tongue and still on his fingers, hung about his head. He looked down and out across a rolling plain framed with the blue hills on which Shaftesbury stood six miles to the north and on the right by downs which lay like a woman upon the earth, contoured so their shape echoed the line that climbs a thigh, dips from hip to waist, then swells into a breast. Below, the coombes were hazed with bosky woods.

Filling the air, making a space rather than an emptiness of it, martins wove cat's cradles of delight so fast all he could follow was the white speck of their rumps above the trees and fields. Higher still, swifts racketed on alternate wing-beats mewing like kittens as they scoured the skies. A scattering of crows chased a merlin from their rookery, and while a male cuckoo made the air ring his mate slipped in and laid intrusive eggs.

It was all one thing, one living thing, bound into one. Even the farms and enclosures, built from the earth and what grew out of it, mingled with it all, were neither alien nor intrusive, adding harmony to what would have been savage without them.

Again he savoured the hawthorn flavour on his lips and saw how the girl, the woman, yellow hair falling on honey-coloured shoulders above the white but grass-stained shift, crossed a meadow where three horses grazed and came to the fence that circled her father's homestead. One step up and there she was astride the topmost pole. She knew he watched for her and she raised an arm and waved. Wild thing. His heart was singing.

CHAPTER
THIRTY-ONE

Tumble-weed and dust devils. Ochre grit, dried-up riverbeds, and distant mountains mauve on the horizon – that's what the great central plain of Asia Minor looks like now as you cross it from Afion or Ankara to Konya, ancient Iconium. But not then, not in the late 1060s. Then it was oak forest, was partially farmed for timber, charcoal, tannin and so forth and pigs both wild and domestic fed sumptuously from the acorns to produce a thick, almost fat-free, dark-red meat. The acorns, those that escaped the pigs, would not germinate beneath the boughs of the parent tree: nothing mystical in this – just that not enough light or moisture got through to them. The forest thus needed very little attention to transform it into regulated park-land open enough for horsemen, hunters or soldiers to gallop through, or, near villages, for the peasants to grow wheat and vines beneath the trees without clearing them.

Why is it now a semi-desert? Because of what Walt and his companions witnessed from a foothill of the Taurus mountains to the south and west of Iconium a few days after they had left the Black Castle of Opium: a battle between the armies of the Seljuk Turks and the Emperor of Byzantium. The plain was spread below them, in the far distance they could see the white walls and towers of Iconium, where St Paul had preached in the market-place one thousand and twenty years earlier, and between it and them, trotting, slow-galloping and marching in tight formations, wheeling, deploying in solid phalanxes, some twenty or thirty thousand soldiers. The Cross against the Crescent. Banners fluttering from spears in the spaces between the oaks, levelled for the charge. Quick-firing archers with small bows, mounted on ponies on the Turks' side, crossbowmen cranking up their steel-leafed engines on the other. Trumpets and horns, some curving above the leopard-skinned heads of the bandsmen beneath the Chi-Rhos, standards hung with bells and horses' tails beneath the silver crescents. Alla Turca. Syncopated drums. It was quite a sight. The ones with turbans round their helmets won. After three hours or so of galloping hither and thither and for no particular reason that the watchers could identify, the ones on the western side of the panorama below them broke ranks and began to flee through the oaks towards the west, leaving a great train of baggage, camp-followers, animals, stores, slaves and women behind them.

Taillefer asserted that this was intentional. By interposing such considerable booty between them the Christian soldiers reckoned to escape their pursuers. And now, from the east, came the women, children and slaves of the Seljuks, filling the spaces left by their victorious army. Ignoring the city, which presently began to burn beneath clouds of black smoke, the main body pitched a thousand black tents amongst the oaks, whilst all around them tens of thousands of russet and black goats moved through the forest.

Goats love oak more than any other food. They will browse every leaf they can reach and they can strip the bark from all but the most mature trees. Their herdsmen, of course, relying on their milk, yoghurt, cheese, meat, wool and hides for all of life's essentials, assist the destruction by cutting down the boughs the goats can't reach. Thus, within a generation or two, the great indigenous oak forests not only of Asia Minor but Central Asia too, were destroyed.

Quint especially had been impressed.

'That is the future and it's unbeatable,' he carolled as he beat the rump of his mule with a stick and urged it up the steep part of a bend.

The woman Walt called Theodora looked at him over the shoulder of her peacock-coloured gown from the back of her white palfrey, whose dainty black hoofs were scrambling at the grit and shingle of the road.

'The Turks?' she exclaimed with some incredulity.

'Not just the Turks,' cried Quint. 'Islam. The crescent.' He warmed to it. 'Truly a crescent. Think of it – the western horn, the Moorish Arabs strike up through Spain, the Pyrenees alone stand between them and

Paris. And here on the eastern point the Turks threaten Constantinople and all the lands beyond. Mark my words. Europe is theirs.'

Taillefer followed him on his big pack-horse with Adeliza clinging to his waist behind him and his saddle-bags filled with the machinery which created his illusions thumping the horse's flanks below his knees.

'One thing I don't like about them though,' Adeliza called out. 'Their Holy Book forbids the use of wine.'

'Until, dear girl, you get to Paradise. Then you can drink all you want. There are even scantily clad ladies there to do the honours.'

Adeliza pouted: 'Personally,' she said, 'I'd rather be served by naked Ganymeds.'

Theodora turned her dark and sensuous eyes on Quint.

'A book of verse, a flask of wine and thou beside me sitting in the wilderness is paradise enough,' she called above the noise of the caravan. 'Why wait for an unearthly heaven?'

Five years later Quint met a poet called Omar, quoted what she had said, and, with a minor improvement or two, the young man incorporated it in a book he was writing.

'You're right, of course,' Quint called again and urged his reluctant mule into a trot which he hoped would bring him abreast with the lady, but she, sensing his intention, shook her reins and urged her game little pony into a trot that took him out of reach. 'From dust we come, to dust we go. The flowers of the field and all that. But the Ancients had it right, had the answer: tomorrow and her works defy, lay hold upon the present hour and snatch the pleasures passing by, nor love, nor love's delights disdain – whate'er thou gets today is gain . . . You see, it's what I was saying the other night – it's the THING that matters, the here and now of it . . .'

She turned on him again, looking down from the path above the next bend so she seemed to be going in the opposite direction, meeting and passing him but on different levels.

'Your here and now,' she remonstrated, 'seem to carry a smack of the essential about them do they not? Are they not essences—'

'Abstractions merely. Not the same.'

Like a distressed cat, Walt, following Quint, growled.

'Men died down there,' he muttered to Taillefer. 'Limbs hewn from torsos, the arrow in the stomach, the black blood in the mouth and what do they know of it all? They're high on what they saw, but what do they know . . .?'

'More than you, young man,' Taillefer said. He reined back and fell in beside him. 'That battle was a civilised one. Oh, a few men got hurt, deaths even, but once the Infidels had paraded their might and let the Christians see their numbers and their strength the Christians evinced a clear desire to be off and the Infidels let them. Quite a different sort of business from the bloody shambles you got caught up in.'

Clip-clop, clip-clop.

'Well, you were there. You should know,' Walt muttered after a time. 'But there was glory there, honour and everlasting fame. The shield-wall and the faith a thegn owes his ring-giving lord.'

He and Taillefer looked inward and back to the shattered men, a handful only at the end, beneath the grey sky deepening to night, the wheeling crows, back to the blood-bespattered shields that swung and wavered where for hours they had remained firm, the rain that fell like arrows on them, the arrows that fell like rain, and the swirling horsemen, circling beyond the reach of axe-blow and sword-slash, waiting like the crows for the last shield to fall, the last man to die.

Taillefer sighed and pushed his horse on, rejoined the theologians who were still discussing Islam.

'They have their problems,' he called out.

'They have?'

'Like the Christians they have their sects, their divisions, their heresies. A house divided and all that. It'll be their undoing.'

'Ah, but one day they'll get it right,' Quint exclaimed. 'Once they've fixed on the true fundamentals of their religion, there will be no stopping them.'

Clip-clop, clip-clop.

'You'll turn Muslim, then?'

'Why not? It's a more rational religion than the one we've got. How about you?'

'Perhaps. Certainly there is one sect amongst them has a special appeal.'

'Yes?'

'The Ismaelis. They have a new leader, a young man, who has provided in one sentence all one needs to know.'

'Which is?'

'"Nothing is forbidden. All things are possible."'

'I make that two sentences.'

'Pedant!' And he dropped back again.

'But that was the end,' he said to Walt. 'The outcome – that dreadful obscenity of a battle. There was trouble, before that, was there not, when Harold returned from Bayeux? Bad news waiting for him. Is that not where it began?'

'The worst news. At the time none knew how bad it was.'

'Tell me,' Taillefer pleaded. Walt looked at him. The dark face was now pained and pleading, the grooves in his cheeks deeper than before. Walt glanced at his still bandaged hands. Russet stains on the back of them, pain in the palms when he gripped the reins. It was as if he needed to know that he was not solely responsible for the fate which had befallen the English king. Taking pity, if not actually forgiving, Walt took up the next part of his tale.

PART V

THE LAST ENGLISH KING

CHAPTER
THIRTY-TWO

The boat slipped into the lower reaches of Chichester harbour towards midday. The fat, grey, mottled seals still basked on the sand-banks; the terns, sea-swallows some called them, still hovered and struck, coming up with small-fry. The sea was calm, velvety, purple, with only the slightest of swells, the sky clear apart from a haze over the lowlands in front of the downs. The golds of late October had begun to stretch along the shore-line amongst the tired greens of summer – the old white gold of oak and elm, the red gold of beech, the new-minted yellow of coins spinning against the silver and pewter of birch and poplar boughs.

The tide was out but flowing. Men with buckets and mud-shoes, small discs of black wood, swung their awkward gait shorewards from the oyster and mussel beds or laid nets against the incoming flood. Wood-smoke drifted up through the still air from the settlements of the shore-folk and as the boat left the swell of the sea and the banks came closer, Harold and his men caught on the air the sweet-sour fresh fragrance of apples crushed in a cider-press.

It was good to be back. As he usually did, Helmric the Golden had a song for it, something about seafarers home from the sea. In the waist of the ship Walt and Daffydd taught Wulfnoth and Hakon, the young lads they had brought back from Le Bec, how to play dice, while Harold stood in the prow with the look-out, hoping news of their approach might have reached Bosham ahead of them and that Edith Swan-Neck would be standing on the quay to welcome them. Already the oath wrung from him weighed on his chest like a huge dead, white bird. It was something he wanted to talk about, quietly, with someone he trusted.

But as they rounded a headland and came in view of the steeple, Canute's thrones and the landing-stage, he could see a group of armed and mounted men clustered around one taller and fairer than the rest. With his long hair, coarser now, with some white in it and pulled back so the dome of his head was bald, fastened in a pony-tail which hung down the back of his leather-studded jerkin, he was, even at a distance, unmistakably Tostig.

The boat nudged the huge and heavy timbers, covered with barnacles and limpets, the sail rattled down with shouts of warning from the crew lest the yard should crack some ignorant land-lubber's skull, the ship's boy leapt up on to the quay with a tarred hawser. One of Tostig's men gave him a hand and together they hauled it in and looped it over a bollard. Behind them Harold was already breaking out of Tostig's embrace.

'What brings you here then? Not just a brotherly desire to welcome me back.'

Tostig, the third-born of close siblings, had always been demanding, attention-seeking, unreliable, always ready to take what he wanted as his birthright, regardless of convention or law. It was his belief that Harold existed merely to ensure that Tostig got what he wanted – especially now that Edward had clearly booked an early passage across the bourn from which no traveller returns. With middle-age approaching, he had grown even more proud and petulant, ready to see slights where none were intended, not willing to see reason, impatient. What charms, both of physique and personality, he had had in late adolescence had long gone. He remained cunning, cruel and ambitious.

He exploded . . .

'Fucking bastards have chucked me out,' he cried.

Harold stood back.

'You'd better tell me about it.'

'Of course I'll fucking tell you about it. That's why I'm here.'

'Calmly. In the hall. Is Edith still here?'

'Your fancy piece? Yes, she's still hanging around. But what I've got to tell you—' He saw how the dark blood rose in Harold's face and his voice faded.

'What you have to tell me can wait until I and my men have eaten, and drunk, and I have spent some time with Edith. I'll see you in the hall. At dusk.'

Through the meal Tostig chafed and fretted, spilled his mead, hit an over-friendly mastiff hard on the nose with a sheep's femur, ignored Edith when she offered him more mead and then called her back with a barely suppressed curse on his lips when she had moved on. Not wishing to put up with this more than he had to, Harold signalled to the women and servants and his bodyguard that they should withdraw. Wulfric, as the eldest and senior of his men, led them down to the far end of the hall where they played dice amicably enough against Tostig's bodyguard, polished their weapons, drank some more and listened to Helmric's strumming.

'So,' Harold began, once he and his brother were on their own. 'They turned you out. Who? Why? How?'

He had already heard from Edith some of the answers to these and other questions but wanted to assess Tostig's version.

'First. The Northumbrian thegns. They used the shire moot as a cover, slipped into York, killed most of the men I'd left there—'

'Where were you?'

'On the Britford estate, near Salisbury. They also seized my armoury and my treasury . . .'

'Why? What brought this on?'

'I taxed them. Extra taxes. For your sake, Harold. The King's dying. He hasn't collected heregild for ten years. When he goes we'll need all the men and arms we can get hold of . . .'

'We?'

'Us. You. The Godwinsons. If I'd been there and armed, if I'd had my sword, I'd have . . .'

And eyes burning he smashed his right fist into his left palm, then pushed his hair back from his temples. In the torchlight the sweat glistened on his jowls and his full lips pulled back in a snarl. 'You know I would.'

'Yes, I know,' Harold murmured. And thought to himself and you would have been butchered like a bull and I should have had no option but war. Wessex against Northumbria. Saxons against Danes. Like the good old days.

'And who put you up to this idea of collecting heregild?' He doubted Tostig had thought of it himself.

'Our Edith,' he said truculently, 'the Queen.'

'Why?' Harold was incredulous. Ever since the débâcle of 1052 which had put her for some months in a particularly spartan nunnery, his sister had kept out of state affairs.

'Poor Eddie's dying. You were away. We all thought the Bastard would get you off the list while he had the chance. She took other steps too to protect us.'

He left this hanging in the air. Harold, aware of quickening heartbeat and a pricking in the palms of his hands, wiped them on his jerkin and drank. Beer. He'd had enough wine in Normandy and mead was for feasts, celebrations. Nothing much to celebrate right now.

'You'd better tell me.'

Without looking at him Tostig began to poke his nails with the short seax he always carried.

'She contracted two men to kill Cospatric.'

'And?'

'He's fucking dead, isn't he?'

'Shit.' Then: 'Why did she do that?'

Tostig pulled in breath and let out a heavy sigh.

'She reckoned,' he said, 'that with both you and Eddie gone, we,' he meant the Godwinsons, and Harold understood as much, 'would back the Atheling. So, he's under age, but some sort of regency could be set up – her and Stigand, maybe . . .'

'Stigand is in on all this?'

'Yes. In fact it was he arranged the contract. She reckoned Aelfgar's sons,' Edwin and Morcar, Earl of Mercia and his younger brother, 'would be looking for a candidate they could support. They've no royal blood any more than we have so she thought they'd go for Cospatric.'

Centuries earlier Northumbria had been two kingdoms – Bernicia and Deira. The royal line of Bernicia had survived in the person of a youth called Cospatric, whom Edward had kept at court, like the Atheling, and for similar reasons – elsewhere he was a threat.

'How much of all this has come out?'

'Most of it. They tried to drown the lad but he struggled and they had to hit him about the head a bit. They caught one of the murderers and under trial by ordeal he confessed our Edith paid him . . .'

'Bloody, bloody hell! So what's the situation now?'

'Edwin wants Morcar Earl of Northumbria in my place. That's what it's all about. That old rogue Aelfgar's fucking brood coming home to roost. And because of the taxes and then Cospatric it's a fucking sight more than just the Northumbrian thegns. They've raised both kingdoms (he meant Mercia and Northumbria), not just the housecarls but the levy too, and marched south.'

Eight years earlier, after several of his earldoms had been given to the Godwin family because of earlier treacheries, Aelfgar, Earl of Mercia and the last great lord in the land who was not a Godwinson, had plotted with both Griffith, who had become his son-in-law, and the Norwegians. Only after Harold and Tostig had finally scotched Griffith in 1062 and Aelfgar had considerately died, leaving Mercia to his young son Edwin, barely a grown man, had the threat been neutralised. Apparently. Now, three years later, they were back – the old alliance of Northumbria and Mercia, albeit with new and immature leaders, challenging the King and the rest of England.

He thought it through, leaving his brother chafing with impatience. At last he sighed.

'How is the King?' he asked.

'Bad. He'll be gone by Christmas.'

'Where is he?'

'Oxford.'

'And Edwin and Morcar?'

'I just told you. Got an army together. Welsh bastards in it too, heading for Northampton when I left the King three days ago.'

Harold sighed again, finished his beer. Suddenly he felt tired, almost old, and his knees ached a little as he stood.

'Wulfric,' he called. 'Get saddled up two hours before dawn. We're going to Oxford.'

He pushed past Tostig and went to the lady's bower. Four hours back in England after nearly two months away and already he was about to be off again. Edith Swan-Neck took him to her couch, and since they had already made love and she knew he was tired and distraught she put his head on her breast and tried to get him to sleep.

But he had much to talk about. First, their sons, Egbert and Godfric, now eighteen and seventeen years old.

'They're all right,' she insisted, smoothing his forehead and pulling the coverlet up over his shoulder. 'Conchobar will see they're all right, don't worry about them.' Conchobar was old Cuthbert's younger brother, her brother-in-law; after her husband Cuthbert had fallen into senility Conchobar and his family had looked after her children whenever she went to England, where neither she nor Harold believed they were entirely safe.

'All right. But I want you to go back to Wexford too. Until everything is settled.'

She ran her hand down his long flank, digging a little with her fingers into the hard muscle below the rib-cage.

But still he was restless and turned away.

'What else is there?' she asked. 'I know. You found a beautiful maiden in Normandy and you want to go back to her.'

'Worse than that.'

He told her about the oaths he had sworn to William, especially the last one.

'It was forced from you by sheer trickery. By the devil's work, for I don't see how else that charlatan could have made you see the things you saw.'

She sat up and leant over him, spoke with all the forcefulness she could muster.

'Listen. It does not count. But already it sits in your heart like an ugly little worm eating away your resolve. Pluck it out. Stamp on it. Forget it.'

Nevertheless, often during the few months that were left, it came back to him like bile at the back of his throat, like a heaviness that sat in his chest when he woke in the morning.

They left when it was still dark. In the yard Edith Swan-Neck held the bridle of his horse.

'Go,' and it was almost a whisper, 'by the Vale of the White Horse. Leave Her some flowers or, better still, a branch of oak. And maybe She'll protect you from that stupid oath.'

He stooped down in the saddle to kiss her, and cradle her cheek with his hand.

'I'll do that,' he said.

Over a hundred miles though it was they were there by mid-afternoon two days later. Almost all the land they crossed was Harold's and it had been possible to change horses whenever they needed to. And this in spite of making a small detour to take in the big Hambledon-like hill with the contoured White Horse scored in its side. There, dismounting, he took the small branch of golden-leafed oak he had plucked in the valley below and laid it above the Horse's head. He had wanted to pray, but did not know what sort of words She would find acceptable, or even the language that would be right. She? A fine lady who wore rings on her fingers and bells on her toes and rode on a white horse. You can see a small image of her to this day in the church at Banbury on the other side of the Thames valley.

As he looked down and across the valleys to the haze of smoke above the city the weariness returned. He glanced back at Tostig, now sitting bolt upright in his saddle, his face flaming, his blue eyes narrowed, spittle driven by the cold breeze from the corners of a mouth that looked mean in spite of his thick lips. He shook his reins.

'Come on our Harold,' he shouted, 'let's get the bulgars sorted.' His horse's hooves kicked up clods of turf as he careered down the steep hill, setting it to jump a low hedge of thorn stained with the bloodlike droplets of its haws.

Almost, thought Harold, as he and his men followed at a more careful trot, I could wish him a broken neck between here and there, between now and what's to come.

CHAPTER
THIRTY-THREE

In 1065 Oxford was a prosperous burgh within better walls and with a more capacious castle than the small motte and bailey affairs most English towns had at the time. Built on what had been the border with the ancient kingdom of Mercia and, at the point where the Thames ceased to be navigable, even with portage where there are now locks, it was an important trading post. Hence the castle. No university yet: it would be a hundred years before the busy town unblemished by spires would be transformed into a cluster of lodging houses.

The King, with his court – that is clerks, officials, scribes and so on – occupied the castle. Archbishops, bishops, abbots, ealdormen, leading thegns, called by the crisis for a Witangemot, were mostly bedded in the city which then boasted nearly three hundred town mansions. Outside and to the north of the city walls the four hundred acres of Port Meadow were dotted with the tents of Edwin and Morcar and their men, a thousand or more. It was rumoured a much larger host had occupied Northampton and was ravaging the surrounding countryside which Edwin claimed belonged by immemorial right to Mercia, though Edward had given it to Tostig.

For almost exactly half a century, first Canute and then Godwin and the Godwinsons had kept war confined to the coasts and borders. Not since Ironside disputed the succession with Canute had there been actual serious bloodshed in the heart of middle England. But now the threat was there again as it had been fourteen years earlier at Gloucester, and for much the same reason – rivalry between the two greatest families in the land was at the root of it.

Edwin and Morcar, the grandsons of Leofric of Mercia, had timed their move well. When Edward died the succession of an English King – be it the Atheling or Harold himself – would certainly be contested by William the Bastard, but probably also by Harald Hardrada, King of Norway, who based his claim on a treaty made between his father Magnus and Canute's son Harthacanute, way back in 1039. Only a united country could possibly deal with the double threat. Edwin was billing Harold in advance for the support of the north and north-east, and with a heart that felt more leaden with every last step he took to Oxford, Harold knew that he would have to cede whatever they demanded.

Though substantial, the castle, little more than a fortified settlement set in the angle of the old walls which formed two sides of it, was not in the least like a Norman one. The pitched roof of a large hall dominated the rest instead of the sheer stone sides of a keep and, while there were armouries, stables, and foodstores in the inner yard, there were also thatched bowers for the women and servants, a flock of sheep held in a sheepcote of hurdles, six cows in milk, a lot of smoke from numerous fires and a continual coming and going of scores of people.

As well as housecarls clanking and jingling with that purposeful walk soldiers always adopt when they want to convince their superiors they are occupied, there were monks scurrying about with piles of parchments in their arms and ink-horns at their belts who really were busy, smiths and farriers, cooks, herdsmen and herdswomen, builders and carpenters putting the place hastily in repair, pedlars, beggars, buskers, children and sightseers, cats, dogs and even a flock of chaffinches scurrying through the husks the horses left. The smells were a healthy mix of woodsmoke, cooking, dung, ordure, and home-brewing – the noise a rustic bedlam. It was about as different from the scene inside the inner ward of the castles at Rouen or Bayeux as can possibly be imagined. No question here of the right thing in the right place – though everything had found a space and seemed to function well enough without being told where to go.

Archbishop Stigand met them in front of the great door to the hall. With one foot on the step, Harold turned on Tostig.

'I don't want you around. You've got to let me settle this on my own.'

Tostig's face flared and his knuckles whitened on his sword hilt.

'Take your men. Find lodgings in the city.'

Tostig held for a moment, then spat on the ground between them. But he turned and with a wave of his hand signalled his ten or so men to follow.

Stigand took Harold's hand. Harold bent his head to kiss the episcopal ring, but Stigand took it away.

'Bugger that sort of flummery,' he said and put an arm round the earl's shoulder, so they walked through the door together.

'Was that wise?' he went on, murmuring throatily, referring to Harold's dismissal of his brother.

'Wise or not, it's done now. How's the King?'

'Up and down, but mostly down. One of his feet is cold, looks dead already, and his sight is going. But his mind is still clear. He backs Tostig, of course. Won't give in. How was Normandy?'

The hall was dark, over-heated with braziers of charcoal. Monks chanted penitential psalms. At the far end, lit with candles so it already looked like a catafalque, Edward lay on a bier, propped up on pillows. His face was thinner, his complexion flushed, his white hair stood out like a halo. Harold slowed his pace to give himself time to answer Stigand.

'Bad,' he said. 'The Bastard got an oath out of me, by trickery and threat, that I would be his man. He's got your number too – have you heard of Lanfranc, a Lombard?'

'The headmaster of Le Bec? Nasty little schemer. Why?'

'He's in line for your job. On his way now to Rome for the Pope's blessing.'

'Well. We'll have to make do the best we can. You are, I take it, telling me that right now we should give Edwin and Morcar what they want in return for their backing against the Bastard?'

'I think we must. It won't have to be for ever. We can sort them out later if we want to. But right now we need them. We'll have to give them what it takes.'

By now they were approaching the King's couch. Edward lifted his head, red-lidded eyes glared until he recognised them, white fingers pulled at the hem of his coverlet.

'Harold? Where have you been? We needed you.'

'You sent me to Normandy. Remember? To bring back Wulfnoth and Hakon.'

'I did?'

You did, thought Harold. And somebody, you yourself perhaps, bribed the ship's master to land us in Ponthieu – which was where our troubles started.

'Anyway. You're back now,' Edward went on. 'And you can sort out this mess.' He looked around, peered into the shadows, made a play of pretending to seek out someone who was not there. 'Where's Tostig, then? I sent him to meet you.'

'He's gone into the town looking for lodgings.'

'What's he want to do that for?' The old man was petulant. 'Plenty of room here. Harold. Sit beside me. And tell that fat priest to go away.'

Stigand moved back into shadows. Harold found a stool and sat beside Edward.

'Harold. We mustn't let them get away with this. It's a direct challenge to my authority and I am not dead yet. It's damn little short of treason.'

He wheezed and waited, but Harold kept his counsel so the King went on without it.

'I don't have to tell you what Tostig means to me.' His expression hardened. His opaque eyes seemed to clear, challenging Harold to comment or sneer. 'For ten years, he's helped me, running things, collecting taxes, that sort of thing. And when you needed him he helped you sort out the Welsh. So. I don't have to tell you all this. But I will tell you what you have to do. Get an army together and deal with these northern raga-muffins the way you dealt with the Welsh. I'm not having Tostig giving up Northumbria and that's an end to it.'

He heaved himself up higher against the pillows and flapped the cov-erlet. A sickly stench fell on the air.

'Damned leg gone rotten. Can you smell it? Yes? You get used to it. So. Normandy. How was the Duke?'

'Very well. He sends you his fondest regards and prays for your speedy recovery.'

'I doubt it. And in any case his prayers will not be answered. But he's a fine young man. He'll make a fine king for you all when I am gone. What do you think, now you've met him?'

Harold said nothing.

'Come on . . . . I asked you a question.'

'I admire William. He is brave and he works hard. But England should have an English king.'

Edward met his gaze and held it. Harold did not flinch away.

'You would be king yourself,' Edward said at last.

'The Witan will decide. I shall speak for the Atheling.'

'That bean-pole! He still sucks his thumb, you know. Anyway, for the moment that is by the way. The business now is to see off these Northumbrian louts. And quickly, too. I want to get back to Westminster. We're consecrating the Abbey over Christmas. I intend to be there if it's the last thing I do. And probably it will be.'

He waved a shaking hand, and Harold realised the audience was at an end.

Stigand fell in with him again on their way down the hall.

'Does he know what he's up to?' Harold asked.

'He knows.' Stigand was grim. 'And when he's not sure of the how of it then the other William, Bishop of London, tells him.'

'So he's deliberately fomenting a civil war to let Duke William in. What does he hope to gain?'

'Revenge on the Godwinsons. Canonisation.'

'Sainthood! Edward?' Harold shook his head, walked on. Then another thought came to him. 'What was Edith up to, ordering the death of Cospatric?'

'You should ask her yourself.'

He did. The Queen of England was in the principal bower nearby, had had the clay and wattles hung with her choicest tapestries and the place lit with gold oil-lamps – Moorish work wrought in fantastical designs, all stuff that travelled in big, closed carts, wherever the court took her. A harpist strummed a ground to a wailing flute and the large, high-roofed room was filled with the odours of spikenard and rosewater. She herself was curled up in a big chair, with her knees drawn up on one side and her elbow supporting her flaming head on the other. The redness of her hair strewn with pearls, the whiteness of her skin, the flimsiness of the long but slit samite robe she wore filled the space around her. Her beauty caught Harold by the throat as it always had, and was hardly diminished by age (she was now in her late thirties and some six years younger than him) unless she exposed unpainted the lines in her neck, the crowsfeet at the corners of her eyes, and the thinness of lips to full daylight. And that she hardly ever did.

A shaggy Afghan hound, long-snouted, long coat the colour of white gold, a gift from a Persian ambassador who had been seeking favourable trading terms with England, bared teeth at Harold's approach but sank back at a murmured command.

She offered her brother her cheek. He brushed it with his lips, took her hand and gently squeezed.

Then he straightened and looked down at her. She met his stare through a curtain of lashes made, as was the custom, from spiders' legs.

'You're angry with me,' she said. 'I can tell.'

'Why did you have Cospatric murdered?'

'The news was that Duke William was waiting for an opportunity to kill you in a way that would not attach too much blame to himself. No one expected your safe return. But then no one expected you to swear an oath of fealty to him either.

'Think of it,' she went on; 'England without my dear husband and without my best of brothers. It could have been Mercia and Northumbria with Cospatric, whose royal blood is after all Northumbrian, as figurehead – all this against the Atheling and the rest of England. And William waiting until we had torn ourselves apart.'

'But that's what has happened. The Northumbrians have marched to avenge Cospatric.'

She was not her father's daughter for nothing nor the sister of Harold himself. Her knees swung down and she sat upright.

'Balls,' she said. 'Wherever did you get that idea? They were already on the way, and marching, they said, to put Cospatric on the throne of ancient Northumbria if not of the whole of England. That, at any rate, we scotched.'

He took a turn around the room, chewing his thumb, chain-mail jingling. She was hard, sharp, ruthless as well as beautiful. A priceless ally, a wicked enemy. And he would need her in the coming months, he was sure.

'All right,' he said at last. 'But I'm back now. I intend to rule when your husband has gone, at least until the Atheling is of age. You must help me but mainly by doing my bidding. Don't act unless or until I tell you to. Above all do nothing behind my back.'

Impressed by the strength that seemed to have flooded back into him, and heart pounding too, she offered the promise he asked for, then pressed him to stay and drink a little wine with her. He sat beside her on the arm of the big chair and put his left hand on her further shoulder. She let her head rest against his chest.

'You seem . . . certain about all this. Do you want to be King so much?'

'A crown is a fine thing, but no more than a bauble. Together, you, Tostig, the young ones and I have ruled England since Dad died. A crown makes little difference.'

'What then?'

'William. The Normans. They are, well . . .' he hesitated, laughed, unable to express the way the awfulness of Normandy had focused his understanding, even a love of his people and the way they lived. 'They are . . .' he shrugged. 'Bastards.'

CHAPTER
THIRTY-FOUR

E dwin and Morcar would not meet Harold inside the castle walls.
Harold refused to go down to Port Meadow. Envoys trotted back
and forth between the meadow and the burgh until a meeting
was fixed for the following morning, two hours after day-break, in the
vestry of the big Saxon church. The rule of the King's Peace was to be
strictly adhered to – no weapons within a hundred paces of the meeting
place, ten unarmed men on each side, no more. Both sides, somewhat to
the Northerners' surprise, agreed that it would be better if Tostig, who
seemed to be at the heart of the whole business, should not be present.

It was agreed that Ealdred, Archbishop of York, would speak for the
sons of Aelfgar and, initially at any rate, Stigand, Archbishop of
Canterbury, would speak for Harold, who would represent the King. But
first both prelates and the clerks who were there joined in a brief service
imploring the Holy Spirit to descend and fill their hearts with a sincere
longing for peace and a just settlement to their differences.

With that out of the way, and many a heretofore and whereas, York
then set out the Northerners' grievances against Tostig: his harshness
when dealing with tax defaulters; the way he over-rode local feelings and
traditions where he felt they were irrational or did not work for the
common good; the fact that he often treated the Northumbrian thegns
as little more than heathen louts and had frequently accused them without good reason of plotting with their equals over the border. Some had
even accused Tostig of plotting with the Scottish King Malcolm with

whom he was known to be friendly since he had escorted him over the
borders and down to Westminster to meet Edward some ten years earlier. Then there was the way his officers always expected their southern
dialects to be understood by people who actually spoke a mongrel version of Norse or Danish – wheretofore, enough was enough: the
Northumbrians wanted Tostig out, and were happy to accept Morcar,
brother of Edwin, Earl of Mercia, in his place.

Stigand spoke brusquely, his deep voice rattling in the barrel of his
chest. He was not here to repudiate the lies that had been told about
Tostig, a capable and just administrator as well as a gallant leader of men
in the recent campaign against the Welsh, he was here, he said, simply to
remind all that it was the King's prerogative to reward his loyal servants
with lands and rank, that this had been tradition and custom for hundreds of years, for that is what it means to be a king, a lord and
ring-giver, and that it was the King's wish that Tostig should be and
should remain Earl of Northumbria. And anyone who gainsaid this
might as well leave the room, indeed pack his bags and leave the country, before he was arraigned for treason.

Impasse. Timor, who stood with Walt on one side of the door that led
back into the church – two of Edwin's men stood on the other – yawned
and sighed.

'I reckon we're here for the day, maybe the week.'

'How's that then?' Walt asked. 'It seems pretty clear-cut to me.'

'Neither is talking to the point, and neither dares to. And until they do
we're stuck here.'

'The point?'

'It's not about Tostig at all. It's about how much our Harold is ready
to give these barbarians in return for their support when the King
dies.'

'Oh!'

From their vantage point on a step in front of the door Walt looked
over them all with more interest than he had felt so far.

Edwin and Morcar, brothers. Earl Edwin the older, early twenties, the
fairer of the two, good figure, but something shifty and weak in his
face – a chin that was not quite all there, a narrow forehead. Morcar
darker, scarcely out of his teens, a touch embarrassed, not yet quite sure
of how he should conduct himself at a meeting of this sort, but showing
an inner strength Edwin lacked.

Then there was Ealdred of York, a decent enough old man, still clutching his crozier which shook a little in his hand. He had carefully avoided breaking canon law in any respect and for this, and on account of his age which meant he would have to be replaced shortly anyway, he was tolerated by Rome. Which was not the case with Stigand who was an excommunicated pluralist with at least one wife.

They were complementary. Stigand looked after the church's pastoral duties: his clergy married if they wanted to; they were not devout and often illiterate, but they performed their duties conscientiously and were welcomed and valued by the ordinary people. Consequently there was little trouble on quarter days when tithes and dues were collected, and most peasants seemed to think they were getting value for the one-in-ten or one-in-five days they spent working for the church. Ealdred, on the other hand, made sure that the few abbeys and monasteries were well-run and free from scandal, that the fabric of buildings was kept up, and above all it was he who consecrated new priests and bishops, performed marriages and such-like where the union was of some consequence, and thus gave everything the church did in that way a legality under canon law it would have lacked had Stigand performed these duties.

The clerks from both sides now formed a huddle round a small table in front of the fireplace. They spread maps and deeds and got out their quills and ink-horns, their slates and squeaky pencils, and attempted to draw up a protocol whereby withdrawals could be agreed, de-militarised zones declared, dates when the next meetings should be held, and so on.

The vestry, which was not large, began to fill with smoke from the fire that had been lit in the big stone fireplace – the chimney perhaps needed sweeping, the logs were green.

Edwin detached himself from his followers and moved through the smoke-filled room to the other side where Harold was standing.

They mumbled greetings at each other, Edwin cracked an imported walnut in his palm and offered half the kernel to Harold, who laughed.

'I'll have all of it or none,' he said.

Edwin shrugged, picked the flesh out of his left palm with his right hand and put it all in his own mouth, letting the shattered shell drop to the floor.

'You can't be serious,' he said.

'About what?'

'About fighting us, arraigning us for treason, all that crap.'

'I certainly am. The harvest is over. It's been a good one – there's food in hand, and coin too. We'll have no problem with the fyrd. Between us, my brothers and I can put four thousand housecarls in the field. We'll be fighting in the King's name. You stand as much chance as . . .' he searched his mind for a really telling, original comparison and found one, 'as a snowball in hell. We'll have you well sorted before winter sets in.'

By which he meant: 'before the King dies'.

Edwin shrugged, strolled back to where Morcar was standing.

'Yon fond fyoul wansa fecht,' he said, lapsing into dialect.

And at that moment there was a sudden pounding at the door.

A young cleric burst in. The King had fallen into a deep sleep from which none could wake him. The whole gathering now ran, or in the case of those who had horses to hand, galloped back up to the castle. Harold, with Walt, Timor and the two rebellious brothers from Mercia were amongst the first to storm down the rush-strewn hall. The arch-bishops, carried in litters by their servants, were not far behind.

Edward was lying back on his pillows with his arthritic fingers neatly linked on the coverlet that covered his chest. A crystal and gold rosary was laced through them. His colour was good, but his breath shallow and wheezy. The general air of cleanliness, neatness and peacefulness that sur-rounded him might have been ascribed by the superstitious to the sanctity of an old man about to enter the presence of his Maker. The more practical observer would have noted the presence of Queen Edith, dressed now in black watered silk apart from a white snood held in place by a gold coronet, sitting in the shadow with her ladies in atten-dance.

As the men approached those who wore headgear doffed it and all fell silent, trying as hard as they could without actually walking on tiptoe to move quietly, grasping any armour or chains about them to stop them jangling. They made a semicircle around the King and for a moment nothing was said. Then the monks behind the Queen and her ladies began softly to intone the *Miserere Nobis*.

'End of an era?' whispered Morcar.

'Let's hope not,' muttered Harold.

Edward opened one glassy pink eye.

'Barley soup,' he said. 'And then you can take me to Westminster.'

*

They had had a fright. As they walked out into the open air, where a soft rain had begun to fall and the chickens were running into the stables for shelter, Edwin stopped and turned to Harold.

'Let's not mess about any more. You can't take on William without us. You know what we want. Give it to us and we're your men. Together we'll see the Bastard off.'

'What if I refuse?'

'Then you really will have to raise the fyrd and shift us by force.' Edwin turned and set off down the now greasy cobbles towards the postern. 'Look. If you're thinking we might go back to York without a fight or without getting what we want, that we might even be considering a deal with William, then think again. We're not fools. William's not coming here to redistribute England amongst the English.'

Surprised at this hint of political acumen Harold looked at him.

'You're certainly right about that,' he said. 'None of us, none of us,' he repeated, 'should be in any doubt about that. All right. I'll talk to Tostig. You'll hear from me.'

'Wanker. Fucking wanker. Spineless, spunkless, womanising wanker!'

Harold leant against the door and waited. Tostig continued to storm about the big first-floor room which he had rented from a prosperous brewer, looking for things to smash, but he had already run through what little there was, including a half-filled chamber pot. The bed remained, a stout oak-frame, and even that he lifted and thumped down every now and then. At last he calmed a little, enough at any rate to explain how very thoroughly he understood his position.

'You know what you're doing? This totally dishonours me. It dishonours my wife and her brother the Count of Bruges. Above all it dishonours you. Why are you doing this to me?'

Harold pushed his back off the door.

'I accept all you say. But I think a time has come when we must consider the possibility that there are things more important than individual honour, the honour even of a family.'

'What sort of things? What the fuck are you talking about? The only thing you are putting in front of my honour and your own good name is the chance you might pluck a crown out of all this for yourself—'

'That is not the case. I should as soon see the Atheling on the throne as me.'

'So. What? What is this new thing that is so much more important than honour?'

Harold turned to the window, pushed back the shutters. The room filled with the noise and smells of the street. Busyness and business, trading, making, doing. Distant hills and forests. Raining still, but not much, not much more than a light mist. Evening not far off. Sudden burst of laughter from a pub nearby where he knew his eight men were hoisting a few pints. Perhaps he'd join them. He turned from the window.

'Not easy to explain,' he said. 'But put it like this. This, all this, the hides, hundreds, shires, earldoms and all who live in them, look to us to protect them. If we have a civil war now, over Northumbria, over a matter of honour, many people will be killed. Much of the country will be laid waste, villages pillaged, towns plundered . . .'

'By what right do we rule, Harold? Answer me that.'

Harold shrugged. Tostig went on.

'By right of honour. Our name. Throw that away, as you will do if you turn me out, there's no reason anyone should follow you or yours. You will forfeit the right to rule.'

'Let me finish. If we fight for you we will win. We'll get you back your Earldom—'

'I've not lost it yet.'

'And the name of Godwinson will be hated north of the Trent for a generation. Yet within months, weeks even, we shall be asking them to join us to fight the Norman. What's left of us. And of them. And because we shall have just ripped them apart, burnt their villages, raped their women and killed their best men, they won't. They'll tell us to bugger off.'

'But still we shall have our honour, our good name. Godwinsons may be hated and feared, but we will be honoured still, and they'll be glad to keep us where we are.'

'Oh shit! Just shut up, will you?' It was Harold's temper now that was going. 'You just don't understand, do you? These people have a decent life, they'll fight for it, but they look to us to lead them—'

'But their lives will be the same whoever leads them. So. The Bastard wins. He won't, but suppose he does. He'll raise taxes, demand an armed man from every five hides, just as we do. He'll boot out the thegns who supported us, and put in his own, just as we have in the past. But for the peasants, the farm-workers, the townspeople, ordinary people it'll all go on the same—'

'It won't. It will not. That's what I'm trying to get across to you, into your thick skull. I've been there, I've seen how they do things in Normandy. Nine tenths live in slavery. The lords do what they like, they own everything, there's no law or justice and they seem to believe that's how God wants things to be, I know—'

'Bullshit. You'll bundle me out for the sake of the ordinary people?'

Harold said nothing.

'Oh, for fuck's sake go fuck yourself.' Again Tostig banged about the room, and for a moment it seemed he might even hit his older brother. 'If you were doing it for the crown I would at least understand. But doing it because you think the crap out there in the streets and fields will be better off ruled by you than by William . . . well. Spare me. I'm off.'

'Where to?'

'First through every estate I have between here and Dover, collecting the men whose lord I am. A couple of hundred, maybe five if I'm lucky—'

'I . . . we could use those men when the Bastard comes.'

'They're mine. I'll take Judith back to Bruges, winter it out there, then I'll be back. You bet your fucking fine feelings I'll be back. Now get off my back.'

Next morning the Witangemot met in the castle hall. King Edward presided from his bier, crown on, sitting up, smiling sightlessly as dull shapes passed in front of him. When below him, in the body of the hall, Archbishop Ealdred called the meeting to order, he nodded off and the crown slipped a little towards his left ear.

There were about fifteen of them who were of any importance. The two archbishops, Harold and his two younger brothers Leofwine and Gyrth, Edwin and Morcar, a few more bishops and abbots. Behind them thirty or so of the major land-holding earls, ealdormen and thegns.

Harold took the floor. Edwin and Morcar had, he said, joined with him that very morning at Mass in the Holy Church of Christchurch and given their solemn oaths that, when the King died (and we all hope and pray he may live for many years . . . amen, amen to that, said all), they would abide by the choice of the Witangemot and support by arms, money, land, kin and any other means they had whomever the Witangemot chose to succeed. And in particular they would resist any foreign incursion or invasion that might occur in support of any claimant not elected by the Witangemot.

Moreover, they would withdraw the troops who were now camping outside the city walls and disband these and all other armies at present harrying the countryside round Northampton and other parts, sending all back to their homes without any further plundering or marauding.

In earnest of which he, Harold, acting for the King, here pronounced and decreed that Morcar, brother of Earl Edwin of Mercia, would take upon him the style and all the appurtenances, demesnes, emoluments (and so on, and so on) that went with the Earldom of Northumbria . . .

It seemed to be all over. Sweating slightly and wondering now if after all he had done the right thing, Harold went over to Edwin who came to meet him, embraced him, took his right hand in his left and turned to face the assembly.

'My lords,' Edwin said, 'Harold has spoken wisely and well. A state of perfect amity, love and harmony now exists between his family and mine. And, so all might know the truth of this, I hereby now and in front of you all offer to him Aldyth, my sister, to be his wedded wife, thus seal-ing in holy matrimony not only the bond between two people but two families for the common weal of all.'

Harold's face went white like white lead then the colour flooded back. His hand was still entwined with Edwin's and for a moment Edwin too went pale but with pain as he felt the crushing grip squeeze the bones in his palm together. Harold looked out and over all the people assembled in front of him. On the faces of some he saw barely concealed smirks, on others worried frowns, but most were stonily passive, anxious not to reveal their reactions to what was clearly a carefully planned but still extremely risky move on Edwin's part.

They all knew the situation. Harold was not married, and really a man of his position should be. For thirteen or fourteen years he had had a mistress, Edith Swan-Neck, the wife of a thegn who had land in the ancient Danish settlement of Wexford. She remained just what she always had been – Harold's mistress, a concubine. Such women can and should be cast off if political exigencies demand it. He could, of course, make what settlement he liked on her, and on their children, from his personal goods, that was no one's business but his, but in the world of power and power-broking she was not a factor.

There was, however, a much more serious aspect. Already, by stripping Tostig of his earldom and, apparently, forcing him into exile the sons of Aelfgar had struck a powerful blow against the Godwinsons both in terms of the prestige and the land they controlled – but this was much more serious. If, and clearly it was meant to happen, if Aldyth bore Harold a son quite soon, then that son would one day be a claimant to the English throne. And when that day came in all probability he would still be young if not actually a minor. If that was the case, then the Queen would become regent, and would naturally turn to her own kin to rule with her. In short, Aelfgar's sons were making precisely the same move to consolidate their power and influence on the crown that the Godwinsons had made when they insisted Edward should marry Edith.

Harold shook his head, not in refusal but to clear it. He let go of Edwin's hand. The third factor, the one of most importance there and then, was that a public refusal in front of the Witangemot would be seen to be so discourteous, so humbling to Aldyth and her kin, that all possible alliance let alone friendship between the two clans would be at an end. He chose his words with the greatest care he could muster on the spur of the moment.

'Edwin, my brother. The fame of your sister's beauty and virtue has travelled to the ends of the earth.' Since she was believed to be only thirteen years old her virtue at least would seem to be beyond dispute. 'Such a paragon deserves to be wed with all the pomp and ceremony we can muster. We must take counsel together to be sure that this is the case. This is a matter which, with all the other affairs that beset us now, should not be entered into too lightly or with less than worthy preparation . . .'

'But you will marry her?'

Harold, now much recovered from the initial shock, took a step back and eyed the younger man slowly from head to toe and finally met his eye, until Edwin looked down.

'Of course. When the time is ripe.'

And that was all he said. He turned to go but Morcar now intervened.

'Harold, there is one other thing to settle.'

'There is?'

Harold only half-turned, contrived to communicate a certain impatience beneath a veil of kingly, yes kingly, condescension.

Morcar blushed but pushed on.

'You have granted me the Earldom of Northumbria. When the same Earldom was granted to your brother Tostig, Waltheof, the surviving son of Old Siward, was only eight years old. He is now eighteen—'

'Can Waltheof not speak for himself?'

'My lord, I can.'

From amongst the thegns assembled behind the brothers, a young man, very tall, very well-built, good-looking, too, stepped forward.

'Well, Waltheof. What would you have?'

'My lord, the Earldoms of Northampton and Huntingdon, which your brother Tostig held as well as Northumbria . . .'

'Enough. Tostig is on his way to Dover by now. He has renounced what is more valuable than any lands, namely the love I bore him. Take them—'

There was a sudden stir behind him, and then a long coughing fit. The King.

Recovering from the fit and supported now by his Queen, who had her arm about his shoulder and was mopping his brow, he sat bolt upright.

'Tostig!' he croaked, then cleared his throat. 'Tosty?'

He peered out down the hall, shaded his eyes with his hand, realised his crown was awry. He straightened it.

'Tostig,' he repeated. 'Did someone say my Tosty has gone? Without a proper farewell to me?'

Queen Edith whispered in his ear: 'You were asleep, Eddie. He didn't want to wake you.'

'Ah. He always was a good boy, a good lad. He'll be back, he'll be back.'

With his Queen's help he settled himself again into the pillows.

'Tosty will be back,' he croaked for the last time but with warm satisfaction in his voice.

To all who could hear him it sounded like a threat, a curse even, reinforced by the way a sudden breath of cold wind gusted under the big doors and set the rushes slithering and lifting over the tiled floor.

Chapter
Thirty-Five

It was bitterly cold. A north-easterly like a banshee howled down the Thames from the city three miles away, cutting across the flats and marshes between, silvering the grey water with white wavelets chopped up by the ebbing tide and the river's current. Grey spume gathered in the reeds. The same wind shredded the smoke from the thousands of hearths behind the Roman walls and carried the smells of the city (woodsmoke, the fumes from forges, tanneries and breweries, ordure both human and animal) right to the big west door of the newest abbey church in Christendom.

Around it a vast crowd had gathered but huddled, diminished by the cold, pulling cloaks, animal skins and furs close round their bodies, grumbling, complaining at the delay. The reeves and counsellors of the greatest men in the land were disputing precedence. Since the King was dying a scant hundred yards away, in the Great Hall, precedence was important. The last man into the church would be seen to be the man most likely to succeed him.

Three groups of mounted men stood out, two of them ranged against the third. On one side of the great door the brothers Edwin and Morcar, Earls of Mercia and now Northumbria, sat beneath their standards on shaggy but sturdy ponies that stamped and occasionally bucked with a sharp jingle of harness. Their thegns and housecarls, also mounted, clustered around them, maybe a hundred all told with another hundred or so grooms and freemen standing behind them. The housecarls wore their armour, helmets, byrnies of chain-mail, carried broad-swords or battle-axes, leaf-shaped shields slung behind their backs; the men were armed with seven-foot lances and round shields, bossed and covered with polished leather.

On the other side – Harold Godwinson, Earl of Wessex, whose retinue almost equalled in numbers the combined followings of Edwin and Morcar. And behind him his younger brothers Leofwine of Kent and Gyrth of East Anglia.

Walt, mounted on a pony, carried Harold's standard with the base of its stave on his right foot – the gold dragon of Wessex on a background faded from purple to red. Beside him, in support, rode Daffydd, the swarthy Welsh princeling.

Walt looked up at the huge walls in front of him and shuddered, and not just with the cold. It was a monster, this building whose consecration they had come to witness.

It was, he supposed, the biggest building in Christendom. Certainly the biggest in England. And although its size and grandeur had been apparent almost ever since Walt had first set foot in Westminster or seen it across the bend of the river from London, it had until now always been fenced in, cocooned by a tight cage of scaffolding timbers, wattle hurdles, and surrounded by a shanty town of workmen's huts and halls. Cranes and hoists had risen above it and remained above it even as it grew, and the smoke of fires and the dust of stone dressed on the site had made a cloud which, in the final stages, had contained too the noxious fumes of smelted lead and copper. Sometimes this cloud darkened the sun, turned it red at noon.

It was alien, foreign, out of place, an intrusion. It was too big. It was formed out of big blocks of pale grey stone, not far off corpse colour, that had been dragged and trundled and carted from almost the furthest reaches of the kingdom, after first being laboriously cut from deep quarries. A lot of men had died moving, dressing and finally heaping those banal cubes of stone, one on top of another.

Through the use of giant round pillars, linked by semi-circular arches with galleries of smaller arches above them, it had been possible to raise a roof three, four times higher than any Saxon church and enclose a space big enough to cover a sizeable village. And it had nothing to do with Walt's people, nor his religion. The men who designed it, who instructed and commanded the Celtic serfs who made it and often died in the making of it, were all French, Normans, speaking their nasal harsh tongue, and arrogant with it. Most of the craftsmen too were Normans, the glaziers, the stone-masons, the lead and copper smiths, though some came from even more distant lands and spoke in tongues entirely foreign.

The faith it celebrated was Roman, the Pope's and the Emperor's, not the people's. Its tongue was Latin, and not just during the offices and masses. It was said it was a universal language but Walt had come to think of it as a code, something that set aside its users, gave them a power, a belonging, an exclusivity which shut others out. He had a confused sense of an entity beyond the Channel of which Normandy and even Rome itself were merely parts, a Grendel-like monster which could swallow all and make all part of itself. Europe?

He shuddered again and thought briefly of the churches he had known and felt comfortable in. The best had been no bigger than a thegn's hall, most much smaller, sheds really, wattle and daub filling in timber frames, with floors of impacted red clay, thatched roofs and small altars. And inside, simple things – carved stone and painted plaster that told of Our Lord's life as if he really had been a man with a real mother and friends, who knew hunger, thirst, and cold, but who also knew of weddings and feasting, a man, in short, you could talk to. He thought of the priests who served such churches, who mumbled a Latin mass they understood scarcely more than you did, but helped you mourn and rejoice in your own language, and in hard times when the cattle died of murrain and the children of agues, forgave the peasants their tithe and even found some cheese or barley of their own to help them out.

Noise, and a stir in the crowd broke his reverie. From the back of his pony Walt could see the approaching processions. From London down the narrow road that crossed the River Fleet came William, London's Norman bishop, mounted on a palfrey with a cross and censer in front of him and a choir of chanting monks behind.

Meanwhile Archbishop Stigand crossed the river from Lambeth in a barge beneath a baldachin of some magnificence. Archbishop of Canterbury, yes, but excommunicated by the Pope. Why? Because, never mind the pluralism and his wives, he was a Saxon and the Kentishmen of Canterbury had driven Robert the Norman out of Canterbury.

And from the Great Hall of Westminster, between the abbey church and the river where Stigand would shortly land, carried on a palanquin

as magnificent as the archbishop's, the Queen. Edith. Beneath her snood
a simple gold coronet gleamed above deep-set eyes, high cheek-bones.
Her hand gloved in white kid, jewelled with gold and amethyst, clutched
at the piles of black and grey furs – bear, beaver, wolf – that were heaped
beneath and over her.

Harold swung his leg, gartered with leather above thick woollen hose,
over the pommel of his saddle, dropped himself with animal grace to the
ground and strode towards his sister's palanquin. He was now in his
prime – not the prime of a young man who has thrown off youth, but
on the cusp of fullest manhood, the moment before the wheel turns and
the descent into old age begins. He too wore a gold circlet in his heavy,
grizzled brown hair, a dun tunic beneath a heavy crimson cloak fastened
with a brooch in the likeness of a gold dragon intricately shaped.
Scabbarded in tooled leather, his heavy broad-sword with its elaborate
gold pommel and quills slapped his muscled thigh.

Walt handed the standard to Daffydd and followed him, respectfully
distant but wary too, ready to leap to his aid at the slightest hint of danger.

At the side of his sister's litter Harold reached up, took her gloved
hand, briefly touched it to his lips. Above it he murmured: 'The King is
too ill to come?'

'He cannot hold his water nor his shit. He stinks.'

'How long before . . .?'

'The Norman doctors, priests, give him until spring . . .'

'Until the weather's good enough for the Bastard to make his crossing?'

Edith shrugged bird-like shoulders beneath her furs.

'The Danish shaman our mother sent has cast his runes and says it will
be on the last day of Christmas.'

'I am sorry to hear it is as bad as that.'

The Queen pulled back her hand but a tiny smile spread her painted
lips as she gave a slight snort of suppressed laughter.

Harold looked around him.

'You are poorly guarded for a queen.'

'As sister to the Earl of Wessex I am poorly guarded.'

'Let my housecarls go before and behind you.'

She shrugged assent and Harold signed to Walt that his bodyguard
should form up around the Queen.

William, Bishop of London, hammered on the great door with the stave of his jewelled crozier, and called, in Latin, for all the devils to come out. A smaller door within the great door flew open and a flock of urchins dressed as imps scurried into the icy air. The priests entered the great nave and the chanting of monks rose up and the spaces filled with incense. The Earls of Kent and Anglia, followed by Northumbria and Mercia, entered first, and Harold of Wessex, with the Queen, came last.

CHAPTER
THIRTY-SIX

'Is that you, Morcar?'

'Sire, it is.'

'Come closer. I cannot see you.'

Morcar moved forward from Edwin's side. He had to stop himself from pushing his palm into his face, allowing the muscles there to contract in disgust. A miasma surrounded the king – a brew of liquid faeces, urine, incense and the spiced oils the clerks rubbed into knuckles knotted with rheumatism like the boles of a pollarded willow. It was undercut with something worse, the sickly sweet smell a wound exudes when it does not heal and the flesh rots though the man still lives. The King's feet had gone.

Morcar glanced back at Edwin and then down the long wide lattice of blackened beams that straddled the low hall, at the fires that burned in the middle at intervals right down to the big doors at the far end, at the shifting tapestries and curtains which closed off the alcoves where the household slept. He knelt by the pallet, heaped with furs, and kissed the sapphire ring that gleamed somewhere in the knotted fingers, the way a piece of iron or a potsherd can be absorbed and almost grown over by the bark of an ancient tree. The other hand fumbled over a reliquary which lay upon the King's chest. Carved crystal mounted in gold, it held a sliver of wood from Christ's Cross.

'Morcar, Earl of Northumbria.' The old man rumbled, cleared his throat. 'Come close. I do not wish what we say to be overheard.'

Morcar pushed his head closer to the old man's. He looked into watery eyes from which yellow rheum leaked at the corners, and marked how the irises were almost filled with sugary opacity.

'They tell me I have not set my seal to the charter that confirms your title. To whom will you swear fealty when I am gone?'

A tricky question – under the circumstances.

'To the man the Witan chooses.'

'And in whose favour will your voice be heard when the Witan meets?'

The King stirred and a gust of foetid gas wafted round them. Morcar suppressed the retching fit that threatened him. When one's rights over a quarter of a kingdom are to be legitimated, one discovers powers of self-denial one did not know one had. Nevertheless, he played safe.

'I shall follow Edwin's advice. He is my elder brother.'

Edward the Confessor sighed, or at any rate drew breath over phlegm into rattling lungs.

'These are weasel words. Tell Edwin to approach.'

Morcar signalled to his brother who knelt beside him and also kissed the ring.

'In whose favour will Edwin's voice be heard when the Witan meets?'

'Sir, may you live . . .'

'A thousand years? Don't fool with me, boy.' A hectic flush briefly coloured the dying man's cheeks. 'You cannot give your voice to Harold Godwinson. William, Duke William is the man.'

The young men remained on their knees, but did not speak.

Not far away, in the Abbot's room above the cloister of the abbey church of Westminster, William, Bishop of London, confronted Harold Godwinson, Earl of Wessex. They waited in silence for the mulled wine William had asked for. Still tall and lean, of course, he had, however, lost the last of his hair – and his tonsure with it.

A monk brought in a silver bowl and horn cups mounted in silver. The air filled with fragrances – cinnamon and nutmeg.

'You cannot speak on your own behalf. In the Witan. You gave your oath to Duke William that you would be his man and that you would support his rightful claim. A solemn oath sworn on the toe of St Louis and the ring finger of St Denis. Such oaths are not broken lightly.'

'It was, I believe, St Denis's ear.'

Bishop William scowled: Harold was being frivolous, impertinent, or both.

They drank. William scarcely allowed his lips to touch the steaming amber liquid. Harold relished the warmth that spread from his gullet and stomach. He set down the cup, wiped his dark moustache and laughed.

'It was a jape, a trick. The sort of thing old men do to make their grandchildren marvel and laugh. An illusion. The relics were hidden beneath a cloth. Once I had sworn the cloth was whipped away.'

'Even if that were the case, it remains an oath.'

'It was a trick.' Anger lent more colour to the leathery red of his cheeks. 'I swore fealty to William on his land, in Normandy, anywhere where he rules by right. Nothing more.'

'When Edward dies this too will be the Duke's land. If you do not heed your oath you will be excommunicated.'

'It will not be his land until the Witan elects him.'

'What sort of law is this that allows a gaggle of old men and young bloods decide who is king?'

'A good law.'

'Kings are not elected by people. They are chosen by God and by God's right they reign.'

'And how does God express his will?'

'Through the principle of royalty, through royal blood. William is kin to Edward. You are not. You have not a drop of royal blood in your veins.'

Harold thought for a moment and let the heat from the cup warm his large, scarred hands. But more than his hands the wine was warming his brain. It was strong stuff and it liberated something deep inside which had been waiting to get out ever since he had heard from his sister that the King was dying. Since his father's death thirteen years ago he had ruled in England in all but name. Now that was in his grasp, too. He was not greedy for the bauble, but nevertheless he felt a surge of liberation at the thought, a wonderful feeling that at last he would be his own man and no one else's. He turned away from the prelate and a slow smile spread across his broad face. He gulped off the rest of the wine.

'My Lord Bishop, you have cast the scales from my eyes, shown me the paths of righteousness and the error of my ways.' There was no apology in his voice; it was, rather, a deep crow of delight. 'I shall speak at the Witan, but only for royal blood.'

'Explain yourself.'

'I shall speak for Edgar the Atheling, the Prince. Son of Edward the Atheling who was son of Edmund Ironside, who was King of Wessex, and son of Ethelred, King of England. There is no blood more royal in England than that of Edgar, the Prince.'

The Bishop chewed on the knuckle of his right hand until the bone became red.

'You would give the realm into the care of a fifteen-year-old brat,' he growled at last.

'Since that seems to be God's will, so be it.'

But the Witan would do no such thing, and both of them knew it.

On the first of January 1066, the Feast of the Circumcision of Our Lord, William, Bishop of London, accompanied by his personal chaplain, entered the King's hall in full penitential procession, with the black-cowled monks of the new Abbey behind him and a magnificent silver censer swung in front. Altar boys carried candles on silver holders draped with the purple of penitence, and the crucifer in front of him carried a wood and ivory crucifix, also draped in purple. He had been told that the King's lapses into unconsciousness were becoming more frequent and prolonged: it was time to hear the old man's last confession.

This did not take much time. Long ago he had been absolved of the grievous sins of his youth and middle-age. Having spent his last years in pious contemplation and good works, and made several confessions of past misdeeds, Edward the Confessor now had little to confess to beyond occasional impatience with the ills of old age and extreme vexation that he had not been well enough to attend the consecration of his Abbey. William pronounced absolution then took the King's swollen and gnarled old hand in both of his, stroked it gently, and spoke in a quiet and conciliatory voice of the trials and patience of Job, of how Moses was granted sight of the Holy Land but was not permitted to enter it, and so on.

He then went on to talk of how his holiness the Pope himself knew of and spoke with deep admiration of the old King's sanctity and good works, of the blamelessness of his life, in recent years, at least, that beatification was already talked of, and of how canonisation must follow. Edward would not be the first king to be sainted for serving the Pope and bringing wayward Christians under the holy yoke of Rome. Louis the Pious of France had pre-empted the Day of Judgement and made it to Heaven by the same route.

'One thing remains,' the bishop concluded, 'to set the seal on a holy life spent in the service of the true church. To ensure there is no backsliding on the part of the Celts to their old ways, or of the Danes to paganism, in order to be sure that the abuses of the English church are cleaned up, you must name Duke William your successor. His Holiness in Rome has already blessed his claim and it behoves you to do likewise.'

The furrows between the King's white brows deepened, though his almost sightless eyes remained expressionless. The bishop leant closer.

'But I already have,' he heard the old man mumble.

'But it needs reaffirmation, public reaffirmation if the people are to accept the Duke as their rightful king.'

The frown deepened. With some irritation the bishop accepted that there was a problem. The Confessor had gone too far down the road of terminal decay to speak or even appear in public. He looked round the long room, at the Kings's housecarls and thegns. Particularly he singled out the lean, awkward figure of the Atheling, who, in this time of stress, was sucking his thumb even more voraciously than usual. And he noted the absence of the Earls and their men. Nevertheless, he must do it now – there might not be a second opportunity. Raising his voice and speaking as solemnly as only a prelate knows how, he announced:

'The King has named his royal cousin Duke William of Normandy to rule in his place. I have heard it from his own lips.'

He turned on his heel and cruised down the hall, scattering blessings as he went. The monks from the Abbey and the chapter of his own basilica of St Paul's on Ludgate Hill hurriedly formed up behind him, taking up the *miserere nobis* from where they had left off.

On the threshold William paused, breathed in the cold fresh air. Then he shook his head and in tones of refined disgust muttered: 'That, I must suppose, was the odour of sanctity.'

Christmas comes but once a year and, in a hall which had once served as the dwelling and offices of the master-builders who had built the Abbey, Edwin's and Morcar's men caroused. Presently the earls withdrew behind hangings that had separated the master-builder's office from the rest.

There was a large, smooth table on which a vellum sheet had been left. Its black ink denoted the way the north tower should be constructed to allow for a belfry, yet to be installed. On it were the subtle instruments that measured angles and a pair of pins joined at the top with an adjustable screw that allowed the master to measure distances across the design.

There were chairs, too, leather slung across trestles and backed with leather, which they sat in.

A cheer outside signalled the arrival of a hogshead of brown ale. Presently a youth brought in a jug of it and two cups. Edwin poured out the ale, drank, wiped his thin moustache, and leant back. The room was dark, the only light from a couple of smoking candles, and his face sank into the shadows.

'It's a bugger, our Morcar. Yes?'

'Yes.'

'What then shall we do? Haver and we're done for. Thing is: we don't know what sort of deal he cut with Tostig.'

They'd been through this often enough, but the moment of serious truth was upon them so they went through it again.

'Tostig slipped away so fucking easy, let you put on Northumbria like it was a cloak he'd got tired of.'

'They say he broke up the room he was staying in, and nearly hung one on Harold.'

'They'd say that, though, wouldn't they?'

'And he took his housecarls with him, money too.'

'They had to make a show of it, didn't they?'

'So . . .?'

'I'm not saying it's like this. I'm saying it could be. I'm saying that, once Harold's king, and he'll have climbed on our backs to get there, he'll pull up the drawbridge and tell us to fuck off.'

'Him and Tostig. Tostig, Earl of Northumbria.'

'And Mercia, too, likely. Thing is, he still hasn't wed our Aldyth. Not even named the day.'

'She's awfu' young yet. Just a kid. Like you said she was thirteen, but that's her next birthday. I were just six, I think, when she were born.'

'Twelve, thirteen, who's to know? Buggered if I do.'

'Mam says she hasn't started her monthlies yet. Edwin, she's a kid.'

'So she'll make Harold a happy man. Listen, Morcar. We'll back the bugger in the Witan, but first he has to name the day. And we tell him straight – not a man moves out of the Danelaw on his behalf until he's properly married. And if the King doesn't sign that bit of parchment before he dies, making your earldom legal, then that's the first thing Harold does. Now sup up and we'll try and get some sleep.'

CHAPTER
THIRTY-SEVEN

Three days later, at about two in the afternoon, with a watery sun still occasionally breaking the low cloud in the south and the west, two horsemen left Harold's manor at Waltham. It was where he always stayed when he had to be near London, and the small, domestic abbey he had caused to be built there to house yet another relic of the Cross had been finished some five years earlier. The air was icy, tiny flakes of snow hovered like midges in the air, ice crackled beneath the horses' hooves. They followed the eastern bank of the Lee for three miles with the purlieus of Epping Forest on their left – the oaks and hawthorn black above frosted ground. No sign of life apart from a pair of peasants, so wrapped in woollen cloths and skins you could see no human feature, gathering fallen wood on a sled, and a pair of crows tearing at a rare coney a fox had left on the river bank.

They left the hamlet of Leyton on their left, crossed the Lee on a long low narrow wooden bridge, followed the raised causeway across Hackney Marshes. Occasionally they talked as their mounts picked their way over the awkward ground.

'When will you marry the lady Erica?'

'When all is settled between you and your enemies.'

The hooves crackled and plopped as the ponies picked their way through the icy mud.

'I should not wait so long.'

'I shall not leave my lord's side until I know he no longer needs me.'

Harold laughed.

'That, dear Walt, will be when I am dead,' he said. 'But while a marriage may be a lengthy business a wedding is not. Tell me again, where does she live?'

'Shroton, in the shire of Dorset. Beneath Hambledon Hill. Three leagues or so from Cerne and the Fighting Man. In the Vale of the White Hart.'

'It's good land. Very good.'

Presently they moved into hillier country round the settlement at Islington and briefly from a height caught a glimpse through the rising mists and enveloping darkness of the permanent pall of smoke above London.

With firmer ground beneath their hooves they set the ponies into a slow canter down the hill, but presently were slowed again when they reached the riparian plain with its rich alluvial soil, the turned but unharrowed black earth gleaming above deep furrows filled with snow. Half a mile above Westminster they joined the road called Strand. It was almost dark now and the mist from the river was thickening so they could hardly make out their ponies' ears in front of them. The black shapes of the shanty town around the Abbey floated through the mist towards them and they could hear from behind the daub and wattle walls the grunts, coughing and low talk of workmen, soldiers, lesser thegns and churls eating their last meal of the day, before turning to the giant butts of ale.

Gleams of dull orange light from tallow and oil-lamps cast thin beams through the cracks round the doors. Stabled cattle lowed gently in outhouses and ponies snorted and stamped. Finally, like a great white ghost, the walls, pierced by tall black arched casements, soared above them. They passed round the northern transept and headed towards the flares that burned in front of the Great Hall. From inside the monks chanted dolefully in Latin of fallen grass and the flower withered on the stem. As they approached one of the torches was plucked from its sconce and thrust into their faces so the orange flame burned their eyes through the darkness and mist.

'Who's there? Stand and declare yourselves.'

'The King's men. Harold of Wessex and his man Walt. Come on Wulfstan, you know me.'

Harold swung out of the saddle and dropped to the ground. Walt followed him.

The soldier, fully armed, called up a groom who gathered the ponies' reins in his hands and led them away.

'The King sleeps,' said Wulfstan, keeping his voice low now. 'Probably for the last time.'

'I come to see my kin. Not the King. This is a bad time for a brother to leave his sister on her own, a woman about to be a widow. She needs her kin.'

Wulfstan hesitated. His bushy dark brows were pulled together in a frown beneath the rim of his helmet, on either side of the nose-guard. But he sensed the easy confidence and power of the man in front of him, guessed at the greater power the next few hours might bring. He turned, swung back the bar that held the doors secure, then rapped with the pommel of his seax and growled a command. On the other side a churl shifted the inside beam and heaved the doors open.

The Great Hall was almost empty for the king had been moved to the upper chamber above the further end. However, his bed was still visible from below since there was no wall or door, just curtains which had not been drawn. The monks sang on, acolytes continued to swing the thuribles, and young men with bowls of copper and tin filled with scented water climbed steep stairs to sponge down the fevered, dying man. For the rest, apart from a small detail guarding the door, the thegns, housecarls and churls had gone, preferring halls still decked with holly and ivy.

Harold strode up the right-hand aisle with scarcely a glance at the tedious drama of unravelling death until he came to a large alcove. It was curtained with heavy hangings woven to depict a Queen, mounted on a dappled palfrey, carrying a silver bow, hunting through a forest. A roebuck darted across dark spaces between giant oaks in front of her. The other side depicted the Queen and her King in their hall, sitting at a table with goblets of wine in front of them while huntsmen below prepared to joint and dress the roebuck, with the arrow that killed it still in its side.

Harold tapped the oak lintel above his head and murmured his name. A soft voice answered. Presently two ladies-in-waiting pushed through the gap and, skirts swinging, flitted down the hall to the brazier nearest the door. He turned to Walt.

'Wait. Hear nothing unless I command you to come. Allow no one to pass you.'

He pulled the curtains apart and went in. Queen Edith was lying on a bed on her side with her head propped high on her elbow. She had her furs around and under her. She was wearing the simple gown of white samite again, embroidered in the seams and low collar with gold; most of her red hair was down, but dressed with tiny fresh-water pearls.

Harold pulled a stool in close to her and took the hand that lay along her thigh.

'I hope sister, you have something with you more fitting for a funeral.'

'Of course. But I thought I might wear this at the coronation.'

'Ah. Whose?'

Rich lips pouted.

'God will decide.'

'He will do nothing of the sort.'

She sucked in breath. 'Harold. You are too proud. You tempt the Fates with such talk.'

He shrugged.

'I'll come to the point,' he said. 'What has Duke William promised you?'

'The palace Queen Emma had in Winchester. With my own house-hold.'

'I can do better than that.'

'You can?'

'A real husband.'

She sighed, not without bitterness, and shifted on to her back. Her small breasts, the nipples visible through the fine silk, rose and fell.

'You are not beyond child-bearing—'

'Certainly I am not beyond fucking and a husband with balls would be a fine thing and a prick that doesn't need another prick up his arse before it moves. But I could turn whore if that was all I needed.'

'A king.'

'A king? Where?'

'In Ireland. The kings in the south are our kind. Danes. I was there. You know I was. They are more gracious there, have finer gold and jewels, and much better minstrels and music, the things you like. The Normans will never get that far west—'

'And I shall be well out of your way.'

'No. When all is settled here I shall visit you.'

He took both her hands in his, resting them on the warm swell of her belly.

'So,' she murmured. 'What do you want from me?'

He leant forward and spoke gently in her ear. She shuddered at the touch of his moustache and clenched his hands more tightly.

'Yes,' she murmured, 'yes. I can do that. Yes.'

He pulled back with the smile on his face. She looked up at him, at his blue-green eyes, his heavy brown but grizzled hair, the strong pillar of his neck, his broad shoulders. She released his hands, slipped her own beneath his jerkin and ran them up his sides from the waist to the shoulders, passing them round to his shoulder-blades. She marvelled at the iron muscle and the stone-like ribs. Then she pulled him back down again.

'Twenty years ago you were the first. To tell truth, in any real sense at all, the only—'

'I thought our father—'

'That was rape, and I was fourteen. And after you had had me, you married me to that monk, that holy fool, that bugger . . . I want it again, Harold. Spare some of yourself now for me, and I'll make you King of England.'

Out in the hall, Walt looked up and down the shadowy spaces, to the cave of light at the end and wondered if any but he could hear her. And if they did, would they think that what they heard was the cry of a woman bereft of her dying husband? A monk might, he thought, but a real man would know the difference . . .

His own feelings about what was happening were neutral or, indeed, warmed to their lust. Although punishable by serfdom, such couplings were common throughout the land – they helped bond kin to kin, and kinship was the mortar of society. The old gods did it all the time. It crossed his mind to wonder what the other Edith would think of it, she with the swan's neck, but pushed the thought away. Not his business.

An hour before daybreak Harold came through the curtains, put his arm round Walt's shoulder and led him a step or two towards the great doors.

'Wait here,' he said, 'until the King dies. See what happens. Then ride out to Waltham like a crow in a hurry for I shall need to know.'

He slapped Walt's shoulder, strode down the outer aisle and was gone. Walt settled himself against one of the wooden supports and waited, wondering for how much longer he could endure the wailing of the monks, and if anyone on that day, in that hall, had a mind to break their fast.

Eventually the ladies-in-waiting returned. And after that a boy with a platter of coddled eggs, rye-bread and milk warm from the udder. Walt begged a breakfast from him and the boy said he would do what he could but the eggs were reserved for the women and the sick. He came back with more black rye covered with thin strips of red cured beef and a beaker of ale. In reply to his question, the boy told him it was snowing outside, but not heavily, not enough to choke the roads. He also promised to check that Walt's pony had been fed and watered, was saddled up.

At about four hours after daybreak, with the monks singing Terce, there was a sudden commotion around the King's bed. An acolyte broke away and ran down the hall to the Queen's chamber. On the way he tripped on his robe, went flying and Walt was first at his side. He hoisted the lad to his feet and hissed: 'What's the matter?'

'The King. The death rattle in his throat.'

He stumbled on, but the curtains were thrown back, no doubt one of the Queen's ladies had been keeping an eye on things, and Queen Edith herself came out, dressed now in a long black robe trimmed with ermine that swept the floor behind her, and her head in a snood, similarly trimmed. She swept up the hall, head high, majestic in spite of the spareness of her build. The monks parted in front of her like the sea in front of Moses. She climbed the stairs, knelt and put her ear close to the lips of the King.

His throat rumbled like dry wattle in a wind, a bubble of spittle formed between his lips and burst. The King farted. The King died.

Queen Edith stood up tall, looked down and into the hall, spoke clear and loud like a trumpet, her voice from that height filling all the spaces.

'My lord the King is dead.' She took a breath. 'These were his last words. "I do prophesy the Witan will choose Harold Godwinson to rule England in my place. He has my dying voice."'

There was a glow about her as she said these words, an aura, that none had marked on her throughout the twenty and more years she had been married. Widowhood became her.

CHAPTER
THIRTY-EIGHT

Next day, the sixth of January 1066, the day of the Epiphany of
our Lord, when He was presented to the Three Kings and the
world beyond, Harold Godwinson, Earl of Wessex, was presented to his people as their King.

But before the real business of the day could be taken up the old King
had to be disposed of. Early in the morning, as soon as all who claimed
a place in the Witan were assembled, the west doors were thrown open
and, borne shoulder-high on a litter, the Confessor's cadaver was brought
in out of the cold air into the hall of cold stone. The breath of the pall-
bearers mingled with the smoke of incense above them; the crucifix
carried in front of him was now wreathed in black, the monks behind
chanted the *Requiescat in Æternum*. The members of the Witan doffed
their head-gear and some knelt, then all joined in the procession behind
Queen Edith, wearing her coronation crown, silver set with pearls in
crosses and sapphires, and moved up the great nave. Presently, holding a
shred of embroidered silk to her face, she seemed to pause, and then sway
a little. Her brother Harold quickly left his place behind her and supported her for the rest of the way.

They swung right at the chancel, passed across the north transept and
so came round to the space behind the high altar. There was as yet no
rood screen nor were the casements above glazed. It was a cold place,
though bright with intermittent beams of sunlight. Stone flags had been
crow-barred from the beds they had so recently been laid in. An oblong

pit of Thames earth had been dug out to make a grave below the floor.

A solemn mass for the dead was then sung, with Ealdred of York as celebrant.

The Witan, nearly a hundred of them, stood around. Some quietly stamped feet against the cold, many coughed and sneezed and the ruder of them hawked and spat. Some got bored, and those who had not been in the Abbey before wandered off to gawp at wonders.

At last it was done. An acolyte removed the crown from the Confessor's head and the strands of his white hair floated briefly in the stirring air. Another removed the gold jewel-encrusted cross from his chest and replaced it with a wooden one, and a third managed, but only with great difficulty, to remove the royal ring set with its giant sapphire from the ring finger of his still-swollen right hand.

Using black leather grave strings, the body was lowered into its grave. The Queen came forward and threw in a posy of dried immortelles trimmed with rosemary.

'Sweets to the sweet, farewell,' she murmured, and turned away, dabbing at her eyes.

Hardly had the last Amen been sung than there was almost a stampede, certainly a brisk rush into the south transept where a table, benches and some chairs had been laid out.

Archbishop Ealdred took the largest chair behind the table and called the meeting to some order.

'The King is dead,' he began, 'and it behoves us, the Witan of the Kingdom of England, to choose another. Who will speak first? Let him name a name and so grow to a point . . . Harold, Son of Godwin? You have guided and protected this realm for ten years or more in the name of the King – it is right you should be first.'

Harold rose from a not un-thronelike chair which Walt had quietly bespoken for him during the funeral rites and moved to the space in front of the table.

'Your Grace, fellow wise men of the Witan. Let us not, in this weighty matter, be guided by fear and expediency. Let us rather trust in God and follow the ancient traditions of our people and choose the man of most royal blood in the kingdom – Edgar the Atheling, grandson of Edward Ironside and the last of Cedric's line. I, Harold of Wessex, speak for the Atheling.'

A murmur, more than a murmur, of surprise. It was not entirely unexpected, after all a certain modesty is expected from the chief claimant at such times, a show, at any rate, of reluctance, but the way it was put, without qualification, caused them to marvel and in some cases to remonstrate.

Aethelwine, Bishop of Durham, and the only English bishop who continued the struggle against the Conqueror after 1066, took the floor.

'The rigorous practice of primogeniture is a Frankish custom, a Roman custom. It is not our custom, neither Danish nor Saxon. Let me remind you all that the Witan's duty is not to abide by such superstitious concepts as that of royal blood and the first-born male, but to choose the man, hopefully from the dead king's family or household, who is best prepared and equipped to defend the realm and its people.'

Oswulf, from the northern Borders near Carlisle, now spoke of the grievous dangers the realm was in. He spoke of Malcolm in Scotland, leader of a united country since the death of Macbeth, and of Harald Hardrada in Norway. Oswulf's thegns, and those of Morcar, could not withstand such powerful enemies without strong leadership and support from the southern earls led by a strong king. He concluded by asserting that the Queen had reported that the Confessor's dying words had been a request that Harold should succeed him. After Oswulf, came Edwin and then Morcar who spoke of the need for maturity, wisdom and, above all, experience in the coming months.

At last one dissenting voice raised the problem that none had dared to air.

'I speak humbly,' said the Abbot of Glastonbury, a very old man indeed, 'and with no desire to show disrespect to anyone here, but is it not a hard matter that Harold Godwinson swore, on ancient and holy relics, that he is Duke William's man and will support the Norman claim to our throne?'

A sort of muted uproar followed through which Ealdred's voice, old though he was too, came loud and clear.

'That was falsely extorted from Harold. He gave it out of compassion for his kin whose lives were, he believed, in danger. But even without that the oath is of no consequence,' he boomed. 'The crown is not his to offer. He was promising what is not his to give. Only the Witan itself, assembled here as we are, can dispose of it, only the Witangemot has that power and privilege. The law and yet more ancient traditions of England declare this to be so.'

And so it went on, with more certainty since that particular problem had been faced and dealt with. And soon the meeting reached a point where all knew for sure that Harold would be acclaimed with no dissenting voice – the Norman clergy, led by William of London, had all slipped away, most already with bags packed, heading for the Channel ports. But as always on such momentous occasions many there, young as well as old, wished to leave their mark on the proceedings and say their bit – even though they were repeating what had been said ten times already. But at last Ealdred took Harold's arm, raised it and cried: 'Let us choose and proclaim, Harold – King of England,' and all there repeated what he had said with a great shout.

Edwin and Morcar joined Leofwine and Gyrth and wrapped a crimson gown embroidered with gold round their King and led him to a great throne set on the chancel step below the choir. The globe and sceptre were brought out and handed to him and Ealdred raised the crown that had been taken from the Confessor's head three hours before and placed it on Harold's. The big doors were thrown open and all the most prominent people of London, who had walked the three miles as soon as they had heard of the King's death, flooded in in a great throng.

And on Harold's left Stigand of Canterbury spread his arms and proclaimed:

'*Hic residet Harold Rex Anglorum*. Here is throned Harold, King of the English.'

Harold's first act, performed before he left the abbey church, was to sign the charter that legalised Morcar's title to Northumbria and his second was to name Lady Day as the day on which he would marry Aldyth.

That night he and his brothers filled the Great Hall of Westminster, where the old King had so recently died, with all the housecarls there was room for. They spent it in music, drinking and boasting, as men must do, of the exploits they would dare to perform for their lords. By daybreak William the Bastard had been shaved, stripped, buggered, dismembered and disembowelled after being overcome in a hundred different single combats – and every Norman who dared set foot on English soil with him.

Towards midnight the King slipped away and Walt followed the cloaked and booted figure over the crackling snow, under the glow of frosty starlight, towards the great white building which seemed, from a distance, to fill a whole quadrant of the world around them. Once actually under its walls you felt there was nothing else on earth.

The King pushed open the door to the south-facing transept and paused until his eyes had adjusted to the deeper darkness. There were candles, but not many, and a couple of oil-lamps that may or may not have burned in front of the reserved Host. At all events, Harold showed no inclination to bend his knee in front of them. Enclosed in that heap of white stone, their light was dimmer than that of the stars outside.

Walt followed his master round to the right, leaving to their left the high, stone block that made a sacrificial altar of the table at which Christ broke bread and drank wine with his friends. Thus Harold came to the stone flags that lay like presses over the body of Edward. He bowed his head, but not in prayer. Then he sighed, and then sighed again, almost as if he were in pain. Walt could not resist a movement towards him, which Harold heard.

'Walt? Is that you?'

'Yes . . . Sire.'

'Fuck that, Walt. I shan't trust you the way I did if you "Sire" me. Come here.'

Walt stood beside him.

'You'd think we'd done it, wouldn't you? To hear the cheers this afternoon. "May the King live for ever." I don't think so. If we make it through to this time next year, then maybe we'll have got away with it. But Eddie. Dear Eddie. He's left a path through brambles ahead of us, with hidden traps and pitfalls. Wherever he is, he's waiting for us to fall into them.'

He sighed again, then looked up and around him at the piled-up pillars, the high, rounded arches, the black spaces where the windows would be, at the guttering candles, and he shivered.

'In one single day, Walt, and just one week and a day after it was consecrated, this church has become the grave of an English king and seen an English king crowned. If things turn out as Eddie in heaven and the Bastard on earth want them, there won't be any more English kings. Not properly English, not what you or I would call English.'

PART VI

1066

CHAPTER
THIRTY-NINE

'So,' said Quint, 'the armourers throve, young men sold pasture to buy a horse, and honour was all anyone thought about.'

'Something like that,' Walt replied, pounding the ground with a stick he had cut from a hazel tree an hour or so earlier.

'I have been told it takes two men three weeks to make a serviceable sword,' Taillefer remarked. 'Is that really so?'

They were toiling up the northern side of the very last range of the Taurus to what their guide had promised them was the very last pass from which, he assured them, they would be able to see the ocean and from which, apart from the odd foothill here and there, the way would now be downhill. Which was just as well. After three days in the mountains most of the caravan's animals were exhausted and all but a few of the travellers now walked with their beasts, some chivvying them from behind with sticks, others dragging them from the front with halters.

'That is so.' The slope zig-zagged through scrub oak which clung to the precipices so the roots were often exposed in the fissures of the limestone cliffs. Some of the trees had succumbed and lay two hundred feet below in a river-bed of chalky water that scurried over lichened boulders. Panting a bit, Walt did his best to explain.

'It must have enough weight to smash through armour or deliver a blow so heavy that the recipient is driven to the ground even though his helmet or mail remains unpierced. Yet clearly it must not be so heavy that a strong man cannot wield it from dawn to dusk. This is a matter as much of balance as weight. Second, it must be supple, it must not break. Indeed, the blades of the very best swords can be bent so the point almost touches the hilt before springing back, undistorted. Then it must have an edge that is bright, sharp and will resist denting. The Wayland hardens the edges by adding carbon or even slag. Every time the metal is cooled it is plunged into the piss of a mare. Preferably taken from one in heat. Finally, of course, the sword's quills, hilt and pommel must be decorated, inlaid with gold, silver, copper and enamels in a way that will enhance or reflect the rank and reputation of its owner.'

'That is, of course, very important indeed,' Quint remarked drily.

'Indeed, yes. The quality and decoration will strike fear into the heart of the foe, while at the same time, if he is a worthy contestant, spurring him on to greater efforts of strength and daring.'

Not for the first time Quint sensed a contradiction that lay beyond the grasp of his rational mind, though he supposed it made sense to most Englishmen.

'So, how is this miraculous blade forged?' Taillefer persisted.

'Well, the smith, the Wayland, first of all chooses iron bars that he knows have been properly prepared, with the right spells and so forth. He casts them in sandy grooves some three feet long and an inch or more across. He is no ordinary smith, you understand, this is not a matter of plough-shares or bill-hooks, he has to know all the ancient lore . . .'

'Fiddlesticks,' said Quint.

'Then he takes three of these bars or rather rods of best iron,' Walt went on, ignoring him, 'and he and his fellow-smith heat them until they are beyond red-hot in a brick furnace over alder charcoal . . .'

'Which, of course, has magical properties,' Quint again interjected.

'No,' Walt replied evenly. 'Indeed, rather otherwise. Some woodfolk rate it a peasant tree because it grows by rivers and in water-meadows. The point is that its charcoal burns hottest. Then, using giant pincers, the Wayland and his mate twist each rod through several turns before forge-welding them together. It is these twists that give the blade its suppleness. The whole process is called pattern-welding. They beat them together into a blade shape, but leaving a long groove down the middle called the fuller. This adds to the suppleness of the blade and lightens it too, without reducing its strength. Finally they work on the edges in the ways I have described.'

'The patterns, of course are runic, and carry magical properties . . .?'

But before Walt could give way to the irritation that was mounting at Quint's repeated if mild scoffing, they saw Adeliza and Alain running down the zig-zag of the track, dodging between the camels and donkeys and, where the slope between was not too steep, launching themselves through the low thickets across rather than round the hairpin bends. Adeliza was now on the very threshold of womanhood, had seemed to ripen even in the three weeks or so since Walt had first seen her dance in the darkened room to Alain's harp-playing. Now, in the sunlight, in a short shift which came only just below her knees, and with her long tresses breaking out of the narrow bands that bound them, she looked like a wild young doe or maybe a valkyrie's daughter.

Alain, annoyed that his sister held the lead, cut across the last bend and took a tumble that scoured his knees and brought him rolling to their feet.

'We are at the top,' they cried, 'the donkey at the front's at the top. There's a spring too. And you can see the sea, but it's not blue or green, but gold . . . Gold and all rippled and ruffled like a big gold plate. Or a shield. The shield of Achilles Dad sometimes sings about. And big row-boats on it, with five banks of oars . . .'

'Quinqueremes bound for Nineveh?' Taillefer suggested, feeling a song or lay coming on.

'You couldn't possibly see how many banks of oars at this distance,' cried Adeliza.

'Actually,' said Walt, but no one now paid him any attention at all, 'the patterns, though regular and intricate, and often pointed up by polishing or inlay, are a natural result of the process. Hence the term – "pattern-welding".'

The view was magnificent indeed. In Lydian Pamphylia the Taurus Mountains are never far from the sea and rise to seven or eight thousand feet within some five or six coastal leagues of the beaches. The narrow coastal plain edges a bay like a jade necklace hung with clusters of pearls – Adalia, Perge, Aspendos and Sidé – the four principal cities of the region. So rich is the land, it was able to support these cities, each with its forum, temples, theatre, circus and harbour, though no more than five leagues separated each from each. At the time Walt set eyes on them they were already in decline – deprived of the Pax Romana, they were at the mercy of pirates and suffered conquest and reconquest by satraps, caliphs, kings, emperors and Christians of both persuasions on an almost yearly basis – yet still they thrived.

The first source of this wealth was the mountains themselves with their abundance of timber, game, furs and above all minerals of all sorts from the most precious to the most base. Then came foothills covered with vines and olives, and in the plain itself, already providing a new source of almost inestimable wealth from the rich riparian soil, the finest cotton, better even than that of Egypt. There were the new fruits brought in by Arabs and Turks from the Orient: oranges and citrons, sugar-cane, apricots, aubergines, spices like cumin and coriander, types of melon hitherto unknown in Europe, jasmine, carnations and many other fragrant flowers from which perfumes could be distilled, and, of course, the roots and grain that have always nourished the poor, beasts of burden and beasts of the field.

Finally, fish. That night they dined off a clawless lobster three feet long. Being English Walt felt sure a clawless lobster was an aberration, a creature of the devil, and highly poisonous, at least. It needed considerable persuasion on the part of his friends to persuade him to eat any of it at all.

And of course, this paradise was warm, even in late October, hot at midday and well into the night.

That night? That night they feasted in Junipera's house – for that, not Jessica at all, nor Theodora, was, Walt now believed, the name of their patroness, she of the peacock shawl, emerald snood, red hair and golden slippers. Over the weeks they had been together she had, she said, learnt to value their company as well as the protection they afforded her. She had gossiped with Adeliza, marvelled and laughed at her father's tricks and songs, had been moved to tears by Alain's skill with the harp, and learnt much wisdom in scholarly discourse with Quint. The fact that she valued none of them more than a straw if it had come to a fight or attack by brigands or an assault from one of her fellow travellers, had not worried her at all – the presence of Walt, one-armed though he was, had reassured her for in his bearing and, above all, in his eyes she could sense the presence of a man who set so little value on his own life he would freely give it to save another's.

He was, however, and she had to say it hurtful though it was, one of the dourest, saddest, most miserable old sods she had ever come across –

and now, on the eve of their separation, she wondered why. Quint explained that Walt was a survivor of the innermost band of companions who had served and, for the most part, died for Harold, King of England.

The tale was already the stuff of legend and romance, though much of it reflecting badly on the Englishman who was, such was the cunning of William's campaign of propaganda, already renowned as a simpleton, a barbarian, an oath-breaker, and so on. Walt overhearing this, declared Harold was the best man, save Our Lord, who ever lived.

'In that case,' said Junipera, 'prove the Norman's histories wrong.'

Junipera's servants, who were all women, had cleared away the crustacean's empty carapace, the bones of a peacock, the femur of a ham cured in the mountain air, the stones of apricots crystallised in sugar, and the rinds of cheeses made from the milk of izards. They had drunk a flagon or two each of the country's purple wine, watched and applauded the ever more sensuous undulations of Adeliza's dance in which her round but still small breasts, her navel and her thighs each seemed to have a mind to go their own way to the rhythm of Alain's harp-playing . . . all this, and yet still the last of the sun glowed with opalescent sheen upon the sea beyond the harbour. Clearly it was not yet time for bed.

Taillefer, recalling that it must now be some forty days since he was crucified in Nicæa, and therefore time he completed his programme, briefly amused them by levitating to the height of a tall palm tree on the terrace before his daughter begged him to come down. Jesus, she insisted, had had a smoke-screen laid on to receive His Ascension and since the sky that evening was cloudless and empty apart from swallows twittering in the eaves before making their last dash for Africa, her father had done well enough.

But still the Englishman kept mum, and his face became suffused with a redness that went well beyond that of his now very healthy-looking stump.

It was not, he insisted, a story for an evening of such exquisite and refined pleasures as they had enjoyed but one of horror, blood, pain, destruction, betrayal and tragedy.

Cunningly Quint took him up on this.

'Betrayal? Yes, indeed,' he cried. 'And tragedy, too. That a whole country should be betrayed to bondage and slavery for a thousand years at the ambitious whim of one brother, and the incompetent generalship of another . . .'

Walt spluttered in his wine and reached for a knife.

'King Harold,' he thundered, 'was the greatest general who ever lived – outshone all your Alexanders and Alp Arslans, I can tell, and you had better swallow what you have just said, or swallow this blade.'

Quint rose quickly and stood behind Taillefer's chair thinking if need be the mountebank would raise him up beyond the mad Englishman's reach. At all events, he felt safe enough to go on, with a taunting note in his voice and the red tip of his nose glowing.

'A general? Did he not fight this battle as if it were some barbaric scrap fought between shaggy saga-louts behind shield-walls? Did he manoeuvre? Did he do anything but wait upon the side of a hill until he had been chopped to pieces? Was not his greatest mistake simply to look up at the cloud-covered sky and say "I see no arrows" . . .'

He had gone too far and Walt, hurling himself across the table, was on him, battering his face with the side of his stump and slashing wildly with the knife which being silver and having no edge or point, did little harm. Alain, Taillefer, Junipera herself and numerous maid-servants eventually subdued him and got him back to his place.

'At least,' he gasped at last, when his breath was back and the servants had cleared up the mess he had caused, 'that bastard renegade monk could say he's sorry.'

'Tell us the truth of it, then, if my version is as wrong as you say, and if I believe you, I'll apologise.'

There was a long silence while all looked at their plates, or at the frescoes, some of which were rather rude and others devotional. Adeliza fondled a short-haired, smoky-grey cat which Junipera said had come from Ethiopia, the land of the Queen of Sheba. Taillefer cleared his throat.

'Start, by telling us of Harold's preparations. The coronation was at the Epiphany, the invasion over nine months later. Your Harold had plenty of time to lay on a welcome. If he were as good a general as you say, he must have had all in readiness.'

Walt looked up at him, dabbing with a napkin at his nose which still bled from where Adeliza had hit him with a goblet.

'You were there,' he growled. 'You tell them.'

'Well, yes and no,' said Taillefer.

'Explain yourself.'

'Some other time. Right now it's your turn. But I tell you one thing:

by May your Harold's preparations were so well advanced, William was in two minds about the whole venture. I really do believe if he could have done so without losing face, he would have backed off then. What went wrong?'

At last Walt sighed.

'Well,' he said, 'if you really want to know, I'll tell you.' He held his cup out for Adeliza to fill. 'But I doubt the true story you'll hear from me chimes that well with what the Bastard's been putting about since. But first you must know you are quite right. By the end of April, yes, we were ready. For as soon as the coronation was done we were all sent back to our own shires to raise men, train and arm them . . .'

CHAPTER
FORTY

'Wait outside.' Erica dismounted from her pony, a small russet animal with a white belly and a big head. She slung the reins over a low apple bough, covered with silver and yellowish-green lichen. A couple of withered yellow fruits still clung to it.

She unhitched a soft leather bag from the pommel of her saddle and, scarcely sparing Walt a glance over her shoulder, walked across frosted dried grass towards the hut. Her pointed boots left prints in the crackling grass amongst those of hens, a dog and a small boy, none of whom had worn shoes.

Tall, straight, she wore a belt with an intricate silver buckle which pulled in her long, dark, woad-blue woollen gown just enough to give an outline to her waist and hips. A brindled, half-starved cat arched its back at her, spat and hissed, but, as Erica stooped and murmured to her, pushed her tail in the air and rubbed her cheeks against her ankles. She pushed open the low board door, ducked her head, and was gone.

Walt was relieved. Women's business. Something to do with a reluctant afterbirth. He could hear the new-born baby mewling like a kitten, and then a sharp cry, presumably from its mother.

He had seen men's arms lopped off in battle, heads shattered with an axe or sword blow spilling brains and teeth, but he turned away squeamishly at the thought of placentas and birth cords. His horse snuffled and one of its back hooves clicked on frozen earth or a flint and he too dismounted and hitched up to the old apple tree. He walked over to a fence made of wattle hurdles that ringed the hut and its acre or two of land. It was flimsy, in need of repair, just enough to keep fowl in and foxes out, so he decided not to lean on it while he looked out and over it.

There was a blue-to-violet stillness in the air, a deep quietness of heavy frost jewelling the trees nearby and whitening the woods that climbed the hill out of the bottom they were in. Nothing stirred, no crows in the patches of field or wheeling above the trees, not even a robin on the thatch – it was that cold. He breathed out vapour and some of it settled in his moustache, the droplets freezing instantly. It bit into him in spite of the patchwork coat of mixed furs he was wearing – weasel, badger, polecat for the most part – and his stout cow-hide boots. His hands were warm though, deep inside fur mittens, glossy and black, cut from a bear-pelt – one of many the King of Poland had sent Harold as a coronation present.

Worse than the cold was the knowledge that back at Iwerne his father was ill, almost certainly dying. He would have stayed there with him, but for the duties Harold had laid on him and which, once this business of a difficult childbirth was over, he would have to spend the rest of the day dealing with.

More cries and moans from the hut made him turn back, but then too the crack of broken twigs and presently a thin mist of white smoke gathered above the point of the roof. The door opened again and a small boy came out, batting aside the smoke that came with him. He was about eight years old, with a grubby face and gap-toothed grin, sandy hair claggy with dirt. He looked fat, but his face and legs were very thin – the plumpness came from the fact that he had put on or tied round his body every scrap of cloth and skin he could find.

'She says you're to go back and get milk and fresh bread and some cheese,' he piped.

'She?'

'The lady Erica. And in the store in your aunt's bower there should be some dried penny-royal, maybe, she said, some fresh in a pot if the frost hasn't got to it. She says we're to be quick.'

'We?'

'She says you're to take me too, in case you forget what she sent you for.'

'Bread, cheese and penny-royal.'

'And milk.'

Pleased to have something to do, Walt hoisted him on to his horse's withers, in front of the pommel, and swung up behind him, putting his arm round the boy's waist.

'Take a good grip on his mane. What's your name?'

'Fred.'

'Alfred?'

'No. Fred. What's yours?'

'Walt.'

'Waltheof?'

'No, just Walt.'

'The penny-royal because the herb is a strong abortient. The rest because there was no food in the hut at all.'

'Why not?'

'Her husband, Wink, was a fool. He cut his ankle with a sickle at harvest, it went bad, and he died two months ago. Frieda had to sell her cow and rather stupidly they ate the calf. The last food in the hut is the broth from the bones.'

'Is she all right. I mean, as far as the . . .'

He was squeamish over even using words like afterbirth.

Erica sighed, her knuckles tightened on the reins, and she shook her head. Two hours later and they were moving now at a steady walk up a chalk track which led into the woods and their next call, a clan of charcoal-burners Walt needed to talk to. She turned to him and her pale blue eyes found his across the space between them. A lock of straw-coloured hair had fallen across her forehead from beneath her hood, and he wanted to reach across and touch it.

'Yes . . . and no. It wasn't the afterbirth at all. She had twins. The second was still-born. I doubt the other, a girl, will survive. I'm not at all sure Frieda will either.'

'They should be moved, shouldn't they? Into the farm?'

He meant his father's farm – the enclosure round the hall and bowers.

'Where they can be properly cared for,' he added.

'Yes. But she's afraid to do that.'

'Why?'

'Dear Walt. You'll have a lot to learn, when you finally take it all on.

Wink was a churl, a freeman. That scrap of land round the hut was his and a couple of hides over on the north side of the village. They should be Fred's now, and Frieda's. She's afraid if she moves off the land and into the farm you'll take it over in return for the security you can give them, but they'll lose their freedom.'

'What should we do then?'

'Promise she and Fred and the infant, if it lives, can stay in the farm until they can look after themselves. But to convince her the land stays hers you'll have to give your oath on it at the next folk-moot. She'll not move until you have.'

He remembered the moot was in two days' time. He hoped Fred's mother would live that long. Erica said she would − or die within six hours. If the latter, then she'd die wherever she was.

Presently the track broke out of the beech woods that filled the side of the coombe and on to the long sinuous ridge that ran above the Vale of the White Hart right up to Shaftesbury. They paused for a moment and looked back the way they had come, to Iwerne and Shroton and the whale-back of Hambledon and the rolling plain, grey and white, forest and fields, with here and there a haze of blueish smoke above the scattered settlements. When Harold released him Walt knew most of what he could see would be his. Hers and his. But now it seemed there was more to being a great thegn, even an earl, than feasting in the big hall and hunting.

They pushed down the other side into much deeper forest, with oak, ash and holly slowly taking over from the beech. The even deeper silence of the woods folded about them so the clip of their horses' hooves and the occasional snort and jangle of harness seemed like a blasphemy. Soon they left the track at a point where an axe blow had sliced a white slash into the dark grey bark of an ash tree − a sign Erica had been looking for.

The slope became steeper and broken with churned mud and mast frozen solid so that they feared it could cause one of the horses to stumble and do itself an injury. They dismounted and led them. The holly, the berries long since eaten by thrushes and redwings, had been browsed to a consistent line just above the height of a tall man's shoulder and presently they saw why. A group of red deer two hundred paces away looked round at them from where they had been reaching up into the glossy leaves. One of them even had its front hooves on the silvery trunk. There was a moment of frozen animation then they were off −

and totally silent – not a twig cracked, not a leaf rustled, not even though they all leapt a shallow but quite wide frozen brook, each in turn, heads down as they approached, searching out the right footing for both take-off and landing before lifting them for the actual jump. You felt that with their necks stretched out like that they could grow wings and soar up through the branches above.

'Not far now,' Erica murmured. Then distantly, from half a mile away or more, they heard a dog bark, then another.

They found six huts in a clearing, even lower than Frieda's, no more than circular twig and turf tents above pits dug into the forest floor, and five charcoal kilns, tall, thin tent-like pyramids of oak boughs covered with turf. The air bent with the heat above them.

The charcoal burners gathered round, but at a distance, wary, ready to fight or run, carrying axes and machete-like seaxes, the normal tools of their trade. They spoke a variant of the Gaelic the Cornish used, but some churchmen and their own traditions claimed they preceded even the Celts, were in fact the last descendants of the flint-workers the bronze-workers had driven into the virgin forests. They moved often, disappeared if threatened, lived off the birds and animals they could hunt and trap, and sold or bartered charcoal for whatever else they needed.

They had a Chief, and a Queen they honoured above the Chief, but it was the Chief who dealt with matters concerning the world beyond their world. His name was Bran. He was a big man, built like a smith, clad in furs and wearing on his head a stag's mask with seven-tined antlers. Beneath it a huge black beard, which had not been touched since the day it began to sprout, filled his face. He spoke English, but simply, brokenly, with few verbs and many gestures of his hands and fingers, especially when it came to totting up numbers and amounts. When he could not find the English word he wanted, Erica found it for him.

Walt needed a thousand bushels in excess of what was normally traded for or bought from the burners, and all by the fifteenth of April, the first day of the fifth of the ancient calendar months, the one dedicated to the Willow-Tree, following that of the Alder, which is the best tree for charcoal – 'the very battle-witch of all woods, tree that is hottest in the fight.'

Bran was the King of the Charcoal-Burners between the River Stour to the west and the Amesbury Avon to the east, the two rivers that meet at Twyneham harbour before flowing out into the sea through a fearsome run by Hengistburyhead. Rich iron deposits had been found on the long flat summit of the promontory of Hengistbury and Walt's idea was that the charcoal could be boated down to the new workings, smiths could be moved in, and new forges set up.

The schedule was tight. In the Seine estuary a great fleet had been begun and the Bastard looked like getting together an army bigger than any English king had put in the field since the days of Ironside. The invasion could come as early as late April, as soon as the spring gales were over.

So now they needed arms and armour not for hundreds but thousands, and in the heart of Cranbourne Chase in early February, Bran was driving a hard bargain. He asked for three times the normal price. Not out of greed, he assured Walt, but because they would have to deplete stocks of growing timber and it could be three years before the normal economy of the forest reasserted itself. He would want hogsheads of ale and wine thrown in (mead was a net export from the oak-forest), salted pork, salt too, and so on.

But his final demand was more fundamental.

'Every year,' he growled, and by now he was sitting on the trunk of a fallen ash, and occasionally picking his teeth with the point of his seax and spitting, while the elders of his tribe, women as well as men stood around and nodded agreement with him, 'every year of peace in this land brings greater prosperity, more infants grow to maturity, the villages and the towns get bigger, you need more land for your wheat and barley and for your orchards, and the forest is cleared, slashed and burnt, driven back. Without wars and battles you need no new weapons or armour. Already the waterlands on either side of the Avon have been cleared of the alder you need now—'

'These are not things in the power of one man to control. Not even a king,' Walt replied.

'Perhaps not,' Bran replied. 'But for every five hides of forest cleared, your king or his ealdormen could give us one hide for our own. He could also guarantee our rights to hunt over what is left for as long as it lasts. Give us your word, and the word of King Harold on this, and the five tribes that live between the Stour and the Avon, and our kin between the Avon and the Itchen, can promise you'll get your thousand bushels.'

They bargained on, through noon when the low, blood-orange sun of winter barely grazed the tops of the trees before reddening and sinking to the west. Erica came out of the largest of the hovels, where she had been entertained by the Queen of the burners, and urged them to agree. They were three hours' ride from Iwerne and Shroton and there was barely that much daylight left. Walt promised that by Shrove Tuesday he would get from Winchester the charters and book-right Bran demanded, and Bran undertook to send the first boat-loads the very next day, down the Stour to Twyneham, taking the charcoal from existing stocks.

Walt clasped Bran's shoulder before remounting.

'You would do well, old man,' he said, 'to keep your side of this bargain. If Harold fails for lack of good weaponry and the Bastard becomes King, there will be little left for you.'

'How's that then? A war-lord needs all the ironwork he can get.'

'There'll be no more wars if the Bastard wins – and he loves to hunt.'

'Room for us both.'

'Not so. First, he'll round you up, then have you made Christians, then slaves. William does not like to share the deer he hunts.'

They re-crossed the ridge that separated the Chase from the Vale of the White Hart with the setting sun actually below them on the distant horizon and casting huge purple shadows across the frost and thin snow, sending transverse beams through the smoke of the stoked-up fires above their respective farmsteads. Erica reined in for a moment, reached across and touched his hand.

'Their Queen,' she said, 'gave me gifts. In return for a brooch I gave her that belonged to my mother.'

'What were they?' he asked.

She handed across to him a flint core, rounded, with a blue and white patina. The significance of its natural shape was clear enough – small though it was, hardly filling the palm of her small hand, it was rounded in such a way as to suggest a pregnant torso with enlarged breasts. There was also a twig with oak-leaves the soft brown-gold of late autumn, and three chestnut-coloured acorns still in their cups.

He sensed she took them seriously.

'Keep them,' he said. 'For good luck charms and three strong children.'

She grinned and put them back in her purse.

'You did well back there, with the charcoal-burners,' she went on. 'And with Frieda, too.'

He blushed a little but remained silent.

'You've grown up in the last five years.'

Was she remembering their love-play between the hot summer ramparts of Hambledon?

'You're a man now.'

He wanted to say, as their horses began to clip down the chalk and flint track between the beech-woods, 'and you are a woman too,' but sensed a possible banality in the reply, even a bullying assertion of his manhood.

'The problem is,' she went on, 'are you Harold's man, or the King's?'

This was a puzzle, a riddle. The English love riddles.

'How can I be one and not the other?'

'I mean . . . when the fighting starts, will you fight for Harold or for all this?'

He did not answer because he knew the answer would not please her. For most of fifteen years he had lived away from 'all this', though he had thought of the hearth often, with deep homesickness, then nostalgia. Now he viewed it all with a touch of irritation. The daily round of checking out fences against deer, barns against rodents, that the harrowing-tackle shared by the cottars and gebors was in good nick ready for the spring sowing, that a joiner had been sent for to fix an old woman's loom, that a dispute over land had been settled at the folk-moot, and that he had at his finger-tips the rights and wrongs of a case of the accidental killing of a swineherd by a lad out with a bow and arrow. The lad had been on the heath, where he had no business to be, after red-legged partridge. It would all have to be settled at the hundredsmoot in a month's time with the right assessment of wergild made if the swineherd's kin demanded it . . . and so on.

It was very different from the training, the comradeship, the actual fighting and clash of arms, the feasting and boasting in the mead-halls, the pomp of coronation and the knowledge that he was Harold's man to the death, to the very death, that that was what it meant to be a housecarl, not just a housecarl but a member of the innermost circle of a great lord's bodyguard, a companion, a *comitatus*, one of the last eight in the shield-wall who would die with him if need be.

Yet, he understood what she meant.

They clip-clopped on, past Iwerne village along the track they had had improved that linked it with Shroton, since once they were married the settlements would become one demesne. Starlight now, but plenty to show the familiar way through fields and then a beech-wood, the big trunks silvery in the darkness to which their eyes quickly became accustomed.

'I am Harold's man. But all this is his.'

He sensed the possibility of equivocation here, but also more than a grain of truth.

'And I will hold it for him. This and maybe much, much more.'

The ring-giver, the giver of land. Harold would not take land from loyal neighbouring thegns, but . . . but Walt, already an ealdorman, a Companion of the King, empowered to raise the local fyrd and sit in the Witangemot, might well be made a full earl, the Earl of Dorset perhaps, and then the neighbouring thegns would hold their land through him rather than directly from the King or the Earl of Wessex. But Erica had not finished.

'The land you hold for Harold, for the King, is not yours but lent. It is not even his, but lent by the people who work it in return for their lords' protection. And this double lending demands you should husband it well.'

'So,' he said at last, and this time it was his hand went out to hers, 'your question was no question at all. To fight for the King is to fight for the land and its people.'

She smiled now, satisfied, almost, with his answer. They had reached the gate to her farmstead.

'When will the fighting start.'

He shrugged.

'Who knows?' He took a deep breath. 'At any rate, let us be married first.'

CHAPTER
FORTY-ONE

He pushed his way through the big unbarred gate into the enclosure of the farmstead. Unbarred? Why should it be barred? The small amounts of coin, plate, jewellery, the clothes made from finer furs, Kashmir wools, silks and fine cotton, were kept in locked chests. For the rest there was little he and his father owned that his villagers and those of surrounding settlements did not already have. No one thieved except in times of extreme want, and if they did would almost certainly be accused at the next moot by someone who knew their guilt.

He did so with a heavy heart for all Erica had agreed marriage before the fighting got under way. He had not told her that his father was beyond the normal winter ailments that afflicted men of his age and was probably dying: partly because he had not wished to upset her, nor impose upon her duties beyond what she already bore; but also because he sensed that with his father there would be an end, an end to the old life that had once included his mother and siblings as well as his father. She had been on the periphery only of that old life, which was really his childhood, and it felt right to him that he should see it go on his own, without her.

The hall was dark, save for one tallow candle that burned at the far end and the glow from a brazier nearby. His father lay on a pallet, his old white head pillowed, and with furs, mostly beaver, piled around him. Anna, an old woman, still with a lot of Celt in her, perhaps the oldest person on the farm, sat in a chair near his head and fumbled with needle and thread. There was no wool in the eye of the needle, and the framed linen patch she held in her left hand was almost blank.

'How is he?' Walt asked, shrugging off the coat of varied pelts he'd worn all day.

'A little worse each hour,' the old woman answered. 'Reckon he's sinking.'

Walt leant over the old man's face. The breath that issued from his open, spittle-lined mouth was weak, but came in short, quick gasps, each clearly an effort.

'Should we get the priest?'

'No point. He's made his peace. He's ready to let go.'

'How can you be so sure?'

'At dusk he watched the sun sink over the trees beyond the brook. Just for a short time it showed − a great red ball. Then he had us close the doors and make up the fire. He asked for the pot, he pissed a thimbleful and passed a pea-sized piece of shit like a goat-dropping. Since then he's had nothing to drink or eat. I've seen it often before. They know what they're doing.'

'Tell me.'

'They want to leave no mess when they go.'

Walt sat near Anna's feet. He watched the swollen joints of her fingers pass back and forth like tired crabs across the webbing she held in her lap. He saw now that what she was doing was not the sad, sightless attempt of a failing mind to sew − rather she was, stitch by stitch, unpicking what had been there. She read his thoughts.

'It was an old piece,' she said, 'the colours fading, the thread fraying. The backing's still sound though. Perhaps, when she comes here, your Erica will fill it in again with something new.'

They listened to the noisy silence. The old man's breath, each gasp as short as a heart-beat; a coal falling in the brazier; mice or a roosting bird stirring in the thatch above them. A wisp of straw swung down.

'It was not,' she murmured, 'a bad life.'

She was not, he realised, sitting in judgement. It was inconceivable she should − not just because the dying man was the thegn and she the daughter of a freed serf, but because it was not in the nature of any of them, thegn or serf, to judge people. Actions, if they had to, but not people.

'No. He was lucky to be born when he was.'

By the time Edwin had been ten the wars between Dane and Saxon were over; Canute used the Danes from the Danelaw on his Scandinavian campaigns, all the West Saxons had to find was money. Yes, there had been famine and pestilence, yes, but not often and none had lasted more than a year.

They sat on. The cold bit deeper, and Walt threw some more charcoal on the brazier.

'I could warm you some milk.'

'No. But what about him?'

'I told you. He's beyond all that.'

Presently she began to talk and he had to lean closer to catch what she said.

'When I was young, the monks who used to come here from Shaftesbury told a foolish old story. It went like this. In days gone by, a Roman priest was trying to make Christians of us. And an old man in the Witan said: look at that sparrow that has flown out of the storm and into the firelight. He will leave the firelight and go back into the storm. Before this Christian man came we were all like that sparrow – we did not know what lay beyond the firelight.'

'And that's a foolish story?'

'Yes. It is foolish to think we shall ever know what lies beyond the firelight. But nevertheless the story teaches us something.'

'Yes?'

'We should all share the firelight and the warmth while we have it. Help each other to make the best of it. It's all we've got. There, that's done.' She set aside the linen square in its frame. Tiny holes still peppered it where the threads had been.

Edwin died an hour or so before cock-crow. It was not, after all, as easy a death as Anna had seemed to suggest it might be. He wheezed and coughed, sat up with staring eyes in his hollowed grey face, sweat streamed down the valleys between the cords in his neck, he seemed to struggle to keep his lungs pumping. Anna and Walt held him up between them.

'It's not the man that makes him do this,' the old woman called across the wild writhing head. 'Just the body. The way water boils when you heat it. It can't help itself.'

A little later, with one last wretched spasm, the wilting body fell back, as unstrung as a bundle of twigs.

Next day a priest came from Shaftesbury. He said prayers, and managed to get a thurifer going to cense the body, now washed and laid out on a bier in Edwin's best saffron woollen robe. When asked where Edwin would be buried, they told him that he would be put, like everyone else, in the burial ground.

'The ground, then, is sanctified?' he demanded in his fruity well-fed voice.

No one seemed to know. Certainly, there was no church or chapel.

The question of burial goods arose. Edwin had a fine pewter cup with a ring of uncut carbuncles and a beaded base. It had always been his favourite at feasts. And in a chest they found his sword. Three feet of steel, a fine pommel, a scabbard of willow bark covered with crimson leather. Walt thought about it, drew it, made some passes with it. In the end he decided it was too light for him – he was a good six inches taller than his father had ever been. He already had a sword he trusted – it had served him well in the Welsh wars. Edwin should keep the sword he had never had to use in this life to fight whatever monsters he might find in the outer darkness beyond the light and warmth of the mead-hall fire.

CHAPTER
FORTY-TWO

Harold sat in the saddle of a chestnut stallion, a coronation gift from the Sultan of Granada, and looked down from Portsdown over the big harbour with the Roman castle of Portchester a league or so in front of him. Portsmouth harbour shone like a silver shield around the square tower and crenellated walls. The mud-flats that hemmed the almost landlocked sheet of water were dotted with slipways and boat sheds; behind them teams of horses ten- or twelve-strong dragged vast trunks of giant oaks to the water's edge, and in them carpenters and joiners worked away endlessly with twelve-foot two-handed saws in saw-pits, some powered by water where a river or mill-stream was strong enough. Outside the saw-pits artisans with lesser tools – axes, adzes, borers, planes, augers, hammers and iron nails brought down by the sack-load from the Forest of Dean – hewed, shaped and pinned the sawn planks to the master shipbuilders' specifications.

Out on the water finished long-boats of seventy feet, powered by thirty or forty oars, skimmed across the choppy but shallow water, canvas rattled up and down, the sun flashed from spear points and round or lanceolate shields as the crews practised the exercises of embarkation and disembarkation. The stiff breeze sent the striped and coloured sails flapping, straightened the swallow-tailed pennants. It all looked good, neat, orderly – he must remember to congratulate his brother Leofwine, who was in charge.

In all there were already fifty war-boats commissioned, and another fifty or so almost ready, each crewed by thirty men captained and trained by the few veterans who had been kept on through the decades of peace or who had fought in the brief campaigns against the Welsh. They had rowed up the Usk and the Wye under Harold's command to catch Griffith in the pincer movement Tostig had completed over the Brecon Beacons. And Tostig. Where was he now? In Bruges? The latest news said his men were already scraping the barnacles from the twenty or so ships he had, and that messengers, spies, whatever – scurriers was the word people used – had been seen moving through the manors and farmsteads that he once held in the southern counties, spreading rumour, stirring up ill-feeling.

Harold sighed. He turned his gaze back to the harbour below. Angles, Danes, Jutes, Saxons and even, from the western shires and the Kentish forest, Celts. They were united as they had never been before and all called themselves English, after the Angles. There were fewer Angles than either Saxons or Danes, but no Dane would call himself Saxon, nor vice-versa, so they were all happy to be Angles or English. Yet there were still far too few under arms – barely three thousand men here in the south trained and paid as housecarls and about as many again in the north. Fewer than the brent and barnacle geese, which swept up in great arced flocks in front of the long-boats' bow-waves, preparing for their annual migrations to the breeding grounds in Iceland and even furthest Novaya Zemla, far away in the lands of the midnight sun the sagas sing of.

The horses around him wheeled and stamped, harnesses jingled. In spite of the spring sunshine, they were feeling the cold on the exposed hill-top. The breeze straightened the standard Walt, as usual, was holding amongst them – the gold dragon on the purple ground, now faded to red, the standard of Wessex. Harold frowned. That banner, that very banner they said, had been Edmund Ironside's at the battle of Ashingdon exactly fifty years earlier – Ironside's Mercians had deserted him, Ironside himself became a fugitive. When he and Canute met again, a month or so later, the dispute between them was settled – in the Dane's favour. Ironside kept Wessex, Canute took the rest. Within two months Ironside was dead and Canute got it all.

It had never occurred to Harold before that the standard might be ill-omened – it was known, recognised, men turned out and doffed their hats when they saw it. In a battle they would rally to it as long as it was there. But the coincidences that now gathered like evil shadows about it could not be ignored. Fifty years. A foreign invasion. The desertion of the Mercians.

A little further down the hill, on the sheltered landward side, a small group of mounted women also waited for him. Apart from checking out his growing fleet and army, Harold was conducting Edith Swan-Neck from Bosham to Weymouth. She would sail from there to Wexford to join their children and await the outcome. But now another errand suggested itself to him which he could combine with the first. He called Walt over. Walt handed the standard to Daffydd and joined him.

'Walt, we'll stop at Cerne on the way to Weymouth. I want to see my mother while I have the chance. There's something she can do for me.'

'A detour of ten miles or so and we could pass through Iwerne.'

'We'll see. We'll see. At any rate, I can spare you for a day or so if you want to go there on your own.'

He turned back to the south, shaded his eyes for a moment against the silvery glare that came off the Solent. Beyond lay the green hills of the Island and the doubts flooded back. Anywhere between Exeter and the Thames estuary the hammer could fall. Though perhaps not. The Normans were Normans now, no longer Norsemen. It was a hundred years or more since their high-prowed dragon-headed black ships had forged down the Channel. Like so many before and after them they had brought no women with them and five or more generations breeding with farmers' daughters had wiped out their seafaring skills. They'd take the shortest route – Harold felt sure of it. A landing anywhere west of the Island would need an easterly wind and they'd never risk that. They could be blown past the Fastnet Rock across the Ocean to Vineland. No, they'd come on a southerly or south-westerly, the shortest way they could. And once they'd sailed they'd have this fleet he was building behind them, up their arses, with the same wind in its sails. And the army with the fyrd in support waiting for them on the beach. We'll fight them on the beaches, he thought. And if they do get any further inland then we'll fight them in the fields and on the hills.

Feeling better he touched his spurs to the big horse's flanks and hacked down the slope to his love, not the only love of his life, but the only woman he loved.

'We're fucked,' said William, and Lanfranc raised his eyebrows – his Lombard sensitivity still a touch repelled by his master's brutishness.

With Lanfranc there were present William's half-brothers – Odo, Bishop of Bayeux and Robert of Beaumont, as well as old Eustace of Boulogne, the Confessor's brother-in-law. They had just heard how five more Norman barons had pulled out in the last three days, following two from the week before. They were, of course, as their oaths of loyalty, fealty and what-all required, perfectly ready to help their liege-lord with money and even some equipment, but with rumours of a possible alliance between France and Burgundy, they thought, by and large, it would be better if they stayed put, at least until next year – this just was not the time for foreign ventures. Truth was – why risk a battle or two against odds when you've a snug castle, all the land you want, and your liege-lord has illusions of grandeur big enough to make you think he might be a penny piece short of a shilling?

And that morning William had been down to Le Havre and watched two of his new long-boats turned on their beams in a sudden but not severe squall.

He loped round the oak table, kicked unused stools aside (all the seats were three-legged stools, apart from the big chair he used), and smacked his fists into his palms.

'Totally fucked,' he repeated. 'From Sicily to Poland every fucking king and duke is waiting for me to slip on my arse, and that is what I am about to do. No army and ships that roll over like puppies if you breathe on them. I was a fool to think I could take on this lot. Whose idea was it anyway?'

He glared round the room. None of them dared meet his eye since none dared give the right answer.

Robert cleared his throat. 'Allies?' he suggested. 'The Welsh? The Scots? Harald Hardrada?'

Odo ticked them off, thumb to fingers, one by one.

'Harold's already beaten the Welsh. He's got hostages, they fear him. As for the Scots – well, Edwin and Morcar may just still be dithering a bit until Harold gets their sister in the family way, but one thing that will bind them to Harold more even than that is if you come at them with the Scots on your side. Harald Hardrada? He's old now but probably still the best leader of men in the world – I beg your pardon, second best – and if he lands in the north and wins, which he well might, since all the Norse in Northumbria will side with him, and maybe the Danes too, then he won't stop there. You'll end up fighting Norway as well as England.'

'There's another thing too,' Eustace, whose memory was longer than that of the others, chipped in, 'he's got a reasonable sort of claim to the English throne himself. Not as good as yours,' he hurried on, 'but still . . .'

A sad, evil sort of silence fell over the room. Then Lanfranc, who had been watching and listening with scarcely concealed scorn, cleared his throat.

'Really, you know, I don't know why you're all making such a fuss.'

'You don't?' William put his fists on the table in front of the Abbot. 'Perhaps your holiness would like to share with us whatever reasons he might have for being so cheery. And before you begin, let me tell you they'd better be good ones. I've heard a thing or two about that place you run at Le Bec, buggery and so forth, and I might have to close it down.'

Lanfranc's eyes darkened but he pushed aside a tremor of anger. Always a trimmer, he never found it difficult to give a little here, appear flexible there. He took what he could, which was nearly always as much as he had hoped for, when the chance came.

'Sire,' he said, 'my lords. To me it seems everything is working out rather well.' He shifted on the three-legged stool, tried to get comfortable. 'First,' he continued, 'let's take these barons. If they come over themselves, supply their own men and so forth, then once we've won, you'll be obliged to give them land, they'll end up even more powerful and with even more potential for being pains in the arses than they are now. But they are obliged to give you money in lieu of men. Collect their dues now. Use their gold to employ directly anyone with a horse and a suit of armour who wants to come. Go outside Normandy. Every second son from Lithuania to the Pyrenees will be ready to have a go, and many will come for nothing if you promise them land.'

William slumped into his throne-like chair, pushed himself forward, big hands clasped in front of him.

'It'll take months to recruit a proper army from abroad.'

'Fine,' Lanfranc smiled, stooped sideways and pulled a roll of fine vellum from the flat leather bag he had brought with him. He undid the ribbon that tied the roll, spread the top sheet of lamb's skin in front of him. It was covered with spidery black writing, done in haste, with blotches here and there, no ornamentation. His finger ran down a list, paused.

'First. We're in too much of a hurry. Even after we have beaten Harold's army and dealt with the Godwinsons, there will be resistance. To put this down we must be sure we can feed ourselves and our troops and without relying on supplies from this side of the water. In short, the first advice I would give is that we postpone the invasion until the harvest is in. If we turn up before the end of July every barn in the country will be empty, and if we have to fight and destroy the fyrd, there'll be no one to reap the corn . . .'

William banged the table with his fists and grinned.

'Let the bast . . . bulgars get in a full year's supply of food first, *then* screw them! Why could none of you think of that?' He turned back to the foreign, Lombard churchman. 'So when do we make the crossing? September, October? By that time we might have men who can fight and ships that float the right way up. But gales, Lanfranc? What about gales? Don't we get a lot of storms round then?'

'End of September, beginning of October you usually get good spells of calm weather. The worst is over by the middle of September. Usually.'

'You're the Vicar. Speak to the Boss. Just make sure that when the time comes God doesn't blow it. What next?'

'My lord, Tostig, Harold's . . .'

'You don't have to tell me who Tostig is. What does he want – apart from Northumbria?'

CHAPTER
FORTY-THREE

They took the Roman road along the crest of Portsdown towards Southampton. The hawthorn was almost out again, briars and honeysuckle in bud. Bluebells carpeted the woodlands; cowslips nodded in the sheltered folds of the downs. For a time they dismounted and walked, side by side. Edith Swan-Neck stooped to pick three cowslips. She undid the brooch that held his cloak on his shoulder to pin them to his jerkin, but he caught her thin wrist in his strong hands and bent his head over the flowers.

'I've never noticed these red spots in them before,' he said.

'Fairy favours,' she said. 'In those freckles live their savours. Go on, smell.' Then she took his elbow: 'Listen. Cuckoo.'

They walked on a bit. Rip came up and took their horses' bridles; and all their train, men and women, hung back a little. Edith took his hand, spoke softly.

'What actually did happen?' she asked.

'I didn't fuck her, you know?'

'I know.'

'You do?'

'Of course.'

'You had a spy beneath the bed?'

She laughed again. 'I wouldn't be asking you what happened if I had. But go on, tell me. I want to know.'

He thought back. The wedding had taken place in the big church in

Oxford. Edwin and Morcar had wanted the Abbey but Harold had said no, we'll save that for her coronation, once all this business is over. It was a ploy and they knew it. They'd stay on board knowing their sister could get pregnant, that she would be a proper Queen too. They suggested York, but Harold said no again. It was too far north. Even back in March he had not wanted to leave the south. He told Edith all about it.

'It was cold. Remember March? Not a daffodil to be seen. And the poor thing was shivering until I made them cover her bridal dress with a proper fur cloak.'

'Not just with the cold.'

'No. She was terrified.'

'What's she like?'

'They say she's fourteen. I'd guess no more than twelve. Very thin. Mousy dark hair, not too clean. Too cold to give it a proper wash. She actually had a cold, nose streaming, sores on her lips. And spots on her forehead and cheeks.'

'Come on. You're going too far. I'm not jealous, you know?'

'But you want to know.'

'Yes. You'd want to, if you were me.'

'I suppose so.'

They walked on in silence for a few steps until she squeezed his hand.

'All right,' he said at last. 'But no one knows this except the poor thing herself, and me, and now you. And they had better not. If her brothers knew she was still a virgin the whole thing could fall apart.'

'So what did you do?'

'I read to her. Until she fell asleep.'

'You don't read too well.'

'It was stuff I knew by heart. Stories my mother told me.'

'In Danish?'

'Sort of half and half.'

'What sort of stories?'

'Fairy-stories, riddles. Some of the Irish ones you used to tell our kids. Battle of Maldon.'

'That must have thrilled her.'

'Sent her to sleep anyway.'

Gytha, mother of the Godwinsons, was an old woman, as old as the century or nearly. Born a Dane, sister of Ulf, whose wife was Canute's sister, she had been married to Godwin in 1018 shortly after Canute made Godwin an earl and one of his chief men in England. Thus her Danish lineage was not in itself royal, but she was a connection of Canute by marriage – a fact that made the English Danes revere her, and her sons too. Before Godwin died she had already withdrawn to a nunnery close to Cerne in Dorset, where, it was said, she became a priestess of the old religion. In her first years there she had studied with the old lady who had concocted the spurious ritual of betrothal which had been intended, for a matter of a few minutes at any rate, to give Edward the power to penetrate Gytha's daughter Edith. But that was all well in the past, and actually eight years before Gytha herself turned up at Cerne.

In 1066 she cultivated her garden, bred new types of fruit trees and roses by cross-fertilisation and grafting, and created the first herbaceous border since Roman times to flourish on a south-facing wall, with irises, giant daisies, acanthus, asphodel, carnations and pinks. And when the weather was cold or wet she retired to a small study where she laboured both with ancient books and even more by interviewing poets, minstrels, milk-maids and midwives to create a picture of an ancient religion that united the paganism of her Danish childhood with the remnants of Goddess worship that survived west of the Stour. In short, she was ideally suited to invent and weave a personal standard for Harold, a standard whose potency, he hoped, would ward off whatever was ill-omened about the gold dragon of Wessex.

She was tall but stooped, heavily built, had scant white hair, and cheeks lined like a walnut shell. When Harold and his small train arrived, she was wearing a purple fur-trimmed robe and a huge floppy black velvet hat. Round her neck dangled a heavy silver necklace providing mounts for a selection of large polished gem-stones – amethysts, topazes and garnets. It got in the way and banged into things.

She embraced Harold warmly and Edith Swan-Neck too; led them into an enclosed garden and made them sit at a table while mead and verjuice were sent for. A large late-flowering cherry filled most of the air above them; its clustered white blossoms, an almost orgasmic delight beneath the blue sky, fell, swirled when the breeze came, littered the grass.

'White for Eastertide,' Harold remarked. 'Two weeks late.'

'Rubbish,' said Gytha. 'Wearing white for Odin and the annual sacrifice of the king. Make the seed of the spring sowings germinate.'

The mead and verjuice arrived. Gytha insisted they both drank some verjuice – made from pressed crab-apples and vinegary in the first week of May as well as plain sour.

'Good for your bladders and purifies the blood. So. Why have you bothered to call on me?'

Harold explained about the battle standard – how he felt Ironside's dragon on its own was ill-omened, and, anyway, he wanted something a bit more personal. Had she any suggestions? Could she make one for him?

Gytha threw up an arm and pointed dramatically above the low tiled roof through a small stand of willows that stood by the brook and at the holly-crowned down beyond.

'The Fighting Man of Cerne,' she cried. 'I'll copy that exactly, on a brilliant green ground for you. Eight feet by six. Why not?'

Edith and Harold looked at each other.

'All of it?' Harold asked.

'Of course! Figure of manhood. In every sense. Our lot will love it . . . and the Normans will hate it.'

'It,' remarked Edith slyly, and neither were in any doubt as to what she meant by 'it', 'is a bit big.'

Harold blushed.

'How soon before it's finished?' he asked.

'Soon enough. You won't need it before Michaelmas.'

CHAPTER
FORTY-FOUR

Junipera popped a large translucent grape between her lushly painted lips. Beyond her head, red hair piled in coils and bound with a gold fillet, through cypresses and past the dark sweep of the theatre, Walt watched the eastern horizon darken to plum colour. His nose had stopped bleeding. 'And then it all turned sour,' she said. 'Serve him right for meddling with the old religion.'

'Poppycock,' said Quint, stroking a last sliver of white mountain goat cheese on to a crust. 'I'm sure the Fighting Man achieved all Gytha said it would. These things exist only in the mind you know, and if the image carried a potency for the Celts and simpler folk in his army then I'm sure they fought all the better for it.'

'It is true,' said Walt, 'that it was within a week or so of his visit to Cerne that things began to go wrong.'

Junipera smiled sweetly but with self-satisfaction.

'Go on,' she said. 'What was the first? Let me guess. That comet?'

'No. That was already just about gone by then. It appeared on the twenty-fourth of April. Of course, a lot of people said it was ill-omened – but Harold laughed it off: ill-omened, maybe, he said, but for whom?'

'He was wrong,' Junipera was insistent. 'Such things always signify profound change. He was in place. William was not. William was the change.'

'But the comet was everywhere,' Quint interjected.

'And there weren't changes here? We'll all be Muslims before the century is out because of them. Alp Arslan? William the Conqueror . . .?'

'Don't call him that!'

There was agony in Walt's voice.

Junipera shrugged, eased another grape from its hold.

'All right,' she said. 'Not the comet. What then?'

'Tostig turned up. On the Island. Bembridge, forty ships and a thousand men.'

'So what happened?' Alain asked, twanging the harp, but, young lad
as he was, suddenly interested in a story that looked as if it might yet
move to fighting and suchlike.

'Not a lot,' Walt went on.

Leofwine, duly commissioned by Harold to do so, chased Tostig out of
Bembridge and east along the coast as far as Sandwich which Tostig
briefly occupied. He seized the shipping in the harbour and press-ganged
sailors to sail them. Leofwine kept a watchful eye on him but did not
engage him. Meanwhile Harold went on to London where, for the first
time, he raised the fyrd, and, with a nucleus of housecarls, marched on
Sandwich. Tostig, faced now with two armies as well as a fleet, sailed
again, first up the River Burnham in Norfolk and then on to the
Humber. He headed south and was heavily defeated by the militia of the
ancient kingdom of Lindsey under Edwin of Mercia. He got clear and
ran into Morcar on the Yorkshire coast, who finished off what his
brother had started. Finally Tostig escaped north with only twelve small
ships from his original fleet. He went on to Scotland, where he was welcomed by his old friend King Malcolm.

By and large Harold, when he heard how the Mercians and
Northumbrians had behaved, was well-pleased. Some of the doubt he
felt for Edwin's loyalty lifted, even though he knew both Edwin and
Morcar had been fighting to keep Tostig from getting Northumbria
back. Moreover his defences against invasion had proved reliable – the
fleet had sailed and handled itself well; wherever the invading host landed
it was met within a day or two by loyal troops.

The summer wore on, June into July. Scurriers nipped to and fro
across the Channel: there was no way, they said, that William could be
ready to sail before the middle of July. During three days' feasting at the
beginning of August, Erica and Walt were married, then Walt returned

to Portchester to continue training the newly recruited housecarls and the fyrd which Harold dared not disbandon. The scurriers revised the probable date when William would be ready to mid-August at the earliest. It was about then, in the first week of August, Walt declared, that the mood changed and some began to feel that things might not turn out as they had expected. There was talk again of the oaths Harold had taken on holy relics at Bayeux the year before.

The harvest came in and Lanfranc's strategy paid off. The fyrd, committed to serve for only two months without pay, and desperate to make sure that there would be food for the winter, became more and more discontented. They were laid off piecemeal to begin with, then more or less completely, but warned to return at a moment's notice. And then the weather changed. A solid anticyclone with high pressure set in: weeks of fine weather, not a cloud in the sky and what wind there was from the north and north-east.

'Isn't all this a bit boring?' Junipera asked.

'But,' Walt tried to ignore her, 'a wind from the north may have kept William at bay, but it allowed Harald Hardrada to sail from Norway . . .'

'Another Harold? How confusing!'

'Har*ald*,' said Walt. 'King of Norway. You must have heard of him. He served your Emperor, and the Empress Zoë before that . . .'

'Oh *that* Harald. I never knew he was King of Norway. My goodness, what a man. I saw him once. So handsome, that red-gold hair, and seven feet tall. I didn't even know he's still alive—'

'He isn't.'

'But you said . . .'

'What I'd like to know about,' Quint interrupted, 'is William and his army. How they were getting on all through this summer—'

'Well, I don't know, do I?' Walt was a touch petulant. 'I wasn't there, was I?'

'But Taillefer does. You were in Normandy. Could you fill us in on that side of the story before Walt comes to his conclusion?'

Taillefer leaned across the table, knife in one hand, pomegranate in the other.

'They said the devil was in him, the devil was his father, and I can see what they meant – assuming you believe in the devil . . .'

'The devil exists, no doubt of that,' Walt muttered grimly.

'Every doubt in the world,' said Quint, robustly. 'But tell us exactly why you are led to speak in such extreme terms about a man who was, after all, no more than a man.'

'It's difficult to put in words.' Taillefer worked the knife across the hard rind of the fruit, then tore it in half revealing two heart-shaped caskets filled with jelly-covered seeds. Using his teeth he tore out a mouthful and began to chew, sometimes crushing the seeds, sometimes spitting them out into his cupped left hand. Juice ran down his chin.

'Treat that fruit with respect,' Junipera interjected. 'It has its place in the holiest of places.'

'I know. I am hoping it will inspire me.'

'What mumbo-jumbo is this?' Quint expostulated tetchily.

Taillefer and Junipera glanced at each other with expressionless meaning. Walt yawned. Too much wine.

'There was always emptiness in his eyes which were dark. There was nothing behind them, no soul, no inner man. He was driven, but driven by things outside him. He had no desires of his own – he always did what he thought was expected of him. Which, of course, is not to say he was in any way humble or obedient – not in the least. Put it like this – he always had to prove himself, and he set himself to achieve whatever others had said would do this. Of course, they were never right, so he was always driven on and on. Was this attributable to his upbringing? Perhaps. A mother whose first-born he was, the only child she bore to his father, a woman whose status as the daughter of a respectable tanner had been ruined, but who was never made the duchess she should have been. One can imagine: "Billy, whatever people say, you are a duke, a duke's son, behave like one, get your due, make sure you have what is yours . . . and so on." Something like that, but something more.

'In some ways he was like the living dead. As if possessed by a spirit that did not belong in his body, had come in from outside, from somewhere else. It even informed his ordinary movements, walking, drinking, eating. He walked jerkily, often with his head on one side but questing forward, with long strides, his hands clasped behind his back. Sometimes it seemed they had been bound there, that he had even asked to have them bound there to keep them out of mischief. Mischief? He could have used them to tear and eat the liver from a new-born baby if he felt it would say something about himself he wanted others to believe.

'But you must not get the idea that this gaucheness led him to be in any way physically unskilful. He rode well but always with a sort of bullying savagery. One cannot imagine any horse ever felt happy beneath him. And, of course, he fought like a lion for strength, speed, and bravery. He did not believe he could be hurt and when he was he brushed it aside as of utterly no consequence—'

'But was he intelligent?' Quint asked.

'He was cunning. Could always work out or accept from someone else what the next step should be to achieve what he had set himself. But stupid over anything long-term.'

'Really? How so?' Junipera asked.

'There was no possible way that Normandy could conquer England. Normandy was smaller, poorer, in almost every respect more backward. He lacked almost all the resources needed for such a project . . .'

'Yet for twenty years he had fought Brittany, France and Anjou . . .'

'Fought them, yes. But those wars were basically defensive.'

'But there was, is, more to him than mere cunning and an ability for physical savagery.'

'Oh yes. He was utterly determined. Completely single-minded, steadfast, tenacious, unflinching, unwavering once his mind was made up. Nothing would shift him. He would listen to and follow, almost humbly, any amount of advice or wisdom, experience, call it what you like, so long as he could see it helped the drive to his final objective. But he was totally deaf to anyone who questioned this final objective, totally incapable of accepting the possibility of obstacles that could not be overcome. Once the men close to him, Odo, Robert, Lanfranc, realised this they became a good and reliable team. Once they sought not to find out or do what was best, but concentrated their minds and bodies on being their master's tools, the servants of his ambition, then they worked for him extraordinarily well. We don't have enough armed men in Normandy – we'll get them elsewhere. We don't have ships or seamen – we'll build the former and, as for the latter, we'll wait for fair wind, quiet weather, and take the shortest route possible. We lack money – we'll screw the last ear of corn out of the peasantry, we'll melt down the gold and silver in every church . . . and we'll borrow. It'll all be paid back in the end. Did you know, already, the plate, ornaments, reliquaries, vestments and all the rest in every Norman Abbey, cathedral and church, are English-made, looted from English churches to replace what he took to pay his army with?'

Walt groaned.

'He must have a prodigious eye for detail, a huge capacity for continuous work,' Quint suggested.

'Not at all, not at all.' Taillefer was adamant. 'Well, work perhaps, in a way. He never rested, was always restless, impatient, bullying, chivvying people to do yesterday what he was asking of them today, often meddling in things where the people he had given the tasks to knew far better than he how to achieve them. Often this "work", this unrelenting effort, got in people's way, hindered things—'

'Was counter-productive?' Quint, as usual, ready with an appropriate neologism.

'Just so. But no eye for detail at all. He never noticed anything at all until it went wrong. Then, of course, he had a tantrum. But while he has no particular eye for relevant detail he does have a mania for neatness. Show him a line of wrong details with one right one and he'll smash the right one. It's because of this he's got this great reputation as an organiser, and in a way it worked. I mean the crew that turned up during that summer—'

'Mixed bunch were they?'

'Mixed? They had one thing in common. What I'd call a criminal bent. There was nothing that gang wasn't capable of in the way of savagery or mayhem. You know how it is. If a man has a good horse, good armour, and the ability to use them, and they're his own, not given to him by some king or prince or lord who can take them back, then he virtually has *carte blanche* to do what he likes . . . until he meets two men with good horses and good armour. Well. If you have something worth keeping – land, a family, even a sense of honour or knowing the difference between right and wrong – then you might use your horse and armour for reasonably civilised purposes, like defending the people who depend on you, or keeping your land out of some other guy's hands. But this lot had nothing. Second sons. Bastards. Lots and lots of bastards, almost all Fitz this or Fitz that . . . Some were people of family or property who had committed some crime where they came from and were on the run. Others plain straightforward mercenaries. There were Vikings, Lithuanians, Lats, Poles, Franks, Lombards, Basques. A few Moors too, believe it or not.

'They began to trickle in with the spring. And of course, lined up on a beach on the Normandy coast they looked like a rabble. The Bastard of all bastards was furious. No one would cross the Channel unless they were wearing a standard conical helmet with nose-piece, a coat of mail to the knees but split from the waist both fore and aft, so it wouldn't get in the way on a horse, but protect the soldier's thighs, a spear, a lanceolate-shaped shield and a side-arm. Only with the side-arm would he allow any variation, knowing that this was the one most of the killing would be done with and they'd get on better with what they were used to: could be mace – ball and chain or spiked – axe or sword. Boots with spurs. And a damned good horse, preferably a stallion or a gelding. If the arms and armour they had didn't fit, then either they bought a new lot out of their own pockets or they chucked in what they had to be melted down and reforged according to regs for free. Nearly all took the second option since very few of them had any gold or money. This was April, May, and since they'd settled on September, he reckoned he had time to do all this.

'Then he split them up into three divisions. All those from the west and south were called Bretons and would fight on the left. Those from east of the Rhine and the north would be called Franks and would fight on the right. And those who were Normans or claimed to be so (a lot of them came from Norman colonies in places like Sicily) fought in the middle where he himself would be. At least he could be pretty sure that the middle lot would understand what he said when he gave a command. And within each group there were Norman commanders or people who pretended to be Norman by taking on Norman names: Howard, Keith, Waldegrave, Howe, Hague, Warenne, Fitzosbern, Malet and so on. What you've got to remember about this gang of dissolute adventurers, often convicted murderers, lootists, church-burners and rapists, is that they had nothing to lose when it came to a battle: an arm, a leg, a life, but they were lucky to have survived as long as they had, and all knew they'd be chopped up or hanged sooner or later. Nothing to lose and everything to gain. While the English had everything to lose. Put it in one word – England. When you have something worth fighting for you want to stay alive to enjoy it; when you're fighting to get something you never had you might as well die if you're not going to get it. It's a hairbreadth between the two, and it's more a question of blind, evil desperation against real courage . . .'

He had realised that Walt was showing signs of distress at what he was trying to say, and his voice faded away. Junipera stood up.

'Time for bed,' she said. 'Your children are asleep already. Tomorrow evening perhaps Walt can resume telling us the final chapter of this tragic tale. Personally I can't wait to hear what happened to Harald Hardrada.'

As they struggled with weariness and tipsiness down the marble passages to the rooms Junipera had set aside for them, with Taillefer carrying Adeliza in his arms and Quint leading Alain by the hand, Walt overheard their postscript to Taillefer's account of William's army.

'What a crew! I think I've thought of a word to describe them – and their leader. A word which means sickness of the soul, morbidity in the spirit, so no action is unthinkable. Psychopath. What do you think? A bunch of psychopaths. And to think, if they hold on in spite of rebellions and uprisings, these people will become the rulers of the English for . . . Well, I suppose for ever.'

'For a thousand years anyway,' Taillefer answered.

Rebellions? Uprisings. It still went on, then? It hadn't all ended at Hastings with the slaying of the King?

Walt felt a cold clutch of terror, self-disgust and sheer misery close round his heart.

Later, lying on his bed in the near dark, Taillefer was haunted by a memory, a vision – that of the tall mad duke, pulling at his goatee, lurching along with his head on one side, spitting and raging in his high nasal voice at some minor breach of order he had spotted. 'A place for everything and everything in its place,' he howled. 'Write it down. Write it all down. Only way to be sure we know where we're at. I want it all on record, till Doomsday, if necessary.'

Odd, really, considering the man was virtually unlettered.

CHAPTER
FORTY-FIVE

'You actually *saw* Harald Hardrada.' Quint looked across the table at Junipera, fixed her violet eyes with his pale blue ones. She blushed a little.

'It was a long time ago.'

'Nineteen years since he left this part of the world. He went back to Norway to be King when Magnus died.'

'I was just . . . a chit, a child. He was in his early twenties. But so handsome. And . . . huge. I was actually at Ephesus at the time with my first husband,' she looked round the table, her face as bland as milk, 'I married at a very young age, you know? It was a meeting of merchants, men of wealth and so forth. Harald was raising money for an expedition to Crete and Malta to reclaim them for the Empress.'

'Did you meet him?'

'Actually, yes. Quite briefly. After he had got promises of funds and promised in return, in Empress Zoë's name, to reduce the tariffs if he were successful, there was a small social function, not a feast you understand, more a sort of soirée . . .'

She tightened her lips, stared them all down.

'Go on Walt,' she concluded. 'Tell us about Harald Hardrada in 1066. He must have been an old man by then.'

'Yes. I suppose so. Just turned fifty, I should think . . .'

Junipera gave a tiny sigh.

'He was a great warrior,' Walt went on. 'Some have called him the last of the Vikings. But he was a good leader too, and a good general. I don't know why he thought he should be King of England—'

'Actually,' said Quint, 'I believe it went something like this: when Canute died Magnus claimed the English throne. Then Harold Harefoot died and that left Harthacanute. He and Magnus came to an agreement . . .'

'This is getting boring again,' Junipera declared.

'Certainly is,' agreed Adeliza and Alain. 'Go on Walt, get to the exciting bits.'

'I'll try. Well. What went on between Tostig and Hardrada, how long they'd been in touch with each other, no one knows for sure—'

'So we don't have to be told about it.'

'Anyway, early in September, with the weather still bright and what wind there was from the north, Hardrada brought a big army and fleet across from Norway via the Orkneys, where he probably met Tostig, and landed on the Northumberland coast. He sacked Scarborough . . .'

'Big? How big was this army?'

'Two hundred long-boats. Getting on for ten thousand men.'

'Oh dear, that is big.'

'Precisely. We were in London when we heard about Scarborough. It was the twelfth of September . . .'

'Ten thousand? You're joking.' Harold was horrified.

'Two hundred boats anyway,' said little Albert who had brought the news. 'I counted them myself. So it can't be far off ten thousand.'

'Let's look at this sensibly.' Gyrth leant across the table. 'Horses, back-up, auxiliaries, with luck it might be as few as six thousand fully armed warriors.'

'That's still double what Edwin and Morcar can get out.'

'Oh, come on. The harvest's in, they can raise the fyrd – ten, twenty thousand.'

'That will need a month, maybe longer. Hardrada will have cut them up by then. Anyway. Hardrada could take on a stripling like Edwin with half the numbers and beat him. For Christ's sake, bloody Tostig could.'

Silence. Six of them, Harold's brothers Leofwine and Gyrth, with Walt, Wulfric, Timor and Albert, looked at the King and waited. Harold pulled his palms down across his face and got up. They watched him walk down the small hall and out into the sunlight. Leofwine made as if to follow him, but Gyrth put a hand on his arm and held him back.

Outside Harold walked slowly, head bent, down a narrow sandy path flanked with rosemary bushes to the west door of the abbey church. His abbey church. Waltham Abbey. He paused in front of oak doors framed in a rounded arch and for a moment or two let his eyes wander up and down the pillared sides and then across the semi-circular tympanum above the doors. None of it was on a grand scale, indeed he could easily put his hand on St Helena's foot at the bottom of the tympanum without really stretching. Along with most people, he believed her to have been British, indeed as far as he was concerned, never having much bothered himself with the minutiae of history, English.

She was kneeling in front of the True Cross which, inspired by a dream, she had just caused to be uncovered, and was surrounded at a lower level by workmen with spades and picks, smaller than her, since they were less important, but with angels above her and finally the Trinity. The whole thing, done in very deep relief, in places almost free-standing, was painted brightly with lazuli, vermilions, and gold leaf amongst other tinctures, was filled with swirling life.

He pushed open the doors and walked slowly up the nave towards the main altar. On either side of him the round solid pillars stood sentinel, each carved differently with dogstooth patterns, herring-bone, lozenges and with differently foliated capitals through whose leaves little ogres and imps occasionally peeped out. They supported oak beams and vaulting which continued the illusion of a forest or tree-temple as well as supporting the barn-like roof. Again gold leaf and other colours glimmered from bosses and supporting brackets sculpted to resemble angels singing or playing harps, lyres, hautboys and trumpets. He stopped a yard or two in front of the chancel step and let his eye wander over the marvellous intricacy of the gold and crystal reliquary, enamelled and studded with jewels, in the centre of the cross. He could not quite see, not without going right up to it, the splinter of elder set in amber. But he knew it was there, knew it was a piece of the Cross itself.

Harold was not devout – not in the Christian sense, anyway. But he understood and felt the numinous, that he was in the presence of an object which, though it did not inspire him to conventional veneration, emanated power.

Slowly the agitation which he had felt faded and a calm peacefulness filled his mind. It was as he had expected. He had not needed to know what to do – that was obvious. What he had needed was courage and certainty. The certainty that he was right, and the courage to carry it through with unwavering resolution, and that was what those few moments gave him. He walked back to the hall.

'We march north,' he said.

For all his certainty they looked up with doubt, even dread, though in their hearts they, too, knew he was right – it was the only possible decision.

'But,' he went on, 'we must cover our arses.'

The housecarls, four-and-a-half thousand of them now, were stationed in five companies along the coast – at Portchester, Bosham, Littlehampton on the Arun estuary, Pevensey, and Hastings – each with enough ships to carry them to a concentration whenever the Norman threat should develop. They were of course also mounted, so if they were faced with a contrary wind they could move by land. Indeed, Harold had made sure the coastal tracks were clear, the bridges in place, the fords passable. Behind the coast, up in the downs in front of the great forest of the Weald, were the twenty or so camps where the Sussex and Kent fyrd, a further five thousand strong, were already regrouping since the harvest was now in.

Harold made three crucial dispositions, bearing in mind that William would cross the Channel as soon as he had a fair wind and that this might happen even before he could move against Hardrada or, even worse, at that moment when he and the housecarls would be at the furthest point away from the south. He ordered the housecarls to concentrate on London – thus they could move south again right up to the moment he committed himself to a move to the north. He ordered the fleet into the Thames estuary too – without soldiers to man it as a fighting force, it could do little or nothing to hinder William while he was at sea. From London it could go north or south as . . .

'Hang on,' Quint grunted. 'The general understanding we have now of the campaign is that thanks to William's strategic brilliance in delaying his crossing for so many months Harold's ships were falling apart and had to be refitted, supplies were running out, and the fyrd had more or less disbanded itself.'

'Rubbish,' cried Walt. 'No such thing at all. Harold was far too good a commander to let anything like that happen.'

Quint shrugged, popped half an apple into his mouth.

'So,' he went on, munching through it, 'what was his grand strategy?'

Harold laid it all out there and then, in the hall at Waltham, within ten minutes of hearing the news of Hardrada's landing.

He ordered the fyrd to break up into yet smaller groups so they could sustain themselves without being a burden on the countryside, but to maintain the line of the Downs in front of the forest.

'If,' he said, 'William lands before we get north of Watford Gap, we turn back and face him. The fleet sails back and destroys his, wherever it is. The fyrd harry him but avoid general engagements until we come up with him on ground of our choosing. If, however, we get to Watford Gap without news of his sailing then we push on and deal with Hardrada. If Edwin and Morcar can keep out of trouble until we get there we'll see him off, no problem.

'Then if William still hasn't sailed, we come back and nothing has been lost. But if he has, and he lands when we're up in Northumbria or wherever, then we let him march inland, as far as the Thames if he likes. He'll have left his fleet, and with luck ours will be able to catch it. The fyrd will be scouting round his tail all the time he's in the forest. By the time he reaches the Thames he'll have the armies of both the north and the south in front of him. If he fights he's licked. If he sues for peace we make him eat shit. But the whole thing depends on one factor. Edwin and Morcar must not fight on their own. They must fall back in front of Hardrada until we can get there.'

Hardrada and Tostig sailed up the Humber and then the Ouse towards York. This was Tostig's first objective. York was a big town. A big manufacturing town, a big trading town, a port, for though it was thirty miles or more from the open sea the land between was a flat marshy plain and the Ouse and other rivers were navigable far inland. It was almost as big as London – some say bigger. Although Tostig had been genuinely unpopular north of the Tees he had got on well with the burghers of York and he told Hardrada that with reasonable guarantees given on both sides it would surrender without a fight.

They sailed up the Ouse, through Selby, which paid handsome tribute to avoid being pillaged, as far as Riccall, where they learned that Edwin and Morcar were concentrating at Tadcaster, some eight miles to the east. The invaders left their ships at Riccall and prepared to march on York with the River Ouse protecting their west flank, their left, and in response Edwin and Morcar moved to York too, about ten miles. Timor caught up with them half-way between Tadcaster and York, on the evening of the eighteenth.

They were strung out over three miles on the Roman road that links Leeds and York, much of it raised above the levels of the waterlands around. It was a grey day, but not cold, cloud filling the sky to the south and west beneath the high white cirrus above. For sure the weather was breaking at last after one of the longest dry spells anyone could remember.

With the sun dipping towards the Pennines Timor tried leaving the road but soon found his horses, he had five men with him, couldn't cope with ground that was marshy even after that dry late summer, so they had to stay on the Roman road and use the bridges and causeways. But it was virtually blocked. The fyrd at the rear of the column simply filled the space and moved forward at a steady stroll – you couldn't call it a march. Further up the mounted housecarls rode four abreast and none would move to the side until they had been cajoled, sworn at and occasionally pushed. The result was he couldn't get to Edwin and Morcar personally before they reached York by when they were having supper in the great hall there.

He showed his documents to a lackey who took them to Edwin. Edwin scanned them, turned to Morcar who shook his head: tell me, he seemed to say. He went back to the bone he was chewing. A lackey brought Timor a lump of bread and cheese and a flagon of dark watery ale, the 'brrun' of the region. Eventually, when the earls had eaten and drunk as much as they could, they sent for him. Nevertheless, he was made to stand in the body of the hall and look up at them, across the table.

'You're from Harold?'

'Yes.'

'One of his war council?'

'Yes.'

'What's he got to say, then?'

Timor took a deep breath.

'He asks you not to fight Hardrada until he gets here,' he said.

The faces of both brothers darkened. They muttered to each other. The lesser earls and thegns around them fell silent. At last Morcar looked up.

'You mean – he thinks we've not got the beating of Hardrada and that bugger Tostig without him?'

'No. But he does think that on your own Hardrada will give you a good day's fighting before you beat him and that you'll lose many men, men we will need when it comes to beating William.'

'Is he saying he can't beat William without us?'

Edward the Confessor would have swallowed his pride and said yes. Harold had told Timor to return the same answer as he had already given Morcar but the other way round.

'He believes he can, but only at great cost. He asks you to consider how much better it will be if both invaders are forced off our land with as little loss of life as possible.'

Edwin laughed, almost mockingly.

'There's no glory to be won outfacing an enemy by sheer weight of numbers.'

They turned away from Timor, ignored him. Edwin called for a pair of dice, Morcar for a refill of his drinking horn. Timor waited. Edwin rolled the dice and the thegn on his left picked them up and rolled them too. There was a lot of laughter at the result. Morcar signalled to a harpist waiting nearby that he should play. Timor took a step forward.

'My lords,' he called, 'it is the King's wish you should not fight Hardrada until the King is here.'

Silence fell, spread down the hall. Again Edwin's face flushed, then he leant back and spread his elbows. Head on one side he spoke quietly.

'Come closer, little man, and listen carefully to what the Earls of Mercia and Northumbria have to say. First. The weather has changed. Your master will have felt the change too. Even if he is on his way north, will he not now march back again knowing the Duke could per-haps be putting to sea at this very moment—?'

'No, my Lord. He asks me to swear to you on his behalf that he will come north first—'

'An oath sworn when the wind blew from the north. Second. Hardrada has come with Tostig, your master's brother. Will Harold treat his brother like the traitor he is? Or will he seek to patch the quarrel

between them? Do not try to answer that question for no one knows the
secret heart of a man where his kin are concerned. And last. If we do not
go out and fight Hardrada we must either leave this city, our city, to be
plundered by him, or seek to defend it if he attacks. The walls are nothing, the defences have not been kept up – not at all during all the time
Tostig was Earl here. The streets are narrow, the houses wood. If we stay
within the walls all Hardrada has to do is fire it and attack us in the confusion. No. We must fight him, and we must fight him in the open. And
that is what we intend to do. Tomorrow. In the fields that lie between
here and Fulford Bridge. You may, if you please, be our guest and watch,
watch while real soldiers deal with this old man and the jerkin-lifter
traitor at his side.'

Timor thought that that was all, and turned to go. Small though he
was and slight with it, he was as loth to plead, cajole or even argue as any
mighty lord or warrior. But Morcar had leapt from his seat, came round
the table and followed him into the hall, caught him by the shoulder and
turned him. He spoke into his ear, almost a hiss, so no one else could
hear.

'After you have told your master how we beat the Norwegian, add
one thing more. Ask him, ask it from Edwin and Morcar, ask him why
our sister, to whom he was wed these six months since, remains a virgin.
We should like to know, for as things stand it can mean only one of two
things. Either he has no balls, but his bastards in Ireland would seem to
suggest this is not the right answer, or he means to set her aside once we
have fought his battles for him. Tell him, I, Morcar of Northumbria,
want a true answer and will challenge him to give it me when we meet,
King or no.'

Timor smelled the mead coming deep from the young man's stomach
and decided that carrying things further would lead to a fight at best, and
a beating at worst. He left the hall. Not at all a question of *Timor mortis
conturbat me*, simply, discretion can be the better part of valour.

CHAPTER
FORTY-SIX

Six days later Harold walked over ground still littered with thousands of corpses. There were not many carrion birds, nor looters of bodies either – by then an even larger killing field lay some eight miles to the east, at Stamford Bridge, and such animals, birds, and men who profit from battlefields had moved on. Timor told him, and Walt, who was there too, how the earlier battle had gone.

'I was standing about here, just behind Edwin's standard. As you can see the city's walls are a mile or so behind us and we felt we could fall back on them if we had to. Although the ground is almost flat what slopes there are were in our favour, especially over there to the east, on the left of our position.'

The ground was uncultivated. There were banks of rushes near the river, reeds and coarse grass and low bog-myrtle and then as the land rose a little heather as well – none of it making any serious impediment to movement. It was clearly common land on which cattle and sheep were grazed, and in places where the river bank was low the ground was churned up where animals had come down to drink.

'Over to the west,' Timor went on, 'you can see the ground is flatter and marshy but the right wing had its shoulder on the bank of the Ouse . . .'

'Right up to the river?' Harold asked.

'Yes.'

'And how many housecarls did they have, Edwin and Morcar?'

'About four thousand.'

Harold shaded his eyes.

'And the left was on that rise?'

'Yes.'

'That makes a hell of a long line for four thousand men to hold.'

'Yes. But the fyrd made up another five thousand or so. They put most of the fyrd down on the right, protected, they thought, by the river, and the best housecarls on the left. The idea was that these housecarls, Northumbrians led by Morcar, should attack Hardrada's right, using the slope for added advantage, while the rest of the housecarls held the centre, and the fyrd the right.'

'But there's a second river running right through the middle of the position.'

It meandered through the coarse grass and rushes and did not look much. Where it ran into the Ouse it spread into a wide triangle of mud – one of the places where the cattle came to drink since for a space both it and the eastern shore of the Ouse had no real banks and the water was shallow. At first sight, it was little more than a ditch.

'It's rained a bit since then, so there wasn't as much water in it as there is now . . .'

'But it was just as wide, the sides just as deep and steep. And the ground between it and the Ouse must have been almost as boggy as it is now. And I'd guess a thousand or more died in it. Tell me. You were in position before the main body of Hardrada's army came up?'

'Yes.'

'So his scouts, front-runners could see it all. And Tostig too, no doubt, who lived here for what, ten years, and knew the land like the back of his hand.' Harold shook his head, pulled palms down his face, grimaced. 'What puzzles me,' he added, 'is how any of you got away alive.'

The first thing that became clear to Timor was that the invaders were in very good order, well armed, holding their positions well as they dismounted and passed their horses to the rear. The pale yellow watery sunlight glittered on their mail and helmets, some of which were the old-fashioned Viking ones with horns or wings. A screen of lighter troops with archers walked in front of them in open order: they would be enough to hinder or slow down an early assault from the Northumbrians and Mercians, give the housecarls time to form up to answer it. The

standards of both Hardrada and Tostig were together and in the centre –
Hardrada's the huge black raven on a white ground, the Land Waster,
dreaded for a century or more.

As soon as the invaders' right came to the foot of the slope and up to
the ditch, which at this point really was little more than a ditch, being a
good half-mile from its junction with the Ouse, Morcar led the
Northumbrians in an attack down the slope which favoured them. The
light troops, all on the English side from the fyrd, briefly skirmished
between the two lines, firing arrows, throwing spears, axes and stones
tied to short handles. Then, the Northumbrian housecarls charged. The
first onslaught was fierce and the invaders fell back fifty yards or more,
but contesting every inch.

'Did they link shields?'

'Only when the pressure warranted it.'

Timor, looking again out over the bare, corpse-strewn slopes, remembered the repeated charges of the English, led by thegns wielding huge
axes, and heavy swords, how they waded into the ranks of the Norsemen
who often played a cunning game, letting the attackers get beyond the first
line, separating them into smaller groups and then cutting them up. Bit by
bit the attack slowed down, the Northumbrians pulled back, regained
breath, and then charged in again, but with every yard won the slope levelled and no longer favoured the English. By midday the invaders'
superior numbers began to tell, and the attacks became weaker. Morcar
was hurt early on – severely enough to make it difficult for him to fight,
though he continued to direct the assault from higher up the slope.

'But they did not counter-attack?'

'Not then. Not yet.'

'What was happening elsewhere?'

'Not a lot. The Mercians crossed the ditch in the centre and the
Norsemen fell back a little but then held their ground. They were very
evenly matched, so much so that for some of the time it seemed they
were just content to throw things at each other and shout abuse, then the
Mercians would come forward in a surge, the Norsemen fell back
another twenty yards, locked shields and held them—'

'Oh, he was a cunning bastard, old Hardrada . . .'

Timor, who had been there, knew what Harold meant, but was
impressed that now, walking over the field, Harold was able to see so
clearly what had happened. The fyrd on the extreme English right, filling

the angle made by the junction of the ditch and the river, began to break ranks and move towards the ditch; some, without orders, even crossed it, urging on the Mercian centre, clearly wanting to join them. At that moment, it was now well past midday, Timor recalled how the horsemen about the Land Waster suddenly moved to their left, and Hardrada himself, dismounting and seizing a huge double-handed axe, led fresh men who had not yet been engaged at all, across the muddy shallow patch where the cattle came for water ('It was firmer ground then than it is now,' Timor said.) They waded into the fyrd, whose ranks had been depleted by their movement to the centre. At the same time the Norse centre suddenly surged forward. Both the fyrd and the Mercian housecarls were now forced back into the ditch where it was narrowest and the banks four, five feet high and steep, the fyrd on the west bank the housecarls on the east, and both in complete confusion.

'He cut them up,' Timor concluded. 'The slaughter was terrible. It went on almost to dusk for the English were by then trapped on all sides, by men, the ditch and the river, and of course outnumbered anyway. They fought well. As well as they could.'

By now they had themselves reached the north-west bank of the ditch. It was still filled by numberless naked corpses – when the battle was over, and the leaders were negotiating terms for the surrender of York without putting it to fire and sword, the Norsemen had forced the prisoners they had taken to strip off the chain-mail, and gather up the shields, helmets and swords of the fallen. A great pile of weaponry still remained above the cattle-crossing, guarded now by Harold's men. But already in England there were more arms and armour than there were men who knew how to use them.

Harold, and the group about him, came to a standstill. Harold sighed and turned away.

'Last week,' he said, 'we got news from Normandy. William got a south-westerly breeze. This must have been getting on for a fortnight ago. He could have crossed but he's a careful, wily bugger and he used it for a dummy run. Moved his fleet from Dives, near Caen, across the Seine Estuary and all the way up to St Valery on the Somme. Remember St Valery and Guy de Ponthieu? He lost a couple of ships and some horses, but the whole trip was longer than the one he now faces.'

Nearby, two crows squabbled with flapping black wings over the eye of a corpse. Behind Harold, Rip from Thornig Hill pulled his jerkin up and his leggings down and pissed, carefully aiming the stream into the mouth of another. His own cheek had been slashed to the bone and, as both hands were occupied, flies settled in the gash. He shook his head to shift them.

'For all we know,' Harold went on, 'he could have done it by now. He could be in London, for all we know . . .'

'I have to confess,' Junipera intervened, 'you've got me a bit lost. What you have just told us is your friend Timor's account of the battle outside York . . .?'

'That's right.'

'But you're telling it as you heard it from his lips almost a week later . . .?'

'Yes.'

'And that was after the second battle, the one where Harold beat the Norsemen.'

'The day after, yes.'

Adeliza chipped in, pert as usual.

'Twentieth of September, battle of Fulford. Twenty-fifth of September, battle of Stamford Bridge, twenty-sixth of September Timor tells you about the battle of Fulford. Got it?'

'Got it. So now you're going to tell us about Stamford Bridge. Which you actually took part in yourself.'

'Hang on a minute,' Quint interrupted. 'Two pitched battles on top of each other and with a third still to come is a bit much. I'd like to hear first what our friend Taillefer can tell us about what was happening in Normandy, this move from Dives to the Somme, and so on.'

'Picture this.' Taillefer took his harp out of Alain's hands, adjusted a couple of the tuning pegs, settled the base on the edge of his chair between his legs and stroked a couple of arpeggios out of it. The rich inlays of gold and mother-of-pearl in its sound-box glimmered in the lamp-light. 'The sea pearly, glaucous . . .'

'What *does* that word mean?' Quint asked with some petulance. Being ignorant about something was one thing he hated more than admitting ignorance – but only just.

'Having a yeasty bloom as on a grape or plum.' Taillefer steadied the harp with his left hand and reached a glaucous plum out of the bowl in front of him. 'Just the day for a sail,' he went on, having first removed the stone from his mouth. His fingers plucked out a rhythmic little ditty, the sort of tune sailors sing as they haul up canvas. 'The breeze light, hardly enough to shift the violet and mauve haze which hung along the horizon beneath a distant chain of pearls that might have marked the coast of the Isle of Wight—'

'A hundred miles away,' scoffed Quint. 'I don't think so.'

'Please, Quint, will you allow our friend to get on with his story? After all, it was you who asked for this interlude . . .'

'A hundred and fifty long-boats and over fifty tubbier transports, and not a tree left standing for five or ten miles inland. They were all pulled up on the long sandy shore beneath the low white cliffs of the area, sometimes not cliffs at all but just a long sandy dune covered with spiky, squeaky blue grass. And in tents and benders behind, in the fields or clear-felled forest, about three thousand knights, that is fully armed men with horses, another couple of thousand without horses, and maybe the same of archers, stick-throwers, spearmen and the like. There was a lot of confusion on that day – psychological as well as physical. For a start many thought that this was it, this embarkation which had been ordered meant they were *en route* for England, fame, gold and glory, land of your own or a watery grave.

'For twenty minutes or so things went pleasantly enough, never more than a mile or so off-shore, the wind still light but steady. It must have been quite a sight from a distance; close-up, I was on the third boat in the inland line, it was pretty bloody chaotic. Lines? Yes, of course. Our anally obsessed leader—'

'Your *what*?'

'It's a mental condition caused by an over-disciplined approach to defecation in early infancy,' Quint supplied. 'Taillefer and I have been discussing it. Symptoms are obsessively tidy minds, outbursts of almost uncontrollable rage when things are found to be out of place or not working—'

'I think we get the picture. You're saying basically that William organised his fleet in two lines—'

'Three, actually.'

'In three lines because his mother smacked him some forty years earlier if he shat in the wrong place or at the wrong time.'

'Yes. You see his mother, always unsure of her position as the unmarried mistress of the duke, self-consciously aware of her low origins, was over-anxious that her son should be well brought up from the very start—'

'Rubbish. Go on, Taillefer, and try to keep it simple. You're in the third boat of the line, nearest the shore . . .'

Taillefer strummed, collected his thoughts and went on.

'The Duke's ship, the *Mora*, was, of course, the leading ship in the outside line, marked by the fact that it was flying a long white and gold banner or pennant given to him and blessed by the Pope. The trouble was that though these ships looked identical they had been hurriedly put together by a variety of craftsmen, some less skilled than others, so under sail they handled very differently.

'First the ship immediately behind him kept creeping up, and once even bumped the stern of the *Mora*; to avoid a repetition, the master let his boat yaw almost broadside on and drift towards the middle line. This caused his sail to take the wind out of the *Mora*'s sail and slowed her down even more, so now the ships in the innermost line began to edge in front of all. The Duke ranted and raged, screamed with fury. This put the fear of death into our master's soul and he ordered the steersman to put up the helm in an attempt to heave-to and of course the one behind rammed us amidships. The effect of this ran through the whole fleet and within half an hour of getting clear to sea, Deauville was still ahead on the starboard bow, the whole lot were milling about, bumping into each other, sails going down, sails going up, horses neighing, stamping and in some cases breaking free and jumping overboard, and all through it, if you were within a hundred yards or so, and quite a lot of us were by then, we could hear the madman bellowing like a baited bull.

'It was Bishop Odo who saved the situation. The Duke's half-brother. He was bigger than the Duke and perhaps the only man in the whole host, in the whole fleet not frightened of him. He found a bucket with a rope attached, slung it overboard, filled it, and emptied it over his brother's head. The Duke's fit left him, he began to give sensible orders, taking advice (something he hardly ever did) from the *Mora*'s master, and contriving to get them passed down the lines. We were all to let the *Mora* get well clear, and then follow, but in much more open order than before, and not worry too much about keeping to our allotted stations. Just so long as we didn't overtake him.

'After that things went well enough for several hours, well into the afternoon. We slipped along merrily up the coast, the waves lapping rhythmically, the seagulls calling, the ropes and timbers creaking—'

The harp seemed to echo these very sounds as Taillefer almost chanted, his eyes turned inwards, seeking out not just the sights he was describing, but reliving the very experience . . . then suddenly the harp switched to a moment or two of shrill lament and he looked up and round the table.

'Only four boats went down. Because they had not been properly caulked they filled, they foundered and all hands and soldiers were lost. Of course the wind died as the sun fell behind us, and the men-at-arms themselves had to roll up their sleeves and heave on the sweeps. It was an exercise few had ever done before. They dug too deep, left the blades in too long, at least a dozen or so were jerked off their benches and into the sea as the handles shot up into the air, oars were broken and again everything was at sixes and at sevens. And by then we were on an ebb tide which was carrying us out to sea. The tide? Living here in Sidé you will not believe this, Ma'am, but the sea in those northern latitudes can pull back a full half-mile where it is shallow, a height of twenty feet, twice in every day and night. Nevertheless, we limped into Dieppe about midnight or beached the ships nearby. Fortunately we were waited for and lights had been left out for us, for there was no moon.

'Next day the wind failed again completely and the men had to row the whole way to St Valery on the Somme. Twenty-five miles is a long-haul on the oars and the whole army was thoroughly knocked up by the experience – hands so blistered there was no way they could have lifted a sword or axe, legs and arms aching, backs so stiff they could hardly move. If Harold had made a pre-emptive strike in the next couple of days, he could have had the lot for virtually nothing.

'Anyway, it was still a clear fortnight before they sailed for England and in that time William saw to it that the ships would be properly handled, repairs done, the men trained up to row and so on. In fact he organised regattas up and down the Somme and awarded prizes for the crews that did best while he and his lords sat on the river-side in tents and drank the fizzy weak wine from Rheims and ate smoked salmon. The smartest whores from Rheims, Rouen and even Paris turned up and a good time was had by all.'

His harp played a lascivious jig.

'On the final crossing he still insisted that, whatever else happened, the *Mora* was always to be in front. He got the wind he wanted on the twenty-seventh but it took a whole day to get everything on board and they didn't actually sail until nightfall. Come the dawn and a sea-mist, the *Mora* was entirely on her own, somewhere in the middle of the Channel. Not another boat to be seen. They told me, friends who were on board, that it was really eerie. Almost calm, a heavy dew in the rigging, the mist, the snort and trumpeting of the whales not far off. The Duke climbed up to where the helmsman stood and looked around. 'All right,' he said, 'we'll conquer the fuckers on our own if we have to. Just see if we don't.' But then the mist lifted and he could see some of his fleet – but the nearest a good mile or so behind him.'

'Is it not true, that when he jumped down on to the beach . . .?'

'Hey, come on. That will do.' Junipera was firm. 'We are getting ahead of the story. Wind the clock back to Stamford Bridge, please? Tomorrow Walt can tell us what happened there and thereafter.'

CHAPTER
FORTY-SEVEN

'It was not,' Walt said the following evening, 'until the actual day of the battle of Fulford that we were ready to set out from Waltham Abbey. Harold was determined to leave as little to chance as possible. He wanted to know the fleet was safely harboured in London, just below Southwark Bridge, and he refused to move until all the housecarls from the south-coast stations had arrived and his army was up to full strength. We crossed the Lee and set off up Ermine Street at dawn on the twentieth, with about four thousand mounted housecarls. Harold had already sent men on ahead of us to raise the fyrd at every major town we went through or near: Hertford, Huntingdon, Grantham and Lincoln, so by the time we got to Lincoln on the third day we had another three thousand, but not all mounted and not all with proper arms. Next day we reached Tadcaster . . .'

'Four days?' As usual Quint was sceptical. 'How far is it?'

'About a hundred and eighty miles. But remember, we were on Ermine Street, a long narrow but dead-straight ribbon of turf. So, by the time we got to Tadcaster we had another three or four thousand . . .'

'It's not possible an army should be able to march that far in four days. Not even Alexander himself—'

'Well, we did. And I told you Alexander was nothing compared with Harold . . .'

Junipera intervened. 'Quint, if you interrupt again, I shall have to ask you to leave the table.'

Quint fell silent, but through the rest of Walt's story crunched almond biscuits noisily whenever he felt Walt had strayed beyond the bounds of credibility.

One thing Harold had developed, almost over the previous week, was a far better system of communications than he had had before. Horsemen were stationed all along Ermine Street and also south of London to the coast, to pick up and pass on news: thus it was just as he was leaving Grantham that Harold heard the news of Fulford, of the northern Earls' disobedience in fighting a major engagement before he could be with them and of how they now had no army at all worth speaking of. It seemed to mean that his four thousand might easily be outnumbered by at least three to two, since the Northumbrians and Mercians had been annihilated. Hardrada's losses had been light – he could still field well over five thousand fully equipped and battle-tried effectives. Of course, the fyrd gave Harold an overall numerical superiority, but they were only reliable in pursuit of an already beaten foe or when given a defensive role behind a wall or ditch.

From the scurriers Harold learnt that, after Fulford, Hardrada had moved his main army eight miles west of York to Stamford Bridge where he was still carrying on negotiations both with the burghers of York and Edwin and Morcar. He wanted hostages from both and a substantial ransom in treasure and food for his men. Otherwise he'd torch the city. With their army destroyed, Edwin and Morcar had little to bargain with, except possibly their support for Hardrada if or when William beat Harold. None had any idea at all as to where Harold was, apart from supposing that, in spite of Timor's message, he would remain in the south at least until William had been defeated.

The army rested for one afternoon and night at Tadcaster while Harold took stock of the situation. At dawn on the twenty-fifth they broke camp and marched the seventeen miles to Stamford Bridge, arriving two hours before midday . . .

'You're not telling this very well. It's boring,' complained Alain. The others agreed. Walt drank off a glass of purple wine, pulled himself together, picked up a knife, slashed it through a candle flame and let out a terrible, harsh cry – something between a scream and a bellow. They all jumped in their seats.

'What on earth was that?' Junipera asked.

'War cry,' he said, and held his glass out to Adeliza, who refilled it. He drank and continued. There were no more interruptions.

It was a sunny, warm, but muggy day, some haze and cloud, maybe a rumble of thunder way in the mountains to the west. There was a long ridge ahead, not much of a climb, but we'd been told that the Norsemen were on the other side of it, and that made it seem more than it was. We passed a farmstead, Helmsley it was called, and the kids ran along the side of our column, telling us we'd never beat the Norsemen, they were giants, but they'd done no harrying . . . yet. Seemed quite friendly in fact.

Near the top Harold called a halt, had a peep over the ridge, then came back. He told us to get the housecarls out of column of march and deployed into a line four deep, two paces between each man, five between each line and then told us, that is the eight of us and his brothers Leofwine and Gyrth, how things were and what he wanted us to do. Down below, he said, there were maybe a thousand on the west side of the river guarding the bridge which was big, a good five paces wide. The main army was spread over the hillside on the far side and was open fields, harvested, not ploughed yet, the fences down so the stubble could be grazed and manured. Only the men on the west of the bridge were standing to arms, on the other side they were just lying about round camp-fires, cooking their midday meal, their arms and armour stacked. Near the top of the hill the Land Waster standard drooped above a handful of big tents.

'Right,' said Harold. 'I want that thousand on this side sorted in twenty minutes and our first men across the bridge before the main body can get themselves under arms. Wulfric, you keep a thousand men behind the main line. When the rest have cleared the ground you get across the bridge and form up to hold the eastern end. You then either wait for the rest of us to get across or, if the enemy are still not deployed, move in on them, but either way you wait for my say-so. All right?'

So we got off our horses and passed them to the rear, and off we went, up the last fifty yards and over the ridge, a long triple line of us, nearly a thousand paces long. It must have been a shock to the poor buggers below when they saw our shining helmets come over the top. They'd no idea at all there was anything like an army against them nearer than London. We were in the middle, in the second line – Harold, me and

Helmric the Golden. Harold had two standards now. Helmric carried the gold lion of Wessex, the flag Ironside had fought under fifty years before, and I carried the new one Harold's mother had made him. It was on a twelve-foot pole, which weighed a ton after an hour or so, though the flag itself was light, made out of fine wool and silk, so it blew out proudly even in a slight breeze. Eight feet by six, just as Gytha had said it would be, but fastened to the pole vertically, so the Fighting Man filled it. Plain bright green, and the Man in white outline just like he is on the hillside, with his great club and his member stuck up in front of him. The message it sent was 'I can bash your brains out with my club, fuck your arse with my prick, and, when they see this, your womenfolk will be glad to trade you in for our lot.' We went down the hill with a shout, a shout like . . .

He pulled in breath again.

'Don't,' murmured Junipera warningly.

'All right then. But imagine that shout coming from three thousand throats at once . . .'

Junipera shuddered.

Of course a lot of them ran for it, most towards the bridge which, wide though it was, clogged up so some fell into the river below where the weight of their armour drowned them; others fled north and south up and down the banks, but a good few got themselves together and held on. But our axes hewed into arms and legs, were swung at heads that ducked and weaved in vain. Soon the red blood flew, splattering shields and mail, and the white bone, shivered like ash-poles splintered for kindling, stuck through wounds and the holes we slashed in their mail. Brains spilled like the meat from an egg. They tried to fight back, to maim and kill us in turn, but their arms were like lead before the fury of our onslaught.

You see, it was only four days since they'd been in a battle, and no one who has not been in one, wielded axe or sword, held shield firm for half a day or more, and traded blow with blow again and again, and taken knocks too, can know what it takes from you. Within ten of Harold's twenty minutes the way to the bridge was clear and Wulfric with his thousand surged through our ranks to cross it, for now just one Norseman, literally just one from all of that thousand, stood in his way.

At first some of us thought it was Hardrada himself. He was big enough. All of seven feet in his boots and helmet. He had the big bull horns on his helmet, there was gold inlay over its brow and down the nose-guard, the lightning flashes of Thor, and you could see he had big red whiskers and beard beneath it. His coat was plate-mail, and the plates shone in the sunlight, and beneath it he had leather guards, also sewn with big studs like crotchless trousers over his leggings, and then heavy boots. Behind him, fastened round his neck by the claws and hung for a cloak, he wore the pelt of a great black bear. His shield was big, bossed with copper and silver, the red leather covering it polished to shine like metal – it was tapered, not round, and so skilfully did he manage it that, with everything else he wore and carried, it seemed he was invulnerable.

In his right hand he had a huge battle-axe. Its curved blade, shiny steel, heavy, wedge-like, but honed to a razor edge was an arc at least two feet long. The haft was a yard and a half at least with a spiked ball at the end which was there to give the whole weapon a balance rather than act as a hammer for heads. In short, he was a true Berserker – a title given to the bodyguards of Scandinavian kings, but only when they have earned it by deeds of reckless courage accompanied by true war-fury.

The bridge itself did not allow more than three ordinary mortals to come at him at once. The first three he quickly despatched, one indeed had his head almost severed so the blood briefly fountained a foot or more above his dangling cranium before his legs folded beneath him; the second had his head stove in from the top, for all he was wearing an iron helmet; and the third took wings and landed in the river to drift into a bed of reeds where the darkness filled his eyes as he bled to death from a wound which, in spite of his mail, left exposed the white foam of his lungs and the shards that had been his ribs.

After that his attackers were more wary, making darting sallies, using one as a stalking horse while another tried to get in from the other side, but he was alive to all their ruses, and only those who backed off got away with their lives, albeit often mutilated. And all through this the Berserker howled, and bellowed with war-fury and killing lust, and in the lulls between our attempts shouted abuse and made obscene gestures.

Harold meanwhile was becoming peevish with impatience, for he could see, indeed we all could, how the Norsemen on the hill were arming and forming up; the Land Waster was already plucked from among the tents and was being brought to a point half-way down the hill to where Hardrada and Tostig, struggling in haste into their armour, were waiting for it. Indeed, as moment by moment we lost the first advantage of surprise, Harold himself drew his sword and made for the bridge. We had to restrain him and it was Wulfric, almost as big as this Berserker, who plucked up a fallen axe and strode on to the bridge.

Now maybe it was that this Berserker recognised in Wulfric an adversary with a strength and indeed a like-minded meanness that could spell danger, for he descended to an unlikely ruse. Carelessly, it seemed, he set aside his shield as Wulfric set foot on the timbers, and with a snarling laugh leapt this way and that, dodging unprotected as he now was the sweeps of Wulfric's weapon. But his left hand was now free and from some pocket or pouch he filled it with sand and, as Wulfric came at him with his fastest and most dangerous charge, he flung the sand into Wulfric's eyes, and sidestepping simultaneously tripped him as he passed. We all heard the thud of his body on the planks. The Berserker quickly took advantage of his stumbling and with one mighty blow hewed off his head. He kicked the body into the stream which now flowed with blood, and held the head up for us all to see – and by some freak of nature we heard a high keening note issue from his lifeless mouth before his eyes turned up in death. The Berserker tossed the head into the water so it actually bounced on Wulfric's back as his body floated down stream.

'That,' said Daffydd, who of late had become closer than friendly with Wulfric, 'was out of order. A long way out of order.'

And he slipped away, upstream into the willows and alders which hung aslant the brook. Presently he reappeared, this time in a large swill-tub he had perhaps already spotted near a deserted pig-sty. This he punted towards the bridge, using an eight-foot ash spear he had snatched from one of our fyrd. Because of a bend in the river just above the bridge, he was approaching the Berserker almost from behind, at least unless the Norseman took a glance over his left shoulder. Seeing what Daffydd was up to we all tried to engage the Berserker's attention by throwing stones and so on, and Timor himself danced on to the end of the bridge on the right-hand side, hurling taunts and nimbly dodging the sweeps of that terrible axe.

The swill-tub came nearer.

Now Daffydd must get it right – no easy thing, for if he was to use his spear as a weapon he could no longer use it to control the passage of his craft. But somehow he managed. As the current took him directly beneath the Berserker our host fell silent and for a second or two the giant looked around him in all directions, suddenly sensing danger but unaware of where it came from.

He was astride two planks.

Daffydd thrust through the gap with all his might and his spear entered the man from below, just between his balls and his shit-hole, and the broad leaf of the spear-head went on, up into his entrails. Daffydd released the spear's haft and drifted out the other side, spattered a little, but not much, with the Berserker's blood and shit . . .

The thing was the man was not yet dead, indeed died slowly over ten minutes or so during which he remained thus impaled and held upright by the spear and as we all rushed past him on to the other side first some- one took off his helmet, and then others spat on him as we passed, and pulled his beard and long red hair. He remained, impaled and upright, a dreadful figure, right through the rest of that day and into the next when the crows and kites came down and worked their way into the places our missiles and weapons could not reach.

Meanwhile, seeing the Norsemen were in line, Harold called for his horse and beckoned to Helmric and me to accompany him up the hill with his standards but also with Albert, carrying a flag of truce. The Norsemen were drawn up in a formation they favoured for defence, namely a half square whose full angle was at the lowest point nearest the enemy, and in that angle flew the Land Waster. Seeing us pull up just beyond axe-throwing distance, Hardrada and Tostig pushed through the line and came to meet us.

Harold addressed himself first to Tostig.

'Brother,' he called, 'there is no need for this. Four days ago you broke and destroyed the army of the north. Edwin and Morcar dis- obeyed my orders and have no army or following. Leave this Norseman now, bring what men you can call your own, fight at my side against William, and you will be as you were, the Earl of Northumbria.'

The colour flew to Tostig's face.

'Brother, you have had a year to say this in. It's too late now to try to make amends.'

'Tosty . . . in the summer I visited our mother. She begged me to do what I could to bring us all, all her sons, through so we could meet again and feast together as we used to. For her sake, leave these intruders and come back to where you belong.'

But Tostig, still handsome for all he had filled out and his cheeks were red, still with his coarse straw-coloured hair pulled back and fastened behind his neck, turned away. Pulling on his helmet he pushed back through the front rank of armed men to where the Land Waster had been planted.

Hardrada himself now looked down the slope, which put his head on a level with Harold's although Harold was mounted.

'You've offered Tostig an earldom. What will you give me?'

But Harold was now filled with anger and sorrow. He looked at Hardrada from head to foot and back again.

'Seven feet of English earth,' he said. 'And that's more than you are worth.'

The battle went on almost to nightfall. In numbers the armies were almost matched, though probably we had a slight advantage having won the fight on the west side of the river. They had the slope in their favour. Both sides were tired – we because we had marched so far in so short a time, they because of the battle four days earlier. It's not just the weight of your weapons, and the mail on your back – it's the men you killed and maimed, the ghosts that still hover around waiting to see you take your turn and join them. That's what the Norsemen felt. And maybe we did too, not three weeks later, when we got to Hastings.

Anyway, it was tough slogging. Both sides knew they had to win. Remember, we had the river at our backs and the slope against us. If we had broken it would have been worse than Fulford. And there was no escape for them for we were between them and their ships. They did not give an inch and we did not let up our attack for to do so would have invited a charge from them. It was just get in there with axe or sword, and kill or be killed. Harold was everywhere, rallying the faint-hearted, urging on yet another attack and, of course, Helmric and I went with him with the standards. Not easy holding a twelve-foot pole with your left hand, fighting off the buggers when they come near with your sword in the right hand and trying to hear what the boss says or tells you to do all the time.

Towards dusk, no earlier, the sun still shone from behind us and in the Norsemen's eyes, Harold sent Albert for the fyrd who were now on or near the bridge, on both banks. They came streaming across, whooping and shouting, waving their billhooks and spears, loosing off their arrows and hurling their axes and rocks. In fact, although it was probably a fluke, their intervention was decisive, for at a moment when Hardrada, just behind the first rank of his men, removed his helmet to mop his brow, a well-slung stone hit him on the forehead and he went down. Probably at that point he was just concussed, but they could not bring him round and soon the word spread through the Norse, encouraged by taunting shouts from our men, that their King was dead.

Kingship is a powerful thing. Tostig did his best to rally them but the fight had gone out of the Vikings . . .

And that's about it. Only Tostig fought on, eventually it seemed Tostig *only*. With dead and dying on the floor around him we all stood back. He stood, bleeding from ten or twenty wounds, and, dropping his shield and sword pulled off his helmet. Harold went to help him but before he could reach him his brother fell. Nevertheless Harold held him there, put his arms round his shoulders and Tostig's head on his breast.

Tostig had two things to say as he died: 'I told you I'd be back.' Then, looking up at the Fighting Man I held above him: 'That's a good flag, Harold. I like it.'

Harold let Olaf, Hardrada's son, sail back to Norway with what was left of his father's army. They came in two hundred ships. It needed only twenty-four for the return journey. Tostig was buried with honour in York Minster. Hardrada got his seven feet out there where he fell. And while all this went on the army, which had marched all but two hundred miles and fought the hardest battle yet fought on English soil, rested up. By Christ we were tired. And we had suffered. Of the four thousand housecarls who marched from Waltham Abbey less than three thousand would ever be properly fit enough again to fight, though all but the five hundred or so dead made it to Hastings. Wulfric was gone, Helmric too – killed by a Saxon axe thrown by someone who thought he was on the other side. Little Albert we never found – but there were three thousand bodies . . .

Two days later, on the twenty-seventh, William sailed from St Valery, landing the next day, in the evening, at Pevensey. Three days later, on the Sunday, six days after Stamford Bridge, we got the news . . .

PART VII

AND ALL THAT

CHAPTER
FORTY-EIGHT

Late next morning Quint, Taillefer and Walt took a walk around Sidé. It was a beautiful town, filling the coastline between two headlands half a mile or more apart. Its new turreted walls, faced with a reddish-brown rock, linked the headlands in a deep semicircle and dominated the narrow plain of cotton-fields and orchards. Beyond the plain the sheer timbered mountains climbed from foothills clad with olive groves and vineyards to high but not distant peaks.

They walked down a short cobbled path into a town which had a pleasant, ramshackle air about it since every twenty years or so it was sacked by pirates: elegant parks and gardens alternated with patches of wasteland where wild flowers bloomed beneath the cypresses and cedars the roots of which had cracked the marble pavings; lizards basked in the warm sunshine or flashed across parterres whose roses had reverted to the briars on which they had been grafted. Narrow alleys beneath lines of washing which were almost dry in the warm and balmy air took them away from the quays. They bought small brown buns crusted with brown sugar from the sugar-cane fields, grapes, figs and slabs of a sticky sweet-meat made from pounded hazelnuts, sesame oil and honey. Taillefer had his leather bottles filled – one with spring water, the other with wine.

Presently they came to the old forum. Many of the temples and colon-nades still stood, but brambles and broom had invaded the area, much of the marble and brick had been quarried to build or repair the streets they had passed through and almost all the statues were overturned. The more fragile extremities – noses, hands and penises – had been broken off. Nevertheless, in a little artificial grotto, a nymphæum, hidden by wild shrubs, protected by gratings, they found three marble Graces holding hands above a still pool of dark water. The two outer ones faced inwards, displaying callipygous loveliness, the middle one faced outwards and looked down at the turning ankle of her companion. The marble was honey-coloured, slightly veined. A small branch with three gold quinces still attached had been left on the nearer side of the pool and was clearly an offering. Sweetly mingled reverence and desire stirred in the breasts of all three men.

On the inland side of the forum rose what was left of the ancient theatre. A half-drum, it was still a substantial structure – the curved wall terraced on the inside above shadowy galleries, the straight one the stage-wall which had been for the most part tumbled not by Vandals but by earthquake. Almost all the facing marble had been stripped away, but the huge mortared conglomerate bricks the Græco-Romans used for such places had resisted the efforts of later generations to pull the thing apart. The three men climbed the terraces and settled themselves on the topmost step from which they could see the quays, and beyond them, across the emerald green and then the deep blue-beyond-blue to violet to mauve sea, dotted with the triangular sails of fishing boats and small cargo-vessels, an unblemished horizon. To the north the mountains, the high peaks of the Taurus and—

'By God,' exclaimed Quint. 'There's snow!'

And indeed there was – pure, unblemished, as brightly white as only the first mountain snow of autumn can be.

They laid their food out on a slab of broken marble that the looters had not bothered with and began to eat and drink – but slowly for there was no hurry and plenty to enjoy. After the first mouthfuls of wine and prompted by the golden quinces in the shrine to the Graces, Walt fell into a reverie, almost a trance.

Walt dreamt. A procession – no, not really a procession, more a crowd of people, followed a chalk track between fields, through a beech-wood. Sunshine filtered by the beech leaves dappled the chalk with flakes of light and purple shadow. Pipes played and sticks rattled on skin-covered drums. Walt was near the front, with flowers in his hair and round his neck. Behind him Bur, the strongest man in Iwerne, carried a ten-foot pole of oak, also wreathed with flowers beneath a floral crown. Streamers of coloured cloth blew in the slight breeze. Walt wore a brilliant green cloak over his saffron shirt, gold round his neck, gold fastening the cloak, gold armbands, and gold inlay on the clasp of his belt, boots that shone.

They were all there, everyone who lived, worked and served in Iwerne, all in their best clothes or any rate clothes washed and stretched to dry on bushes and fences the day before. They all carried food or drink – the strongest men with firkins of ale on their shoulders or leather bottles filled with mead. Two of them carried between them, just, the eighteen-month-old boar they had slaughtered that morning – gutted now but otherwise still whole; two more who worked the manor's forest had roebucks slung across their shoulders. As well as these, there were hens, ducks and geese: all still alive – some carried by their feet, but the geese stupidly waddling along with the rest, flapping clipped wings to keep up. The chattering children carried big baskets filled with loaves of bread, cheeses and cakes made from barley and honey. Their elders had to tell them off for picking at them. All in all there were over a hundred for many had come in from nearby villages and farmsteads. Even Bran, the King of the Charcoal-burners, had turned up with five of his blackened fellows, he with his antlered mask on his head.

At the brook where Erica and Walt had been betrothed ten years before, the elders of Shroton waited for them, with Erica's uncle and aunt and cousins from Childe Okeford, the village that lay round the other side of the hill. Walt and Bur, the pipes and drums, and the older people from Iwerne solemnly crossed the small narrow bridge to be greeted with exchanged embraces, while the rest of the party swarmed down the banks, splashed through the stream and scrambled up the other side.

Now the track climbed a little through fields from which the corn had already been harvested and Walt could see clear across to the other village and farmstead nestled beneath Hambledon, and there, at the gate, still a half-mile away, dressed in white with her yellow hair bound up with a gold fillet, her figure framed in a great arch of apple-boughs bearing fruit, was Erica.

'We ought to get down to the market quite soon,' Taillefer remarked. He spat grape-pips into the palm of his hand, disappeared them, rediscovered them in Walt's ear. 'If we're going to get the sea-bass madame asked for.'

'Where's our Walt gone, then,' he went on, passing his palm in front of Walt's unfocused eyes.

Walt shook himself, laughed – a rarity since the battle.

'Just day-dreaming.'

Quint now had his restless eye on the quay.

'There's a boat just in,' he said, 'flying the Mussulman crescent. And since it came from the west it's fair to think its destination lies eastwards. To Sidon or Tyre, perhaps, or even Joppa. It's worth looking into, at any rate. We cannot trespass on our hostess's hospitality for much longer. We should leave before she throws us out.'

Walt felt a tremor of doubt.

'You are still set on getting to the Holy Land?'

'I think so. I think the places where the Mountebank performed his stuff are worth a look, don't you?' Quint turned to Taillefer. 'You may pick up a hint or two.'

'Oh, I think I have it all off pat. Except perhaps the Feeding of the Five Thousand.'

'Get a grip on that and we're made men.'

They finished their meal, stretched and yawned a bit, except Walt who was now bothered by various conflicting perceptions and emotions. He chewed on the nails of his one hand, but not, Quint noted, on the now unblemished stump at the end of his right arm.

'Right then,' said Taillefer at last. 'A sea-bass for Madame Amaranta, and perhaps we'll book a passage on that boat.'

'Some fennel would go well with the fish.' Quint began the climb down the terraced stone benches. 'Walt, something's bothering you.'

Walt paused on the step above him.

'You just called our hostess Amaranta,' he said.

'It's her name.'

'Not Jessica, not Theodora nor Junipera?'

'Certainly not. Whatever gave you the idea . . .? Ah, I see.' Quint slapped his brow with his palm. 'Theodora because at Nicæa she said she was a gift from God to us, that I understand. But I do not recall she said that was her name. And Jessica? Surely you cannot think . . .?'

'I thought Theodora . . . Amaranta . . . was the murderous, adulterous Jewess in disguise. She who followed us out of Nicomedia, keened in the night and stole the gold from your back-pack.'

They were now in the theatre's orchestra. Quint leant against a fallen piece of masonry.

'You seem to have got into a frightful muddle about it all. There was no Jessica. The wife of David ben-Shimon, who dealt in lapis lazuli, was a gentile. The woman who followed us into the mountains above Nicomedia and keened is a figure of your imagination. I do not know who stole my gold but I doubt it was a woman.'

'And the woman who swam in the mountain pool?'

Quint shrugged: 'A naiad. Why not? Otherwise, as I suggested at the time, a shepherdess. Why should you think these women are the same person as Amaranta?'

'In my mind they look alike. Her red hair is a wig, I saw her take it off in . . . in the caravansarai at Dorylæum. I think. The hair beneath is black.'

'Red wigs are the fashion.'

'She was acquainted with Jewish merchants.'

'So am I. That does not make me Jewish.'

'She arranged to have us killed – first with a poisonous centipede and then with a giant spider.'

'My dear Walt! Those were the normal sorts of accidents that can befall any traveller in lands where such beasts are native.'

Taillefer intervened.

'You were not well. Certainly after receiving the blow from the Nicomedian soldier or constable, you were in pain, had fevers . . .'

'And then, of course, there was the opium. It can have pronounced side-effects. But my dear Taillefer,' Quint turned to the mountebank, 'our friend here was already deeply disturbed. He suffered terribly in his mind after the battle: not just physically but his soul, I believe, was torn in two, and has remained so for two, three years. Only now is it coming together again.'

'Nevertheless,' Taillefer plucked a silk scarf from the air, balled it, put it in his mouth and drew it inch by inch from Quint's ear. 'It's odd how it all links up – each person, each incident flowing into the next with a sort of logic of its own, a sort of sub-plot to the main story.'

'Don't *do* that!' Quint batted the scarf away with an angry palm. 'Yes. Precisely. Walt's fantasies have exactly the logic of story-telling. Almost as if he were stringing together events in such a way that a listener would foresee connections Walt himself could not see. Thus creating a cheap sort of dramatic irony. It is typical of the way the human mind works, always trying to make reality and events follow or fit into a predisposed pattern. Just as we seek essences behind things to bind together a pebble and a rock instead of concentrating on the thisness of each, so we seek to impose the pattern of, in this case, narratives, such as the Golden Ass of Apuleius, on actual events, which in themselves occurred once and once only, never to be repeated or linked.'

'I like the Golden Ass . . .'

'How can you? In the first place the dignified, the ludicrous, the voluptuous, the horrible succeed each other with bewildering rapidity—'

'But is not this precisely like life, as opposed to the patterned constructions of more formal narratives . . .?'

Quint ignored him and continued almost without a break.

'. . . fancy and feeling are everywhere apparent, but not less so affectation, meretricious ornament, and that effort to say everything finely which prevents anything being said well. Moreover, and worst of all, it conceals within itself a load of hermetic neo-Platonism, the dire enemy of Aristotelian empiricism which alone can uncover for us the secrets of the universe . . .' He turned on Walt who was now lagging behind and rubbing the back of his head with his stump. 'And wherever,' he asked, 'did the name of Junipera pop up from?'

'I don't know,' said Walt. 'I must have made it up.' He took a turn round the orchestra, and to change the subject, asked: 'What is this place we're in?'

'A thee-a-tor,' Taillefer pronounced. 'A place of illusion and entertainment where once marvellous fictions were enacted to an enraptured audience.'

He leapt up on to the stage, struck a pose and declaimed.

'"The raging rocks, and shivering shocks shall break the locks of prison-gates – and Phoebus' car shall shine from far and make and mar the foolish Fates . . ."' He dropped the pose and sketched an elaborate bow to his friends below.

'So what happened?' Walt asked. 'Why is it a thee-a-tor no more?'

'Fucking Christians,' muttered Quint. 'Spoil everything.'

CHAPTER
FORTY-NINE

'So,' said Amaranta, using a silver knife to lever a substantial morsel of fish from the bones that lay in her plate, 'you aim to be off the day after tomorrow? Joppa, is it, and then on to Jerusalem?'

'I think so,' Quint replied. 'If the wind stays fair. There is no cabin room, but I doubt we should have been able to afford it if there had been. We shall be deck-passengers, unless the master manages to fill every available inch with cotton bales.'

He drank – white wine from a glass that hazed with cold. At dawn, traders who specialised in the commodity had sent their fittest slaves up into the mountains to fetch down sacks and barrow-loads of snow. That evening anyone who was somebody in Sidé drank their wine ice-cold while their cooks prepared sherberts of the stuff flavoured with honey and the juice of pomegranates.

'Then we must press on with the last fits of your story. It would be a great shame if we did not hear the end before you left. Let me see. Where were we?'

She pushed away the sea-bass bones and lifted a tiny braised cutlet of kid from the bowl her cook had placed in front of her. There were thirty or so, pungent with thyme and garlic, lying on a bed of almonds and cracked wheat. Alain strummed his father's harp.

'Harold and Walt,' he said, 'are at York, and have just received news of Duke William's landing at Pevensey three days earlier.'

'Ah yes. And before we return to Harold, your father was going to tell us about the embarkation, the voyage, and the landing, giving us an eye-witness account . . . Will you need your harp for this?'

Taillefer passed a broad hand across his thinning black hair and also helped himself to a cutlet or two.

'I don't think so, Ma'am. Alain can fill in the odd chord where he feels a musical comment is appropriate. But by and large, apart from the mew of the sea-birds, the splash and gurgle of water beneath the prow of our vessels, the creak of timbers and the rattle of tackle, there is little lyrical about what I have to recount. Nor heroic either come to that.'

'Pray continue then as soon as you are ready.'

She dropped the thin twig-like rib to the floor where her grey Ethiopian cat had a spat with her long-haired lap-dog. The cat, of course, won.

'The last days of September were calm and warm, a definite sign that the weather was at last shifting from the prolonged sunny but cool spell that had filled most of the month. However, on the morning of the twenty-seventh a decided breeze got up, a balmy warm breeze just such as the wine-makers long for at that season since it will put the finishing touch of sweetness to their grapes while the rain that may follow will plump them out—'

'That will do. You're no Virgil, you know?'

'What I am trying to say is that we got what we had been waiting for – a steady fair wind from the south—'

'Say it then.'

'I just did!'

Duke William gave the order that we should embark. But after the fiasco, muddle and, indeed, losses that had accompanied our trip up the coast from the Seine, he had drawn up a detailed protocol as to how this should be achieved: which ships would be loaded first, with what and with whom, and so on, and what order we should sail in. So throughout the day viscounts, bailiffs, ships' masters, clerks, commanders, grooms and what have you scurried up and down the quays and beaches, flapping notes and instructions many of them could not read, unlettered as they were, and all desperately fearful that they might be caught out in an error, doing something not prescribed or failing to do what had been ordered.

By midday the Duke became aware that things were not going as they should and took a hand. I can see him now in my mind's eye, storming down the quay at St Valery, waving his arms about, sending soldiers this way, sailors another, pulling horse fodder out of one boat and refilling it with wheat for bread, ordering horses into the narrow gap between the rowers' benches of a long ship and then taking them off again when the ostler told him they had not been watered. By late afternoon, evening really, with the sun sinking into cloud on the western horizon, he was in a filthy temper. When one of Lanfranc's clerks from Le Bec tried to point out to him that the fleet would sail in exactly the reverse order from that which he had previously ordered if he did not countermand his latest instruction, he pushed the poor man into the harbour, grabbed the reins of his black war-horse from the hands of the groom, and marched on to the *Mora*. Without further ado he ordered the crew to hoist sail and put out to sea.

Of course, everything went much more smoothly once he had gone and within an hour, and just before darkness fell, the rest of the fleet was pulling away from the coast and we were only a league or so behind him. It was not a big army – something like two thousand fully armed horsemen with horses, three thousand fully armed horsemen without horses, another three thousand light troops, not knights, mostly archers, and then the usual cooks, ostlers, farriers, armourers, commissariat and so on. In all, less than ten thousand.

During the night the wind dropped or shifted a point or two, so the first landfall, a couple of hours after dawn on the twenty-eighth, was Beachy Head, an impressive headland of very high, very white chalk cliffs a couple of leagues to the west of Pevensey Bay. Considering it had been a night crossing this was accurate navigation indeed – the French pilot, a St Valery fisherman, knew exactly where they were, but then French fishermen very frequently trespass into English waters and know the way.

Within an hour or so the fleet entered Pevensey harbour, having first ascertained from an English fisherman that the Roman fort was ungarrisoned. There was a beach of mud and fine shingle between the moles the Romans had built and as the *Mora*'s prow nudged into it William, in full armour, leapt down, being determined to be the first of his host to touch English soil. Of course he fell over, in a foot or so of water, and had to be helped to his feet.

There were no more mishaps and by early afternoon the entire army had disembarked within the walls of the Roman fort, with their ships pulled up on the shingle behind them. It was all going well, too well. There was not a sign of an English soldier or ship to be seen. Naturally William suspected a trap. The locals, an old man or two and their wives, were threatened with torture and revealed that the troops who had occupied the fort, and also the ships in the harbour, had left a full fortnight earlier. William tried torture just to make sure, but got nothing more out of them and when one of the old women died he gave up.

Being more than naturally prone to suspicion and feeling suddenly rather frightened in this new and unprecedented situation, he now took the unnecessary precaution of building a second fort within the confines of the one already there, throwing up earth walls even higher than the Roman ones, and shoring them up with timbers he had actually brought over for the purpose. Meanwhile he sent horsemen scouring round the countryside and even up into the Downs with the task of finding out just what was going on. Not a man, not a horse, not a ship to be seen – but the barns were full, Lanfranc had been right about that, and there were cattle and sheep in the fields.

As day followed day, he grew more confident, and indeed some garbled news did reach him that Harold had had to go north to deal with some unspecified threat and had taken his army with him. Nevertheless he still suspected some trap, some ruse, and feared that if he exposed himself at all, or moved any distance from his ships, the English army would rematerialise and annihilate him inland while the English fleet burnt his ships behind him. However, once he was sure there was no army within five leagues or a good day's march by his standards, he scuttled up the coast as fast as he could, six miles it was, as far as Hastings.

Pevensey was surrounded by marshland which made it difficult for him to get supplies in from the surrounding farms to feed his army, and as a base Hastings was even safer. It was on a promontory between two rivers, the Brede and the Bulverhythe, had a harbour less exposed to attack from land or sea and was surrounded by rich farmland which he plundered extensively and thoroughly. There were very few men about – the fyrd was quartered up beyond the hills in the forests waiting for Harold's return – and the few there were he hanged. The women were dealt with in the usual way and the children herded into stockades from which they would, eventually, be sold as slaves. The infants were impaled. Racial sanitation, he called it.

Over that first week it became clearer that Harold and his army were many many miles away, certainly way north of London, and it was guessed that he had gone north to deal with a substantial threat – Tostig perhaps or even Hardrada and the Norse. This pleased William no end – the idea that his enemies were at each others' throats definitely appealed to his sense of humour . . .

'You didn't really like William, did you?'

'No, Ma'am. Not at all.'

Walt, chewing on the last of his kid cutlets, spoke through it.

'Then why the fuck did you do what you did to Harold twelve months before?' he asked. His face was a touch flushed – they had all perhaps drunk a little more wine than usual, the way you do when it's served really cold.

'Maybe I'll tell you one day. Or Adeliza can, if she remembers it clearly enough.'

'Oh, I remember, Daddy.' She shook her head so her hair swung about her neck; she looked down at her plate, her lips tightening into a pout.

'Go on, then!' Walt was truculent. Amaranta intervened.

'Later, perhaps. It would be an unwarranted digression just now.'

'At all events I hope he'll tell us just why he felt ready to lead the Bastard's army into battle, singing and playing a guitar.'

'Yes,' Taillefer spoke drily, 'I'll do that.'

Nevertheless, when his war council proposed that under the circumstances he should march on London and either get the rich burghers on his side or burn and loot the lot, he refused. He felt snug and secure in Hastings where he was already building a castle, the first of many – he really was obsessed with castles, and always he had his ships at the back of him. Clearly it was in his mind that if Harold came at him, as many said he would, with a vastly larger army, he'd just call it a day, re-embark and sail home.

On the seventh of October, nine days after the landing, news from London got through. Harold had arrived there from the north with the vanguard of his housecarls, on the fifth, and William learnt of the two battles, Fulford and Stamford Bridge. It was good news. Hardrada was dead, out of the way. And, up until then, he had believed that Harold could probably field up to twenty thousand men, including the armies of the north. But they had been smashed at Fulford and Harold's own Wessex and southern army, although victorious, had suffered serious losses at Stamford Bridge. It now seemed likely that they would meet on equal terms, even that William would have the advantage. The war council again urged him to advance on London before Harold's army got up to full numbers. But he refused for one other thing had come clear from these reports – Harold was no slouch as a general, a leader, and his men were fighters. Hardrada was no pushover.

Of course that was not how he put it, though his given reasons were just as germane.

'Number one,' he said, rounding on Odo and Robert and the rest, 'he's still got that fucking fleet in the Thames estuary, and from all accounts re-fitting and well manned. If we move away from our ships they'll surely come by sea, burn them and thereby shaft us. Number two. If we move north and into the countryside all he's got to do is fall back in front of us until his army is as big as he wants it to be. He can scorch the earth in front of us and starve us, and, finally, he can choose the ground he fights on. If he wants he can carry on a war of attrition through to Christmas or beyond, sucking us into a hostile countryside where we'd be done for in three months.'

'But your grace—'

'Sire, Odo, sire. Or Your Majesty. We're on English soil now, my soil.'

'Sire. What else can we do? We can't just sit here and wait for him.'

'Yes we can. We have a snug castle now, and I want every barn and granary for forty miles around emptied, and the contents brought here. I want every sheep and cow, and every horse—'

'There don't seem to be any horses.'

'Never mind, and every pig, chicken, duck and goose either killed or brought here, too. And while we're at it, every village and town burnt, every woman raped, and every brat impaled . . .'

'We're doing that anyway.'

'Do it properly. Make it hurt. Think of new ways of being nasty but always leave someone alive to tell the tale. I know these English. Milk-sops where their folk are concerned. They'll put pressure on Harold to stop us. And he'll only be able to do that by coming here. And if he doesn't we'll move up the coast to Dover or Sandwich or wherever and do the same all over again. Come on, Odo. Give our boys a good time and let them see the sort of goodies they're here for, let them realise, one big push, one big battle won and they can live out their lives like pigs in shit . . .'

Evening of Friday the thirteenth we heard the first of Harold's troops were taking up a position five miles away in the Downs, just on the edge of the great forest, having marched from London in a night and a day and that it looked as if he would have no more than five thousand men. Before dawn on the fourteenth Roger Montgomery, a Flemish soldier who knew what he was about, went forward with five or six men on good, fresh horses to see what was happening. He was back, in William's big tent, before the sun cleared the plain that lies to the east of Hastings—

'You were there? You saw this?'

'I was there.'

'It's a strong defensive position,' Montgomery said. I can see him now, a lean mean-looking man with high cheek-bones. He wore a black woollen hat with two silver talismans in it over his right eye, the body of the hat pulled to the left. 'I doubt he expects to be attacked there, not unless we can field double the numbers. And the truth is we can't.'

'What's he up to then?'

'I reckon it's a meeting place. The levy are coming out of the forest to join him, there must be more troops on the way from the north. He'll stay there till all are up and then he'll move on down—'

'What do you think he expects us to do?'

'That depends on how many more men he'll get in the next few days. If he gets enough he'll expect us to parley with him for safe passage home . . .'

'Well, then. Let's get moving, bustle, and get at him.'

'My lord . . .?'

'Sire.'

'Sire. It really is a very strong position he's in. I don't think we can get him out of it—'

'Fuck that, Roger. We march, the moment we're ready to go. No we don't. First, l shall give the men a short chat and then we'll be off. Yes, Taillefer? What is it?'

For yes indeed, I now tried to get in my two-pennyworth. This plan to give the men a chat before they started had made me realise that the

Bastard had gone over the top. He was seeing it all in theatrical terms, already writing the history of what would happen, tarting it up to make sure it impressed the world beyond, the empires, the Pope, posterity. I reckoned I could play my part in this.

'Sire,' I began, 'let me go ahead of the very first rank of your men as they march up the hill. Let me take my rebec. Let me sing to them of ancient deeds of valour unsurpassed until this very day, of glory and sacrifice, of how their names will be recorded in history to the last syllable of recorded time.'

'All right, but make sure they know they're on to a good thing too when they've won.'

He turned to his valet and signalled to him to bring his hauberk of mail from its cruciform hanger. He was in a tearing hurry now and got the thing on the wrong way round so Normandy's lion pranced across his back. Of course he was livid, mad with rage when Montgomery pointed out the error. I felt sure the day's first casualty would not be yours truly, as I had planned, but the poor valet.

'Sire,' I cried, as he shrugged himself out of the thing, reversed it and put it back on again, 'what a good omen this is of the great change-about you will go through today, from being a duke to a king no less.'

And arrant fool as he could be, he swallowed it, roared with laughter, and banged the poor valet on the back.

Of course very few actually heard his pre-battle speech. They weren't particularly meant to. It was for my ears mainly, so, as I said, it would figure in the epic I was to write and perform.

The front ranks of knights were drawn up in column of four down the road out of Hastings, with their pennants fluttering from their lances under a cold, grey sky, with just a thumbnail of red sun showing in the east beneath a long black cloud and the moon in its last quarter setting in the west with the morning star almost sitting on its higher point. There was a snuffling of horses, a champing on bits, a jangle of armour, so even those in earshot heard only snatches. He rode, walking and trotting up and down the vanguard division of four hundred. Since they occupied the road he had to use a chalky bank above it on which his horse kept slipping. A couple of times it nearly dumped him.

'Normans, countrymen,' he began, 'and of course chaps from other parts as well. We are gathered here today not to praise Harold but to bury him. Make no mistake though. He is a worthy foe and no push-over.

What I mean is this: some of us will fall in the coming hours and they shall be honoured. Their names shall be recorded. And remember − every loss we suffer means just that bit more for the survivors in the carve-up that will come afterwards.

'But that is not the point. Not the point at all. We are here today to initial . . . to begin a new chapter in world history. Make no mistake about that. Today this little off-shore island with its barbaric folk will be drawn into the wider world of continental Europe, will enter the mainstream of history, setting aside the barbaric squalor of its humble way of life and becoming cultured, yes cultured, like, as indeed, we are already. And if you can't keep that fucking banner upright I'll have your balls off.

'Where was I? Harold calls himself King of this fair sceptred isle. Why? Because a bunch of old men said so, with his sword at their throats. That is, the swords of him and his brood of brothers. Yes, brood of brothers. Snakes in the grass. Not grass-snakes but vipers. But many of you saw how, a year ago, he swore to be my man, to serve me as his King and liege lord, yes swear it on these very relics, these holy relics that you see . . . Where the fuck are they? Roger, they must be in my tent, be a good chap and get them for me. Lanfranc said I should wear them round my neck.

'So. All I want to say is this: right is on our side; might is on our side. Let's let loose the famished hounds of leashed-in war and famine and let them have it where it hurts. Cry God for William, England and Saint . . . Who's the patron saint of England, Odo? You're a fucking bishop, aren't you, you ought to know . . . ?

'St George? Who's he? All right, then. God for William, England, Normandy − and St George!'

Taillefer scraped out the last of his sherbert.

'There you go, then,' he said, and his face was pale, sheened with a slight sweat, 'that was it. Quick march and off we went. Is there a drop more of that wine left?'

'But St George came from round these parts. Yes, of course. Help yourself. Killed dragons and suchlike. Saved princesses. He was nothing to do with Normandy or England.'

'Cappadocia, I believe,' suggested Quint.

'Wherever.' Taillefer poured wine and drank off a glassful in one. 'It was the first saint came into Odo's head. I doubt it'll catch on.'

CHAPTER
FIFTY

As Walt approached his room along a marble-floored verandah which looked out not over the harbour but the sea, rather choppy tonight beneath a half-moon intermittently shadowed by flitting clouds, a hand reached out from the darkness of an empty recess and closed on his forearm above his stump.

'Walt?' murmured Adeliza, and she eased him gently into the space beside her. It had been designed to hold a statue, but at that particular time Sidé was ruled by a bishop who relied on the support of the devout artisan class and the commandment against graven images was quite ruthlessly enforced (though apparently the nymphæum in the forum had escaped his attention). Consequently Amaranta had had all the statues in her villa that were visible to the outside world put in the basement and the mosaics whitewashed.

The moonlight penetrated hardly at all into the niche and Walt was aware of the young girl's presence more from her warmth and the odours of her body than from what little he could see.

'Walt,' she repeated, having made sure that it was indeed him by cupping the end of his stump in her palm, 'Daddy would like you to know the circumstances under which he performed the trick which made Earl Harold swear allegiance to William.'

'Can he not tell me himself?'

'He would rather it came from me.'

'Go on, then.'

'There is no real magic in my father's performances. He relies on machinery, on falsifying appearances, on making the day-to-day laws that govern natural objects work in hidden, unusual but perfectly explicable ways. But above all, he uses or abuses the willingness of his audience to be duped. In most cases they have paid to see wonders and what one has paid for one is usually determined to get.'

Bemused though he was by her fragrant closeness, Walt was not bereft of reason.

'On that occasion,' he said, 'Harold had every reason not to be duped and was a most unwilling subject.'

'Exactly so. Which is why on that occasion the illusion was devilishly tricky to organise. You will recall the central, deciding factor was the presence of two figures, standing on a gallery rail many feet above the body of the hall, with nooses round their necks, the ends of which were attached to the beam above their heads.'

'Yes. They appeared to be Harold's young cousin and his even younger nephew. '

'They were nothing of the sort. They were in fact Alain and myself, dressed and made-up to fit the parts. Harold, you remember, had not actually seen them for many, many years, the hall was poorly lit and smoky, so it was not at all difficult to suggest to him that he was about to look on the death by hanging of his close kin, the very people he had come to Normandy to protect . . .'

Sensing another interruption from Walt she hurried on.

'So, they, that is we, were corporeally real enough and no illusion, and neither were those nooses.'

Her hand caressed her neck – he could see the whiteness of it now as his eyes became accustomed to the darkness.

'And the threat was real enough. William had warned Daddy that we would hang there and then if Harold did not give his oath. What else could he do?'

What else indeed? No father could have done otherwise. Of course, in the general calculus of good and bad, far more, far worse things had followed this deception than the deaths of a young girl and a young boy, but at the time—

Walt sighed, deeply, heavily.

'Well,' he said at last, 'it was beyond mending then and it is beyond mending now.'

She raised herself on tiptoe to kiss his cheek and fleetingly he felt the pressure of her young body against his groin, but it was not a desire to prolong the embrace that made him catch her hand with his one good one as she made to leave him.

'But why has he never told me this before?'

She hesitated and turned back.

'Quint is always with us,' she replied, 'and Daddy knew that, with his questioning, sceptical turn of mind, he would have cast doubt on Daddy's account. To be precise, he believed Quint would find the revelation which made you and Taillefer good friends an example of a narrative that followed the logic not of the real world, where unpredictable chance and contingency always rule, but rather that of conventional story-telling. Daddy feared that Quint would fail to see that the actual events were themselves a sort of fiction and that therefore it was proper, indeed predictable that the logic of fiction would prevail. Anyway, he hopes that you may now be truly friends and that you will not hold it against him any more.'

Walt made little of this, but one thing still puzzled him.

'Was it guilt, then, that prompted him to lead the Normans into battle and be the first to fall?'

'Oh no. He is sorry. But not that sorry. No, he foresaw a battle. People get killed in battles, but usually only once. Therefore the safest thing to be in a battle is dead. And dead early on, at the outset. He had a bladder of pig's blood in the sound-box of his rebec, and as soon as the English started throwing things at him, he squirted it in his face and fell over. There were other things too. He'd had enough of William and reckoned this was the best way of leaving him.'

And with that she broke away with a last kiss and was gone.

Walt took with him to his own bed not the questions that were prompted by a certain untidiness in her tale, but the memory she had stimulated of other warmths, other friendships, of happier times he had for some years now pushed away whenever they threatened to cross the threshold of consciousness. No memory of pain is as unbearable as the actual pain of remembering the happiness one has lost.

CHAPTER
FIFTY-ONE

Followed by the vast crowd of guests from Iwerne and the surrounding settlements, Walt crossed the sun-drenched grass, climbed the rise on to Shroton's playing field. Dressed in white pleated cotton, Erica stood on the far side of it with her bridesmaids in green about her, framed in a hoop of apple-bearing boughs. Behind her, amongst and in front of oak and ash trees, he could see the thatched roofs of her bowers and barns, the shingled ridge of her hall and church. And beyond that the ground climbed gently at first through stubbled fields and then steeply through hawthorn and blackthorn to the grassy ramparts of Hambledon. Blue smoke spiralled from her farmstead and hazed the air between. The round field was already ringed with trestle tables, small makeshift tents, braziers filled with as yet unlit charcoal. On the edge furthest from the village men had begun to build a bonfire big enough to roast an ox for the evening feast and provide light and warmth deep into the night beyond.

But now the morning, even in early August during a long dry spell, was still fresh though what dew there was had gone. This freshness extended to everything and everybody – the scrubbed faces of the children, the new or newly washed clothes, the light spring in the way the grown-ups walked, the ambience created by bustle and greeting and chat, with odd snatches of song already breaking out, the confident air that everyone had that today at least there was a good time ahead, a good time to be enjoyed by everybody.

Erica exemplified this mood. Twenty-four years old, she had taken on a perfection that yet remained unused but ready. It was not just a physical perfection though no one there would question that, nor was it merely or entirely sexual. Tall, but not lanky, strong but not overtly muscled, with a skin that had on it the fresh bloom of youth without the plumpness of adolescence, she stood like a goddess in her pleated cotton shift which came below her knees, with a fine wool cloak, russet in colour, over her shoulders. Her long, blonde hair was tied up and dewed with fresh-water pearls, revealing her high forehead. Beneath brown lashes, her pale blue eyes held a serene but lively smile that was echoed by the upturned corners of an angel's lips. But there was an earnestness about her, too, tiny lines in the corners of her eyes and lightly etched above them that spoke of responsibilities already taken on and carried through, of decisions made, of grief at early bereavements, of an understanding of and the ability to work with and make the best of whatever was around her or chance might bring.

When Walt was five paces from her, and already in his face revealing anxiety as to how the situation should be handled, she passed the posy she was carrying to one of her companions, and almost ran across the small space between to throw her arms round his neck. With his hands firm in the small of her back, she kissed him warmly and not briefly on the lips. A small cheer circled the field. Breaking away, and with a touch more colour in her cheeks and across her breast-bone than there had been before, she took his hand and led him through the arched apple-boughs.

Shroton, unlike Iwerne, had its church – recently built out of flint cores bound with mortar filling a timbered frame, it even had a tiny steeple with a bell which was not rung at festive occasions but only at funerals or to warn the people in the fields of danger. The closest surviving relatives on both sides, with also the oldest and most respected of the freemen, now formed up behind the couple and followed them into it. Though small it was a bright, airy place lit by unstained arched windows and with no furniture apart from the small altar – a slab of Portland stone set on four oak trunks. It was filled with flowers and greenery taken from the cottagers' gardens and the woods as well – roses in abundance, lavender, and big meadow daisies, and fruit – apples, pears, strawberries and sheaves of nodding barley.

The priest listened to their brief, extemporised but formal vows, witnessed their exchange of rings, blessed their union. It was over in ten minutes.

Back out on the field, they sat for half an hour or so on chairs placed on the floor of the largest cart to be found in either village, surrounded again by flowers and beneath a canopy of thatched straw, while almost everybody there came in no particular order to offer gifts, pledges of loyalty, blessings and hopes for long lives and many children.

After a while Erica showed signs of impatience.

'Let's enjoy ourselves. Every one else is. But first take off all that gold – it's far too showy for the likes of us.'

He handed her down on to the turf and immediately she span away, twisting and dancing with her maids, followed by the drums and pipes which quickly whistled up a frantic jig, weaving in and out the tables until all the women there joined in with them.

They feasted and played until dusk by when the roasted ox was ready for anyone who still had room for it. Already they had eaten kid stuffed with apples and roasted over hazel twigs (the traditional meal for the beginning of the Apple and Hazel month), cheeses, chickens, geese, mountains of bread and freshly churned butter, cakes larded with clotted cream, hazelnuts with shells still soft and green, the flesh white and yielding, and apples fresh from the tree or cored, stuffed with cloves and cinnamon dipped in honey, skewered on hazel sticks and charred over the many small fires that circled the field. And they drank too, by the hogshead, countless gallons of last year's cider and beers brewed from last year's barley: the new harvest was in, the old had to be finished to make room for it!

As well as feasting and drinking there were games for prizes donated by Walt. Three wooden balls carved from the boles of elm trees were trundled rumbling down a long row of wide planks to knock down nine skittles at the far end. Everybody had a go, though everyone knew that it would come down to two experts, one from Shroton itself and one from Childe Okeford who could knock down all nine with one bowl each to score twenty-seven each time. They would go on doing so until one of them left a single skittle standing. The usual prize, the eighteen-month-old pig, was duly awarded to the Childe Okeford man. There were horse races round and round the field with hurdles for obstacles; archery contests with arrows fired not at targets but at mock hares and birds pulled across the ground or whirled through the air. There was a ploughing competition over the stubbled fields which every freeman who had his own team of oxen entered – points awarded more for the straightness and depth of the furrow than for the speed with which it was cut. Fred's uncle with Fred riding on the beam above the coulter was the winner. His widowed mother, assured that land tenure would remain with her and hers, had survived her post-natal illness, though Fred's twin had died within a week of birth.

There were many other contests. Men chopped wood to fireside lengths (one of Bran's men won that one), tossed leather boots to see who could throw furthest, marked with pegs where they thought a tethered cow would dump first, cut and wove withes into hurdles (Bur won this one). Erica, with Walt somewhat sheepishly behind her, judged straw dolls made by the children, cakes, home-brewed liquors and possets to be kept for winter illnesses (old Anna who had sat with him through his father's death took this one with a tarry embrocation made from pine sap), spinning, weaving, dyeing and embroidery, woodcarving, joinery and furniture.

Hearing of the feast, and indeed probably seeing the coils of smoke that drifted into the hazy sky, people began to come in from all around, but all with some contribution – a skinful of mead, a bag full of pasties, or drums, pipes, rebecs and the rest to add to the growing cacophony.

Through all this they all kept almost mum on one subject alone, though it must have weighed with all of them. No one mentioned William or the threatened invasion, though they knew it could not be far off. The harvest was over and most of the men would be marching back to Sussex to rejoin the fyrd within the next week or so, and of course all knew that Walt, now a major thegn in his own right, was one of the king's innermost bodyguard, and likely to be made an earl if all turned out well.

Night came – the sun a big red disc through the mauve haze, the sky jade-green above it then deepening blue, the air filled with swifts, swallows and martins, now fledging their second broods, the rooks swirling back into the tree-tops and the buzzards and kites either relishing the thermals above the fire or the smell of hot meat soaring to where their wings caught the sun, even after the last sliver had dipped behind the hills on the far side of the Vale. A moment to pause in, to sit on the warm daisy-strewn grass and chew at beef bleeding or charred, swig ale and talk of what had happened during the day, of feasts in the past and feasts to come. Only the children still scampered about in tireless games of chase, though the infants slept.

Then the moon rose, huge and orange in the east, just past full, some-one threw more branches on the big fire and sparks rolled upwards on a billow of smoke, and from the big cart still on the other side of the field a pair of pipes wailed a spiralling, twisting, dancing tune into the air and drums fell into a beat which at first followed the pipes then drove them. Pair by pair, sometimes falling into lines or squares, sometimes remaining as couples, some staggering wearily or drunkenly, others quick, grasping the moment they had been waiting for, the whole throng, maybe now as many as five hundred, filled the field and the dancing began.

Until then the feast, the party had been communal – a celebration of their lord's and lady's wedding, an affirmation of the hierarchies, and pecking orders, of the freedoms and restraints that bound them all together – now it became something different, wilder, unrestrained, a swirling, floating world through which each sought in their own way the ecstasies that dancing, drink and love-making can bring.

For a time Erica and Walt joined in, but he was not the greatest dancer in the world, was too content to sway back and forth on his heels, watch her twist and turn, her profile flash from left to right, her loosened hair swing so occasionally it touched his cheek, the way the now dropping pleats of her simple dress flattened with her movements to the curve of her thigh or breast and the sweat spread from beneath her arms. Presently she stopped, grinned, took his hand.

'Enough of this. It's their party now,' and gently but firmly she pulled him towards the fields that filled the lower slopes of the hill.

They were not alone, other couples already threaded the hawthorn or, having got to the top, wandered down the hollows between the ramparts, looking for a place where the tussocky grass provided a softer bed above the chalk, or a spot that conferred a minimum of privacy, but Erica would have none of that. She took him through the two deep ditches, over the last rampart and on to the long rising hump-back of the top of the hill. The grass here was cropped short and sheep drifted away from them as they approached, though still the fragrance of thyme after a hot day lay heavily across it all.

At the highest point she stopped and embraced him again with a long slow kiss, then broke away and made him turn slowly through the compass to look north first across the Vale towards Shaftesbury and then down into the field below where the big fire glowed and showered sparks when a bough fell into a cave of heat whose orange and red brightened and waned with each passing breath of air. The muted sounds of music, laughing and singing, the thud of the drums was a distant presence.

Then west to where there was still a warm glow in the sky and the planet of love burned like a green spark above the broken hills; then south where the River Stour was a silver snake through the darkness of woods, and the square hill of Hod, once a Roman camp, was caught in one of its loops; and all of it lit by the huge moon shining from the east, more silver now than orange as she climbed into the clear sky, ruling the night far more surely than ever the sun rules the day. Erica, still holding his hand, offered her a shy, slight curtsey and, almost without knowing it, he found he too had bowed his head and as he did so his whole being – heart, mind and soul, from the top of his head where his hair stood on end to his curling toes – was flooded with an ancient joy.

She made him take off his clothes then lifted her dress over her head. He wanted to take her in his arms, take her to the ground, but she took both his hands in her palms and gently made him go on to his knees and then his back. She straddled him, her knees on either side of his thighs, and reaching forward and down, slowly caressed him, neck, shoulders, arms and chest, while he reached up with his hands, cupped her breasts, and stroked her sides and hips, and, as she came in closer, her buttocks too. At last, by shifting a little this way and that, and using her fingers and encouraging him to use his, she took him inside her, with all the gentleness both could muster. For a moment or two they were perfectly still then her head came down almost to his face and she whispered:

'There, then. That hardly hurt at all.'

Then she began to ride him, slowly at first, then more and more fiercely, calling him to hold on, which he did, by biting his lips until they bled, gouging into the turf with his nails and then, remembering something Daffydd had told him, counting in thirteens up to three hundred and thirty-eight and then down again until she threw her head up to the moon and let out a long howling cry.

Almost he felt excluded, but after that she came down and curled herself up into a ball between his knees and his chin, before starting a slower, gentler love-making, much of it marked with gurgles of laughter as well as sighs and groans, until the moon began to sink on the other side of the sphere they inhabited, the eastern horizon brightened and the sun chased off the chill that had preceded the dawn. Larks sang and swifts switchbacked silently over the tussocks and mole-hills around them. Not far off a shepherd's dog barked. They pulled on their clothes, kissed once more and . . .

'Catch me if you can!'

And she was off down the slopes, leaping like a deer, a white hind across the ditches between the ramparts.

CHAPTER
FIFTY-TWO

The stiff breeze which had chopped up the sea the night before was from the west and, early in the morning, a ship's boy – small, Arab, skin the colour of cinnamon, barefoot beneath a yellow singlet and a striped headband – was banging on Amaranta's street door and calling for Quint. The master had concluded his business quicker than he had expected and now wanted to take advantage of the fair wind: if the travellers who had booked deck-room on his vessel were not on board within an hour, he'd sail without them.

Quint and Walt travelled light, but not Taillefer and his children. Their horse and mule were still stabled half a mile away near the city's inland gate and had to be fetched. It would not be possible to take them on the boat but they needed to get his trunks and bags of tricks, his harp and the rest down to the quayside – it was that or hire porters who, trained by experience to recognise a crisis when they saw one, would double their charges. The animals arrived within the half-hour, were loaded in fifteen more minutes, and all then bustled, ran and trotted down the cobbled alleys, spilling the odd vegetable stall as they went, and made it on to the quay with a good five minutes to spare. All? Amaranta, with two of her maids came too.

The wind was indeed brisk, plucking at their cloaks and skirts, filling the flapping, half-hoisted sail and, even in the harbour, rocking the boat. Gulls cruised on it before dropping to scoop up scraps thrown from the fishing port on the other side of the harbour where the women were already gutting and filleting the fish from the night's catch. Ropes slapped against the masts of this and other boats moored nearby. Beyond the moles the sea was almost black so deep was its blue beneath the white horses that stormed across it.

Taillefer watched his goods hoisted on to the deck by means of a temporary derrick then came over to Amaranta.

'Sell you a good pack-horse and a mule?' he offered.

'Daddee!' Adeliza exclaimed, taking his hand. 'After all our dear friend's hospitality, the least you could do is give them to her.'

Amaranta smiled.

'You could auction them,' she suggested, looking round at the small crowd of traders, stevedores, pedlars and passers-by.

And when he did just that, she made the highest bid and insisted that he take the three gold pieces her oldest servant took from the household purse she carried for her mistress.

'It's a fair price,' she said, 'though I shall make a profit if I sell them on at a proper horse fair.'

That moment of awkwardness now, which always comes when farewells have to be made and one is not quite sure how soon the boat will sail or the caravan move off. Walt, feeling heavy in his heart and filled with doubts, wandered off down the quay, communing with himself about the voyage to come. To his fear of death by drowning there was now added a sudden and recognised nostalgia for hearth and home.

He heard English spoken and looking down found he was above a small open trader, a long-boat really, not much more, a bit fatter in the beam perhaps, and higher in the prow and stem than the war-boats, but a fifth of the size of the Arab galley bound for Joppa that he was booked on. It was even smaller than the boat that had taken them from Bosham to St Valery back in '65, since this lacked a cabin for the master. It too, like the Arab freighter, was loading bales of cotton, though he could see below them boxes of salted fish and mountain-cured hams. Up in the stern, perched upside down on a bale, there was a tiny tub of a row-boat, no more than a coracle.

'We could do with another hand, though,' were the words he had heard.

'Another hand and a change of wind,' came the reply.

The accents were those of Wessex, mid-Wessex, Southampton perhaps. And they were English all right – a podgy man with slightly protuberant eyes, wearing cotton or linen dyed blue and impregnated with oil, had spoken first. His mate was shorter and more compact, had ginger hair and a melancholy cast about his mouth.

With heart pounding, mouth suddenly dry, Walt hunkered on the quay above them.

'One hand is all I have,' he said. 'But it may serve to earn my passage back to England . . .'

They looked up at him.

'Have you ever worked a boat like this?' the master asked.

'Yes,' Walt lied, 'how else would I be here?'

They came to a quick agreement, one tenth of all profits made between Sidé and Southampton for Walt. Light-hearted now, even light-headed, he made his way back to the others. Quint was impatient: 'We're sailing in five minutes,' he called.

'But not with me. I've travelled enough. There's an English boat up there. It'll get me back where I belong or drown me first . . .'

Explanations, expostulations, resignation, thanks especially from Walt to the travellers: to Adeliza for making his stump heal finally and cleanly, to Alain and even Taillefer for the magic of their illusions and the greater mystery of their harp's music, and, above all, to Quint: 'For looking after me when I could not look after myself, for talking to me and listening to me, for helping me to—'

His voice faded.

'To understand?' Quint supplied. 'I think you'll find it's been a healing experience.'

He used the Greek word – therapeutic.

'But we won't hear the story of the great battle,' Alain complained.

'When does your English boat sail?' Amaranta asked.

'When the wind changes to the east.'

'Then I shall hear it,' she said, with some satisfaction.

By now the Arab master, showing signs of serious impatience, was urging the travellers on board.

Kisses and handshakes, embraces and slaps on the back all round and an especially warm hug from Adeliza and up the gangway they went. The hawsers were slipped, the sail hoisted fully and the reefs shaken out. One bank of oars on each side to take them between the moles and then the sweeps were shipped, the sail bellied and all Walt could see of the friends who had been so close was the scarf Adeliza waved from high up on the stem, by the helmsman. He thought for a moment of where they were going, of the Holy Land and the Orient beyond, of the long trails across deserts beneath star-studded skies, of the illusions Taillefer and Alain would perform and the scrapes these would get them into and out of, of Quint conversing with philosophers and men of science or knowledge, Arab, Tartar and those in Cathay, and of the sweet harp music they would take with them wherever they went, the music Adeliza would dance to, and his eyes filled and for a moment he regretted his decision.

But then he thought of home, of Iwerne and Erica and a greater regret and longing filled him. When his eyes cleared the ship was a speck on the eastern horizon.

'Come,' Amaranta said, 'rest for a time and then tell me the story of the battle.'

CHAPTER
FIFTY-THREE

On hearing the news of William's landing at Pevensey we marched as soon and as quickly as we possibly could and made it from York to London, Waltham Abbey, in four-and-a-half days – a few hours less than the march north had been. But that was only the vanguard, the first thousand men, Harold's personal bodyguard, and at their head, always with him, his five remaining closest *comitati*, companions – Daffydd, Rip, Shir, Timor—

'And you.'
  'And me.'

During the next two days a further two thousand fully armed housecarls under Leofwine and Gyrth came in, with another five hundred, mostly suffering from minor injuries, trickling in behind them.

What was to be done?

The choice was clear. Stay close to London and wait for reinforcements or move south now and contain William on the coast until they arrived. Many in Harold's war council argued for staying put, or at least for moving no further than across the Thames to protect London, taking up a position in the North Downs and waiting to see what William would do. But this left the initiative with William. While London would indeed be a valuable prize, he could just as well move west along the coast, taking his fleet with him, from port to port, right up to

Southampton. From there he could attack Winchester – which, as far as Harold was concerned, was as important as London, especially as that was where the treasury remained.

Meanwhile, as the days relentlessly succeeded each other, reports came in of the truly ruthless ravaging William was carrying on, coupled with pleas from the burghers of the Cinque Ports that Harold should come to their rescue before they, too, fell to the invader.

On the morning of the eleventh Harold made up his mind. His men had rested for nearly a week; Edwin and Morcar were believed to have left York. The final factor which tipped the balance was his intimate knowledge of the countryside north of Hastings.

He called his leaders together in Waltham's small mead-hall. He pulled a piece of charcoal from the cold hearth and hunkered to draw on the unglazed tiles in front of it. They all crowded around, the front ones also bending or even kneeling so those behind could look over their shoulders. Harold looked up and around – clear blue eyes earnest but sure – sure of himself, his brothers, and his men.

'Many of you will know the place I am going to describe,' he began. 'It's about six miles north of Hastings. The road south through the forest from Ton Bridge and London meets the old coast road on the crest of the Down . . .' With broad sweeps using the side of the charcoal he indicated the Andredesweald up under his knees then showed the coast road running east-west in front of it and the cross-roads with a spur turning south towards the town.

'After the place where the roads meet and become one, the one road runs along a spur that runs out from the Down and then rises into a round hill above the plain. The road skirts the top of this hill before dropping down to Hastings. The hill has coombes on each side of it with brooks running through them and the land below it is heavy and marshy. In front of it the ground drops less steeply though the last two hundred yards to the top have quite a slope on them. On the crest, just west of the highest point there is a solitary apple tree.

'Right. This afternoon we leave here and we aim to reach that apple tree, which will be our meeting-place, by nightfall tomorrow, Friday, the thirteenth,' he gave a hasty little shudder, but pressed on, 'and we will camp in line of battle along that ridge. I shall be in the centre, close to the tree, Gyrth to my right, Leofwine to the left, with all our companions and housecarls about us. Meanwhile the fyrd will be told to meet us there too. The first to arrive will occupy the wings of our position and the rest will form up behind the housecarls. We shall leave guides and messengers here at Waltham to tell the northerners where we are, commanding them to make as much haste as they can to join us.

'That hill is so strong William will not be able to shift us from it. Hopefully he will see this is so and not make the attempt. But if he does we'll hold him. The battle then might end in a stalemate, but it is we who will be receiving reinforcements to replace our losses, whereas he'll be stuck with his. Once our numbers exceed his by half as many again, which they will within a week, we shall offer him terms, demand hostages, indemnities for the damage he has done, a renunciation of his claim to what is not his and let him go . . . Any questions?'

Leofwine looked at Gyrth, who nodded, then straightened and faced Harold who straightened too. Both shared a reputation for selfless courage and strength. Like all of Godwin's son, they were handsome, well set-up, proud.

'Brother. Gyrth and I have talked long about what I am going to say and we are agreed on it. The oath that was forced from you in Bayeux a year ago means nothing to us, but there are many, perhaps some even in this room, certainly in the ranks of the fyrd and the housecarls, who say because of it you should not lead an English army against the Bastard. Please hear me out. We think your plan is the best there is and sure of success . . . but you must admit,' and here a hint of a smile lifted the corners of his mouth beneath his moustache, 'it is not complicated, it requires little in the way of finesse or cunning. In short, Gyrth and I are quite capable of carrying it out without you. Moreover, if anything should go wrong then at least England shall still have its rightful King around whom resistance and indeed armies will gather again, whereas if we lose you then, indeed, all will be lost.'

The colour that had filled Harold's face faded and left him almost white beneath skin coppered by years on campaign or hunting through forests and over hills. He bit his lip and then turned, left the room. Again he went to his abbey church. When he came back to the hall he looked calmer but somehow sad as well, yet determined. He paused as soon as he was over the threshold and the men at the other end of the room turned to look at him.

'Brothers,' he said, 'I am the King. No one else. And I must defend my right and my title. If I do not then, indeed, will the hearts of our men be filled with doubt as to who should rule – he who hangs back behind his younger brothers or he who leads his men into battle. Now . . .' and he came firmly into the hall and took up his place again by the fireside, 'let's sort out the details.'

Next day, just as the light began to fade, Harold himself, with his five companions and his two standards, was the first to arrive at the meeting place. From the crest he could see the Norman camp, nearly six miles away, just north of the small town and port, how already an earthen motte and bailey castle dominated the fields and marshes around it and even the masts of the ships beyond. The sun shone on the sea, turning lead into gold beneath the grey clouds. The breeze was stiff enough to shift the folds of the gold dragon and the Fighting Man and cold enough to make the men shiver as the sweat from twelve hours' steady riding dried on them.

Walt looked around, at the Normans and the sea, and then back to the forest they had come through. A long line of men, spears and helmets glinting, wound out of it and the sound they made was a sibilant rumble punctuated by the squeal of cart-wheels. Then he glanced at the tree by his side.

The bark and twigs were covered with a friable, grey lichen which crumbled at the touch. A handful of tiny, wormy, wizened apples still clung to its brittle twisted twigs. Possibly the long, cold, dry summer had deprived its roots of water on the chalky top of its hill, but, whatever, it was dead.

CHAPTER
FIFTY-FOUR

By seven o'clock the next morning it was clear that William had decided to attack. Scouts rode back from the Norman camp with news that they were arming and forming up, and presently the first columns began to wind up the road. Harold immediately deployed the housecarls across the ridge from coombe to coombe, from brook to forest, in a line four deep and a thousand yards wide, so each man had room to wield his battle-axe or sword and leave gaps through which the skirmishers drawn from the fyrd could filter out and in. Daffydd and Walt, with help from Rip, Shir and Timor, dug holes into the chalk next to the grey apple tree and planted the staffs of the standards in it, thus leaving their hands free to fight.

Harold called his brothers in from either side and gave them final orders. They were to fight in open order unless William massed a large number of well-armed men in one place, in which case the housecarls were to overlap shields in a shield-wall – especially this was the tactic to be used against mounted attack. They should not, he insisted, be awed by men fighting from horses – no horse would charge a wall, they all knew that, and as soon as the enemy came close, they should go for the horse first, then the man.

'You have only one thing to fear,' he concluded, 'and that is their superior numbers. But it doesn't need a single man more than we have to hold this ridge, three thousand can defend it as well as ten thousand could. But remember, it is the ridge, the hill, that makes this so. Break ranks either in flight or attack and, as long as they have more men than we do, they'll carve us up. That's my last word. Stay in the wall. Stay put.'

He embraced his brothers, shook their hands and turned away. There was a solemnity in what he said and in the way he shrugged on his byrnie and helmet and allowed Walt to fasten the collar of the one to the neck of the other. His fingers touched and then lingered for a moment on the small gold crown that circled it, then he grinned.

'Is it straight?' he asked.

'Yes.'

'Right, then.' He pulled in breath, smacked his leather gloves together. 'Let's go for it.'

The Normans were now just over half a mile away and, behind a screen of light troops, mostly bowmen, were deploying into close-knit lines − foot-soldiers first and then mounted knights − in three main blocks across the slope. The English could easily make out which was William himself. He was taller than almost anyone in either army, a gangly figure occasionally lurching on his big, black stallion as he cantered and trotted this way and that with a handful of men and his lion standard behind him. They could even make out his high voice shouting, almost screaming as he got his men into line, just so, just as he wanted them. They could see the white and gold banner the Pope had sent and the small reliquaries that were slung round his neck from gold chains, the reliquaries on which Harold had sworn his oath.

At last they moved forward, and, since bowmen and light troops remained as a screen in front of the leading files, Harold ordered the first wave of the fyrd to filter through the ranks and engage them. As he did so a solitary figure broke through the Normans, a weird capering figure, in a bard's purple cloak, but bareheaded, almost bald, black-bearded, carrying a small guitar.

> *Paien s'adubent desobsercs sarazineis*
> *Tuit li plusur en sunt dublez en treis*
> *Lacent lor elmes mult bons sarraguzeis*
> *Ceignente spees del'acer vianeis . . .*

The pagans put on their Saracen hauberks
Most of them triple-linked
They lace up their helmets from Saragossa
And buckle on their swords of Vianian steel . . .

★

'And it really was Taillefer?'

Oh, yes. It really was.'

A shower of missiles was slung at him and down he went, with blood streaming across his face. Within moments the front rank of the advancing Normans, bowmen for the most part, had trampled over him and he was not seen again – not until he turned up outside the gate of Nicæa, busking for a living.

The thousand or so of the fyrd who had filtered through our lines were carrying as many missiles as they could manage, in their hands, slung about them from leather straps, in bags, stuck in their belts – small throwing-axes, rocks tied to the ends of short hafts, just plain stones. The Norman bowmen were no match for them – the bowmen were shooting uphill, their arrows rarely did more than graze a neck, a shoulder or a thigh, they fired at will which meant there was no concerted volley and each separate churl or freeman was able to dodge any arrow that threatened his face. Meanwhile the English flung what they had brought with them, downhill and from close quarters, laying the archers low or driving them back through the ranks of the oncoming soldiers.

These were different – with their long leaf-shaped shields, their hauberks of mail and their steel helmets, they moved slowly but relentlessly, and while a few took a serious knock or two, sticks and stones were not going to stop them: the fyrd fell back before them, mostly in good order, some scampering not out of fear but with battle-glee at having played their part so well. And we, housecarls and companions, drew swords and hefted our axes – took breath, and held it.

The first thrust as a spear probes your guard, the first clang as a sword edge smashes across the rim of your shield, the first metallic crunch as you swing your axe or sword-blade into the chain-mail just below your adversary's ribs and you see his face contort with rage and pain as the blood spouts from his side – these are shocks, physical and psychic, and suddenly you realise, yes, the bastard really does want to kill me and the only way I can stop him is by . . . and he falls aside but there's another one behind him.

Face to face, line to line, the battle at this stage resolved itself into a series of single combats – short and long, shifting as a fallen man allowed you to help your neighbour or brought in two on one against you, each man deploying his own particular skills and weapons – sword, axe or mace, making the best of his physique, denying his weaknesses to his adversary. The big and strong relied on a solidly held shield, a weapon swung with such force that it would break down the defences of the men they faced; the smaller, like Daffydd or Timor, on nimbleness of foot to dodge a blow and strike under a careless guard. Where numbers were not a consideration, the victory tended to go to the side that had the advantage of the ground, whose members were fittest and whose weapons and armour were most sound. The weight of mail began to tell on our backs and arms, the repeated sickening jar of blows taken on shields or parried, the mounting heat although the day was cool, and, before long, hunger and thirst – for the fact of the matter was the Normans had rested for a fortnight, during which we had fought at Stamford and marched much the length of England twice.

But at last trumpets called them back. For a moment some of the housecarls hallooed with the battle-joy of victory and began to break ranks in pursuit. Harold's voice rang across the hillside and most of us remembered our orders and held back. The wild ones, seeing themselves out on their own, paused, hurled insults and what missiles they could pick up off the ground at the retreating Normans and then regained the line.

Clustered round the apple tree and the twin standards, Harold weighed up our situation. To left and right the standards of both his brothers still stood, the slope was strewn with dead and wounded, and most were Normans. Our line still held, and looking back north he could see more men now winding down the track out of the forest: a Mercian ealdormen with a hundred housecarls, and maybe twice as many levies, their billhooks over their shoulders, their round shields on their backs. He looked back over the Norman army below him and smiled. With luck, by midday or a little later, our numbers might match or surpass those of the invader.

I also took stock. Since Wulfric's death I was the most senior of the companions. Daffydd was on the ground with Timor hunkered in front of him bathing a nasty gash on the Welsh princeling's cheek. Shir was just returning from taking his brother Rip to the rear with a broken arm. My own right arm was badly bruised and possibly grazed beneath the mail and ached terribly, but still seemed to work, and when the battle-joy came again I knew I would forget the pain. But so far we were all still alive, and more important, so was our chief, our man, our King.

Trumpets again, and this time it was the mounted soldiers who were forming into lines below us. Pennants fluttered from lances, helmets stood out black against the sheen of the distant sea, hooves rattled on the loose flints in the turf, harnesses jingled, horses snorted and some neighed with the trumpets. Harold, and his brothers to left and right, brought all the housecarls forward from four lines into two and the front line overlapped their shields to make a solid wall eight hundred yards long while those behind waited to fill any gaps that occurred or deal with knights who got through.

Duke William himself, with gold circling his helmet above the nose-guard, and behind him the white and gold banner of the Pope next to his own gold lion on a crimson ground, was out in front. Behind him, a regiment of horse, three deep across a front of a hundred and fifty troopers, broke into a slow trot, holding their line steady. Out on the wings, similar formations also moved forward and the ground began to shake.

For many of us English this was a moment of deep uncertainty. Few of us had ever faced mounted soldiers before and, though we had been told what to do, and been assured that it would work, it was suddenly difficult to believe. For a start the horses were much bigger than we had expected, gleaming blacks and bays for the most part, four-year-old stallions, several hands taller than the ponies we used, not for fighting but for hunting or travelling.

At twenty yards the Normans hurled their lances, which did little damage though those that were aimed high above the wall did get in the way. We were tripping over them for most of the rest of the day. Then, drawing swords and maces (William himself had a spiked mace a yard long), and giving a great shout, they spurred their mounts into a slow gallop and thundered across the space between. The urge to run before such an onslaught of metal and heavy horseflesh was almost irresistible but the wall held. For the most part the horses turned sideways on as they reached us, refused to lead with their heads but used their shoulders and haunches to barge into our shields while the knights reined blows on helmets and shield rims from the advantage their height gave them.

Here and there the wall did break, a shield buckling forward, a man dropping backwards with blood pouring from his smashed-in forehead, but when that happened and a knight urged his big, heavy horse into the gap, the cry went up: 'Kill the beast, then the man, kill the beast first!'

Not as easy as it sounds, although the horses themselves carried no armour. Swords slashed into their necks and flanks, axes hacked at their legs. They dealt out almost as much grief and damage with their heavily shod hooves as the knights on their backs did, until at last over they toppled in a maelstrom of whirling limbs, the weight crushing the men they fell on in the dense throng. Sometimes an unhorsed knight got through the line but then the men from the fyrd hurled themselves, five or six at once, on to him, weaving past his whirling sword or mace, grasping his knees and neck, hauling him to the ground where a seax could cut his throat or search up for his genitals beneath the split skirts of his mail.

Yet, for all the line held, we suffered heavy losses, for most knights who went down took three or more with them. William himself lost his horse in the wall, and for a moment was circled, only yards from Harold's standards, by thegns and housecarls. This was the nearest they came to each other in the fight. For a second their eyes met above the helms of those who stood between them, and a moment of cold silence passed. Then, bellowing and swinging his terrible mace, William fought his way out without hurt, and, spattered with blood, left smashed skulls and rib-cages behind him. One of the men he killed was Shir from Thornig Hill.

After twenty minutes of this the trumpets sounded again and, to a derisive cheer from all of us, the Norman horse pulled back – but it was no defeat, simply that their horses were winded, their arms leaden. Almost immediately the foot-soldiers repeated their first attack. But this time Harold ordered the line to remain with shields locked and there was little the foot-soldiers could do against the wall apart from win a respite for the troopers, who re-formed behind them and in many cases took second mounts.

It was at this point, as they pulled back and the horsemen came on again, that I felt my spirit overwhelmed by fatigue. Where there had been a sort of glory and hope if not certainty, there was now disgust edged with the bitter, sharp taste of fear. All around and in front of me men were dying of fearful wounds, faces once proud and handsome were twisted in grimaces of agony, rage, and, as they realised they were dying, of fear. There was blood everywhere, and shattered bones in it, spilled brains and purple guts. The smell was appalling, too – blood and shit, the slaughter-house and the shit-house.

For a moment I covered my eyes with my hands and briefly was overwhelmed by longing – for Iwerne, for the bower at night where Erica held me in her arms with my head between her breasts and I could hear the slow, steady beat of her heart and savour her nesty warmth, the blissful comfort of satisfied desire, the sweet givingness of muscles relaxed and rested.

But the Normans too were feeling the strain, not those in the middle, still led as they were by the Bastard, now mounted on a frisky chestnut, but over on the English right, the Norman left, where the advance was slower and more broken up than before, with those who were better mounted getting ahead of the rest. At the far end there was a slope down into marshy ground before a steeper climb up the other side and it seemed some of the horses were almost dragged down into it. The result was that the Norman line was broken even before it got to the shield-wall and the knights were arriving piecemeal, ten or a score at a time. The English, seeing an advantage, broke out of the wall, surrounded these small detachments and hewed them to pieces as they isolated them man by man. Those further down, instead of coming up the hill to their comrades' aid now hesitated and milled about indecisively. Seeing this the second line of our housecarls broke out and, followed by the fyrd, went careering down the slope to fall on them. The Norman cavalry broke back up the hill down which they had come and rolled back on to their own infantry who were also thrown into disarray.

In the midst of the mêlée round the standards, Harold did not realise what was happening, but from the back of his horse William did. Breaking off from the fight in the centre he went careering across the slope. He screamed with rage, hurled abuse, battered his own men with the flat of his sword (he had lost his mace), and turned them round, got them into some sort of line just as the English, now climbing the reverse slope into the Norman position, got amongst them.

And at that moment a member of the fyrd, seeking immortality, cut his horse's throat with a slash of his razor-sharp seax and William went down for a second time.

A great cry went up around him, of triumph and despair, and all along the line men paused in mid stroke or wheeled their horses away and with eyes shielded peered down into the wide hollow.

William flung one of his own men out of his saddle, heaved himself into his place – but his crown or coronet had gone and none knew it was he until he tore off his helmet, hurled it at the Englishman who had slain his second horse, plucked his standard from the lad who still contrived to be only yards behind him, and went careering along the broken line, showing both sides he was still alive. His men, cavalry and foot alike, recovered in body and spirit, now surged down the slope into the marshy hollow where most of the English right were now gathered. The slope was now against the English, Gyrth and his earls, fearful of disobeying Harold's orders, were not there to rally them, and three or four hundred were slain before they could regain the ridge behind them.

It was there and then the battle turned ineluctably in William's favour. The English had suffered that worst of all moments of despair which follows hope betrayed, they had lost an unaffordable number of men, and, above all, everything that rumour had said about their adversary seemed to be true: William was invulnerable – either because he was the devil's whelp, as some said, or because round his neck he still wore the relics on which Harold had sworn away the throne.

CHAPTER
FIFTY-FIVE

Dead on noon with the sun a lemon-coloured disc glowing through cloud, the Normans – would you believe it? – broke off for dinner. All through the morning sutlers in carts containing baskets filled with bread and the big round cheeses of Normandy, also the flavourless, floury, yellowish apples they insist are so delicious, had been trundling up the track from Hastings. Without leaving their lines, but maintaining a watchful eye on our shield-wall, the whole fucking army spread cloths on the churned-up turf and fell to. We were not so well prepared and, while most of the fyrd had brought their snap along with them and were prepared to share a little with us housecarls, there was nothing like enough to go round. Taillefer might have done something with five loaves and two fishes but he had gone. There was bugger all to drink apart from the brooks at the bottom of the hill, but these were within arrow-shot of the Normans, and whenever a man went down with his helmet off to scoop up the water he was peppered with arrows, which did little damage so long as they kept their heads out of the way, but left them looking like pin-cushions.

Anyway, when they came on again at dead on two hours after noon, they were in better shape than we were, though another two hundred or so had come down the road from London to join us.

'Not enough,' said Harold. He put them on our right to replace the losses we had suffered when our men went down into the valley after the retreating Normans.

However, in the next phase William concentrated his assault on our left, where there had been less fighting than elsewhere. Again it was the foot-soldiers who came on first, but he'd put the horse of the regiments far out on his right – they were mostly Franks and mercenaries from east of the Rhine – to a point where the ground was flat, and even sloped in a little towards the space between the two armies. Something like what had happened with the Bretons in the morning happened again, though this time it had a look of preparation, planning about it. Make no mistake, I do not think the foot-soldiers feigned a retreat to pull Leofwine's men out of line, they were well beat, but when they did retreat in poor order and the housecarls broke out after them, the horse were on hand to charge amongst them, cover the foot-soldiers' retreat, and inflict heavy losses. Leofwine plunged in amongst his own men, urging them to regain the ridge and re-form as quickly as they could before the wall could be turned, and in doing this was struck down, skewered from behind on a horseman's lance.

This so confused his men that they hesitated, and milled around in a leaderless fashion like so many headless chickens, which gave the Franks a chance to re-form and attack again, both horse and foot together, before the remnants of Leofwine's men regained the ridge.

Harold concealed his grief with rage. He stormed down the line – we, Daffydd and I, had to pluck the standards out of their holes and follow as best we could – urging on his commanders that, come what may, they must now stand and hold the ridge and not leave it, no not even if the whole Norman army pulled back or even, though now it did not seem possible it could happen, broke and fled.

Again there was a respite, for although the afternoon fighting had been heaviest at the east end of the line, all had been engaged and both sides had suffered badly, and both armies were dead tired, the Normans perhaps even more than us, even though they'd had a decent meal, for we had mainly just held our ground, while they had marched up and down that hill as many as five or six times. About four hours after midday, and about two after the resumed fighting, the whole ugly field, churned-up mud, dead horses, dead men, dying men and dying horses, blood and shit everywhere, had the weary sick look of a stalemate about it.

Which was fine with Harold, fine with us. If they didn't break us by nightfall they were done for – they couldn't stay where they were, exposed below us, they'd have to pull back to their fortified camp and maybe even Harold would let our light troops harry them as they did. And all through the night and the next day reinforcements would come in from the north and the west, and William would have to sue for peace on the best terms he could get and all would be well. So for twenty minutes we thought we were there, that we'd made it, but all the time we could see William cantering up and down the lines, standing in his stirrups, bellowing orders, sarcasm mingled with threats, and bit by bit he got his line into shape again, this time with the horse in front for they had suffered less loss than either of the other arms and were the ones who had had most success against the wall.

Harold sent messages down the line: 'This has to be the last push they can make before sunset – withstand this and we've won.'

William brought his front line up the hill and stopped them about fifty yards below us, just within lethal arrow shot had we had any bowmen left who had not shot off their last arrows, and then he came out in front, and turned his back on us! But we could hear him. The voice high now, cracking occasionally, the phrases coming in short bursts:

'Land for all. Castles and slaves and women, because there will be no men left. Mutton, beef, boar's meat every day. Hunting whenever you like, your own hounds, your own horses. Enough mead and wine to keep you drunk till you die . . .

His horse, his third of the day, a big bay this time, gave a shiver and tried a pirouette which maybe jogged his mind to higher things.

'This day you will begin a new order. A reign which will last through generations. Your sons will inherit this earth and your sons' sons, maybe to the crack of doom, certainly for a thousand years. Yes. Follow me now and claim your share in a lease of a thousand years, albeit a thousand years has all too short a date. Summon up all your strength, stiffen your muscles, and once again cry God for William, the England that will be ours and Saint . . . Saint . . . George? Yes. Saint George.'

'Christ and his Holy Cross defend us,' Harold muttered.

And William pulled his horse round to face us, lifted his mace (someone had got another for him), and thumped his spurred boots into the beast's sides. It took off and almost had him on the ground, but he held on, got it back under control and was off again on a short rein in a slow trot, and all his men followed. And at that moment we realised, and maybe his army did too, that he did not mean to give in or go back. And

for all his screeching, and manic posturing, for all his bullying and attention to minute and pointless detail, for all he lacked perfect control over
his long limbs, he had a power about him, a sort of black aura that
made you shiver. *You* knew he was vulnerable, *you* knew that scratch him
he'd bleed, but he didn't. He didn't know it.

Within seconds we were at it again. The horses pushing sideways
into the shields, the maces and swords flashing above our heads, the
screams of the wounded, the clash of arms on armour, the neighing of
horses, the sudden fountain of blood that blinded you, yours or someone
else's, the throng so thick at times you were crushed and could hardly
move at all, at other times giving bewilderingly away and leaving you
where a horse could fall on you or a mace take off your head . . . Then
the horse wheeled away and the foot-soldiers came in and it was back to
single combat again, but now it was not so single for more and more it
seemed there were three against two even two against one, if at all we
parted shields and tried to make a real fight of it. The thing of it was, at
the beginning of the day we were able to stand shoulder to shoulder in
two lines along the whole of the ridge or in four lines in open order and
now, in spite of reinforcements, shoulder to shoulder we could barely
hold it in one. No doubt the Normans were as depleted in numbers as
we were, but they could concentrate where the line seemed weakest, and
this they did, bringing up the horse behind the foot and storming in
wherever a gap appeared.

There was only one thing for it. I think I said this ridge, this hill was
linked to the Downs and the forest by a narrower isthmus. The only way
we could shorten our line was by pulling back on to the end of this and
about an hour before sunset we did just that, carefully and in good
order, it was the sort of manoeuvre we had been trained for. But when
he saw it happening the Bastard realised he might lose the advantage he'd
gained and he tried to gallop round our right with about twenty horsemen. For a moment, he moved so quickly, it looked as if he might, but
Harold's brother Gyrth rallied enough men in front of him and they
turned him back. But not before the Bastard himself smashed Gyrth's
face in with his mace – he was going at him at almost full gallop.

Harold saw it this time. He had no room for anger now. His eyes
filled, he almost wept, then he shook his head and said: 'Later, later.'

For a time, a short time, it seemed we had done enough.
Concentrated again, we were solid. But the movement had two bad side

effects. First, it meant we had abandoned the apple tree. Thus far and no further is what the apple tree had said to us and now it was swallowed up in the Norman advance, although we were only a hundred paces behind it. That sort of thing shouldn't count, but somehow it did. Second, we no longer had the advantage of the slope. At first this didn't make much difference, it was level ground, more or less.

Again there was a short pause, I suppose while the Bastard sorted out the new situation. It came on to rain. Not heavily but enough to question your grip on your sword . . .

'You have not said anything about your sword. Was it not in any way special? Like an old and trusty friend, forged by goblins? An heirloom?'

'No, nothing of the sort.' She's heard too many Romances, Walt thought. 'Lot of nonsense sung about that sort of thing. Excalibur, Durandil, whatever. It was just a sword. One picked out of many because its weight and balance suited me.'

He went on.

That greasy rain made things seem slippery, though heaven knows there was enough blood about to have the same effect. What the Bastard did now, and of all the things he did on that day it seemed about the most stupid, was bring back his archers. Until then his bowmen had been shooting uphill and their arrows, which were light and more of a nuisance than anything else since they would not pierce leather let alone steel, had hit our shields or passed over our heads, and most of them had run out.

Anyway, he called them up again and of course there were a fair number of their own arrows on the ground we had left, so they got together enough for a proper volley or two. And when the first lot didn't seem to do much damage, someone, maybe the Bastard himself, rode amongst them and told them to shoot up in the air so they'd fall on the other side of the shield-wall. Stupid idea really. Almost impossible to judge the right trajectory and they were close enough to make it possible for some of the arrows to fall on his own men. And anyway we all had helmets on . . .

'But.'

★

Four swans flew out from over the forest, heading towards the estuaries, and Harold looked up at them. We heard the wingbeats coming from behind us and to our left. You know, there are some sounds you just have to look round and up for. He counted them, not with numbers but with the names of his brothers: 'Sweyn, Tostig, Leofwine and Gyrth.' And a stupid little arrow hit him in the right eye.

It wasn't fatal, not even serious, though almost certainly he'd have lost that eye, but naturally he went down. Well, you do. Even if it's just a finger or something, if it comes hard enough, and of course it bled a lot, all over his face, and he stayed dead still for a minute or so, again the way you do when the pain is bad, until you've worked out just how bad it is. And that was it, enough for the word to go down the line that he was gone. Well, both wings had already lost their leaders and now the King, too. It means something – the King. More than just the ring-giver, whatever Quint might say. And both his brothers who might have been king after him, they'd already gone. Quite a lot of the housecarls out on the ends of the line just broke and ran for it, and, of course, the fyrd in the rear went with them before we could mop Harold up enough and get him on his feet and show them he was still alive.

We were down to as few as five hundred now and there was no way we could block off even the narrower part of the hill. We formed a circle round the King and the standards. The sun had almost gone. There was still a chance if we held on we'd get Harold out, under cover of darkness. One thing, though. William sent a lot of his horse down the hill on the west side after the fugitives and we could see how, just before he launched his final attack, they got caught in a deep ditch down there, many were thrown and there were enough English still about to cut their throats.

But, anyway, here they came again. And now they could ride right round us, swinging in at us, smashing at us with their swords and maces from all sides and all angles. Of the eight companions there was just Daffydd, Timor and me left round Harold. He was in a lot of pain, but he kept telling us: 'Keep the standards flying, keep them up.' Then there was a lull, and we could just make out how the Bastard called together four or five of his heftiest knights. They were only fifty yards away and they had torches flaring now, and they were silhouetted against the sky and the very end of the sun. Then those five came at us, riding at a full gallop, and the men in front of us, they were all wounded, and near dead

with exhaustion couldn't hold them and four of them broke through . . .
and then it happened.

'Harold got killed.'
  'Worse than that. In a way. For me. I should have been killed, too.'
  'Why?'
  'It's . . . what . . . one should do, really.'

Walt wanted to live. He wanted to go back to Iwerne, to Erica, to the
hearth. These were the things he was fighting for. In that critical moment
he turned his back on a millennium in which the mead-hall, the feasting,
the boasting, the oaths, the training, the loyalty, above all the loyalty to
the Chief, dominated the lives of young thegns and housecarls. To die for
one's chief in the shield-wall might still be the greatest glory but to live
amongst one's family and people and serve them is better than glory.

When the first blow fell, a sweeping stroke from a sword held two-
handed, his body could have been between it and that of the King –
instead he tried to parry it with his sword and arm. At that moment, perhaps, with that choice, the civilisation of the English reached its zenith –
it turned its back on the savagery of war and embraced hedonistic willingness to live as well as one can and help others to do the same. And –
at that moment its decline began.

Not Walt's fault, though – the battle was already lost. Nevertheless, the
companion should have been killed with his chief and it was the presence
in his soul of all that the hearth had come to mean which denied him
that glory. He walked away from the battle with three insufferable bur-
dens – guilt that he had not died with Harold, guilt that he had allowed
the hearth to betray him, guilt that he could not force himself back to
Iwerne where he knew he would now be more desperately needed than
ever before . . .

'Walked?'
  'Yes. Daffydd was dead but Timor survived. In the darkness he bound
up my arm. He said he owed me one because I had saved him from
drowning when we were kids. Then he left me and I passed out. I came
to not long before dawn. The crows and kites were already gathering
over the hill. There were people moving about. With lanterns.
Women . . .'

'Don't cry. Tell me about it. Who were they?'

'Edith Swan-Neck. Next day Timor took me to Dover and on the way he told me how she had made him take her and her women back to Bosham instead of Weymouth. They had to gather Harold up. He had been, well, more or less chopped in pieces. Only his mail, slashed and torn though it was, held his torso together. Edith knew him though.

'William found them shortly after dawn. He said Harold had broken his oath to God and would not let them bury him in holy ground. So Edith and Timor and a few others of us buried him on the beach beneath a cliff near Hastings. We wrapped him in the Fighting Man of Cerne, made a shroud of the standard his mother had woven for him.'

Walt wept.

Eventually Amaranta asked: 'What will you do now?'

'I'll go back. There's an English boat in the harbour. I'll work my passage with them.'

'I can give you money.'

'No. I shan't need any.'

'It's a very small boat. Aren't you frightened of drowning?'

'Terrified.'

EPILOGUE

It took a year. Piræus, Venice, Messina, Moorish Valencia and Cadiz, Santiago de Compostela. On the way they picked up news of how things were in England, of how the resistance had gone on and still continued. Of how Harold's and Edith Swan-Neck's sons from Ireland had landed in the West Country and been driven off. Of how East Anglia had risen, but the rising had been betrayed by a turn-coat called Hereward the Wake. And of how the north was still in arms against the man they already called the Conqueror. And of how wherever he was resisted he laid the land waste, of how his men burnt villages in reprisals and how castles were built everywhere from which the Normans and their mercenaries, armed and horsed as they were though still only a few thousand in number, looted and raped at will.

Ham and Cedric could have dropped him at Weymouth but he asked them to cross the bay and drop him at Lulworth Cove. They lowered the coracle into the water and Cedric rowed him ashore. At five paces or so from the beach Walt stepped over the side into shallow clear sunlit water. His feet stirred fine glittering sand into brief swirling clouds above a shingle of small smoothed fragmented seashells and flints. He gave the small black coracle a push and waved a farewell. With his face set to the land, he climbed to the top of the shingle bank and walked along it to a point where a steep chalk track climbed to a saddle of grass between the white headland and the country inland. Salmon-coloured valerian still bloomed in spikes above its waxy leaves, choughs wheeled against the cliff faces. He was nearly home.

The sun went in. He glanced up at the dark clouds that were gathering in the west and north, then, as he reached the saddle between the two headlands, he looked back over the sea. The sun still shone on the boat that had brought him; its sail was now up again, the coracle safely lifted and stowed on board. The sea gleamed silver to the high horizon beyond but, even as he watched, the white cliffs turned grey and purple cloud shadow slid across the waters in pursuit of the ship. The Wanderer turned his face inland, and followed the track down into the woodland and scrub on the northern side. A host of starlings whirled like dust motes over the valley ahead, gathering for an autumn moot. Summer was fading. Winter lay ahead.

Now you can order superb titles directly from Abacus

☐	Hannibal	Ross Leckie	£6.99
☐	Samarkand	Amin Maalouf	£7.99
☐	Ancient Evenings	Norman Mailer	£8.99
☐	Live From Golgotha	Gore Vidal	£6.99

──────────────── ⟨ABACUS⟩ ────────────────

Please allow for postage and packing: **Free UK delivery.**
Europe: add 25% of retail price; Rest of World: 45% of retail price.

To order any of the above or any other Abacus titles, please call our credit card orderline or fill in this coupon and send/fax it to:

Abacus, 250 Western Avenue, London, W3 6XZ, UK.
Fax 0181 324 5678   Telephone 0181 324 5517

☐ I enclose a UK bank cheque made payable to Abacus for £ . . . .
☐ Please charge £ . . . . . . to my Access, Visa, Delta, Switch Card No.

Expiry Date ☐☐☐☐   Switch Issue No. ☐☐

NAME (Block letters please) : . . . .

ADDRESS . . . .

. . . .

. . . .

Postcode . . . . Telephone . . . .

Signature . . . .

Please allow 28 days for delivery within the UK. Offer subject to price and availability.

Please do not send any further mailings from companies carefully selected by Abacus ☐